JULIA

Recent Titles by Cynthia Harrod-Eagles

A CORNISH AFFAIR *
DANGEROUS LOVE *
DIVIDED LOVE *
EVEN CHANCE *
THE HORSEMASTERS *
LAST RUN *
THE LONGEST DANCE *
NOBODY'S FOOL *
ON WINGS OF LOVE *
PLAY FOR LOVE *
A RAINBOW SUMMER *
REAL LIFE (*Short Stories*) *

* *all available from Severn House*

The Bill Slider Series

ORCHESTRATED DEATH
DEATH WATCH
NECROCHIP (*USA Title:* DEATH TO GO)
DEAD END (*USA Title:* GRAVE MUSIC)
BLOOD LINES
KILLING TIME
SHALLOW GRAVE
BLOOD SINISTER

JULIA

Cynthia Harrod-Eagles

This first world edition published in Great Britain 2002 by
SEVERN HOUSE PUBLISHERS LTD of
9–15 High Street, Sutton, Surrey SM1 1DF.
This first world edition published in the USA 2003 by
SEVERN HOUSE PUBLISHERS INC of
595 Madison Avenue, New York, N.Y. 10022.

British Library Cataloguing in Publication Data

Harrod-Eagles, Cynthia
  Julia
    1.   Adultery - Fiction
    2.   Illegitimate children - Fiction
    3.   Love stories
    I.   Title
  823.9'14 [F]

  ISBN 0-7278-5891-2

Except where actual historical events and characters are being
described for the storyline of this novel, all situations in this
publication are fictitious and any resemblance to living persons
is purely coincidental.

Typeset by Palimpsest Book Production Ltd.,
Polmont, Stirlingshire, Scotland.
Printed and bound in Great Britain by
MPG Books Ltd., Bodmin, Cornwall.

Go from me. Yet I feel that I shall stand
Henceforward in thy shadow. Nevermore
Alone upon the threshold of my door
Of individual life I shall command
The uses of my soul, nor lift my hand
Serenely in the sunshine as before,
Without the sense of that which I forebore—
Thy touch upon the palm. The widest land
Doom takes to part us, leaves thy heart in mine
With pulses that beat double. What I do
And what I dream include thee, as the wine
Must taste of its own grapes.

Elizabeth Barrett Browning
Sonnets from the Portuguese no. 6

One

May 1953

Lady Margaret's let out earlier than the other schools, at three thirty. The girls spilled out into the empty streets of mid afternoon. All the world was at work. The only traffic was a few delivery vans and a trolley bus moaning past under the tall plane trees. A row of tradesmen's carts queued up for the horse trough across the road, the ponies' ears limp at half mast in the bright heat.

The senior girls – upper fifth, lower and upper sixth – were allowed to use the front entrance, a great and gravely-bestowed privilege. Most of them seemed conscious of it as they dawdled down the steps. They walked with an air, as if expecting to be looked at; chatted to each other loudly, as though someone might be taking down their words for posterity.

Julia came down with the rest, neither leading nor holding back, somewhere near the middle of the flow, but always a little apart. No one chatted to her.

At the foot of the steps, the flow split into distributaries as girls walked off to various bus stops, to the underground station, to their nearby homes. Some headed for Fred's, the transport café down the road, which they used as a coffee bar, though the coffee was made with Camp syrup and the comfort was meagre. The proprietor was a misogynist with one eye and several fingers missing. He hated schoolgirls using his premises, and if they lingered too long he would drive them out, complaining they were taking up room wanted by honest working men – though there was rarely anyone else in there at that time of day. Once Rhoda Edwards, the sixth form bad girl, had boldly told him so. He had scowled and cursed her and waved his stumps at her, and told her he hadn't fought a war to take cheek from the likes of her. His unpredictability gave an added zest to proceedings. Not that any was needed, for Fred's was where girls from Lady Margaret's met their peers from St Anthony's, the local boys' grammar.

At the foot of the steps the girls called cheerful goodbyes, confirmed plans to meet later, over the weekend.

'See you outside the Gaumont at half past seven.'

'I'll come round tomorrow about fiveish.'

'Are you going to the Palais tomorrow night?'

'Are you coming to Fred's?'

No one said goodbye to Julia. She had no arrangements with anyone, and she never went to Fred's. She walked off alone, and the lingering, chattering girls bent their sapling bodies to let her pass without looking at her. She was an outsider, she knew that. She had always been different, so she was used to it, and what you are used to, you come hardly to notice. The other girls did not treat her with hostility – most of them didn't. Once or twice she had overheard cruel remarks, or glimpsed the bright-eyed malice of a group that stopped talking abruptly as she passed. But on the whole they were not unpleasant to her. They simply ignored her, not deliberately but as if she didn't impinge on their awareness.

It was another hot day. The heat seemed to stand motionless between sun and earth like an enervated dog. The air tasted dusty, smelled of hot pavements – a smell Julia liked. She turned her face upwards and felt the sun press on her like a hand. She squinted into the sky, which seemed bleached of colour. As she tilted her head she felt her plaits bump against her back with a familiar, friendly weight, like the nudge of a dog. No one else in the senior school wore plaits. They were old-fashioned, kiddish. She knew the others thought her queer for sticking to them, and even queerer for not minding what they thought.

She couldn't help it. She couldn't make herself care about the things they cared about, clothes and lipstick and boyfriends. She had nothing to say when they talked about Elvis Presley and Buddy Holly and Tommy Steele. She had tried listening to that sort of music and she understood why they liked it. She quite liked it herself but it seemed to her

2

too simple and limited to listen to over and over. Just once she had misguidedly tried to explain this to Rhoda Edwards and Gill Gallico and their set when they were twitting her about not liking rock and roll. They had reacted so violently she had recoiled in surprise.

'You beastly snob!'

'You think yourself so superior, don't you?'

'Smug cow!'

'I suppose you think you're better than us!'

The more she protested that it was not conceit or priggishness, the more pathetically she asked weren't people allowed to be different, shouldn't people's differences be respected, the more shrill they grew. At last she had had to beat a hasty retreat before they reduced her to tears, which she knew instinctively would make things worse. She had been bullied at junior school, and had learnt you never let them see you cry.

Now she kept her opinions to herself, and lived mostly inside her head, in the rich and satisfying world of thought. She wasn't unhappy. Life seemed to her too amazingly full of a number of things for happiness: variety and possibility, books and music. She had no friends, but she wasn't lonely. Well, hardly ever.

She turned off the main road into a side street of neat Edwardian terraced houses. There was a small flight of shops on the left: ironmonger, grocer, butcher, barber with his striped pole forever magically regenerating, greengrocer spreading out on to the pavement with stacked orange-boxes of fruit and veg, and at the end a tiny shop that sold wool and baby clothes and which she had never seen anyone enter. The shop doors, all except the last, stood open for the air, and their interiors seemed invitingly dark and cool in contrast to the blinding sunlight.

As she reached the grocery, she saw the grocer himself standing in his doorway, rolling himself a cigarette. He was a tall, lean man who had been handsome in his youth and had retained the automatic expectation of being found attractive by the opposite sex. Julia found him attractive without in the least knowing why; assumed, if she ever thought about it, that it was simply because he was a nice man. She got on better with grown-ups anyway: she knew how to please them, while her peers remained a potentially hostile mystery. As to many a bright child before her, adults seemed her natural constituency, so she was disposed to like him even without his extra, mysterious allure.

'Hello, Mr Johnson,' she said.

He paused, the thin roll-up half way to his lips. 'Hello, love. Early, aren't you?'

'Not really. We always get out before the other schools, because we start earlier.' She had twigged by now that adults asked questions just as a way of making mouth-music, but she had not quite yet got out of the child's habit of answering them properly, as if the information were really required.

'Belter of a day, isn't?' he said, wetting the end of his cigarette before putting it between his lips. She watched his lips and his tongue without realising it, but he saw the direction of her eyes. Still got it, he thought. Still got the old magic. And little Julia Jacobs was growing up. Got a bust somewhere under that school uniform. Ugly clothes. Shabby too – second hand. There was no money in *that* family. Queer set-up. No wonder Julia was such a queer little thing. Not shy, quite – you couldn't say she was shy – but a bit of a loner. She'd be – what? – fifteen or sixteen now. Didn't look it, not in those clothes, but put her in something a bit more modern . . . His practised eye made the transformation. Yes, she was growing up.

He came back from his thoughts to meet her frank open gaze, and embarrassed himself. He became brisk by way of compensation. 'I'm glad I caught you – can you take a bit of shopping home for your mum? I said I'd drop it round, but my boy hasn't come in.'

Julia nodded. 'I'd have had to come for it anyway.'

'Can you wait while I slice the bacon? The rest is all ready.'

She followed him into the dim, fragrant interior. There was no one else inside, and she was vaguely glad. She didn't like it when his wife was present – a smart, rather hard-faced woman who had kept things going alone through the war when her

4

husband was away, had seen a thing or two, and was coolly suspicious of all other women. Julia had not yet worked out why, but she was always glad when Mrs Johnson wasn't there. He seemed nicer when she wasn't. He went behind the counter now and she stood looking round and sniffing appreciatively.

'You are lucky to be here all day with these lovely smells,' she said.

'I don't notice it,' he said, amused at her idea of luck. 'What is it, then – tea?'

'Oh, tea, and bacon and sawdust and cheese and furniture wax,' she said. She paused, and added, 'And some other things I can't identify. Lovely!'

He had put the piece of green streaky in the machine and was setting the blade. 'What is it, number four your mum has?' He wound the handle and the regular whirr and hiss deposited thin rashers on to the greaseproof paper on his palm. There was a good joke he'd heard the other day about a grocer's shop with a big sign on the wall: 'Would customers kindly stand further away from the bacon slicer. We're getting a little behind in our orders.' He considered telling it to Julia, but then thought better of it. She mightn't get it – and if she did, it might embarrass her.

He weighed the bacon, wrapped it and put it on top of the rest of the order, already packed in a cardboard box. As he lifted the box up on to the counter something caught his attention and he said, 'Here, if it's smells you like, how about this one?'

Julia looked at him expectantly. He rummaged around out of her sight and then brought up, like a trophy, a small package about the size and shape of a sugar-bag, but brown instead of blue. She raised it to her nose, and snuffed delightedly at the hot, maddening, glorious smell.

'Coffee,' she said. 'It's wonderful.'

'Yes, one of the best smells there is, I reckon – that and bacon frying. Used to do a lot of it before the war, but people got out of the habit, I suppose, when you couldn't get it. Only two or three of my customers take it now.'

'We only have tea,' Julia said. But hadn't they used to

have coffee, *before*? She couldn't quite be sure, but the smell seemed to trigger something in her, some vague remembered sensation of pleasure and comfort. 'Who's it for?'

'Mrs Kane.' He took the package back and snuffed at it himself. 'D'you know her? She lives in your street.'

'No,' Julia said. 'At least, I don't know the name.'

'They live in that big house with gables, down the end, corner of Milton Street and Spenser Road – there now!' He stopped himself, and looked at Julia speculatively.

'Yes?'

'I wonder, now, how would you like to earn yourself a few bob?'

'What would I have to do?' Julia remembered his saying that his boy hadn't come in, and supposed he wanted her to deliver for him. She wondered what her parents would think about that. She guessed her mother wouldn't approve.

Somehow he divined her thoughts. 'Oh, nothing for me. Mrs Kane was in here today with a card for the window, and what with one thing and another I forgot about it until just this minute. She's looking for a babysitter.'

He reached behind him to the part of the shelf beside the till where he kept odds and ends like his order book, pen, and tobacco tin, and picked up a white postcard that was lying there.

'She wants a babysitter one or two evenings a week so's she can get out a bit. Two young kids and her husband works evenings. She asked me if I knew anyone. I suggested a card in the window – business is business even if it is only thruppence.' He gave her a very professional wink that left the rest of his face immobile. 'What do you think?'

'I'd like to,' Julia said, 'if my mother and father would let me.'

He nodded, pleased with the idea of doing her a bit of good. He didn't suppose she ever had any pocket money. No money in *that* family, he thought again. Of course, they might not let her do it. People like that sometimes got a bit sniffy about their girls working, especially if they thought it was anything like going into service. He didn't actually think 'decayed gentry', but the shape of the idea was in his mind.

'You tell your mum it's quite respectable. My young niece does it. Sits and does her homework for a couple of hours, and gets paid for it – *and* her couple give her supper too. I should think the Kanes would see you all right – they aren't short. Here, I'll give you the card. You can bring it back if you don't get the job.'

'Thanks very much,' Julia said. It sounded very easy, undemanding – enjoyable, even – and it would be lovely to have money to spend. The grocer was right that there was no pocket money. Even if she had been keen on lipstick and clothes and records like the other girls, there would have been nothing she could have done about it anyway. It was one of the things that made her different. Scholarship girl, poor girl, hand-me-down-clothes girl – that was her. The others disliked her for being clever and for not liking what they liked, but she knew they also despised her for being poor – something, she reasoned, she couldn't be expected to help. She thought the attitude ridiculous and therefore contemptible, like despising Fred of Fred's café for having only one eye. But that didn't stop it hurting.

But the grocer must like her, to be doing her this favour. And he looked at her as though he liked her.

'You're very kind to think of me,' she said.

He came to attention and gave the sketch of a salute. 'N'tall. The pleasure, as they say, is all mine.' She turned to go, and he recollected himself. 'Here, your mum's shopping.'

'Oh, yes, sorry. I forgot.' She received the grocery box into her arms, balanced it for a moment on the edge of the counter while she picked up her school briefcase and put it on top, and then with another smile of thanks took up the burden again and went out into the dazzling sunshine.

Milton Street was a long one and, perhaps simply because it had presented a larger target, seemed to have taken most of the bombs that fell in that area. One side was almost untouched, and presented the long-familiar façade of Victorian semi-detached houses, each with a minute front garden bound by a half-wall, along the top of which the row of metal stumps showed where the railings had been amputated for the War

7

Effort. Some showed the remains of minor damage – cracks in the stucco, missing chimneys or garden walls – but the road was wide enough for them to have escaped most of the blast that had almost flattened the other side.

Living opposite the ruins – only now beginning to be rebuilt – made the war an omnipresent memory, like the men one saw on crutches with one trouser leg pinned up, the men with an empty sleeve, with an eyepatch, the men in wheelchairs. The war was always there, in the background of thought; an assumption that coloured and supported everything, a taken-for-grantedness which united everyone at a certain level – just as rarely-seen relatives at a family 'do' were joined together by the fact of their cousinhood, however little they had in common.

Julia's father had been too old to be called up – another factor in her differentness. Other girls' fathers had served in one way or another; one or two in her class had a widowed mother; one had a divorced and remarried one, a war casualty of a different sort. But Julia's father was much older than theirs. It was only recently that she had begun to notice her parents' age as an influence in her life, though there had always been those occasions when classmates had come to school excitedly announcing that their mother had just had a baby, and she had thought wonderingly what that must be like. Having another baby would surely make your mother seem suddenly different, mutable; would alter everything in the household. To have another baby would be a very human and living thing to do. But she had come to realise that she did not see her parents as real in that sense at all. They seemed to her as static as granite statues. Nothing about their family would ever change. Certainly there would be no more siblings, and she, Julia, was the end of the line, so to speak, the terminus at which the bus turned off its engine and fell silent. From here onward there could only be her life – hers and her sister's. Her parents had no future, in the sense that future was change. They had said the last word about themselves and that was that.

She would have loved to be part of a large family, to live with noise and movement and personality. Perhaps in a large family she would have had someone – surely *must* have had one sibling she could feel close to and confide in. But there was only her and Sylvia. There had been another sister, Lydia, but she had died in infancy long ago, before she or Sylvia had been born. She did not know in what circumstances Lydia had died. Her mother did not say, and she could not ask. It was impossible to talk to her mother about quite simple things; how much more impossible to ask about something so personal and, she supposed, distressing as the death of a child.

Thus she was thinking as she let herself in at the front door, the box of groceries balanced on her hip and cutting into the flesh of her waist in a way that was oddly almost pleasurable. She had a rare moment of seeing her parents as separate from her, not just familiar shapes labeled 'Mother' and 'Father'. What was it *like* to be them? She paused, trying to imagine, but the effort was beyond her. She lacked not imagination but information. They were both so reserved, so formal, so withdrawn, that she had nothing to go on to estimate their feelings or requirements as individuals. Perhaps, she thought tentatively, they didn't have any? Perhaps one could outgrow them? Did age rub away passion and longing and even opinion, as wind and rain eroded stone and made it smooth and featureless?

The house was a typical London dog-leg semi: narrow hall with stairs straight ahead, front room with bay window, back room – the original dining room – with French windows, and back addition comprising kitchen, scullery and servant's lavatory. They had no servant, though she thought she remembered that *before*, there had been. At any rate, she remembered someone who came in daily, a woman in a flowered cotton overall who she associated with yellow dusters and the smell of lavender wax. The door to the back room was closed, as always. It was her father's study, and one did not go in there without invitation. The back addition, originally the kitchen, was now their dining room, and the scullery had become the kitchen by the installation of a gas stove against one wall, an enamel-topped wooden table against another, and a hot-water geyser over the porcelain sink.

Her mother was sitting at the dining-room table reading the paper over a cup of tea – something about the forthcoming Coronation, Julia saw. She did not look up as Julia walked past her into the kitchen to put down the grocery box.

'Mr Johnson asked me to bring the shopping. His boy didn't come in.'

'Hmm,' said Mrs Jacobs.

Julia came to the kitchen door and stood there, looking at her mother, trying to see her as a separate person. She was neither fat nor thin – what Julia thought of as a grown-up's shape, bulky and hard with no ins and outs, the effect enhanced by a grown-up's shapeless clothes: a dress with buttons down the front and a cloth belt, usually with a cardigan over it, but not today, because of the hot weather. When she did anything around the house she thought of as 'dirty' work, she wore a sleeveless wrap-around flowered cotton overall instead of an apron. She had three, one in shades of yellow and orange, one in shades of green, and one in shades of pink and mauve. Julia was aware, without actually thinking about it, that her mother hated doing those things, and that doing them put her in a bad temper. By transference, therefore, Julia had come to hate the overalls and always felt a lifting sense of relief when she came home and they were not in evidence.

Mrs Jacobs was tall for a woman, and her arms seemed powerful – muscular below the elbow and almost meaty above. She was thirteen years younger than Julia's father, which made her fifty-three. Her hair, which had been blonde, was now faded-fair mixed with grey, what was sometimes called pepper-and-salt. It was brushed smooth over the crown and curled up and pinned in a roll from ear to ear around the back of the neck. Julia didn't remember it ever being in any other style. Her face was smooth, unwrinkled, with fine arched brows, a straight nose, a wide, thin-lipped mouth that always seemed clamped shut lest anything should escape: an incautious word, a smile perhaps?

Julia realised, without actually feeling it, that she must have been beautiful as a girl; but it was hard to visualise her mother as a girl. She was this, as if she had always been: the woman who kept house, cleaned, cooked, served meals, sat reading or

10

knitting in the evenings, and sometimes, if Father was working late in his study, tuned the wireless in to dance music, turned down low not to disturb him, and tapped her feet to it while her fingers flew unregarded, knit-one-purl-one-knit-two-together, with her eyes fixed blankly on some other time or space.

She felt Julia's eyes on her now and looked up from the paper, raising an eyebrow in question. Her eyes were blue, like Sylvia's, but faded like her hair. They unnerved Julia, seeming so expressionless, concealing what might be coming. Sometimes in her early childhood it had been a slap. Now it was usually a denial or a criticism – differently but equally painful.

Julia knew in some dimly-sensed way that her mother did not like her. It had to be dimly-sensed because mothers loved their children, that was the way things were. As a child she had neither been able to suppose anything so unnatural as, nor bear the thought of, her mother not liking her. But she saw the difference in the way her mother was with Sylvia. She liked Sylvia. Sylvia was like her. Sylvia was not 'clever' as Julia was. Sylvia had gone to the secondary modern, left school and gone to a commercial college to learn typing and shorthand with a view to getting a job in an office, which was what Julia knew her mother thought of as a 'good' job. Sylvia was pretty, as her mother had been. She was nice and ordinary and conventional, did not think or say strange things, or have strange desires. Her mother liked and approved of Sylvia, but Julia was an alien thing to her. Julia was like her father, and it should have been he who loved her, to balance things up and make everything fair and all right. But her father loved no one, and Julia was left feeling cheated of what should have been hers. She was the outsider even within the four walls of 'home', where she should have belonged.

'Can I ask you something?' she said. Her mother waited impassively. She did not waste words. 'Mr Johnson said there's a lady down the road who wants a babysitter for a couple of evenings a week and he thought I might like to do it. He said to tell you it's quite respectable,' she hurried on, to get all the information out before the expected refusal. 'His niece does it for another lady and she does her homework

11

there and gets paid and gets supper left her as well, and . . .' She ran out of invention. 'I'd like to,' she finished feebly. 'If you don't mind.'

She waited, standing square before the impassive face, the tightly-tucked lips. She did not often ask for things, knowing that any request usually elicited a negative. Better, she always felt, not to ask than to be disappointed. She knew by now, more or less, what sorts of things were all right and what were not, but babysitting was something new and strange, outside her experience – rather American, even. Her father disliked all things American for being responsible for the erosion of standards and What This Country Has Come To. Once, when she was quite little, another child had given her a stick of chewing gum, which had earned her a more than usually harsh rebuke from her father – delivered, as always, by her mother, along with a slap and a banishment-to-bedroom.

The thin lips unlocked. 'Who are these people?' Julia silently offered the postcard. Mrs Jacobs studied it lengthily, as if memorising the details. There was a telephone number as well as the address. 'They must be well off.' If it was a question, Julia had no answer, and remained silent. 'I think I've seen her. They've got a car. There's one parked outside sometimes, anyway.'

'Mr Kane works in the evenings,' Julia offered. 'I don't know what he does. Mr Johnson didn't say. But he knows them well, so they must be all right.'

At last Mrs Jacobs thrust the card back at her, as though she had lost interest in the matter, and Julia thought it would be 'no'. But she said, 'Do it if you like. As long as it doesn't affect your homework.'

Julia felt a surge of gratitude, absurdly extravagant, out of all proportion to the boon. Why did she care so much? But while her mother had deliberated she had felt suddenly that it was terribly important that she should do this, that it mattered *dreadfully*, and the more sure she had been that she would be denied it, the more she wanted it.

'Oh, *thank* you,' she said. 'May I go round now and see them?' She was aware of a panicky sensation in her stomach that some other girl was this very minute closing in on the

Kanes' house – perhaps a string of girls – and that her chance – of what? Not just a job, surely? Freedom? Hardly. Something new in her life, anyway – was about to be snatched from her.

Her mother made a small waving-away gesture of her fingers, having already gone back to the newspaper. Julia did not wait to change out of her school uniform but went just as she was, before anyone's mind should be changed.

The corner plot was a large one, the house was detached, and it overlooked the park on the other side of Spenser Road. It was Victorian, red brick to halfway up and stucco above, with a large gable with imitation Tudor black beams on it. It had fancy chimneys and some of the upstairs windows were mullioned and had diamond panes. The front garden was neglected – shaggy grass and overgrown shrubs. They didn't like gardening, then, or have a gardener. There was a garage joined to the side of the house and Julia noticed that the doors were open and a car was inside. Mr Johnson said that the husband worked evenings – presumably he hadn't left for work yet. It seemed a quite large car – but ownership of any car was proof of wealth, or at least a way of life above and beyond Julia's experience.

She walked up the path to the front door, feeling suddenly nervous, and strangely apprehensive, as though she was about to initiate something that would have unforeseen and perhaps dangerous consequences. She shook the feeling away. It was absurd. She should be excited, rather. She was going to meet some new people, see the inside of someone else's house, do something *different*, which in a life as static as hers and in a world which valued unchangingness above all else was devoutly to be wished. She knocked, and waited. After a decent period she raised her hand to knock again, and saw the doorbell. It rang distantly. Almost immediately there was an upsurge of noise as if someone had opened a box of it, and then the door was opened and Julia had her first sight of Mrs Kane.

'I've come about the job – I mean, babysitting,' Julia said nervously. The tall young woman with a stout, solemn-faced child on her hip looked her over for a moment. She was slender – perhaps almost too thin – and very smartly dressed. She had make-up on, and her hair was cut and permed and looked as though she might have had it done by a hairdresser. Julia wondered if she was about to go out somewhere, but then decided, rather bemusedly, that this woman would always dress and look like that, even just for staying home.

Mrs Kane said unsmilingly, 'You'd better come in. Michael, will you *stop* that noise!' This latter was to another child out of sight who was banging a tin monotonously with some metal implement. Julia followed her into the hall and shut the door behind her. The hall was large and square – a real hall big enough to have furniture in it, not just a passage – and the wide stairs led up and round on the right. She was always sensitive to smells, and the house smelt unexpectedly but pleasantly of rosin and old books. The rosin she remembered from the ballet lessons she had taken when she was very little – that was *before*, of course, and the classes had broken up when the two women who ran them had packed up and joined the Wrens – and the old-book smell was one she knew intimately from her father's study which was mostly full of them.

Mrs Kane led her across the hall and into the sitting room. The centre of the floor was covered in a thick, pale-coloured carpet, and Julia felt herself sinking into its pile. She had a brief impression of luxury, thick carpet and thick upholstery, shining wood and lots of space, before her attention was drawn forcibly to the child who was sitting on the floor in front of her beating a biscuit tin with a spoon and smiling with the expression of one who knows he is making an unholy din, perfectly intolerable to all but himself – although it didn't seem to be upsetting the man who sat on the large sofa with his legs crossed and the evening paper up.

'Michael, stop this instant!' Mrs Kane cried with exasperation. She dumped the child she was carrying ungently on the floor and descended like the proverbial Assyrian on the offending tympanist, leaving him spoonless and momentarily nonplussed.

'How you can just *sit* there,' she hissed at the man with an acidity that even Julia noticed.

14

'He's only exercising his musical talent,' the man responded lazily.

'I thought he must get it from you,' she retorted. The man looked up at her, and she closed her mouth and breathed loudly through her nose in a way that was meant to show disapproval.

All this time Julia stood very timidly at the edge of the carpet, looking mostly at the children from embarrassment, for she had never heard grown-ups arguing with each other like that. Her parents hardly spoke to each other at all, and would never have dreamed of quarrelling in front of her and Sylvia, let alone strangers. It was one of the many things Julia knew her mother would have called 'bad form'.

Now Mrs Kane, pushing the confiscated spoon back and forth through her fingers, said, quite politely, to her husband, 'This little girl's come about the babysitting.'

Julia looked at her, indignant at the label, and then at the man to see how he took it. He put down his paper, and as the vividly blue eyes fixed her she had the impression almost of being run through, pierced by a sort of terrible significance, or connection – she could hardly say what, but something, at least, out of the ordinary, which made her feel that she and he were in some way on one side of a line which divided them from everyone else she had ever met. It lasted only an instant, before giving way to a more usual feeling of confusion and weakness as, unable to remove her gaze, she began to blush.

All he said was, 'Oh, good,' in a perfectly normal voice, but he continued to look straight into her eyes – something she suddenly realised hardly anyone ever did – while he stood up and went on politely, as if she had been an ordinary guest, 'Won't you sit down?'

The contrast between being 'this little girl' to Mrs Kane and a guest to Mr Kane left her unsure of her status, and in caution she took the hard upright chair by the door and only sat on the edge of it. Mrs Kane picked up the baby again and sat down in an armchair with it on her lap.

'You saw the card in the shop, did you?' she began.

'Yes, Mr Johnson showed it to me,' Julia said.

'I must say I wasn't expecting quite such a prompt response. What's your name?'

'Julia Jacobs.'

'And do you live near here?'

'I live at number fifteen – Milton Street.'

'Oh, just round the corner. That's handy. Have you lived there long?

'Ten years, nearly eleven. We used to live on the other side of the park until we got bombed out.' Used though she was to being questioned by grown-ups, she didn't quite like it from Mrs Kane. She sensed something – a faint hostility, a desire to catch her out, perhaps? – which she didn't understand; and she was at the same time burningly aware of Mr Kane looking at her, though she was definitely not looking at him. She wondered suddenly if they had been quarrelling before she arrived and their sharp exchange and the present atmosphere were the leftovers from that.

'And what does your father do?' Mrs Kane asked, but her husband interrupted her.

'Oh, don't interrogate the poor girl,' he said. 'You'll frighten her off. Offer her some coffee or something, before she takes fright and leaves us in the lurch.'

He stood up as he spoke and crossed the room to a large and gleaming radiogram in the corner. The lid was up and there was a record already on the turntable, and he lowered the needle on to it.

Mrs Kane breathed out through her nose again, and said, 'Would you like some coffee?' But she said it in the sort of tone that so clearly expected the answer 'no', that Julia would have refused even if she had wanted it, which she didn't. She had a brief memory of the smell of the packet of coffee; but to negotiate the social hazards of drinking anything in this house at this moment was beyond her.

'No, thank you,' she said, and then, as Mr Kane returned from the radiogram to his seat, the music began, and caught her attention. The very first phrase was one of instant delight, and felt familiar to her, fitting down into the spaces of her brain like a jigsaw piece, though she had never heard it before. 'Oh,' she exclaimed with pleasure. It drew the attention of Mr Kane

16

to her again, but now that the first shock was over she found his blue gaze less disconcerting – bearable, anyway. 'What is it?' she couldn't help asking.

'Brahms,' he said. 'Serenade No. 1 in D major.'

'Brahms!' she said. 'That's why I felt as if I knew it. I love Brahms.'

'It's musicians' music,' he said.

She didn't understand the remark, but it caused a different enlightenment. 'Are you a musician?'

'For my sins,' he said. 'I am a fiddler and I play for an orchestra. Nothing exciting, just rank and file, lest you leap to the idea that I am a glamorous soloist or something of that sort.'

'I think it's very exciting,' Julia said, interested out of her shyness. She remembered the smell of rosin and slotted that piece in with satisfaction. She liked to *understand* things.

'So, you like music, do you?' he said.

She liked the way he didn't feel the need to define it – not 'classical music' or 'serious music' but just music, as if that was all there was.

'I don't see how anyone can't,' she answered. 'It's – like *life*, isn't it?' He seemed to understand what she meant, and nodded, smiling. Mostly when people smiled it was just a different decoration on the same basic façade, but his smile seemed to change his face in some profound way, and it caused a strange small quiver deep in her stomach – something that felt almost like a pang of hunger.

'Do you play?' he asked.

'No,' she said. She felt bad about saying no, as though she thought he *wanted* her to be able to play and was disappointing him. Musical instrument lessons could be taken at school, but they were extra, and there was no money for extras. She had never been to a concert, either, and she felt embarrassed about that, feeling it would sound like a snub to his chosen profession to admit it. In explanation, as if he had been privy to her train of thought, she said, 'My father has a gramophone and I listen to that, and the wireless.' This sounded so meagre that she added, 'My father says that music is like mathematics, that the relationship between notes is fixed so you can always

17

work it out logically, like a theorem.' It was one of the few things her father had ever told her, which was perhaps why it had made such an impression. She understood more than she had words for: principally, that if the relationships were fixed by something other than man's ingenuity, then music must be part of the ordering of the Universe – like the atomic tables – which meant it came from God. She thought for a moment of voicing this, but it seemed impolite to be bringing God into it in someone's sitting room at half past four on a weekday afternoon. Instead she finished feebly, 'I suppose that's why it's like life.'

She wanted to keep looking at him to see if he understood, but Mrs Kane said at that moment, 'And what does your father do?' She said it in exactly the same tone of voice as she had said it before, as if she had simply torn up all the words in between and was going back to the only ones that mattered.

Julia turned to her. 'He's a mathematician,' she said, and because people always wanted clarification at that point she added without being prompted, 'He writes text books. Jacobs and Underwood?'

Mrs Kane looked blank, but Mr Kane said, 'Oh yes! The good old J and U! We used those at my school. So your father is *that* Jacobs, is he?' He flung his wife a significant look.

'We use Townshend at my school,' Julia said.

'Just as well,' he said. 'As I remember, everyone always hated maths. It wouldn't make you popular to be the daughter of the chief torturer, would it?'

He and Julia smiled at each other, and she felt the warmth of sympathy, immensely powerful in her solitary life. She thought that if only she had a chance to talk to him, he would understand whatever she said, whether she got the words right or not.

Mrs Kane intervened firmly: 'Now, Peter, if you've quite finished talking nonsense, what about the babysitting?'

Julia almost felt him withdraw, and had an instant's annoyance with Mrs Kane for spoiling things. His blue gaze had become mocking, and he surveyed both the females from a distance of superiority, on no one's side but his own.

18

'Oh yes, I'd forgotten you came here for a purpose. Well –' he made an outward gesture with his hands – 'you see us, you see the offspring. He of the tinny tympani is Michael; he of the unwashed visage is James; that is my wife, Joyce, and I am Peter. Do you think you could bear to babysit for us? Much of my work is evening work and my wife complains of being left so often alone with the children and never seeing me. She would prefer to be present while I draw my horse's tail across the stretched intestines of lambs, as someone so ably put it—'

'Never mind the smokescreens,' Mrs Kane said – to Julia, at least, incomprehensibly. 'Get on with it.'

'Well, that's it really. If you would come and sit in our house now and then and make sure the children don't play with matches or eat soap or do any of the other things that children are suspected of secretly longing to do, we should be appropriately grateful. To the tune of half a crown, to be exact.'

'One or two evenings a week,' Mrs Kane broke in briskly. 'We should be back by ten thirty at the latest, and we'd leave you your supper.'

'Thank you, I'd like that,' Julia said gravely. Now Mrs Kane was the comfort. Mr Kane, from being as familiar as the inside of her own mouth, had moved back immense distances, and his wife seemed kind and reassuring, a normal sort of grown-up, saying only ordinary, comprehensible things.

'You have asked your parents, I suppose?' she went on.

'Yes,' Julia said obediently. 'When would you like me to come, then?'

Husband and wife exchanged a glance, and then Mrs Kane said, hesitantly, 'Well, I suppose you'll be going out with your friends tomorrow night.'

'No, I don't have any friends,' Julia said, and thinking how odd that sounded when said out loud, went on quickly, 'Do you want me to come tomorrow?'

'Well, yes, that would be very nice, if you don't mind.'

'I can do some swotting. I've got exams coming up,' Julia said.

'If they'll let you,' Mr Kane said, following her gaze to

the children and jumping back into the middle of her thoughts and disconcerting her all over again.

'Yes,' she said, as if she didn't know what she was saying yes to.

Two

Peter Kane was driving home with Joyce asleep beside him. The concert, a Coronation Gala affair, and the subsequent reception for VIPs and orchestra, had been rather heavy for her and they had left early, though they had half promised Jimmy Hill, Peter's co-desker, and his wife to dine with them after the reception.

Joyce thought she might be pregnant again. Peter was not sure what he felt about that yet – surprise had been his first emotion, for he could not clearly remember when the evil deed might have been done. Still, if she was pregnant, it was his deed, that he could be sure of – Joyce was not the type to be unfaithful. Apart from doubting whether she had sufficient animal spirits to want to – she seemed to have little enough for him, anyway – he could not imagine her doing anything shifty, underhand, or likely to ruffle her appearance. An affair would simply be too undignified to be contemplated.

He glanced at her as they drove down the well-lit main road. She looked attractive even asleep with her head rolling on the seat-back. Her curly dark hair was short-cropped to show off the length of her neck and her fine shoulders. Evening dress suited her, especially this austere affair of dark-blue silk with its bias-cut bodice and narrow knife pleats; you could never imagine Joyce wearing anything either loose or frilly. She was attractive – handsome, perhaps, with its Austen echoes was the word to use – in a kind of open-air, county way with her long limbs, clear eyes, healthy, high-coloured face. She knew how to dress, and she knew how to behave. He could always be proud of her on his arm. Even pregnant.

Peter Kane had never been in love; he didn't expect ever to be, and most of his acquaintances would say that he was incapable of it; though in fact there were already two loves in his life – his music, and himself.

The second of these loves had been with him for as long as he could clearly remember. He knew that he was not generally well-liked amongst his own sex: he had heard himself called variously 'a bit of a rotter', 'a cad' and 'no fool' – all of which contained about equal proportions of disapproval and envy. Any man who shows ability to look after his own interests, and ability to pick up any girl he wants, will always be both admired and disliked by his comrades. This was precisely what he wanted. He had little use for male companionship. At his first boarding school he had been miserable and homesick, bullied by the bigger, ignored by the more self-confident boys. Having to make do with his own company for so much of the time, he had soon learned that he was better company for himself than they were.

However, for one with his pride, self-sufficiency was not enough: it had to be obvious to everyone else that he didn't want or need their company. For that reason, he had to excel at something. Games seemed the obvious choice at first, and for three terms he exerted himself at rugger and cricket, with immediate success, for he had a neat, strong body and good co-ordination. But others were good at games too, and they tended to be the very people he wanted to dissociate himself from – the popular boys, the school stars and heroes. Thrown into their company, he found them beginning to like him and himself beginning to enjoy their liking. Comfortable mediocrity seemed to beckon, and he sheered away from it in instinctive horror. It would not do. He needed to stand apart from and above his peers. He must find something else to excel at, something more individual, where there could be no emulation.

It was this that led him to concentrate on his music, an area in which he had already shown some promise. Out of a desire to lead where his peer group would not follow, he dropped the flute – too easy, reminiscent of junior school recorders, too dangerously popular, and lacking in sufficient intellectual rigour to keep off rivals – and concentrated on the violin. Almost from the first moment of taking it seriously, he found himself captured. To coax out of the indifferent school fiddle not just sounds but *music* invested him with a power beyond thought, gave him a bone-deep satisfaction which had nothing to do with competing with other boys. It was exciting, fulfilling, yet paradoxically left him hungry, with a sort of hunger that felt as though it could never be satisfied. His rather discreditable desire for superiority, he soon realised, had led him to the place he really wanted to be.

From then on, there had been no doubts, only logical steps. From the school music teacher he progressed to a private tutor. The double circumstance of being only fourteen and immersed in music had meant that he did not even notice the outbreak of war. Youth orchestra experience and the Royal College followed; his particular talent got him excused from National Service, and for the past seven years he had been with one of the leading orchestras in Britain, where he had moved up to third desk. These were all logical steps on his path to fame, and another of them had been to marry Joyce Mary Markham, only daughter of Richard Markham of Milton Abbas, a girl with the right looks, the right blood, the right connections. He would not always be rank and file, and when he went places he meant to have the right sort of wife to support and enhance him.

He glanced at her again, sleeping defencelessly beside him. It hadn't turned out quite as he had expected. For one thing, Joyce had wants and needs of her own, something he had unaccountably left out of the equation. For another, the statutory two children had turned up rather too promptly for his liking and almost, it seemed, without his express orders. These two circumstances had led to the first unpleasantness between him and his bride. It had genuinely surprised him when she complained that she hardly ever saw him and could never accompany him to concerts because of the children. He had not expected her to crave his company, and it forced him to realise that Joyce had had reasons of her own for marrying him, one of which presumably had been love. That had not entered into his calculations; of course he had told her he loved her while he was courting her, and during their first nights together, but that was a matter of form, of custom – simple good manners, for heaven's sake! He hadn't meant it, not in the grand MGM passion sense, or, indeed, thought that she meant it like that when she said *she* loved *him*. It perplexed him to be forced to consider that it had *not* only been to get away from the rural village, where she had been imprisoned most of her life, that she had accepted Peter's proposal of marriage.

He had had to do some quick thinking. He loved the freedom and unaccountability of his life, the sense of shucking off his impedimenta when he stepped out of the front door, and becoming his untrammelled lone self again. He didn't want Joyce to come with him to concerts and on trips out of London, but he couldn't refuse without good reason. He didn't want to arouse suspicion in her as to what other fish he was frying, and of course her presence would put the frying pan at least temporarily out of commission. He also didn't want her to know that he had only just realised she loved him, for fear of what conclusions she might draw about his feelings. The only thing to do was to let her come with him sometimes, however much it cramped his style. He must humour her: he must get a babysitter.

The result had been the advert in the grocer's shop window, eliciting an unexpectedly quick response – privately he hadn't expected any response at all – from the girl who seemed to be so eminently suitable. The hand of fate must have been involved to come up at short order with a respectable, quiet girl who lived practically next door, and who seemed to be available at all hours and at any notice. A funny little thing, she was, with her noticing eyes and her solemn face, and those long fair plaits, like a – well, one couldn't really say nowadays 'like a German girl' – but anyway, like a Swiss girl. The children adored her already, and the sight of her coming up the front drive in her school panama, clutching her school bag, was enough to send them into ecstasies of anticipation.

Joyce grunted and stirred, and Peter slowed down a little, driving more carefully so as not to waken her. He didn't particularly want to talk now. His thoughts drifted back to the Jacobs kid. One couldn't be too careful about what one's offspring might pick up, and he had taken the precaution of writing to the girl's headmistress for a reference. The result had been satisfactory, as far as it went, but it did nothing to lessen his opinion that she was a funny kid; in fact the beak had almost said as much herself, mentioning that she was gifted and intelligent, but seemed very independent, a 'loner', always reading – that sort of thing.

The kids adored her, talked of nothing else. To James, 'Dula' was little more than a pick-a-back and cuddle machine, for both of which blandishments he had an insatiable appetite; but Michael was full of what Julia said and what Julia did, the new games she thought up, the things she knew, the pictures she drew for him. She seemed to have a talent that way. She drew them wonderfully lifelike and animated rabbits and mice, pigs and dogs and kittens; and he had seen – though she had not wanted him to – some sketches she had done of the children. While she was 'sitting' them, he thought, they had been sitting for her. Ha! He must remember to tell Julia that next time he saw her. He liked to see her laugh. Anyway, Joyce seemed to be quite taken with the girl, and couldn't speak highly enough of her, so the half crowns he laid out could hardly have been better spent.

Left off the main road, left again, first right into Spenser Road; there was the park, the only thing of any attraction anywhere near his house. God help them all when they decided to build over that: with the post-war chronic housing shortage nothing was sacred. And here they were at home. The address was Spenser Road but the drive up to the garage was round the corner in Milton Street. In the thirties, when a lot of new development had taken place in the area, the local council, or whoever it was that named roads, had come down on the side of Culture and adopted a Milton, a Shakespeare, a Dickens, a Spenser and a Scott, surfaced the roads and given numbers to the existing houses. New houses had been built on the vacant plots, and it had become a suburban estate. Then the German bombs had knocked them down again; not thoroughly, however, only enough to make the area look shabby.

Well, there was nothing wrong with their house anyway, once they had taken down the imitation oak nameplate inscribed in curly writing 'Shangri-la'. Victorian mock Tudor was not what he would have chosen if given an unlimited choice, but the house was well and solidly built, and the location was convenient for him, with good road and tube connections, which was important for his work.

There was a welcoming glow in the hall window, the sort of glow that comes from a standard lamp shining behind closed curtains of some warm colour. It was good not to come home to an empty house. Peter turned the car into the drive and pulled up outside the garage. No point in putting it away, really, when he'd be going out again early tomorrow. He shook Joyce gently.

'Home darling,' he said. She groaned, murmured, and woke, opening her eyes just enough to verify his statement. 'Straight to bed with you. I'll see to Julia. Come on, best foot forward.'

She stumbled drowsily behind him to the front door, swayed on her feet while he opened it, and as soon as he let her in climbed obediently upstairs, her eyes already shut again. Peter listened. Everything was quiet, with the warm, breathing quiet of a house where people are sleeping safely. He put his fiddle case on the hall table and laid his car keys on top of it, unwound his white silk scarf and dropped it on top of the keys, and then glanced at himself in the mirror above the table. The taking-off of the scarf had ruffled the hair on the crown of his head, and he put up a hand automatically to smooth it; thin, fine hair that he would not keep, and an ugly hand, not the traditional idea of an artistic hand – Joyce had that, with the long, fine, graceful fingers. Breeding, he supposed. His was square, strong, with a great pad of muscle behind the thumb. But he admired it anyway. It was a hand that knew its work, a hand that he could trust to anything, a hand that would not let him down.

He turned to the line of light under the sitting-room door, and opened the door softly. The standard lamp was positioned behind the sofa and was the only source of light in the room. She was sitting on the floor in front of the sofa, leaning her back against it, just inside the circle of light. Her knees were up, supporting a board on which she was drawing, and she was absorbed, childlike, in what she was doing, so that she didn't look up at first when he came in. He walked over to stand beside her. She finished the part on which she was

26

immediately engaged and then put down her pencil with a gesture that seemed to say, I will not work while you are watching.

She looked up at him, gravely, expecting him to make the first comment. She had tied her plaits together behind her so that they would not interrupt her, and her sleeves were rolled up, workmanlike. Her forearms were long and smooth and tenderly curved – somehow touching, like the limbs of a young animal.

He didn't quite know what to say. He rolled several opening gambits over in his mind, but could not decide on any of them. At last he said, casually, 'All serene?'

'All serene,' she said. 'We had floods at bedtime because Jamie didn't want to take off his vest, but he did it in the end.'

'Dirty little beast,' Peter remarked cheerfully. 'He must get that from me. His mother would never have such a sordid desire as to sleep in her underwear.'

Julia made no reply to that remark; she was enchanted with him, as always, for the things he said, so unexpected, so very much *there* that she felt what he said was specifically for her, and not just mouth-music, like other grown-ups.

Peter thought, There she is, just watching me again, as if she were absorbing information, like one of those beastly electronic brains. He decided to make her pay for it by talking to him.

'I'm going to have a cup of cocoa,' he said. 'Come on – come into the kitchen and I'll make you one, too.'

'All right, but then I'll have to go,' she said, and stood up quickly, still holding her drawing board. She followed him into the kitchen, and stood by the door watching as he got out milk, sugar and cocoa and began the ritual.

'I love cocoa,' she said after a moment. 'We hardly ever have it at home. Only tea.'

'You should have told me before. I'll see to it that you have cocoa every time you come,' he said.

Perhaps he was rather too jovial, for she said coolly, 'Then it wouldn't be a special treat any more, would it? Thanks all the same, but I'd be happy just to have it now and again.' She watched him set out two cups and spoon the ingredients into the saucepan, and said, 'Where's Joyce?'

'She's gone on up to bed,' he said, starting at the sound of her name and glancing up to see what was on the child's mind, but there was only that same quiet nod – information-gathering again.

'You do it well,' she observed next. He met her eyes. 'Make cocoa, I mean.'

Could she possibly be as innocent as she looked? But her face was guileless. Damn it, he was supposed to be unnerving her, not vice versa. How old was she? Fifteen? Sixteen?

'How old are you?' he asked abruptly.

'Fifteen,' she answered. 'Sixteen in August.'

'And what are you studying at school?'

'General subjects at the moment, but next year I hope I'll be doing art, English and music. They're my best subjects now.'

'You didn't tell me you were studying music.'

'You didn't ask. But it isn't exciting, like playing an instrument. It's just theory and history of music. All in books. We hardly ever actually hear any. Funny, isn't it, to teach music just with words? Once in a blue moon we go down into the hall and Mrs Anderson puts a record on the gramophone. Otherwise it's just –' she paused as if searching for the right expression – 'a dry run,' she said at last.

He laughed, thinking the expression apposite, and felt comfortable with her, the tensions of the evening slipping away.

'Can I see what you were drawing?' he asked next. She said nothing, handed over the board with obvious reluctance, but obediently, having no idea of her rights. It was a drawing in soft pencil of Michael, to which he guessed she had been adding the background when he came in. Michael sitting on the chair by the window and reading: he had one foot tucked under him and the other dangled, the foot turned in at the ankle to reach the bar of the chair. One hand held the page down; his head was bent, and the other hand was creeping up for the thumb to slip guiltily into his mouth. The effect of the light coming in from behind was very well done, he thought. Also the likeness was unmistakable, and the forbidden thumb

28

about to be sucked was so much a gesture of Michael's that Peter laughed aloud.

'It's very good!' he said, and looking up he saw her smile of sudden pleasure at his unmistakably genuine praise. 'You're very good,' he said, and her cheeks grew pink. For something to do, she put her hands up and behind her head to release her plaits from their band. She was wearing her white school blouse, without the tie, and as she lifted her arms he saw her young breasts move under the cotton: she was scarcely grown yet.

'I like to draw people,' she said. 'I can understand them when I draw them – like my father. I did some good things of my father, and when I showed them to him he was surprised. But – well – he didn't like them. He seemed –' she paused, not this time because she did not know the right word, but because she did not want to admit the fact – 'uneasy.'

This struck Peter, and he looked again at the drawing and thought, yes, it could be unsettling to be sketched like this, to find oneself revealed all unknowing, pinned to the page like an entomological specimen and dissected by those quiet, watchful eyes. And yet, he thought, he would like her to draw him one day. He'd like to know what she saw. It would be an exciting, intimate thing. The sudden image in his mind of sitting for her – having her look up at him and down, her eyes touching him, taking him, translating him – made him shiver.

He needed to change the subject. 'Tell me about your father,' he said, leaning himself against the kitchen table to exhibit his complete ease. 'What does a mathematician do?'

'I don't know, really. He stays in his study nearly all the time and we aren't allowed to go in there. I think he's working on some very obscure formula.'

'You mean, like the highest prime number, or pi to ten thousand places?'

'Oh, more obscure than that, I expect. I don't know, but of course I could never ask him. I don't suppose I'd understand anyway, even if he told me. He writes papers sometimes, for journals and learned societies. And he has to do changes and appendices to the text books too. There are always new editions coming out.'

'Doesn't Mr Underwood help?'

'He's dead now, so he can't. He used to do the geometry bits – that's not Father's specialty. Now there's a professor in Reading who does them, but he never comes to the house and Father hardly ever goes to see him. It's all done by post.'

'But when it was Mr Underwood, it wasn't done by post?'

She looked up at him, clear-eyed, as though the answer were obvious. 'Oh no. We all lived together, you see, in a big house on the other side of the park. The house was sort of divided – I don't mean we lived *together*. We had our own side, and he had his, but he and Father saw each other nearly every day. Uncle David had a big room – the library, we called it – where he worked, and Father would go in there.'

'Is that what you called him? Did you like him?'

'I don't really remember much. It's what Mother calls him when she refers to him to us, but I was quite little then. I think I remember thinking he was nice, but a bit daunting.'

'He must have been super-intelligent.'

'Yes, and people like that are daunting. Anyway, *I* never went into the library. We were never allowed to disturb Father's work.'

'Doesn't your father lecture or anything? He must be quite famous. I mean, lots of schools must use Jacobs and Underwood.'

'Oh yes, thousands of them. And not only in this country – they use it in Indian schools and African ones and all sorts of places. That's what makes it all right. The royalties on text books are very small, you see, but they're sold in such huge numbers it adds up to enough.' She smiled. 'I suppose it's a good thing that schoolchildren are careless with books. It wouldn't do us any good if they kept them in perfect condition.'

'And does he lecture?'

'No. I think he used to, *before*, but he hardly goes anywhere now, only to the Royal Society dinner and things like that.'

'Before what?' Peter had not recognised the stand-alone nature of the word.

She hesitated, looking into her thoughts for the right words. *Before* had always lived in her mind as a picture and it was hard to put it into words. 'A bomb fell on the house in 1944 and completely destroyed it, and Uncle David was killed. We were all right because we'd gone down the shelter but he didn't believe in them so he stayed in the library working. So after that, we had to move to Milton Street and I think that's when everything changed.'

'What changed?'

She shook her head, frustrated. 'I don't know, because I can't really remember what it was like before that, but I think everything was different.' She couldn't convey to him the silence and lack of conversation in her home, the absence of communication either man to woman or parent to child. She didn't *remember* things being different, only felt that they had been; and she felt, besides, that no one could have been like that all their lives, or how would they ever have managed to do anything? Her father and mother had married each other and that at least, surely, must have necessitated some speech and perhaps even a smile or (she mentally shook her head in wonder) a kiss? She couldn't bear to think that someone could live their whole life without ever connecting with another person – couldn't bear it because she was afraid it could happen to her.

Peter watched her, trying to fathom her thoughts. He saw that something troubled her, and from what little he had gathered about her home life he didn't wonder. She came back from a reverie and looked up at him again, looked into his eyes in a searching kind of way, and he felt an odd sense of connection with her, so that for a moment she ceased to be the funny little schoolgirl who babysat his children but was just – well – herself, too complete and familiar an entity to need a label.

The sudden closeness disturbed him, and he sought a grown-up, *de haut en bas* question to restore the normal equilibrium.

'Do you want to go on painting when you leave school?' he asked.

She didn't seem to notice the apparent non sequitur. She seemed completely relaxed in his presence, ready to answer anything it might please him to ask.

'I would like to, I think. It's the only thing I'm any good at, and Mrs Thompson says it would be a pity if I didn't. But I don't know if I'd be good enough to earn my living at it, and I've got to do that somehow.'

'Do what?'

'Earn my living. My father did say that if I pass my A levels well, he'd think about letting me go to art school. But my mother wants me to go to secretarial college. She says you are never short of a job if you can type and do shorthand.'

The gloom that had crept into the last sentence made Peter smile. 'It sounds like a fate worse that death,' he said.

'You don't know how lucky you are,' she said solemnly, 'to be able to do something you like for a living.'

Which pitched him on the instant back into a recollection of the evening just passed. As it was a gala, he had been pretty well forced to take Joyce, but his Current Entanglement had not been pleased about that, having had a fancy for it herself. She had come to the damn concert anyway, buying her own ticket, and there had been one or two moments when he had feared there would be an unpleasantness. But it had all passed off all right, and he was sure Joyce had not noticed anything, though Jimmy Hill had given him a wry look that told him *he* knew what was going on. Still, it had not been an evening to cherish in memory, and now that he *had* remembered it, he felt tired. The cocoa was finished, this little interlude was over.

'I think it's about time you were getting home, don't you?' he said.

Julia understood herself dismissed, accepted it without hurt. 'Yes,' she said obediently, draining off her cup.

'I'll see you to your gate,' he offered politely, and she as politely refused.

'No, that's all right, thanks.'

'Just as you please,' he said with relief. 'Let me see, I owe you half a crown, don't I?' He reached into his trouser pocket, and she stood watching him, still too young to be embarrassed about receiving money. He held out the coin and when she lifted her hand he placed it in her palm, feeling uncomfortably like a rich uncle 'tipping' a favourite niece. For the first time it seemed an incongruity.

'Thank you,' she said. Her hand dropped to her side, and she still watched him, as if waiting for further instructions. He wanted his bed.

'Off you go, then.'

She turned away, went through to the sitting room to collect her things, and let herself out of the front door, all in silence, but as she was about to shut the door after her she poked her head back in to say, 'I'll pop round after school on Friday to see if I'm wanted this weekend.'

The door shut quietly, and Peter turned off the light in the kitchen and made his way upstairs. He stopped at the door of the kids' room to look at them: James round-faced and poppy-cheeked, sleeping on his back in his undisturbed cot, Michael beginning already to grow angular with boyhood, sprawled on his front, his brow corrugated with concentration, his bedclothes wound round him like a cocoon, snorting his way through his complicated and heroic dreams. Peter smiled with the softness he dared not show when they were awake. He fought softness in himself as he had all his life, because a career in music demanded hardness, focus, determination – sacrifice, even – and he intended his career to go as far as it could. He intended to be an international celebrity one day, as soon as possible, and nothing must get in the way of that. But alone and unobserved in the doorway, he indulged for a moment that perilous tenderness that affected him at the sight of his sleeping boys.

And then went on to his own bedroom. Joyce was asleep, and didn't stir when he climbed in beside her.

Three

Throughout the following year Julia's relationship with the Kane family developed to everyone's satisfaction. She performed her babysitting duties twice or three times a week on a regular basis, but as time went on she took to calling in at other times. The children always liked to see her, and Joyce was often glad of extra help. She was not robust, and clearly found looking after two children alone a daunting task, not to mention keeping house, shopping and cooking, and all with no servants except a cleaning woman who came in twice a week. It became natural for Julia to call at the house on her way home from school to see if there was anything Joyce wanted. Even if there was not some little errand or task, Joyce would usually ask her to have a cup of tea with her. Occasionally – though her pride prevented it from being often – Joyce would ask her to keep her company through the evening when Peter was out. Solitude was not Joyce's forte. The children might wear her out, but the silence of the house when they were in bed asleep and Peter was not due home until late got on her nerves.

Through the summer Julia got into the way of presenting herself at weekends, too, to take James and Michael to the park, do bits of shopping for Joyce, in fact make herself generally useful. Joyce was often in doubt as to how much she owed her young helper. She disliked not knowing how many hours were official and how many unofficial, for she was a methodical woman and liked to pay her way. But she was too glad of Julia's help and company to try very hard to sort it out.

For Julia's part, the money had become a secondary consideration. She loved the children, she admired Joyce, and she was glad to have a place to go that was not her parents' home, a place where she was welcomed, smiled at and talked to. The house seemed grand and gracious to her in comparison with Milton Street. It was not stuffed with belongings nor fabulously luxurious, but there were nice carpets and pieces of good furniture that Joyce had brought with her from her parents' house in Dorset. There were one or two paintings, a fine clock, a few selected ornaments – things that spoke of harmony and thoughtful choice. To Julia it seemed delightful that someone had cared enough to select and place articles for the purpose of creating a pleasing surrounding. She became aware, through the contrast, that her own home jarred her. The furniture there seemed ugly and awkward; she learned now that it was cheap, some of it Utility, some merely old without being antique. She supposed if they had ever had good things *before*, it must all have been destroyed by the bomb. But she saw also that her mother had no interest in making the best of things. She kept the house clean, but that was all. Had she always been like that? Julia wished she could remember. It seemed that a heart had gone out of her, but if that were true, when had it, or why?

Compared with the Kanes' house, home was cold – not physically, but emotionally. Joyce was not a spontaneous, outgoing person, but compared with Julia's mother she was a bubbling extrovert. She clearly liked Julia, and liked having her around; and the children poured love on her. It was like waking up from a frozen sleep, Julia felt – like Snow White in her glass coffin, or like a green shoot pushing up through the earth after a long winter.

As to Mr Kane – Peter – he remained to Julia a delight inside an enigma wrapped in a mystery. She didn't see much of him, as it was most often his absence that caused her presence at the house, and when she did see him, she never knew what his reaction to her would be. Sometimes he ignored her or treated her distantly, and sometimes he cornered her and involved her in long conversations, or asked her endless questions about herself. She had no explanation for his arbitrary changes of mood, but they didn't worry her: she put it down to mere grown-upness, and never saw any connection between his tempers and herself. But when he was in a mood to talk to her, it was the best thing in the world. With no one else in her life so far had she ever had that sense of connection: it seemed, at those best of moments, as if the physical walls between her mind and his could dissolve, leaving some essential quick of her to speak directly to his. She felt she could say anything to him, anything at all, and he would understand. What she said would never make him ridicule her, sneer at her, shrink from her, or worst of all simply look a blank incomprehension. He would never say or imply those deadly words, 'What do you mean?' He stood apart in her mind, distinct from all else in creation, limned in a special light of known- and knowingness. To talk – oh the bliss of it! It must be what it was like to have a friend, she thought. When he was in that approachable mood, there seemed no barrier of age or standing between them. He chatted to her as if she were simply *like* him.

The autumn and the new school term brought changes to Julia; the sixth form meant new responsibilities and new privileges. She was made a prefect, and her timetable was spotted with blank patches, marked 'private study'. She spent them reading in the school library, though others, less conscientious – or perhaps merely more sociable – spent them in the prefects' room playing cards. She abandoned the plaits at last, had two inches trimmed off her hair, and began experimenting with styles, wearing it 'up' in a different way each day. Her body changed shape subtly, and after an anguished half-hour of embarrassed attempted conversation with her mother, she had her first bra bought for her, and wondered if everyone could tell she was wearing one when she went in to school the next day.

One or all of these factors – being a prefect, the hair, the brassiere – made her suddenly become visible to the St Anthony's sixth formers. She saw them looking at her when she came out of school and they were idling about at the bus stops waiting for other girls: not long or deeply fascinated looks, but they noticed her, and she saw the other girls notice them noticing. She wondered what it would be like to have a boyfriend, covertly watched those that paired off, noted the handholding and sometimes the arm about the waist, the mouth-to-ear conversations, sensed the small local field of tension they generated. Some of the boys were good-looking, but none of them looked kind, and she found the idea of having to talk to one of them alone frightening. She would have no idea what they might say, or what answer she would be expected to give, or how they would react if she said or did the wrong thing. It would be like walking over a minefield, all hidden hazards ready to explode. She would get it all wrong and they would *laugh*; and their scorn seemed to her the worst of hazards, far worse than if they had been likely to hit her. She could have hit them back, but scorn would shrivel her like salt on a snail. So when they looked at her she looked away.

But one boy, bolder than the rest, did make the attempt on her. Having waited outside the school gates for four days running on purpose to say good afternoon as she went past, on the fifth he asked her to go with him to Fred's, a recognised precursor of a proper 'date'. Frozen with terror, she felt unable to refuse, and walked with him to the café. He did not recognise her terror, and believing her cool remoteness came from innate superiority, was a little daunted, and managed nothing more stimulating by way of conversation than the weather and a forthcoming match he was playing in. At Fred's, he bought her a cup of tea and they sat opposite each other at a corner table, sipping and avoiding each other's eyes, neither able to think of a thing to say, until the cups were drained and they were able, each with secret huge relief, to go their separate ways. Unable to explain it to himself in a way that squared with his pride, the boy afterwards made up a suitably horrific story of rejection by an Ice Maiden, which he told, with suitable embellishment, when anyone asked him at school how it had gone, and even sometimes when they didn't. As a result, Julia gained a reputation and wasn't bothered again in that way, though she was still looked at. The story inevitably got back to Lady Margaret's and, oddly, it made things easier for her. She had come in for a certain amount of mockery for not having a boyfriend, but once it appeared that it was because she didn't want one rather than that no one had ever asked her – which meant she was 'queer' rather than 'wet' – her classmates left her alone.

37

Michael started school, and Julia solved another problem for the Kanes by meeting him from school every day and bringing him home. Joyce now always offered her tea along with the children, and she didn't refuse too firmly, for quite often Peter was home at that time, and sometimes he would have a 'fit of the fathers' (as Julia privately called his paternal moods) and join them. She loved to watch him with his children, seeing them and him in a different light, each redrawn and redefined by the relationship of one to another. Everything about Peter Kane fascinated her, and she was happy simply to be in his company and to be allowed to look at him while he rough-housed with Jamie, or played a construction game with Michael, or read a story to them both. She hadn't the least idea why she found him fascinating, but then neither did she know that she needed a reason. He was unlike anyone she had ever met or heard of.

His attitude to her remained changeable, and she accepted that as a function of him. Coolness from Joyce would have hurt her and made her wonder what she had done wrong, but then Joyce inhabited the real world of ordinary mortals and was bound by their rules. Peter was just himself. She didn't resent being put through her paces now and then to amuse him, and as she grew more skilled at turning these catechisms into proper conversations, she found his treatment of her gradually changed, and the distant and loftily amused moods came less often. More and more he treated her as if she were one of the family – though quite what relation she could not determine. Autumn gave way to winter, and winter to spring, and the Kanes became part of her natural and unspoken landscape, and she was happy.

Summer came round again. Joyce Kane had not been well for some time. The baby she had suspected last year turned out to be trouble of a different kind. She had received medical treatment for it, but it became obvious that this wasn't working, and that in the end they would have to resort to surgery. Julia, being by now almost one of the family, was let in on the plans, which were that Joyce should go into hospital at the end of July for the operation while Peter was away on tour with the orchestra, and the children were to go to stay with Joyce's mother in Dorset.

Then, one evening towards the end of term, Julia came round to the house to return a book she had borrowed and found Peter and Joyce looking harrowed. She hesitated at the door of the sitting room, having let herself in at the side door as usual, sensing an atmosphere. 'I'm sorry,' she said. 'I only came to bring back the book.' And she made to go away again.

'No, it's all right – come in, Julia,' Joyce said. Julia came into the room, glancing quickly at Peter, and then back to Joyce, who, she noticed, was looking strained, almost haggard, and as if she had been crying. 'Sit down.' Julia removed some pieces of Lego from a chair and sat. Joyce noted the action and said, 'I'm sorry everything's in such a mess, but I've just been –' she paused and shook her head for lack of words to explain – 'I've done nothing today – literally nothing. I've just been sitting around like a stock.'

'Is something wrong?' Julia asked cautiously. She wanted to be sympathetic and tacitly invite a confidence in case Joyce wanted to unburden herself, for she had obviously been crying; but Peter was there and Julia was afraid it might be something to do with him, something that she should not know about. Married people, she knew, had huge and complicated secret lives with each other beyond her experience and therefore anticipation. Beyond the comic world of marriage portrayed in books and films and comedians' jokes, there was a dense and deadly serious thing that went on out of sight, all but the iceberg tip that protruded into daylight. She thought of her own parents. She could not imagine what they might say or do to each other when they were alone, or in what ways it might become a problem; and the same was true of the Kanes. It was like the boyfriend business multiplied to the power of n.

But Joyce answered her at once, 'Oh, everything! I've had a letter . . .' She made an uncharacteristically vague gesture of her long hands, which seemed to aim towards the mantelpiece, and Julia looked up there, expecting to see the letter. It was where her mother put letters and bills, edging them behind the clock to keep them upright. But of course Joyce did not do such things. The mantelpiece was as elegantly bare as ever, holding nothing but a pair of brass candlesticks, two porcelain figurines, and the clock, which had nothing thrust behind it.

'Bad news?' Julia asked, still tentatively. Out of the corner of her eye she saw Peter turn away to get a cigarette out of the box on the piano by the window and felt relieved at the break in his attention.

'It's awful,' Joyce said, with a slight break in her voice which told Julia that the tears hadn't long been finished with. 'The hospital have written to say they can't take me after all. The soonest they can do the operation now is the twenty-third of August.'

'Oh, I'm so sorry,' Julia said, thinking how awful it must be for Joyce to be condemned to a whole extra month of waiting.

Joyce went on: 'All the arrangements will have to be changed. We'd booked a bed in a convalescent home, and that'll have to be cancelled. Peter will be home, and he'll have to look after himself in the house. And worst of all, we'll have to find somewhere else to send the children.'

'I thought your mother was going to take them?'

'Yes, she was, but she and Daddy have booked their holiday for the end of August, to fit in with having the children in July, and now she says she can't alter the arrangements. I phoned her up the moment I got the letter, but she says she can't possibly change it. The villa's booked and they've got friends coming to stay with them there. Oh, it's such a nuisance.'

Julia was listening to Joyce, nodding sympathetically, when the startling thought came into her head as suddenly and completely as if it had been planted there whole. She shot a glance at Peter, and was disconcerted to find that he was looking at her from his vantage point by the piano with his most enigmatical smile. She turned her eyes quickly back to Joyce and listened with a sympathetic expression to her exposition of the trouble. At last Joyce wound down, and a silence followed, broken by the sound of Peter exhaling a mouthful of smoke and then clearing his throat. The two women looked at him expectantly.

'Julia is the answer,' he said.

Joyce looked impatient. 'Peter, don't be portentous. What do you mean?'

'She'll be on school holiday in August, when you go into hospital.'

And Julia heard herself say, as if without volition, 'I could look after the children.'

'You mean, here?' Joyce asked.

Peter answered. 'Well, obviously. Where else? She couldn't take them home with her, now could she?'

Joyce looked at Julia, and read her expression with dawning hope.

'I wonder – is it possible? You could come over in the morning – Peter could get them breakfast before he goes off. But you wouldn't want to be at all that trouble, to give up your holiday time for us? No, it's too much to ask.' She said the last part firmly, but Julia had seen the hope dawn in her eyes, and could not refuse now, even had it not been her own idea.

'Really, I wouldn't mind,' she said. 'I'd like it. And it wouldn't be for long, anyway, would it? They'll both be going to school when I go back, won't they?'

'There'd still be after school, and the evenings when Peter wasn't home. And for the first two weeks it would mean looking after them all day, every day. I can't believe you'd want to do that.'

'But why? They're good children, and you know I'm very fond of them.'

'It's different having complete responsibility for them, without anyone to hand them back to when you get tired of them. But, if you really wouldn't mind, it would be *such* a relief – you just can't imagine what it would mean to me.'

'Then I'll do it,' Julia said. 'Really, I'd like to.'

For a moment the tears threatened a return, and Joyce did not speak. Then she regained control and said, 'Naturally, we'll pay you for your time. Peter will stay home as much as possible, and Mrs Coleman will do the cleaning. You needn't worry about that. I can get her in to do a grand clean-up when I'm back. It's just the children, really. Of course, it would mean your staying late when Peter's working in the evenings.'

'That's all right. It isn't as if I have far to go home,' Julia said.

There was another brief silence, during which she seemed to hear her own words unnaturally loud in her head. The skin crawled on her scalp and though she was looking at Joyce she saw Peter's face in her imagination, and it was almost as if she could feel his thoughts pattering into her mind like little stoat feet.

Then he said, as if thinking it out as he spoke, 'I don't see why you need to go home at all. Wouldn't it be easier and more comfortable for you to stay here for the duration?'

Julia turned her head with what seemed agonising slowness towards him. There was an odd expression of satisfaction in Peter's face, as if some complicated chess problem he had been engaged in was just working out. Julia suddenly felt that she had been manoeuvred, that she had been coaxed quietly and stupidly into not exactly a trap, but a pen, perhaps, like a sheep. She had spoken the words of the offer herself, but who had put the thought in her mind? He had known all along that this was going to happen.

Joyce was speaking. 'That does sound like a good idea – what do you think, Julia? It would save you going backwards and forwards. You could bring all the things you needed and settle in here, in the spare bedroom, if you think you could stand it?'

There were many considerations, not least among them that the Kanes' house was far more comfortable than her own and seemed to her now much more like home than her parents' chilly dwelling; but there was nothing for her to decide – it had been decided for her in Peter's catlike smile.

'I'd love to come and stay,' she said. 'It's always fun staying in other people's houses. Sometimes Sylvia and I used to swap beds, just for the fun of it.' All attention was on her, and she felt as though she had found herself in the middle of the empty stage in the school hall with everyone waiting for her to say something, while she didn't know in the least what she ought to say. She went on helplessly: 'It'll be fun keeping house, too. And I'll be able to practise cooking – Mother never lets me at home, in case I make a mess and waste good food.' Why didn't one of them stop her talking? She looked from one to the other, and then in desperation said, 'By all means, I'll come. Shall I make a cup of tea now?'

Out in the safety of the kitchen, she wondered what the Kanes were saying to each other. She felt as if a gentle trap had been sprung on her – but after all, why should she think that? Joyce had so patently been upset, and now was genuinely grateful and relieved. And it had been her own idea. And there could have been no necessity to trap her when she would have said yes to a direct request. Thinking about it while she made the tea, she discovered that she really was rather excited about it. It would, at the very least, be something different, and change was always welcome in a life as static as hers had tended to be. There were slops in the saucers when she carried the tea in, but Joyce, who was usually fussy about that, was too grateful to her to mention the fact.

Julia had not considered that there would be any other interested parties in the matter, and was astonished more than anything when her mother objected to the scheme.

'I'm surprised at Mrs Kane suggesting such a thing,' she said. 'A young girl like you to be left in charge of two small children. She must be a strange sort of mother even to think of it. To leave two small children for weeks on end with a girl with no experience—'

'But I've been left with them before, often,' Julia broke in.

'In the evenings, yes, for a few hours. That's different from having them all day and all night as well.'

'But it isn't different, really. They aren't both going away, you know, only Joyce. He'll be coming back every night, and he'll be there some evenings and sometimes during the day as well. I shall never be left with them for more than a few hours.'

'Never mind, what would you do if one of them should choke, or cut himself? You'd be in a fine pickle then. Any number of things could go wrong. And who would get the blame? No, it's too much responsibility for a girl your age.'

'There are lots of girls my age have children of their own.'

'That's got nothing to do with it,' her mother retorted, and so it hadn't. 'That's their business, and in any case, other girls aren't you. I'm surprised really that they've kept you on so long, a daydreamer like you. Look at you now!' Mrs Jacobs burst out, for Julia had disappeared behind her vague look which she used for protection. 'You're standing there in a

43

dream this very minute. I don't know about you, Julia, I just don't. You must get it from your father.' An unusual burst of irritation made her animated and brought her to the brink of criticising Julia's father, something that was absolutely not done. 'All this reading books and art and so on – it's not going to get you far when you leave school, you know! If you don't buckle down and look to the future, start thinking about what you need to get a proper job, you'll end up in a factory packing biscuits.'

'I don't want to be a secretary,' Julia said doggedly, knowing that was what was meant by a proper job, knowing the lines of the argument from here onwards.

'How do you know? You don't know anything about it. Art is all very well as a hobby, but it won't earn your bread and butter. Get yourself a proper job as a secretary, something that'll bring you home good money and keep your hands clean, and you can have all your spare time for your art and your books.' Mrs Jacobs' voice was growing calmer as she felt the unassailability of her position. 'It's for your own good I'm telling you. Heaven knows, I wish your father had been well enough off for you not to have to think of a job, but I'm afraid you've got to, you and Sylvia. I want to see you in a position where you never have to worry about being able to keep yourselves nicely. And there's always a call for secretaries. Years ago you wouldn't have had the choice, you know.'

She paused here, and at this point Julia normally said something like, 'But that was before the war and things are different now,' upon which her mother said – but she didn't want to argue it all over again, and she said nothing.

Put off her stroke, Mrs Jacobs had to ad-lib, and said unguardedly, 'Of course, you might get married, and if you get yourself a good job you'll have more chance of meeting the right sort of person. I hope you do. Though mind you, what man in his senses would take on a dreamer like you – how you'd ever manage to run a house—'

'Well then,' said Sylvia who had been sitting at the table behind them, supposed to be practising her shorthand, but in fact nibbling the end of her pen and listening, 'this is just the chance for her to learn, isn't it?'

Mrs Jacobs shot her other daughter a suspicious look, but Sylvia's head was bent diligently over her books.

Julia picked up the line from there. 'It would be very good practice for me for when I do get married, and even if anything did go wrong, they've got a telephone, and you're only just down the street, so I can always ask your advice if I get in a muddle.'

'Well,' her mother began, and Julia knew she had won, 'in any case, your father will have to say what he thinks.'

'I'll go and ask him,' Julia said quickly, and went out of the room before her mother could think of an objection.

She tapped on the door of her father's study, and at his automatic 'Come in' she opened the door quietly and looked in.

'Father?'

'Yes, come in,' her father said vaguely. He wasn't writing, but leaning back in his chair and staring into the distance. He looked, though neither of them knew it, remarkably like Julia at that moment.

Julia went in, closing the door behind her, and stood on the other side of the desk in front of her father. His books and papers were spread across it, and before him was a stack of his foolscap writing paper, the top sheet covered in his tiny, black, meticulous writing, paragraphs of words followed by lines of numbers and symbols. His fountain pen was uncapped and lying across the paper, the ink dried on the nib. He had been in a reverie, she deduced, for some time.

The walls of the room were shelved all round and up to the ceiling, with the exception of the space taken up by the filing cabinet, and by the French windows – closed, always closed, because draughts of air might blow his papers about. Beyond the glass was the side slice of the house leading down to the back garden. Outside there was sunshine slanting down between the houses, a blue sky lightly fretted with wisps of cloud, a tree in a neighbour's garden blowing gently in a delightful breeze, birds hopping about and chirruping to each other. Inside there were dark ranks of books, a faintly churchy smell of dry decay, and that desk, like a rock on which, she thought, her father had been washed-up and stranded all these years, far from the world, and out of the swing of the sea.

Everything had a neglected air, including her father. He looked worn and shabby, and his vague expression made his face, by contrast with her mother's, look as if it had been worn away too, so that all the features were blunted and rounded into indistinctness. Even his hair was worn away at the front and on top, as though all the thinking had fretted and rubbed it off. Many of the shelves that seemed to hedge him in were lined with the familiar green of various editions and levels of Jacobs and Underwood. She tried to think of it as her father's achievement, like a portfolio of paintings, like the output of a Somerset Maugham or a Du Maurier. He was the Jacobs of Jacobs and Underwood: he was famous in his way. This not unimpressive stretch of green spines was his oeuvre, his life's work. But she could not make the thought real to herself. The solid, cloth-bound volumes seemed rather like the bricks with which he – or fate? – had walled himself up.

He paid no attention to Julia, and she examined him in silence while she waited for him to come back, respecting his train of thought as one who had them herself. Children can rarely see any resemblance to themselves in their parents, and the fact that she was blonde and her father dark-haired threw her off the track. All she could see was that they both had dark eyes. But in fact they were very alike, so alike that Mrs Jacobs sometimes felt almost hatred for Julia when her face took on that same opaque expression that her husband had always used to shut her out.

Carefully, so as not to disturb him, Julia picked up the pen and put the cap on it, and put it down again; but the movement brought him back to the present.

'Did you want to speak to me?' he asked her. He spoke courteously, as he did to everyone, whatever their age, sex or station. When she had first come to an age to appreciate it, and to realise how rare it was for an adult to speak to a child like that, Julia had thought it was a mark of his respect or at any rate love for her, and had been deeply moved and flattered by it. But after a few weeks of observation and analysis she had come to see that it had nothing to do with her, but was simply a function of him – just as when a quadratic equation worked out, it did not do it to please you. And she now

believed it was not a genial thing in him, this courtesy: it was
his way of keeping everyone at bay. She remembered suddenly
something that Peter Kane had said, that Roman Catholics had
to be more virtuous than non-Catholics, because they started
with such an advantage in *being* Catholics that God expected
more of them. She thought now that that meticulous courtesy
was what her father expected of himself because he started
with the advantage of a vastly more powerful intellect than
everyone else.

He was surveying her now with the same kind of vague
attention as that with which she had surveyed him earlier. It
was an allowance he had made her, meting it out from the
teeming demands of his brain, and she felt obliged not to waste
it. She assembled the words for economy.

'I wanted to ask you if I might go and stay with the Kanes
for three weeks and look after their children while Mrs Kane
is in hospital,' she said.

'Who are the Kanes?' Mr Jacobs asked without interest.

'The people I babysit for, in Spenser Road,' she said.

'Stay with them where?'

'Oh, at their house. In Spenser Road,' she clarified.

He looked very faintly puzzled. 'Why should you want to do
that?' He seemed to be having to bend his mind from a great
height to comprehend something utterly trivial, and she felt,
as she had so often before, guilty about wasting his time. But
what could she have talked to him about that he would have
regarded as worthwhile? Very occasionally he might make a
comment to her about music, but she felt that he heard it from
such a very different standpoint that it was barely a shared
interest. She could not talk to him about what it *felt* like to
her, as she could to Peter Kane. Feelings, she thought, were
not for her father, would involve his bending so far down from
his intellectual eminence that he might break something.

She inwardly debated what reason to give. Not the same
as for her mother, of course. She couldn't think of any angle
on it that would interest him. He had, she had gathered, not
much opinion of women's intellect. Her mother had once said
to her in an unguarded moment, 'Your father has a mind
above things,' without specifying what things, and when her

mother had said it, it was evidently meant to be a criticism. But Julia thought it was just the truth. She was academically much cleverer than Sylvia, was in the top half of her class at what was anyway a very selective grammar school, but still as far as her father was concerned she might as well have been on a different planet.

'They've been kind to me, and I want to help them out,' she said at last.

Her father considered this gravely, as he did everything. Uninteresting, but unexceptionable, his expression seemed to indicate. 'If you really want to do this,' he said in a tone that seriously doubted that anyone could want to do something so entirely lacking in appeal, 'I can see no reason why you *should* not.' He paused to give her the chance to say that she really did not want to. He resumed: 'It is encouraging, I suppose, to learn that you can aspire to an altruistic act – since I cannot suppose it will entail any pleasure for you.'

Julia felt she could not now say, 'Yes it will – a great, great pleasure,' especially as she had only just realised, because of his words, how much she was looking forward to it. So instead she said, greatly daring, 'How is your work going, Father? Is it a revision? A new edition?'

He looked at her for a long silence, and she had a rare moment of understanding with him. He was hovering on the brink of answering her question – he *wanted* to tell her – but the thought that she would not understand, and the wearisomeness of the very prospect of trying to explain, daunted him. She wanted to cry out, 'Yes, I know *exactly* how you feel!' She wanted to tell him she had felt like that almost every day of the life she could remember. She couldn't, of course. Instead she smiled at him.

He was surprised and, strangely, shaken by her smile. It changed her face, made her look almost beautiful, much older than he had grown accustomed to thinking of her, and, oddly, somehow wild. There was a sharpness to the mind behind a smile like that, and an unpredictability that woke an appetite in him – which he had almost forgotten – for communication. It reminded him of his lost, lamented partner Underwood, who had made life so interesting, who had made everything possible, whom he missed so unexpectedly much.

But the brief upsurge of emotion died down as quickly as it had arisen, and he lost the impetus to break through the barrier of inertia between them.

'If that is all, I must get back to my work,' he said.

She prepared to go, saying with emphasis, 'Thank you.'

'For what?' he asked.

'For making me think,' Julia said. Her father's rare smile turned up the drooping corner of his mouth, and even the darkness of his eyes seemed less faded, for a brief moment invested with an adamant brightness.

'Not at all,' he said politely, and for that instant they looked at each other with sympathy and satisfaction.

Four

Julia took over her new charges on Saturday morning. Peter was to take Joyce to the hospital, and would then have to drive straight on to a recording session in Maida Vale, which would run from two until five.

Joyce was near to tears when she finally came downstairs in her coat to where Julia stood in the hall with the children, watching through the open front door as Peter put the suitcase into the car.

'I hope everything will be all right,' she said. 'You two must be very good and do everything you can to help Julia,' she added sternly to her children, and then swooped down to hug them both. Michael rocked on his feet at the onslaught, and James withdrew his face to avoid being impaled on the spike of Joyce's brooch, but otherwise they were not too troubled by their mother's excess of emotion. They, of course, had no notion of why she was going; they were merely rather excited at the thought of being alone in the house with Julia for days on end. 'Goodbye, darlings. Julia will get your lunch for you – they eat at about twelve thirty, Julia, and it's all in the kitchen. You only have to cook the vegetables. They like to have a little butter mashed into the potato, and Michael likes pepper, but only a very little. Oh, and James is to drink his milk, no excuses.'

'Ready, darling?' Peter came back to the door, and winked at Julia over his wife's shoulder.

'Yes, I'm just coming. I was just telling Julia about the children's lunch.'

'Listen, Julia, just tie the brats up in the dog's kennel with a crust of dry bread, and I'll eat their lunches when I get back in. Three dinners – oh my-my!' Peter pantomimed rubbing his stomach and rolling his eyes in bliss, and the children giggled delightedly.

'You won't get mine, Daddy!' Michael shouted boastfully.

'You won't get mine!' James squeaked.

'Oh yes I will!'

'Oh no you won't,' they chorused.

'You'll have to eat it all up, then, so Daddy won't have the chance,' Joyce chipped in quickly, improving the shining hour.

'Right, now, let's be off,' Peter said briskly. 'I'll be home around six, Julia. Did you leave something for my dinner, darling?' to Joyce.

'Yes, there's a little bit of steak, and—'

'Right-oh. Come on then,' Peter cut in quickly to stop another flood. 'Bye-bye kids! Say goodbye to Mummy. See you later, Julia. Don't let them bully you.'

Joyce, following Peter out, turned at the car to wave. Julia was standing in the doorway looking peaceful and secure with a child's hand in each of hers. As if she lived there, Joyce thought with a little pang.

'I hope she'll be all right. I hope she'll manage,' she said to Peter as he got in beside her.

He glanced through the side window at the group in the door and gave a tucked-up little smile. 'She will. Don't worry.'

He looked again, and saw Julia stoop her head to say something to Michael. Michael giggled and turned to wave once more to Mummy. 'She'll be all right,' he said again, and then, mindful of the occasion, turned to Joyce and patted her hand comfortingly. 'You just concentrate on getting well as quickly as you can, so that we can have you back home again.'

He was rewarded by a smile from Joyce a little less tremulous than before, and he set the car in motion before the sight of Julia looking so very much at home in the doorway with the children unsettled Joyce again. Or him.

Now, thought Julia as she closed the door having waved the car out of sight, the first thing is lunch. That should be easy enough.

'Are you two hungry?' she asked.

51

'Yes!' they hooted.

'Well, I'd better get on with it then,' she said, dropping their hands and turning towards the kitchen.

'Can we help you?' Michael asked.

'Yes, if you like,' she said, and was greeted by another hoot of hilarity.

'Mummy never lets us help her,' Michael said.

'She says we get in the way,' James chipped in. 'And break things.'

'Oh,' said Julia, wondering if she had thought enough before she answered. 'Well, you won't break things if you're careful, and if you're not careful I won't let you help again.' That seemed to cover it, she thought. In the kitchen she let them lay the table while she cooked the vegetables and laid out the cold meat on the plates. James was soon sidetracked from his 'helping' and, leaving Michael breathing stertorously with concentration, laying out the knives and forks exactly parallel with one another, he wandered over to watch Julia.

'Can we have tomato sauce with it?' he asked her suddenly.

'Oh yes!' Michael called, looking up at the words.

'Does your mummy let you?' she asked.

'Yes,' James said promptly, but Michael said nothing, just fixed his eyes on her pleadingly. Julia had already learnt that James was entirely self-interested, and would lie without the least compunction if it was to his benefit, but Michael, through so often having to answer for the little one's transgressions, had a prematurely developed sense of responsibility. Having been told so often that, being the eldest, he ought to know better, he did.

'I don't see why you shouldn't have tomato sauce,' Julia said, since she didn't.

'Yippee,' James crowed and danced over to the cupboard to get it out.

'Where is it?' he asked after surveying the shelves for a moment.

'Well, how should I know?' said Julia.

'There isn't any,' Michael said.

'Get some more,' James ordered.

'Don't be silly,' Julia said, 'where would I get some more from?'

'From the shop.'

'I haven't got any money.'

James eyed her with disbelief. 'Grown-ups always have money.'

'Well, I'm not a grown-up.'

'What are you then?'

'What do you think?'

There was a long pause while they considered this, and then Michael said, slowly and doubtfully, 'I suppose you're a sort of a girl.'

Despite the lack of tomato sauce, they ate their lunches without fuss, and drank their milk, and then went up for their lie-down. Joyce insisted on half an hour after meals, and when Julia had seen them upstairs in their rooms with their shoes off, lying on their beds, and with the curtains closed, she went back down to do the washing-up, thinking what good children they really were. I'll make something nice for their tea, she thought, and having cleared up the traces of luncheon, she eyed the stove with satisfaction. The cooking was the part she was really looking forward to, for she never had the chance at home, but here she could experiment to her heart's content; and Joyce's stove was a modern one, and bigger than the one at home.

'Jam tarts,' she said aloud. 'They're easy, and it'll be a chance to practise pastry.'

Her mother had said that it was very difficult to make good pastry, and that it was by her pastry that you judged a cook. Julia, having heard the theory, couldn't see why it should be difficult, and rolling up her sleeves she padded round the kitchen finding ingredients.

The children, during their half-hour, were supposed to lie still on their beds, but it was perfectly obvious from the thuds and occasional voices that they weren't. However, as long as there was no actual sound of destruction, Julia decided to let them be. Her pastry was much more satisfying. She had got to the cutting-out stage when Michael appeared in the doorway in his stockinged feet, looking tousled and rather sheepish.

53

'Is it half an hour yet?' he asked hopefully.

'What were you doing? Fighting?' asked Julia, amused.

'Well, not a-zactly,' he said carefully. 'Jamie wanted to play with my fire engine, and I was playing with it.' Julia could imagine the rest. 'Is it half an hour yet?'

'I expect it might be,' she said kindly.

'What're you making?'

'Jam tarts for tea – at least,' she added honestly, 'that's what they're supposed to be going to be, but they might not.'

'Can I help?'

'If you like. What's Jamie doing?'

'He's playing with my fire engine in his bedroom. What can I do?'

'Well, you can't really help with the ones I'm doing, but you can make one of your own, if you like. Here –' she gave him some trimmings – 'shape that into a little pasty. Go round the other side of the table, so we keep out of each other's way.'

It wasn't long before James tired of his triumph with the fire engine, since there was no more struggle involved in it. Intrigued by the silence, he padded down to see what they were up to. He rushed into the kitchen and his feet in their woollen socks skidded on the polished floor and he went down with a bump.

Julia saw his mouth open in surprise, and before it could give vent to a yell, she cut in on him. 'Here, this isn't a skating rink, you know.'

Michael giggled, and Jamie changed his incipient wail for a smirk. 'What are you doing – can I do some?' he asked all in one breath, trying to get to his feet and skidding again.

'You'd better take off your socks, or you'll be shooting about like a hard-boiled egg.'

James sat down again and hairpinned his foot round to take off his socks as directed. 'Take off my cargidan as well,' he said. His speech had become very clear in the past year, but this was one of the words he still got wrong.

'Cardigan,' Julia corrected automatically.

'Cargidan,' he said obediently.

'No, car-di-gan.'

'Car-gi-gan,' he said doggedly.

'Oh, never mind. Just say woolly,' Julia said resignedly.

It kept them quiet for some time, standing at either side of the table and squodging the pastry about, making it into snakes and ashtrays and people until it was grey and limp like putty. Julia, meanwhile, cut out and filled her tarts and put them in the oven, and then came to clear away, at which point the children insisted that their own efforts went into the oven as well. She tried to persuade them otherwise, but they clamoured eagerly, and she shrugged and put the grey, coiled snake (Michael's) and the greyer aeroplane (Jamie's) in too, on the corner of the baking sheet.

They were like bullets when they came out, but the children were immensely proud of them all the same, and insisted that they were kept for Daddy when he came home. Julia's tarts were not a tremendous success, for she had made the mistake of jamming them too generously and they had overspilled like volcanoes and stuck to each other and to the baking sheet. She detached them with a philosophical shrug, and scraped the sticky lava off as best she could, and gave it to the boys who ate it with delight.

'What do you call it?' Michael asked.

'Jam toffee,' Julia improvised.

'I like it. Mummy never makes it.'

I bet she doesn't, Julia thought.

Six thirty was the children's bedtime, and since Peter was supposed to be home at six she decided the best thing was to get them bathed and pyjamaed straight after tea, which was at five o'clock, so that they could have their last half an hour to play with their father, if he was in the mood. And that, she thought to herself efficiently, will give *me* the chance to make his dinner with them out of the way.

They were being angelic, she knew, because it was her first day, but it was very satisfying to manage them so well, and she found them flatteringly good company. Everything she told them they absorbed with interest. Her jokes they found side-splittingly funny. Her unsuccessful jam tarts were eaten with unfeigned relish. And when she directed them upstairs to get ready for bed, they obeyed her without a question.

She put them in the bath together to save time and washed

them in turn. Michael had a fit of modesty and wouldn't let her wash him below the waist, so she let him get on with it, and five minutes later had to do the same with James, who took his lead. The only thing was that they seemed to spread waves of disorder behind them wherever they went, and she was still mopping the bathroom floor, with the thought of the sea of crumbs under the kitchen table that hadn't been dealt with yet, when she heard Peter's key in the front door.

'It's Daddy!' James yelled excitedly through his toothbrush, turning as if to head downstairs.

'Finish your teeth first,' Julia said sternly, and they both resumed brushing with frantic haste.

'Anybody home?' Peter called cheerfully as he closed the door behind him and laid his violin case down on the hall table. A muffled reply came from the bathroom and he smiled to himself and looked around as he took off his coat. A pair of grey socks hung over the bannisters where James had abandoned them on his way upstairs, and a cardigan was hanging from the kitchen doorknob. Through the kitchen door he could see Michael's fire engine on the floor under the table and what looked like a crust of bread just beyond it. He smiled again, and then turned to steady himself for the blow as the children came hurtling downstairs and threw themselves at him from two steps up.

'Hello monsters! Have you been good? Lay your hands upon your hearts and tell me you haven't driven poor Julia insane.'

'You're a monster,' James shouted, overexcited.

Peter winced. 'Ouch! Not in my ear. Down you get, you weigh a ton. Michael, what have you done with her? Show me the mound of freshly-turned earth in the garden, my son, and I will forgive all.'

Michael giggled, not knowing what he was talking about, and Julia appeared at the top of the stairs with her sleeves rolled up, her hair in wisps, and the front of her blouse soaked.

'I'm here,' she called. 'They've been very good, really they have.'

'Saved at the eleventh hour,' Peter said, tweaking Michael's nose. 'I can see you've been bathing with them.' Her wet blouse was clinging to her, showing the outline of her breasts and the darker points of her nipples, but when she glanced down she did not see that, only the wetness.

She smiled at him and said, 'I suppose it does look like that. I never knew anyone could make so much mess just taking a bath.'

'You wait until you see me in the bath,' he said solemnly. 'They don't get it from their mother, you know.'

'Are you going to bath Daddy as well?' Michael asked, intrigued at the thought, and Julia only laughed and said, 'Of course not, silly. Grown-ups bath themselves.'

'Well, who baths you, then?'

'Never mind that, whose socks are those, and whose cardigan is that, and whose fire engine?' Peter changed the subject and distracted them with a rapid fire of questions, before he started to think about Julia in the bath, which wouldn't do at all.

'I'm sorry, I didn't have time to clear up yet,' Julia said.

'My dear girl,' Peter said, putting a hand on her shoulder fondly, 'we didn't ask you to come here to be a slavey, just to look after the children.' Her shoulder under her blouse was hot and bony like a bird. 'For heavens' sake, you mustn't be doing housework and that kind of thing.'

'Oh, I don't mind, really,' she said, looking up at him from close quarters. The children too looked up at him, and the three pairs of candid eyes disconcerted him. 'It's good practice for me.'

'Nevertheless, we've no right to let you slog away at the housework. You must promise me not to do any more than you actually, actively enjoy.'

She seemed to consider this, and then nodded. 'All right.'

He removed his hand, and used it to shoo the children forward. 'Go on, you two, pick up those things. Right away. Chop chop.' They moved off inch by inch, and he followed in the direction of the kitchen.

'Did Joyce settle in all right?' Julia asked politely.

'Oh yes. She has a very nice room, and the nurses all seemed very pleasant. And she managed not to cry until I'd gone.'

'How do you know? I mean, that she cried after you'd gone?'

'I know,' he said with a grim kind of a smile.

'It must be awful for her,' Julia said. No one in her family had ever had an operation.

'It must have been awful for *you*. Did the monsters give you a great deal of trouble – really and truly?'

'Really and truly – they were angels,' Julia said.

'Which means they'll be fiends tomorrow. Sheer reaction – you have been warned.'

'Oh, I don't mind. I love them whatever they do. I thought,' she went on delicately, 'that you might like to play with them before they go to bed. And then I could get your dinner ready.'

Before answering he chivvied the two boys upstairs with their tidyings, and then he turned back to Julia and took her by both shoulders this time.

'Listen, Julia,' he said seriously, and her solemn eyes looked straight into his, 'I really mean this. It's very nice of you to offer to cook my dinner, but Joyce and I only asked you here to look after the children, and if you do anything else around the house it must only be because you want to. I can manage to cook for myself, so don't feel that you're obliged to do the dinner. Now, you must be honest with me.'

'I will be honest with you,' she said. 'Actually, I like cooking – at least, I think I do because I've never had much practice – and I should enjoy to cook dinner for both of us. But,' and her teeth gleamed in the half-lit hall, 'I promise I will tell you if I get bored with it.'

'Are you kissing her?' came Michael's voice at that moment. Peter glanced up and saw that the boy was craning over the bannister at the top of the stairs to see them below him.

'No, I'm talking,' Peter called back calmly, and looked quickly down at Julia, expecting her to be scarlet with embarrassment. By rights she should have been, but in fact she was merely looking up at Michael with the tail end of the same smile on her face, utterly unruffled. Peter released her shoulders and turned away, wondering about it. 'All right, you two, if you come down now I'll play a game of cards with you until bedtime.'

The three of them sat on the floor in the sitting room with just the standard lamp on to augment the dusk and played Beat Your Neighbour until Julia appeared in the doorway again to say, 'It's nearly ready. Will you eat in the kitchen or do you want me to lay up the dining room?'

'Oh, in the kitchen, by all means,' Peter said. He liked the informal idea of it. He and Joyce never ate there – she'd have been horrified at the thought. 'Can you hold it off for ten minutes while I get these two to bed?'

She nodded and disappeared again. Peter collected up the cards and chivvied the boys upstairs, got them into their beds and tucked them in.

'All right now? Sleep tight,' he said with his hand on the light switch of Michael's room.

'Will Julia come and say goodnight?' James called from his room, and Michael came in eagerly, 'Oh yes!'

'I'll ask her. Goodnight, kids.'

'Night, Daddy.'

In the kitchen, Julia was just straining off the potatoes, and as he came in she looked round with a frown of concentration on her face.

'They want you to say goodnight. Will you go up? I'll serve up while you do.'

She nodded and put the potato pot down without a word and slipped past him and up the stairs. She seemed to have gone very quiet, and he wondered what was wrong. When she came back a few moments later he saw that she had changed her blouse and brushed her hair, but he decided not to comment on it, in case she was feeling upset about something.

They sat down, one at either side of the table, and began to eat. Peter, his eyes wandering round the kitchen as he tried to think of something to say by way of conversation, saw the remaining jam tarts on a plate on the side table.

'Did you make the tarts?' he asked her kindly.

'Yes,' she said in a normal voice. 'They weren't very good. I put too much jam in them. It said in the recipe only half a teaspoonful, but it looked so mean I topped them all up.' She suddenly smiled. 'And they spread and spread and spread.'

'I once did something similar with rice pudding,' he said cheerfully, glad she seemed all right again. 'That spreads and spreads, too. But what on earth are those? Beside your jam tarts?'

Julia looked round, and then laughed. 'Oh, that was the boys' efforts. The snake is Michael's, and the other thing is supposed to be a plane. That's Jamie's.'

'But what are they? I mean, what are they made of?'

'Pastry. They wanted to join in, so I gave them the trimmings to make pies of their own.'

'You let them play in the kitchen while you were cooking?'

'Shouldn't I?' Julia looked worried, in case she had broken some domestic law.

'Oh, it's all right, I'm just surprised,' Peter said. 'Joyce can't stand them messing about in the kitchen while she's doing anything. You must be very patient.'

She didn't answer that, but simply smiled. When they had finished eating, she got up and said, 'Shall I make some tea, or coffee?'

'No, I'll make it,' he said quickly. 'You go and sit down in the other room, and I'll bring it in. What would you prefer?'

'I'd prefer tea, if it's all the same to you.' She hesitated. 'I'd like to finish off a sketch,' she said, rather as if she were asking permission, and he realised that she, for all her appearance of being at home, still felt like a child on a visit.

'Yes, OK,' he said, and she went out. While the kettle was boiling he hastily washed up, to make sure that she wouldn't feel obliged to do it later, and smiled to himself at the thought of doing the same thing for Joyce. When he took the tray of tea-things in, she was sitting, as she had once before when he came in, on the floor with her back against the sofa and her sketch pad in her crook'd knees.

'Here we are,' he said, putting the tray down. He poured out two cups, handed her one, and then sat down in an armchair opposite her and unfolded the morning's paper, which he hadn't had a chance to read yet. The room was silent, except for the soft sounds of pencil and rustling paper, and now and then the chink of a cup being laid down in its saucer.

From time to time he glanced up quietly to look at her. The lamplight shone on the crown of her bent head, and her fingers moved surely and strongly, like his own did when they were about their own, known business. Her shirt was V-necked, and because he was sitting higher than her, her long throat seemed to plunge down into it, rather than rise from it. She was – what? – sixteen now? Not really a child at all. He stirred uncomfortably in his chair and went back to the review he had been reading.

The next time he looked up, she was looking at him. He raised an eyebrow in query, but she didn't seem to see it, and her eyes flicked back to her page, and then up to him again. She was sketching him, of course, and so absorbed in it that she didn't register that he was looking at her. He kept quite still, looking at her indirectly now, not to disturb her. Her eyes seemed to touch him physically each time, giving him a prickling sensation at the back of his neck. It seemed odd to him that being sketched should be sexually arousing – but then, many odd things were, like having your hair combed by someone else, for instance, or doing up a woman's zip (though undoing it was better). He had known a girl once who loved to have her feet held. Odd little things trigger off odd little nerves. He kept as still as he could until she finished.

She didn't, as he had expected, study her work and compare it with the original when she had finished, but after one glance turned the page and looked up as if she was going to start again. This time, however, she saw his eyes on her, and gave him a perfunctory smile.

He said, feeling that she knew he was going to say it, 'Can I see?'

She did not hesitate, but said frankly as she held out the book, 'It isn't good. Parts are all right, but I haven't got the proportions right.'

He stood up and instead of taking the book went over and sat on the sofa to look at it over her shoulder.

'I started it too big,' she explained. 'I was only going to

do head and shoulders, but I wanted to get the hand in, and I squashed it up rather.'

She had, making him look stunted, or as if he were leaning forward over a camera lens. But it was – as far as anyone can ever tell about themselves – a very good likeness. Not only that, but it looked like a person, not like a drawing. It looked, to use the only expression that came to mind, very professional. She moved her pencil about the drawing, unselfconsciously, explaining it to him.

'The mouth is good, I think. I've managed to keep it flexible this time. The sketches I've done of Michael have all been very wooden about the mouth, and a child's mouth is actually easier to do than an adult's. More curves.' She looked up at him appraisingly. 'You do have a very difficult mouth. And nose. But your eyes are beautiful.'

Now, what the hell? It should be her that was blushing, but in fact he alone seemed to be disturbed by her look. And although she was looking at his eyes, it was not *into* them with any kind of intimate look, but at them, as one might look at a view or a vase of flowers.

He debated making some flippant remark, but in the end what he did say was only, 'You, too, have beautiful eyes.'

He saw her focus change from looking at his eyes to looking into them, and he felt seared by the clarity of her gaze. The moment extended itself perilously, and it became more and more impossible to draw back from the position he had thrust himself into, more and more difficult to think of anything to say that was not more perilous than this excruciating silence.

At last she said, 'Of course, I've only ever seen them in the mirror, so I can't say.' She turned the page of her book again and said politely, 'If you wouldn't mind going over there again, I would like to do another.'

He returned to his chair with relief, tinged with disappointment, and said, 'Just five minutes, and then I must practise.'

'All right,' she said, her eyes flicking up and down and her fingers busy, 'I'll be quick. I shall be off to bed soon, in any case. What happens tomorrow?'

'I've got a rehearsal in the morning, so I'll have to leave here at nine, but I'll be back by about two, so we can have lunch and then go out somewhere. Or –' thinking of the cooking business again – 'go out somewhere and have lunch.'

'That would be nice,' she said, sounding as if she meant it. 'What time do the children get up in the morning?'

'About seven, usually, but we don't breakfast until eight on Sundays when I'm home.'

'I'll get breakfast then,' she said.

'No, I'll get it. You can lie in if you like.'

She smiled at him ruthlessly. 'I always get up early.'

'I'm not going to fight you for it. But I'll cook breakfast, if you'll keep the boys out of my way until it's ready. Unlike you, I can't do with them under my feet in the kitchen.'

'All right.' More rapid glances, but this time she was smiling as if at some private wickedness. 'There, I've finished.' She handed the book over to him, and after a startled glance he burst out laughing. Not a sketch this time, but a cartoon, of him with a stubborn frown on his face, his fist clenched, and his lip stuck out like Jamie's when he was told to drink his milk. 'That's you fighting me for the breakfast.'

'Bad girl!' he exclaimed. 'You're dangerous, d'you know that?'

'I don't mean to be,' she said, and stood up, collecting her bits. 'Well, I'll be off to bed now.'

'So early?' he asked, wanting her to stay.

'I'm going to read in bed,' she said simply. 'I love to read in bed, and then when I get really drowsy, just slip down and go to sleep.'

The thought of her in bed, growing warm and drowsy, prickled him again. He stood up too, wondering just what exactly he was going to do.

'Goodnight, then,' she said, and hesitated, as if there were more to come.

'Goodnight, Julia,' he said. He noticed she never said his name now. He wondered if she was waiting for him to kiss her goodnight, if she wanted him to, or expected it. He wouldn't have known how to, anyway. She smiled quickly, and went out.

Peter turned out the standard lamp, fetched his violin from the hall, and went into the room he used as his music room.

He got out the music they would be playing tomorrow, and began to go over it, and after a little while he had cleared his mind of her and was in the place where nothing existed but the wordless ideas of a man a hundred years dead.

Upstairs in the spare room, Julia lay in bliss in her comfortable bed in a circle of lamplight, reading. She thought there was no delight on earth ever discovered to compare with the delight of reading in bed, the unutterable comfort and security of it. The day had gone well, and she had loved having dinner alone with Peter, and the quiet, intimate comfort of being in the drawing room with him afterwards, drawing him while he read. This, she thought, must be what it was like to be married to him – oh, lucky Joyce! (Not lucky having to have an operation, of course, but otherwise . . .) She remembered that moment when he had said she had beautiful eyes. What had he meant by it? It had filled her with a perilous, fluttering joy, and for a moment she had thought that he wanted to kiss her. That was ridiculous, of course, and she had punished herself for such a fanciful thought by going up to bed early, depriving herself of his company. But it wasn't much of a punishment. He was in the same house, she would see him tomorrow morning, and every day for weeks – oh the bliss of it! But she must be sure to keep a tight rein on her imagination, and not let herself think about his liking her in any special way. He was a miracle to her, but to him she was just the babysitter. She didn't suppose he saw anything different about her from any other girl of her age.

She read on, and began to drowse a little over the printed words. She could hear from below the sound of the music Peter was making, and that added to her happiness. Her book was *Jane Eyre* – again – and Jane, sitting in the alcove watching the grand ladies and gentlemen in the drawing room, had as yet no idea that Mr Rochester loved her. She was watching the door with longing, waiting for him to come in; and when he did come in, Edward Fairfax Rochester was the image of Peter Kane.

Later that night, Peter Kane lay in his half of the double bed and found sleep elusive. He was disturbed by the thought of Julia lying only a few yards away, under the same roof, accessible, inaccessible. What the devil was she? She not only disturbed him – that was straightforward – but she bothered him too. She was so imperturbable, too self-contained for a girl of her age, and when she looked at him like that with her terribly noticing eyes, he felt she read everything in his mind – at that point he laughed at his own thoughts. My God, if she could read *every*thing, she'd be out of the house like a bullet from a gun.

He turned on to his side, stretching himself across the unaccustomed space, and his thoughts grew more tranquil. She was there, after all; there to be found out about. Never mind that she disturbed him. Something could be done about that, he thought drowsily. Something would have to be done about that.

Five

He woke on Sunday morning with a sense of well-being. Glancing at the clock he saw that it was five past seven. It was the sun that had woken him, for he had omitted to draw the curtains last night, and it was streaming in unchecked. He could hear the birds singing outside, and inside, in the peace of a happy house, he could hear a chirruping kind of song from downstairs.

He smiled to himself, stretching luxuriously. Julia! He would bet she was down there doing something about breakfast – not cooking it, of course, because she was too honest to break her word, but in some way preparing to cut down his task. He liked the sound of her singing, and as he lay listening to it, it gradually grew familiar – not a song, but the music he had been practising last night. She was trying, bless her, to sing the whole thing, all the different parts, which accounted for the chirruping, as she tried to da-de-da the first violin part, diddle-iddle-iddle the woodwind part, and pom-pom in the basses. She was doing pretty well, too – better than he could have, for instance, though probably no one who didn't know what it was meant to be would have recognised it.

It was going to be hot. Already his skin was soft and damp, and his pyjamas were twisted about him limply. Pyjamas! He hated the things. At home (strange how one went on referring to one's childhood home as 'home') he had never worn them, not after the age of about ten, but Joyce had been brought up differently, and on returning from their honeymoon he had bought some in deference to her. Now it was habitual to wear them, but, damnit, she wasn't here now. He flung the covers back and pulled the pyjamas off and threw them on the floor.

That's better, he thought, stretching again. He wished he could have a shower. When he had been in America with the orchestra there had always been a shower at every hotel, and he had loved to shower in the morning. One of these days he would get one fixed in his own house. He didn't see why it should be too expensive – if one could find a plumber who knew what a shower was! He listened again; the singing had stopped, but he heard voices out in the garden. He jumped out of bed and went over to the window and looked out. There was Julia with the two boys running round and round the garden in bare feet. He couldn't determine the object of the game, but it looked as though the boys were chasing her. Like dopes, they didn't unite their efforts, and so she, twisting and dodging, kept away from them, but at last she slowed down, probably deliberately, and they flung themselves bodily at her and she went down, rolling over under their two solid bodies, bowled as cleanly as a puppy by a dog.

They lay panting for a moment, and then Michael spotted his father at the window and began to call and wave, no doubt asking him to come down. Peter made a vague gesture in reply, and then realised he was naked, and turned quickly away. He washed and shaved and dressed in slacks, shirt and cravat, took out his double-breasted blazer from the wardrobe, and then stood in front of it to comb and meticulously part his hair. Then, taking his jacket in hand he went downstairs to see about breakfast as promised.

She had been preparing, as he had thought. The kitchen table was laid, and before each place was a small tumbler filled with orange juice (another of the habits he had brought back from America – he must have told her about it). The salt and pepper were in the centre of the table flanked by butter dish and marmalade jar and toast rack. Bread had been cut and was lying on the side table by the gas stove. The kettle was heating over a low light, and four eggs and four rashers of bacon were lying on a plate ready to be cooked.

He stared around, and then he smiled, and then he laughed. Well, she had kept her part of the bargain – she hadn't *cooked* breakfast, but it was a close thing. He looked out into the garden through the window, and saw that she was now keeping the rest of her part, and was tirelessly giving the boys coley-buckies round and round the lawn, pretending to be a seaside donkey. James was riding at the moment, and Michael was leading her by the hair, pretending (only pretending thank the Lord) to whack her with a stick, and saying shrilly and officiously, 'Come along, come along, or you shan't get any nice grass.'

James then added to the poor beast's burden by kicking, and Peter was on the point of interfering when the donkey herself decided enough was enough and did a neat twist, depositing her rider on the grass on his back. She then raced off round the garden giving a very good imitation of bucking, while the erstwhile rider and owner pursued her with a mixture of coaxing and threats. Eventually she allowed them to bowl her over again, and the game had come full circle.

By the time he called them in, Julia was breathless. The three of them came into the kitchen rather more slowly than they had gone out of it earlier that morning, and when he told them to wash their hands, Julia, for the time being, could only stand in the doorway and pant, supporting herself by one hand on the jamb.

'I'm not sure if I admire you, or pity you,' Peter said to her. 'Such energy! And put to such poor purposes!' She bared her teeth in the midst of her panting, which was all she could manage by way of a smile.

He put the plates out on the table and they sat down, he and she opposite each other with the children between them – the lay-out he and Joyce had adopted automatically for the greater ease of cutting up dinners and wiping chins.

'I see you did everything this morning *but* cook the breakfast,' he said to her sternly.

'Well, I woke up,' she said apologetically. 'It seemed so silly to wait until you came down when I could be doing it.'

'That's no excuse. It is a kind of cheating, you know, to obey the letter of the law and not the spirit.'

'Do you think so?' she asked. She really wanted to know. This made him pull himself up a little. Most people did not listen to what you said; most children too; so it did not matter whether you meant everything in all sincerity. But he would have to be careful with her.

'I've only just thought about it,' he said honestly, 'but I have always believed that a lie was a matter of intention rather than a matter of fact.'

She was silent, masticating bacon and digesting his words, and then said, 'Yes, I see that. I think I read it somewhere, that if you tell the truth in such a manner that it cannot be believed, then it is a lie.'

'It's all part of the same thing, isn't it?'

'Mmm. But then –' she hesitated, and he made an encouraging grunt of enquiry – 'by the same rule, wouldn't it be true that when I said I wouldn't do the breakfast, you didn't believe I wouldn't, and therefore my promise wasn't valid?'

'And therefore you didn't break it by obeying the letter and not the spirit?' He finished for her, and grinned delightedly. 'My dearest girl, you weren't intended to take my reprimand seriously. And, yes, you are right in a way. Provided you knew that I knew that you wouldn't.'

'Would.' She corrected him, and he shrugged having lost the grammatical thread several clauses ago. Breakfast made a little more headway, and it was when he had got up to make himself a second slice of toast to have with marmalade (Joyce's mother's own make, now sugar was off ration at last) that she asked him, 'Is it a rehearsal you are going to this morning? What is it like? I mean, is it like a dress rehearsal of a play?'

'Hardly,' he said with a short laugh. 'Undress rehearsal more like. Especially the Sunday ones. Most of the chaps come half-dressed, half-asleep, and completely unshaven and unwashed.'

'And what do you do?'

'Generally with a rehearsal at this stage – on the morning of the performance – we play right through each piece and then pick up anything the conductor's not happy with. Most of the work has already been done at earlier rehearsals. But it depends very much on the conductor – some of them change everything at the last minute.'

'Didn't Toscanini use to change things actually during the performance?' she asked.

'Apparently – but then he was a genius, he could carry them along with him.' He smiled at her quizzically. 'How do you know about Toscanini?'

'I know lots of things about music,' she said.

She sounded offended, and he laughed at her assumption of dignity. All the same, he apologised by saying, 'I'm not used to musical companions. These two –' he gently batted the back of Michael's head – 'don't know music exists, and Joyce, poor dear, is a musical moron.'

He looked at Julia as he said this last, to convey the force of the apology to her, but she looked faintly shocked, as if he had committed an indiscretion – no, a solecism – and he realised she had misunderstood his use (admittedly esoteric) of the expression 'musical moron'. He did not wish to embark on an explanation, and couldn't conveniently do so with the children listening, so instead he changed the subject.

'Where would you like to go this afternoon?'

'Are we going out this afternoon?' Michael enquired, suddenly interested away from his breakfast.

'Yippee!' from James, accompanied by his usual drumming of his fork-handle.

'I had thought of taking you out – not, I hasten to add, for your sake, but as a reward to Julia for being so good.' Her analytical gaze was turned on to him at that, while the children protested variously about their virtue.

'All right, all right, I said "you" meaning all of you. But where would you like to go?'

'To Grandpa's,' Jamie shouted deafeningly, pounding the table rapidly again, and Michael, though equally excited, agreed quietly.

'Oh yes, let's go to Grandpa's.'

'I know why you want to go there, you miserable little hooligans – it's because Grandmama spoils you horribly. That's my parents,' he added in explanation to Julia. 'My father's very stern with all young creatures, human or otherwise, so my mother tries to compensate by being doubly soft. Hence most of my failings.'

'What failings?' she asked with interest.

'I couldn't possibly tell you here,' he smiled. 'I would very much like to take you to my home – you'd love it. Loads of horses.' It was one of the things he knew about her, that she had a rather hopeless passion for horses. 'But unfortunately,' and he repeated the word more loudly to attract the children's attention over their noise, 'unfortunately, there wouldn't be time this afternoon.'

'Oh, Daddy!'

'Silence, the both of you. The fact is that I won't be home here until nearly two, and I'll have to leave again at about half past six for the concert. And it takes two hours to drive to Grandpa's, so you can work it out for yourself.'

Michael obediently did so, putting down his fork the better to wrestle with his bunch of recalcitrant fingers.

Peter went on to his diminished audience, 'If nothing comes up next weekend, we'll go then. But for the moment, it'll have to be somewhere nearer.' Julia's eyes seemed to be fixed on him earnestly. 'Any ideas?' he asked her.

'Your toast is burning,' she said. He whipped round to see it just beginning to catch.

When he had effected the rescue and sat down with the results, Michael said, 'Could we go to that place where we had a picnic that time?'

'Which place was that, boy?'

'That place – there was a hill,' he said, screwing up his face in fearsome concentration as he tried to remember it. 'There was a hill with a kind of building on the top. And there were poppies all on the side of the road.'

'We picnicked on the side of the road?'

'No, that was going there. It was a kind of a field, all lumpy, and then a hill and bushes and things.' He stopped, and then agonisingly squeezed another thought out. 'There were lots of cowpats everywhere.'

James laughed shrilly, and the cowpats clinched the memory.

'You mean Radnage?' The name rang familiarly in the boy's head and he nodded happily. 'Yes, we could go there, if you like. Do you want to take a picnic?'

He asked it thoughtlessly before remembering that Julia would be the only one available for preparing the food, but she

71

concurred as eagerly as the children, so he mentally shrugged and accepted the arrangement.

'All right, that's what we'll do.'

'I'll have all the food ready,' Julia said answering his unspoken thought, 'if you'll show me what bags you have to carry it in.'

'Right you are. And, listen, you boys, I want you ready to go, dressed and *washed* when I get back, and don't get in Julia's way while she is making the sandwiches. I'm serious, James. No shenanigans.'

He felt guiltily relieved when he left the house soon afterwards for the comparative peace of *The Pines of Rome* and a Grieg piano concerto. He knew Jamie in those kinds of moods, and only a complete rotter would leave that poor girl as his sole victim. So he was leaving her, as any sensible person would.

When he returned home, not without trepidation, however, he found everything peaceful and ordered, the picnic packed, the boys clean and clothed, and the three of them lying on their stomachs in the sitting room reading.

'My God, how did you do it?' he exclaimed, and Julia, looking up from her prone position, did not pretend not to understand.

'I just let them mess until it was time to get ready.'

'Mess?'

'That tin bath you have in the outhouse. I filled it with water and stuck it out in the garden.'

'We had a *smashing* time, Daddy,' Michael said almost in awe. 'It was just like the seaside.'

'With no clothes on,' James said with relish. Peter's eyebrow lifted involuntarily but he managed to suppress the laughter that went with it. The thought of those two cavorting round the garden in the nip, and the thought of the neighbours twitching their lace curtains in outrage at the sight of them, and the thought of what Joyce would say next time one of them demanded a tin bath and nudity and cited precedent to support his case – oh dear oh dear, two laws in one household! But it really was very funny.

'I see you are a student of psychology,' he said to Julia,

72

who accepted the observation incuriously. 'I'll just run up and change, and then we'll be off. No, I don't need any help, thank you, son. You just stay there and read until I get back.' And he darted off to laugh in comfort.

Radnage Common was, as Michael had described it, a kind of lumpy field full of cowpats and bushes that perched on the top of a steep hill. It was reached by a narrow, high-hedged lane that led nowhere else and was therefore unfrequented. There were rosehips and blackberries to be had in late summer; and despite the cowpats it was very beautiful, very wild, and very peaceful.

The boys were quiet on the drive there, sitting in the back together without fighting or even quarrelling, and Peter had an idea that Julia had somehow managed to tire them out that morning without perishing in the process.

She sat beside him on the front seat with one elbow resting on the frame of the open window and the other arm lying across her lap. She had on a pale blue sleeveless blouse with a V-neck, and a pair of green linen shorts. Her limbs were narrow and straight and brown like a foal's. The oblique sun lighted a down of golden hairs on her arms and shimmered on the strands of her hair that were caught and whipped by the air flow past the window. He glanced at her sideways from time to time as he drove, thinking how young, how beautiful she looked. But it wasn't that that was so arresting; it was some quality about her that he couldn't quite put a name to. Something about her being like an animal, with that quality an animal has when it is free in its own element: a deer, say, grazing, or a lion sunning itself, or a sparrow sitting on top of a drainpipe and surveying its territory. It was a wholeness, a completeness. She lacked nothing, perfectly in accord with herself and her body, fulfilling her function just by being.

And although he desired her, sometimes quite painfully, he was content merely to look at her. That was probably the fascination of wild animals for people – their impregnability – and why the soul revolted at the killing of them by man, while the slaughter of a domestic calf was accepted with a shrug. Virginity: that was the quality. Not the conventional idea of the flaxen-haired martyr with her hands folded across her breast, but the virginity of an animal, whose innocence is too intrinsic to need protecting. Here was one utterly innocent person – not the innocence of a child, for a child had no knowledge, and Julia had knowledge, and understanding. That was her quietness and completeness. That was her beauty.

The thought stayed with him throughout the afternoon, mixed up with other things, other thoughts and impressions, but steady through them like the line of the continuo. She was, after all, an ordinary human girl, sixteen, nubile, energetic and happy. She ate almost as ravenously as the children, and with as good cause, for she ran about with them and played quite as roughly. They played with the big inflatable beach ball, and Peter threw it to her high for the pleasure of seeing her jump – a skilled, vertical thrust of a jump which she had learnt at school playing netball, which uncoiled her spring of a body so that for a moment it was stretched out and suspended a few inches above the ground.

He watched her ravenously, her lithe movements and easy unconscious gestures; the flick of her head that threw her hair away from her face; the hairpinning of her slender arm to scratch between her shoulder blades; the quivering of her small rubbery breasts as she ran and jumped; the opening of her face in laughter to the children; her eyes, both solemn and merry, when she looked at him.

He wished he did not have to go out that evening. He would have liked the day to continue unbroken into eventual sleep. He was afraid of the disruption that was to come; but like everything else that day, she seemed to have provided for it, for the children were so worn out that they slept on the journey back, and when they arrived home consented to be bathed and put to bed immediately. There was no noise and no fuss and practically no conversation, so the mood was not rudely shattered. Peter washed and changed into his tails and ate a light meal at the kitchen table with Julia opposite him in sympathetic silence and the children already banished to their other kingdom.

When he eventually left, she came to the door with him, and she did not say, I wish I were coming with you, and he did not answer, I wish you could; but each knew the other had thought it.

'I'll see you later, then,' he said, and there was the ghost of a question in it.

'Yes,' she said, answering it. 'I want to finish my book.'

He thought about her all evening. While he was actually playing, he thought about the music, as he always did, but she was there in his mind anyway, woven into the fabric of the sounds, just a dim, blurred picture of herself. While he played he saw only pieces of her, the shape of a word, a small movement, her hands holding the ball, the shape of her shoulders, and all the features of her face individually, in detail.

When he was not playing, in the intervals between movements and between pieces, and even in the rests during the movements, she would break through into his forward mind whole and vivid and clear. It was like shelling a chestnut. In the interval, he went to the bar to try and exorcise her with conversation and whisky, but it was only partially successful, for he found that he kept wanting to talk about her and twice started on an anecdote about the day, twice having to stop himself when he realised what he was doing and what he might be about to give away. He wanted her achingly, and the whisky didn't help, but simply made him feel restless and reckless, so that he began to think that he could – would – do something about it. After all, he told himself in justification, I can't have her interfering with my work; and he heard himself and sneered at his own conceit and cheap sophistication. It sobered him a little – metaphorically speaking, at least – to realise that he had been on the verge, even if only mentally, of seducing a young girl to whom he was *in loco parentis* for the time being. She was a child under his care, said one half of his mind, and the other half of his mind rolled its eyes despairingly.

Prokofiev's seventh symphony was the second half of the concert, and it called for plenty of concentration from him. Julia receded into haziness again and merely danced a kind of ghostly jig to the music. While they were standing for the applause at the end, Peter's new co-desker, Tom Streeter, invited him to join a party at the local pub – 'My sister and a couple of friends' – and Peter, thinking to put off the evil moment, accepted.

'I'll drop in for a few minutes,' he said. 'I won't be able to stay long – got to get back for the babysitter.'

They sat again, the applause still going strong.

'You're lucky to get a reliable babysitter, I can tell you,' Tom went on, pleasantly, just making conversation. 'Every time Kay and I get one properly trained she moves, or gets a boyfriend, or gets married, and we have to start all over again. They start on the old boy business so damn young these days –' they stood again at the conductor's signal – 'Sixteen, and they're off.'

'Not mine,' Peter said, unable to prevent himself.

'Not mine what?' Tom was trying to catch the eye of a pretty girl in the front row and was not really attending to Peter.

'Babysitter. She's not like that.'

'Go on! She's probably got her boyfriend round there while you're out. You'll catch her one day – happened to us with Stephanie, the one before last. Got home from a concert and found her on the sofa with a great beast of a teenager, snogging.'

'Mine doesn't have a boyfriend,' Peter said.

Tom looked at him oddly. 'You don't say?'

Peter realised perhaps he had sounded a little too vehement, and added, shrugging, 'Well, apparently not. Not the type. Probably more interested in horses.'

'Oh,' Tom said, as if that explained it.

The clapping died away, one last stalwart in the gallery doing a solo in the hope of infecting his neighbours, but it lacked momentum. People were standing up, gathering their coats, and the orchestra began to file off, while the woodwind dismantled and stowed away their instruments and the basses clothed up theirs.

Peter and Tom joined the slow file for the steps down off the platform, and as he reached them, Peter said to Tom over his shoulder, 'Look, old man, I think I'll just trot off straight home, if it's all the same to you. It's been a long concert, and . . . well, those two brats of mine can be a handful.'

'Just as you like,' Tom said. 'Can't be too careful.' And as they parted in the dressing rooms, Tom gave Peter a large wink and said, 'Enjoy yourself!'

Damn, he thought. Am I being obvious? No, it's just Tom's dirty mind. He hurried out to the car, eager to be home now, and unwilling to analyse why. He was tingling all over, and not all of it was the whisky. The car started obligingly easily, the roads were almost empty, and Peter began to relax as he drove quickly north-westwards. It was a warm, calm night, and he wound his window down to enjoy the freshness of the air, resting his elbow on the frame and thinking as he did so of Julia's arm, brown and silvered. He found himself humming the beginning of the second movement of the Prokofiev over and over, and it urged him on; good driving music.

He was still humming it as he turned left at the park into Milton Street, and saw ahead the rosy light of his own bay window with a lamp shining behind the drawn curtain. Home. He drove into the driveway, thinking of Julia hearing the sound and being glad he was home. 'Good, Peter's home.' Or did she think of him as 'Mr Kane'? She never called him anything at all. Most people didn't, of course, with people they lived close to. He got out, locked the car door, changed his grip on his bunch of keys to bring the front door key into the operative position, and went in.

The house was quiet. He had imagined, for some reason, that she would be playing a record, probably the Prokofiev that was still running through his mind. The sitting-room door was shut, and there was a line of light under it. Delaying the moment, he went through to the music room and put down his fiddle case. He went back into the hall and listened, his ear tilted towards the upstairs regions – no sound. He turned, breathed slowly, opened the sitting-room door.

She was standing by the window, but facing towards him, as if she had been looking out of the window and had just turned away, frozen in the act like a child caught stealing jam. He stood in the doorway looking at her but neither moving nor smiling, and as the seconds passed the incipient movement in her died away and she became very still.

Peter did not know it, but he presented a forbidding aspect to her as he stood in the doorway almost lowering, and she was afraid of him. To her, despite her crush on him, he was very much a grown-up, and she was afraid of him firstly in the normal way that a child might fear being 'told-off'; and secondly she was afraid of doing anything to anger him or make him dislike her. It was her way, when she was afraid, to stay very still, play possum, but Peter did not know that. To him, it looked like self-possession.

'Everything all right?' he asked eventually.

She made a guilty kind of movement with her head, as if looking round the room for the clue left unconcealed, and said, 'Yes. Oh, yes, everything's all right. Did you have a good time?'

He laughed at the idea of that, and she went very still again. He was just enjoying himself looking at her, not aware that his standing in the doorway looked vaguely threatening to her.

She said tentatively, 'I'd better be off to bed, hadn't I?'

But he broke across that cheerfully. 'No, no, come and have some cocoa. You like cocoa, and I promised you should have it every night. Come and have some cocoa in the kitchen and talk to me for a little while.'

What could sound simpler? How could she refuse? She followed him obediently and stood leaning against the back door while he made the hot drink and talked to her about music. She did not know the Prokofiev he had been playing, and he found himself describing it and waxing enthusiastic on the subject.

'I know his fifth symphony,' Julia said in reply to his question. 'I like that, it's rather – I don't quite know the word for it – rather like Chaucer's poetry.'

'I know,' he said delightedly, 'just what you mean. It's vulgar but vulgar without losing its musicality.'

'Isn't it strange,' Julia said, 'how there are no proper descriptive words for music – they're all borrowed from other senses, except for "loud" and "quiet". And yet, you'd think that they'd come first, sound-words and smell-words.'

'The antics music critics get up to describe sounds are incredible,' Peter agreed. He had made the cocoa now and poured it out, and thrusting one mug into her hand he took the other and preceded her back into the sitting room, without pausing in speech. 'I read one the other day who called Mozart "muscular".'

Julia smiled. 'And they'd call Prokofiev "robust", I suppose – like Breughel,' she added more musingly. 'But it isn't really like Breughel. Breughel is soft and rounded, like big, fat fruit, but Prokofiev is edgy.' She stopped abruptly, and with a rare percipience Peter saw it was because she felt she had used the wrong words, that they were inadequate. He had sat on the sofa, but Julia had wandered over to the window and was sipping her cocoa, holding the mug in both hands like a child, while she looked out through a crack in the curtain.

After a while she said, 'It's so different here. You'd never think it was only the other end of the street. It's like being a world away.'

'Do you like it here?'

'Oh yes,' she said unemphatically, as if it were a thing to be taken for granted. 'It's like home to me in a way. But,' she added frankly, 'it's much more comfortable than our house. And bigger. Have you ever seen –' she said quickly, turning to him with the eagerness of a new thought – 'a dog that lives in a slum house? It always has its tail tucked in and its hind legs half-crouched, because it's forever getting trodden on. That's the way I feel sometimes at home.'

'But surely,' he said very gently, because he felt she was likely to be frightened off if she realised she was confiding in him, 'it isn't all that crowded at home?'

'No. I don't mean physically,' she said, making a cancelling gesture. 'I feel as if my mind, or my, I don't know, *essence* is being trodden on. Even my father . . .' she stopped.

'Go on,' he encouraged her.

'I don't think he really likes me,' she said slowly. Then she smiled. It might or might not have been what she was going to say. Peter neither knew nor cared. At her smile he had surged up painfully; his hand shook slightly as he set down his cup.

79

'Come here,' he said.

She obeyed him, probably automatically, walking across the room to stand in front of him where he sat on the sofa. He took her cup from her unresisting hand and set it down, aware that she had gone very still again. Watching me, he thought – not very clearly – like a predator. Her dark eyes were wide and curious but seemed unafraid. She was wearing the same shorts, and a striped T-shirt, and her hair was in two absurd short plaits. She looked like an American tomboy.

Julia had obeyed him automatically, but now, standing very close to him, she felt his tension. She ached and trembled inwardly with a terrible love for him; she longed to touch him and be touched by him, but still was unable to believe that anything would happen. He was a grown-up and had all a grown-up's apartness for her, despite the sense she often had that she and he were alike in a world of aliens. She had told herself sternly that any idea she had that he liked her specially was just her fancy. All evening she had thought of him, played out (rather guiltily, because it was a self-indulgence) daydream scenarios where he came home to her, spoke of his feelings for her, perhaps even kissed her, knowing that a foolish daydream was all it was. She loved him so fiercely, longed so from the depths of her unloved life to be loved, to be touched; but she knew it never could or would happen. He was as magnificent and adored and unreachable as a god to her.

But now, he was looking into her eyes in a way that was different from anything she had ever experienced, so it could not be imagination. Half-frightened, she looked at his mouth. Did he really mean to kiss her, then? She couldn't believe that he would, that he might, and yet, and yet . . . She knew that whatever her god asked of her she would do without question. She hardly breathed, living in a daydream that had suddenly slipped over into reality. She saw his hands move. He *was* going to touch her, she though deliriously.

He reached up and took off the elastic bands that held back her hair and with both hands ran it out loose. She shook her head to make her hair lie naturally, and smiled at him. As a smile it had some qualities of the purr a cat makes when it is in danger, to placate the enemy; but Peter saw only that it was a smile, and took it as encouragement. Without taking his eyes from hers, he put his hands up inside her T-shirt, shuddering a little as he touched her skin at last.

She was wearing no bra, her small breasts were unexpectedly naked, smooth under his hands, the tips more satin than satin, turning hard immediately at his touch. Her skin was silky and warm over hardness like the coat of a thoroughbred horse. He had to swallow before he could speak – whisper – 'Take your clothes off.'

The shock of his touch and his words – gone far beyond anything she had imagined in bed over *Jane Eyre* – threw her out of any ability to make decisions. This could not happen in the real world. She felt dislocated, drunk, and wonderfully released. Her painful, passionate love for him was about to be set free. She felt like flying; her hands seemed to be a thousand miles away as they tugged off her clothes.

It was done in a moment, for she was only wearing three garments, and he could look and look, and then reach out and touch her again. She was as small and slender as a weasel. Her body seemed long, a long slope from armpit to groin; she was all long curves, narrow, flexible. He ran his hands again and again down the line of her flank, down the harder, more muscular curve of her back, looking at her eyes but without seeing her. He looked at her mouth – a troubled smile – and pulled her down to him to kiss the long curving lips, warm, silken and hard. It seemed dreadful that he had to let her go even for as long as it took him to take his clothes off, and his hands felt naked until they were filled with her again.

He laid her down, he hardly knew where, and lay beside her, gathering her in beside him, warm and flexible, nowhere soft, all to be touched, smelled. Her skin had the warm biscuity smell that he remembered from hot summer days in his childhood, and when the round of her shoulder came under his mouth he licked it, and it tasted like the smell. What had she said? – sound and smell come first? No, it was

81

touch and smell, like animals. Animals were beautiful in this
– beautiful. God, everywhere he touched her his hands could
encompass her, she was so small, so narrow. He put his hands
about her neck and his fingers met under her hard jaw and he
held her head up off the floor to kiss it. The skin of her face
tasted salty, and when he kissed her mouth again the outside
was salty too, but the inside gave back the metallic taste of
himself.

Inside her mouth, inside her, to be in her: his hardness and
wanting were no longer separate from him, they were just the
forward edge of the drive of his body; he wanted to be in her
entirely, in her and outside her, all around her like water. Her
long curves were curves leading inwards and he slid into her
without effort but with a murmur of relief, and there was a
long moment of quiet before he was driven into movement
again. She filled his mind as she had filled his hands, and
now even her body was not separate from him but yet another
part of his great desire. And then he climaxed, and it was
indescribably lovely.

Julia felt dazed, battered as though she had been swimming
in a rough sea, completely detached from reality. She had
known nothing, nothing! Was this love, this pounding and
battering? Nothing she had half-heard or read or understood
could have prepared her for this: it was beyond her imagining.
Her mind and body felt swollen and almost numb, but she
was aware most of all of the great possession of herself by
love, which had wiped out, blasted out like a great explosion
every other consideration. She loved him, oh, she loved him;
and more than that, more than all, she was one with him, had
him, possessed him, encompassed him as he did her. For that
moment, though wordlessly, she felt her continuous sense of
aloneness was gone. Not herself and lonely, but of him, and
complete.

Slowly awareness seeped back to him as the thundering in
his head quietened and the throb of his nerve ends dimmed.
He whispered, 'Julia', and she whispered 'Yes' in reply, and
he was aware of her as suddenly as that one word. Now she
was inside him, small and curled like an embryo right inside
him as she was curled in his arms against his body. He felt her

hands on his back and her face in the hollow of his shoulder, felt the quick shallow breathing, the dampness of her skin, felt *her* as she was to herself where before he had only felt what she was to him.

'You're beautiful,' he said. 'Julia. Julia.' And then, feeling no response, he put her back a little from him to look at her. 'Did I hurt you?' he asked. Her face looked too sensitive, as if the least touch would be agony: bruised with loving. He kissed it, small soft kisses on mouth and cheeks and eyes to recreate it for her – this is your face, this your body, this is what you look like and what you are. Be for yourself what you are for me: I want you to have it too, feel what I feel. I give it all back to you, your face, your body, your little warm animal silken body, now sweat-soft, damp – oh very human now!

'Are you all right?' he asked again. Her mouth moved, starting to say many things and saying none of them, but her face looked peaceful now, collected together again as something she knew, an entity she lived inside and was at ease with, and he gathered her to him again comfortably, coming back to normal. Very human it all was now – the smell of sweat, smell of semen, smell of the carpet they were lying on; and, by God, the hardness of the floor communicating itself to the parts he was lying on, getting harder by the minute, as did the sharp bone of her hip that was digging into him. Fantasy was blown away, reality was back. Time to be getting up!

He eased himself out of her, and she made a small sound like a protest. Gently he detached himself and sat up, and then got to his feet.

'You'd better have the bathroom first,' he said gently, looking down at her bent head with infinite kindness. She stood up, an all-of-a-piece movement that he could no longer emulate, and would have gone without a word, not even looking at him, had he not caught her back and forced her to stand and meet his eyes.

Now the moment was past and he was his separate, important person again, she was very unsure of herself, and so she stood very straight and held her head high, looking at him directly.

In a horse he would have recognised the stance as, at the very least, wariness; but it seemed to him, then, only like pride, and the quietness of her face satisfied him. He smiled at her, and she smiled back, and so he let her go.

Six

1955

J ulia dreamt that she was dreaming and trying to wake. It was a horrible dream, and when she woke in reality she was sweating and miserable. Her body was hot, damp and cramped and smelled pungently of sweat and semen; her head ached and her mouth was dry and felt unpleasantly coated – in fact, she had a hangover, and though she didn't know it by that name, she knew it was a result of drinking too much wine and sleeping too long in the heat of the evening with no windows open.

Peter had rolled over in his sleep and was half on top of her, pinning her at the furthest edge of the bed against the wall. If she had been sleeping on the outside, he would no doubt have pushed her right out of bed by this time. The hottest and stickiest and most cramped bits of her were those touching any part of him, and in sudden irritation she set her hands against his back and pushed as hard as she could. He groaned and rolled over, away from her, and she was able at last to straighten out and lift the clammy sheet off her. Sighing with the pleasure of cooler air on her skin, she lay on her back and stared up at the ceiling.

It was white, and beautifully moulded round three edges with a pattern of acanthus and hyacinth (or was it grapes?) but the fourth edge was plain, and that and the fact that the ceiling rose was well off-centre revealed that the room had once been part of a much larger one, designed for more spacious days. The other part of the room was now the sitting room of the flat. Together with a small bathroom and kitchen it made up the first floor of the small mid-Victorian house off Queensgate which was the residence and property of one Martin Newman, a freelance fiddle player and friend of Peter's.

Julia knew the flat intimately now, for whenever Martin went away, which was often, he lent it to Peter. Embarrassed though she was by the thought of someone's lending his flat for this explicit purpose – particularly by the thought that Martin knew exactly what went on – Julia had to acknowledge that she was grateful and glad. When she had first become Peter's mistress (though that was only what she called herself; Peter would not allow the word, and when she asked him what she was then, he would reply that she wasn't *his* anything, she was merely Julia) they had made love mainly in his car, wherever it was dark enough, or, if they were out of town, in fields and woods and under hedges. At least in the flat it was comfortable, and private – if you discounted Martin's absent presence.

The first time she met him she had been rigid with embarrassment; but to Martin it had seemed a matter so commonplace as to raise not the slightest interest in him. Shocking as it might have seemed to the general public, a lot of it, she came to understand, went on in artistic and musical circles, which in some ways lived in a moral time-lag in the 'bohemian' thirties. Martin treated Julia with such indifferent friendliness, and referred to Peter's purposes so off-handedly and matter-of-factly that she was actually more uneasy when he wasn't there than when he was.

But here at least they could conduct their affair at leisure. Normally they would cook and eat a meal as well as make love, which meant that they could talk too; the flat had turned a snatched and uncomfortable rapture into a pleasure for her. That sultry June evening they had met early to celebrate, for Julia had just finished her 'A' levels. Peter had had an evening session cancelled at the last moment, so they could spend longer together than usual. He had bought a bottle of wine which they had drunk with their meal, and that, combined with a large gin and tonic beforehand, the stifling heat, and the strenuousness of their love-making, had made them fall asleep.

Julia leaned up on one elbow to look at the clock. It was across the room on the mantelpiece of the beautiful marble fireplace, and she had to stare for a long time before she could make out the time, for Peter had drawn the curtains and the light was dim. A quarter past eight. They would have to think about moving soon. Always, whatever the circumstances of their meeting, she hated the necessity of parting. Even though she lived in the same street as him, even though she knew she could go round to his house whenever she liked, and so, in effect, see him whenever she liked, it was no comfort. In those circumstances he was a different Peter, which made her a different person, too, a shadowy, waiting thing, watching life going on on the other side of a window. Only when she was alone with him did she feel real and *there*.

She had a private, unspoken ambition to spend a whole night with him, but she could not imagine how it could ever be achieved. She had to pretend to be babysitting in order to spend these times alone with Peter, which was perilous enough. Not only did she hate the necessity of dissembling, but she was terrified of discovery. Only the fact that Joyce and her mother did not mix socially and never spoke to each other even if they passed in the street had kept matters secret for so long.

She looked down at Peter, sleeping heavily with wine and heat and fatigue, and smiled with pleasure at the simple fact of his presence. She loved to look at him, could never have enough of it. She had been his mistress for almost a year, and in that time her schoolgirl crush on him had necessarily undergone a change. Finding that her god was human had not evaporated her feelings but had changed them from the distant adoration of an idol to the real love of a real person. Her outward eye had never been deceived, for seeing him primarily with a view to reproducing him on paper she had never invested him with physical beauties he did not have; and coming to him with no romantic preconceptions, her discovery of his character bit by bit had been exciting rather than disillusioning. He was the hub of her life now, and everything she did, everything she thought, revolved around him like a trapped planet circling its sun.

In many ways she had been lucky, perhaps uniquely lucky, for her particular innocence was an extraordinary thing; as Peter had felt, though not understood. Even in those uncommunicative days, when girls still went utterly unprepared to their marriage beds, most of them built up in their early teens a body of sexual morality composed of cultural pressure, tacit guidance, misinformation and prejudice. Marriage was the right true end of love, as songs, films and stories all showed; girls who were too 'easy' got into trouble, and girls who got into trouble were ruined and never found husbands. As to the awful deed itself, parents were reticent on some points, over-emphatic on others; biology lessons at school provided facts in a vacuum, romantic magazines provided a vacuum without facts; while extraordinary old wives' tales defied all public refutation and were passed from pubescent girl to pubescent girl in whispered conversations in lavatories and at bus stops.

The influences on Julia had been not so much different as absent. Her parents had been not reticent about sex, but absolutely silent, so she had been exposed to no body of adult morality. Biology lessons at school had dealt exclusively with reproduction in animals, allowing her to understand the mechanism without necessarily applying it to humans. She had never read romantic magazines, and having no friends of her own age had missed out on the folklore. To her, a naked human body was a thing of beauty and interest, a thing to be looked at and admired and copied, reproduced on paper; it came unattached to any considerations of propriety or forbidden fruit. As to love, she had no previous experience in it, and so to her, love was Peter, and anything he did or said. She came to him without preconceptions, ready to be moulded by him, ready to accept his evaluation of the situation, since she had no yardstick by which to make her own measurements. Loving him, she could not conceive that anything he asked of her could be wrong.

His evaluation, of course, had not included anything recognisable to her as guilt. He did, in fact, feel spasmodically guilty, but he hid the fact from her, and was interested to note that her reactions confirmed what he had believed, that feelings of guilt were not natural manifestations, but induced by early training. She had no modesty other than a love of privacy: he had noticed that she had been embarrassed at meeting Martin for the first time but had been reassured by Martin's reticence; and she coped with the almost-daily meetings with Joyce so well that he would have been thoroughly suspicious if it had been anyone other than Julia.

For him, her ability to dissemble in front of his wife was just another of the fascinating things about her. It was an instinct for self-preservation in her, as wholly free of moral weight as the actions of an animal. She seemed to him always like some kind of exotic animal, with her lithe, easy movements, her unshadowed passion, her calm, watching eyes – like a cat of some kind, a leopard, perhaps. She was completely different from any female he had ever known. It was that which had sustained his interest in her for such an unprecedented time.

That, and the fact that he was obsessed with her body. It had reached crazy proportions, so that sometimes he would stare at himself in the mirror in the morning and wonder what had happened to him. He even had dreams about her, erotic dreams that he was making love to her, and they were so vivid that just the sight of her was enough to give him an erection. (He thanked providence quietly that he had never been attracted by the modern trend towards tight trousers, nor had ever traded in his braces for a belt.)

And here she was, he thought as he woke just then, next to him in the bed, on her back, spread-eagled to allow the sweat to evaporate. Waking up beside her was a tender kind of torture: he rolled over and reached out his hands for her, and groaned softly as his penis gave an automatic, tired surge. Not this time, old boy, he thought. She turned her head slightly on the pillow to look at him as he touched her. Dark eyes in a white face – soft and hard at the same time, like her mouth, like her body.

He leaned up on to his elbow to free his other hand for peeling back the sheet completely, and he studied her musingly, running his hands over the long curves that he knew in his sleep now. She was quiet under his hands, but not passive. Even in sleep (and often when she fell asleep after love-making he, older and less able to extract his mind from a situation his body led him into, lay awake and watched her sleep) she did not seem abandoned – her body seemed to lie relaxed but self-possessed, ready for instant use, like a dog sleeping with

89

one ear up. Like – what had she once said about crocodiles? – they have eyes in their eyelids, that was it. When her eyes were closed, she seemed still to be watching him.

Oh her body, hard under softness, open to him, known to him, but still secret, secretive! As he stroked it he glanced up at her face, and her face was like that too, not shy or afraid or defensive but still her own, not his. He was aware, in a wondering kind of way, that it was love, this obsession, and not just physical passion. He had to be very careful with himself, not to say too much or be too emotional with her. She accepted his evaluation of the situation, and as long as he never mentioned love or permanence, as long as he never even hinted at anything other than this clandestine affair, with him in the driving seat, he was safe. Oh, but sometimes . . .

'We'd better be making a move,' he said briskly to dispel whatever was trying to come into his head, and climbed off the bed.

'I'm awfully thirsty,' she said.

Peter smiled. 'I do believe you've got a hangover,' he said teasingly. 'Why, you little drunkie – I shall have to watch it in future, keep you away from the bottle.'

'It was your idea in the first place,' Julia said. She smiled happily for she loved it whenever Peter said anything to her that emphasised the permanence of their relationship. She wanted to stay with him for ever. 'I would never have thought of wine. We never have it at home, except sherry at Christmas, and that's more for Father than the rest of us.'

'Do you like wine?' he asked, amused.

'Yes, very much. I like the taste of it, but it tastes so fruity and fresh and good that I would never have thought it could creep up behind and clonk me on the head like that.'

'But a wine drunk is a good drunk – no bad feelings afterwards. Whisky's the worst . . .'

He might have elaborated, unthinkingly, but Julia said quite gravely and quite innocently, 'I don't think I'd like to be drunk,' and he realised that she thought only in terms of being drunk like the old men who fell out of the Green Man on Saturday nights and sat in the gutter peeing their pants. He hadn't the energy to try to explain otherwise, and changed the subject.

'D'you want to wash first? I'll put the kettle on and we'll have a cup of tea before we go.'

'Okay,' she said, and got up obediently to go and wash – she always took his suggestions as orders. He went into the kitchen – ultra modern with matching cupboards and an electric cooking stove – and filled the kettle and put it on, and while it was boiling he went back into the bedroom to make the bed. Who was it had once said that everything worth doing leaves a mess? He went back into the kitchen, enjoying the feeling of nakedness. It was good and private here and he could do what he liked without fear of raising eyebrows. When he was a small child he had sometimes crept out of the house in the early hours of the morning and taken off his pyjamas and danced naked on the lawn, just for the pleasure of the unhampered feeling it gave him.

He felt the same way about horses – after riding, when he had gone to turn his pony out, he had loved the moment when he slipped off the halter and the animal had moved away quite naked and untrammelled again. They always rolled when they were turned out, threshing their lovely silky bodies about on the grass to rub away the last lingering itches left by their tack and their humans. He felt that way about Julia, too, when . . .

Full circle! he thought, laughing at himself. Back to Julia again – I must have it badly. The kettle was about to boil and he made the tea and set out the cups and then headed for the bathroom to hurry her up, meeting her just coming out.

'Just in time,' he said, brushing past her before the fact that she was clean and pink from her washing could start him off again. 'Tea's made. It just needs pouring.'

Julia got dressed – just knickers and a dress and sandals, so it only took a minute – and went into the kitchen. She poured a cup of tea and drank it quickly for the thirst, and then poured another to sip for the flavour. A kind of reaction had set in, and she felt troubled and – inexplicably – lonely. He was out of the room, out of her sight, but she felt suddenly that she had come untied from him, like the string of a kite, and that he might go bobbing away on the wind, leaving her behind, limply earthbound. She heard him come out of the bathroom and cross to the bedroom, and guessed that he was dressing before he came in for his tea, but when the sounds receded further she grew curious as well as lonely and, taking his full cup as an excuse, padded softly out to find him. He was not in the bedroom – she heard his voice quietly from the sitting room and went to the door. He was sitting with his back to her, telephoning.

Joyce, of course – he was phoning Joyce. She had not before analysed the situation between them all sufficiently to feel jealousy – and besides, Joyce was a large part of her life and she liked her and was grateful for her attention and kindness. But now suddenly, in this loneliness, she thought with the beginning of resentment, why does she always have to come between us? Can't I just have him to myself for a little bit? She always comes up to take the shine off everything.

Peter had been listening on the phone, and now he spoke: 'All right, well tell me about it when I get home, darling. I'll be home in about an hour.'

I didn't mean to hear, Julia protested guiltily in her mind. She backed off in a panic, but though she made for the kitchen, slopping the tea into the saucer in her haste, and tried to shut her ears, she still heard his voice going on.

'I'm really bushed. Scheherezade's exhausting anyway, and Grünstein kept us going over and over it.'

He calls her darling, her mind said to her starkly.

He *lied* to her.

Of course I know he phones her, he has to. She's his wife, his wife, naturally he goes home to her, naturally he calls her darling. She's his wife.

She put the cup down, half-empty now, and leaned against the sink, feeling sick, arguing with herself frantically.

He lied to her.

Well, what else could he do? He couldn't tell her where he'd been, could he?

He lied about where he'd been. Had she asked him? Had she asked a direct question he couldn't avoid? It didn't matter, did it? Of course it did!

But he would have lied even if she hadn't asked him.

That thought came to her like a small icy hand clutching the wrist of her panic. It was true, wasn't it? He would have lied anyway. He *liked* lying. It was part of the fun.

And the next thought that came was unbidden too, and shocked her as much: I wish it had never happened, she thought, meaning their affair, everything they had done to each other. She saw it suddenly from the outside in, saw all the conventional, worldly things about it that she ought to have seen from the beginning: the deception, the danger, the disgrace, the potential hurt. She saw it all not instead of, but in parallel with her previous feelings: a dichotomy that threatened to pluck her apart like unravelling knitting.

In the middle of all this she heard the ping of the receiver being replaced, and she struggled to control her face, and to keep back the tears. She thrust herself off the sink which was supporting her and swallowed hard, then put her hands up to her face in a futile kind of gesture, as if she could push her features into place like plasticine. She heard Peter come into the kitchen behind her and she pulled herself up straight.

He said, 'Where's my tea, then? Here, there's a flood in my saucer! What have you been doing to it?' She tried to say something and failed, tried to turn to face him and didn't dare, and as he said mildly, because he suspected nothing, 'What's the matter with you?' she seized on to the only thing she could think of.

'I think I'm going to be sick,' she croaked, and dashed for the bathroom.

He thought it had been the wine, and she let him think so, and they drove back in silence. Now I'm lying too, she thought, by letting him think I was sick. He stopped at their usual corner, two streets away, and let her out, saying, with a cheerful smile as if nothing was wrong, 'Take more water with it next time.'

She smiled back, climbed out, slammed the door shut, and gave a little wave of her hand as he drove off, just as she always did, and then started walking in the same direction. If only she could get into the house and upstairs to the bedroom without meeting anyone. She could not face her mother. She did not want to speak or answer questions. She didn't even want to see Sylvia – though Sylvia knew about it, knew about Peter, had seen her getting out of his car one night. She had guessed some, and forced the rest out of Julia. She wouldn't tell – she had her own secret life to conceal – but her knowing did not make anything easier for Julia, because she disapproved, and thought Julia both venial and a fool.

Julia crept up to the house like a thief, slid her hand into the letterbox and drew out the key that hung on a string inside, then let herself in. Luck was with her. She shut the door behind her, and hearing a movement from the direction of the kitchen she fled upstairs into the bedroom she shared with Sylvia, shut the door, and flung herself on to her bed face downwards.

She didn't cry as she had thought she would. The moment was too far past for her to take refuge that way. She could only lie there hiding her face and thinking round and round in circles. She was confused by the number of contradictory thoughts she could host at the same time. She did not know what she wanted. After a while she sat up and looked around her dully. Home always seemed drab in contrast to Peter's world, whichever part of it she had just visited. This room, for instance, that was so comfortless, was her only resort when she was at home. The walls were distempered in an ugly peach shade that was neither here nor there, not pink nor orange nor any colour at all, really. It had not been decorated for longer than she could remember and there were finger marks round the door and light switch which over the years had accumulated into a grubby smear. The white paint on the door and skirting board had yellowed with time. The floor was covered with a parquet-patterned linoleum, but the pattern had been worn away in a long forking track from the door to the window and the beds where it disappeared under the bedside rug that she and Sylvia shared.

Julia's feet were on the rug, and she looked down at it with dislike. Her mother had chosen it, and years ago it had occupied pride of place in front of the sitting-room fire, but as age had worn it, it had been relegated first to her mother's bedroom, and finally to its present place. It was predominantly pale blue, with a complicated picture of a thatched cottage surrounded with giant lupins and hollyhocks – the woolly attempt at perspective hadn't come off, and the ugly flowers towered chimney-high like something in a botanical horror story. Julia had always hated it, even before her interest in drawing had received any proper guidance at school. At one time she had tried subversively to destroy it by spilling things on it, but the rug always triumphed. 'It's wool,' her mother would explain. 'It comes up beautifully, how ever often you wash it. One of the best buys I ever made, that rug. It'll last a lifetime.' And, gloomily, Julia had known it would.

The house was like that all through. Furnished after the bomb when there was little choice available and hardly any money anyway, it was unlovely; uncared-for except from the point of view of cleanliness. Age had made it shabby, and her father's diminishing income – her mother did not go out to work (only lower-class married women did that, she said) – had prevented anything being done about it. What was merely old Julia had never minded much, but some things that were downright ugly, like the rug, and that dreadful print of the flat, waxy-looking flowers that hung over the mantelpiece in the sitting room, had caused her continual irritation. Now she knew there was something else to be had, a better way, she was less able to tolerate it all.

She got up and went over to the window for relief. The sky was almost dark now, with only a faint red glow still over the roofs to the west. She could not see the Kanes' house from here – the angle down the road was just too much – but she looked in that direction anyway, and wondered what was happening in there now. In her mind's eye she travelled right round the house, into each room, admiring again each thing she had admired before, passing over one or two things she would not have had if it was *her* house. She did not think about the occupants – it was too painful. She kept her mind on the furnishings, until a movement and a quiet voice attracted her attention to the front porch below her.

Sylvia was standing there, and beside her a dark figure somewhat taller, with a crest of backswept hair, stood over her with his hands in his pockets arguing quietly and patiently. Julia watched them without really thinking about it, except to register that this must be 'Tony from the ice rink' with whom

95

Sylvia was currently, secretly, going out – secretly because their mother would not have approved of him (too common, and a manual job). He was apparently asking something which Sylvia was just as apparently refusing, though now and then her muted laugh was carried up clearly. The taller figure removed its hands from its pockets and made a kind of a lunge, and for a moment Sylvia's head was blotted out by the crest, before, laughing again, she ducked away and ran indoors. Julia heard her calling out to their mother, and then running upstairs, and a moment later she burst in.

'Oh!' she halted with surprise at the door, and then turned back to shout downstairs, 'She *is* in. She's up here, in the bedroom.' Then she came in to sit on her bed and remove her shoes, saying to Julia, 'Mother thought you hadn't come in yet. Where've you been all this time?'

Julia, turning back from the window, made a vague gesture but did not answer. She sat down on her own bed, opposite Sylvia, and watched as her sister rolled down her stockings and pulled them off by the toes, and then stood up to undo her suspender belt.

'Oh, Him again, I suppose,' Sylvia said with a derogatory face. She always called Peter 'Him', investing the word with withering scorn. She threw her stockings and belt on to the bed and then sat down again, splaying her legs out with relief. 'That's better. I felt as if I were being cut in two.'

'How was skating?' Julia asked, making an effort to be sociable.

'We didn't go skating. We went to the pictures up the West End.' Sylvia sounded faintly proud of the destination. 'A few of us went to the Corner House in the Strand afterwards. You should've come. It was really funny.'

Julia knew Sylvia didn't mean she should have come – she meant only that the evening had been successful, and that she wished there had been some way in which Julia could witness how pleasurable it had been.

'Tony and I nearly got thrown out.'

'Why?'

'Oh, he kept kissing me, and the manager came over and

said, "No kissing in here. Any more of that and you're out."
Everybody just about died of laughing.'

Julia was seeing double in her mind, one half of her saying
she would not be Sylvia for worlds, being slopped over by
pimply youths, while the other half was saying, how I wish I
could be like that, just ordinary, doing ordinary things, having
ordinary boyfriends. She felt she was letting Sylvia down by
not appreciating her story, but all she could think of to say
was: 'Did Mother know where you went? I thought you said
you were going skating?'

'Of course she doesn't know.' Sylvia made an impatient
gesture with a hand whose fingernails had been painted in the
latest shade. Julia wondered mildly how she had concealed it
from their parents. Their father would have forbidden it utterly
and their mother approved only of clear varnish, for protection
purposes only. 'And I don't know why you're looking so pious
– she doesn't know where you were this afternoon either.'

'I wasn't looking pious,' Julia objected mildly.

Sylvia snorted. 'Can you imagine what she'd say if she did
know? She'd go *blue*! She'd tear you to pieces!' She stared
at Julia, not sure whether her disapproval of her sister's
wickedness wasn't outweighed just then by her admiration
for her outrageousness. 'If she should ever find out . . .
You really are a *fool*, Ju. I mean, what's the point of it?
You know he can't marry you, so what's the *point*? You're
taking an awful risk for nothing, just to give him a bit of
pleasure. I'm jolly sure I wouldn't let a man do that sort of
thing to me unless he married me. Even if he weren't married
already, if you give him everything he wants just like that he's
got no reason *to* marry you, has he? I mean, he won't respect
you for it. And you could get found out any time. Have you
thought what your precious Joyce would say if she knew you
were carrying on under her very nose?'

She stopped as she saw the tears oozing silently from her
sister's eyes. Julia never cried. Even as a little girl, when
she had hurt herself, fallen down and skinned her knees for
instance, she never cried. The surprise of it woke a sympathy
in Sylvia, who was fond of her in a detached, impatient,
older-sisterly way. Though she disapproved of Julia's affair

she did not want the trouble she was sure would break when it was discovered. Trouble for Julia, she knew instinctively, would overspill and complicate her own life. And there was a little thread of admiration in her for the daring of the Julia-Peter situation, for the *glamour* of it. She wanted it to succeed, though she knew it was against all the odds as well as the proprieties that it should.

She said, 'Oh, Ju, don't cry! What is it? Are you in trouble? Here . . .' She sat down beside Julia and put her arm round her, and offered her a handkerchief, not knowing what else to do. Julia took the handkerchief but was crying too much to use it just yet. The sympathy had made the tears flow faster.

'Did you have a row with him?' Sylvia tried.

Julia shook her head, looking in on her own amazement at the idea with a horrid realisation. 'He doesn't – he doesn't care about me enough to quarrel.'

'I thought you said he loved you?' Sylvia said. On her happy nights Julia would convince herself that he did, and would dance around the bedroom in ecstasy.

'In a kind of a way he does.'

'Has he said it to you? Has he told you he does?'

'No, of course not. He doesn't love me in the way you mean. It's different. I can't explain.'

'Well, what did he do to upset you?'

'Nothing, he didn't do anything. I suppose –' she said, pausing to blow her nose – 'I suppose it just all came home to me suddenly, that he's married to someone else, and that I can never be with him the way I want to.'

'What do you mean? How do you want to? You don't mean marriage? Come on, you must have known *that* was out when you started messing with a married man!'

'I never really thought of it,' she said, honestly. 'I wouldn't expect him to marry me, even if he wasn't already married.'

Sylvia was impatient. 'Well, what then? What are you talking about?'

'It was . . .' she paused, wondering how to express what she was feeling for the first time. 'It's just that I discovered today that he lies to her about where he's been. I heard him.'

98

'Well, so do you. So does everybody,' Sylvia said reasonably. This was all double Dutch to her. 'What's wrong with that?'

'It's different with you and me. That doesn't hurt anyone. But with her – he shouldn't lie to her. She's his wife. Suppose I was married to him and he lied to me – how would I feel?'

'You wouldn't know, so you wouldn't feel anything. I think that's silly. Of course he has to tell her a fib or two. You must have known that all along.'

'But I never thought about it.' She wiped her wet face on her arm and frowned, wondering still. 'I never saw what we did as being connected with anything else, or any*one* else. It was just him and me. But now . . .'

There was a silence, and then Sylvia said, 'You'd be better to give it up. You know it's wrong, and anyway it's a mug's game. You don't get any fun out of it – I mean, look at you!'

Julia shook her head, unable to find any words.

'You ought to meet some boys of your own age. Why don't you come skating with me tomorrow,' she said in a burst of generosity. 'There are lots of nice ordinary people at the rink. Make some proper friends and have some fun. Never mind these intellectuals. They're all weirdies anyway.'

The simplicity of the solution appealed to Julia's tired mind. Forget it, go back to being ordinary, leave the intellectual weirdies to their own devices. She nodded slowly.

'Perhaps. I'll see how I feel tomorrow. Thanks, Sylvia. You're very kind to me.'

'Oh bosh, you're my sister,' Sylvia said dismissively.

They prepared to go to bed.

'I did try,' Julia excused herself afterwards. She did try. She went skating with Sylvia, and enjoyed the exercise and the movement to music, the stubborn, gratifying rhythms. She enjoyed the colours, the experts dancing on the ice, tiny children doing amazingly complicated things with no apparent effort, the pretty dresses and the light reflecting off the silver blades. She stored it all up, sketching busily in her mind as she skated around and around the rink on her own. Sylvia had no doubt meant to keep her company, but she was a popular girl in her group and her excitement soon got the better of her charity. On the whole Julia was not sorry. She liked to be alone, if she couldn't be with Peter.

She even allowed Sylvia to arrange a foursome including her, and they went to the cinema. It was a very embarrassing evening. Sylvia's boyfriend was that same Tony, and they of course were well at ease with each other, to the exclusion of everyone else. The other member of the party was a young lad called David Somethingorother, a tall, fair-haired, fair-faced boy of about eighteen who was as painfully shy as Julia was absent. He seemed disconcerted to be thrust so categorically at Julia, relieved when he found that she did not expect him to entertain her. In the cinema the other two began to kiss each other fervently as soon as the lights went down, and did so on and off until they rose again. When the second picture started, David seemed to decide that something was expected from him, and he grabbed hold of Julia's hand in the dark.

She let him have it for much the same reason, and there they sat, unable to get disentangled again, while their hands grew hot and sweaty in each other's grasp, a limp, damp bundle between them, an unwelcome responsibility, like a baby that needed changing. It was a relief to both when the lights came on again, and they could let go.

Outside the cinema Sylvia and Tony suggested going for some coffee in the High Street, where there was a Wimpy Bar that stayed open late. Julia said quickly that she had rather a headache and wanted to go home.

'I'll walk with you,' David said dutifully.

'No, really, that's quite all right. It's only five minutes from here. You go on with the others.'

'If you're really sure?' He was a nice boy, and Julia felt obscurely sorry about the evening, though from quite what angle she wasn't sure.

'Oh yes, really. Thank you very much for the pictures,' she added because he had paid for her ticket, 'and the ice-cream.'

'Oh, that's all right,' he said. He hesitated, not sure how to go, and Julia helped him.

'You'd better dash – they're nearly out of sight.'

'Righto – goodbye.' He bolted, and she turned, relieved and sorry, amused and disappointed, and walked homewards.

It was pleasant to walk alone at this time of night, with one's echoing footsteps for company. The air was mild, and seemed clean because of the darkness. She could smell the grass and trees in the park just ahead of her. I did try, she said to herself, but it wasn't any good. I can't be like Sylvia. I can't be like anyone but me.

She wasn't happy with herself, or with her situation, and still the thought of Peter pulled at her like a leash tugging an unwilling dog. She didn't know what she would do. She didn't want to go home just yet – she wanted to keep walking, to have time to think something out, or at least to calm herself; so she turned at the park-corner and walked the other way, away from home, along the other side of the park. She ran her finger along the railings, smelled the sooty privet, and heard a cat yowl in the silence with a sound like a human baby.

And another sound, the sound of a car's engine. Coming this way. She knew that car, she heard it every day of her life, whether she was listening for it or not, whatever time of night it came home. She glanced around her for somewhere to run, but she was halfway along the road, and it was straight and shelterless for its whole length. The car came round the corner ahead of her and she froze.

She was in the penumbra half way between one lamp post and the next, but he saw her anyway. He saw her as soon as he turned the corner and wondered what she was doing walking away from Milton Street at that time of night. He pulled up alongside her, leaned out of his window and said cheerfully, 'Hello! Running away from home?'

'No,' she said gravely. 'I was just walking. I didn't want to go home just yet.'

'Fair enough,' he said. 'Jump in – it's open.'

The moment of decision – but she didn't decide, she didn't even think of hesitating. In obedience to his wish she walked round the front of the car (he had trained her never to walk round the back when the engine was running) and got in beside him. He made a neat three-point turn and accelerated away down the street, heading in the direction of the Lido.

'Where have you been this past week?' he asked her after a moment. 'You've been missed.'

'Who by?' she asked tentatively.

'Oh, the kids have been asking for you. And Joyce misses you around, especially when the kids are noisy.' He glanced at her sideways, and heard her thought. 'And I missed you too, of course,' he added casually. She did not smile as he had meant her too but looked at him as if assessing how much he meant by it; assessing him and storing him away. He felt a little guilty at his own levity. Where *had* she been for the last week? Had she been avoiding him? (It seemed so.) Was she going to tell him she didn't want to carry on with the business? He couldn't shrug at the thought. Like it or not, he had missed her.

He changed gear, and then reached out his hand towards her, and after what might or might not have been a hesitation he felt her bony hand slip into his palm and her fingers close.

'What's the matter?' he asked gently. She didn't answer at first, and he thought he heard her sigh, but when the driving next allowed him to look at her, her expression was calm, she looked as she always did.

'Nothing, now,' she said.

Joyce's father was ill again, and Joyce went to stay with her mother for a few days, taking James with her. The 'baby', as he was still called, had been chesty for a week past and Joyce felt the change of air would do him good.

'Why not take them both?' Peter asked, not because he thought she might but to hear what excuse she would make. He had formed an opinion that she didn't much care for her firstborn and was now collecting evidence to support his theory.

'I don't think it would be wise to have them both around the house with Daddy ill.'

'Mrs Thing could look after them, surely?'

'Mrs Thurston has enough to do, cooking and cleaning. Besides, you know how they fight – they'd disturb him.'

'James alone is enough to disturb the most robust of—'

Peter began, but Joyce cut across him. She had no time now for his urbane cynicism.

'I can manage James quite well on his own. Or Michael on his own.' She stopped and then added in exasperation, 'You know perfectly well what I mean. Why do you *talk*? You wear me out with your talk.'

Peter looked at her critically, wearing that insolent smile which was both his most fascinating and most irritating expression. He thought how much like a hausfrau she looked now – always perfectly dressed, even though her day had been rushed with preparations and her face was clouded with apprehensions, but dressed to avoid rather than attract notice. She moved like a wife-and-mother, not wishing, not expecting to be desirable, she dressed for her own self-respect and not for her man's libido. She blended into the background of her Maples' furnishings, interspersed with good antiques from home, and smart modern drapery, so that you could hardly see her. Neutral-coloured, she could have been transported into any house in the same income bracket and her protective markings would have camouflaged her perfectly. He began to weave a fantasy in his head about two wives swapping houses and no one noticing anything for weeks.

'Of course,' he said. 'You need a break – you're looking tired. Michael will be all right with me. I'll take him to my parents' at the weekend for a treat – maybe even leave him there. That's an idea – why not leave the pair of them there, so you can have a real break?'

Joyce did not answer for a moment, mistrusting his kindness. He was only ever kind with his own comfort in mind, when he wanted her to do something or wanted her out of the way while he did something; but she was tired, and anxious about her father, and unhappy on several counts, and it was tempting to believe in his affection. Peter, still watching her, read most of this as it passed through her mind. He reached out a hand and rested it on her shoulder; a gesture of casual affection that flooded her with a spurious warmth.

'No, it's better if I take Jamie with me,' she said at last. 'He's too young to be left with strangers.'

'Just as you like, dear,' Peter said, and squeezed her shoulder gently. Joyce lifted her hand and touched his briefly, and he smiled at her without the cynicism. Her resistance to him faded so that she didn't notice a lot of small things that should have been danger signals to her.

Julia was glad to see Joyce go. She had felt choked for the past weeks with the claustrophobic relationship of the three of them and with the, only now appreciated, necessity of deceit when Joyce was around. Peter had never seemed to mind this dissembling, but then, as Julia knew quite well, he could forget both of them for long periods, even when either or both of them were in the same room with him. Sometimes Julia had the horrors that Joyce was going to confide in her about Peter, or that Peter would force a reckoning out of sheer wantonness; and so, though she was heartily sorry for Joyce in her worry about her father, she was heartily glad to see her off, by taxi, for the train on Friday evening. Peter was still working and would not be back until late. Julia was, of course, babysitting Michael.

'I wouldn't be half so easy about leaving him behind if it weren't for you,' Joyce had said, unconsciously turning the knife that Julia had stuck in her own bosom. 'Peter might just go out and leave the boy in the house on his own, and anything might happen.'

'Oh, surely not,' Julia had protested politely.

'You don't know Peter,' Joyce had said, and there had ensued an uncomfortable silence.

Michael went off to bed at his usual time without any fuss, or even so much as a tear for his missing mother. He accepted Julia so completely now that her presence did not arouse any excitement in him, though he preferred her company to his mother's, as most children would prefer to play with a sibling rather than a parent. So Peter arrived home to find his house in order, his child asleep, dry-cheeked, and his mistress in sole possession of the sitting room, crouched in one of her oddly disjointed positions, making anatomical sketches on a sketching block. Propped open beside her was what by its sheer size he knew to be some kind of art book, borrowed, no doubt, from the library.

'Hullo. All serene?'

'All serene,' she replied, and then twisted her head to look up at him over her shoulder. She was kneeling with her behind poked skywards, her elbows on the floor, and her feet crossed, their soft, crinkled palms upwards. He went down on his hunkers beside her.

'What's this?' he asked, of the book.

'Blake,' she said. He drew a strand of her hair out of her eyes as she spoke, and then laid his hand on the small of her back and drew it softly down over each of her buttocks in turn. 'His anatomical drawings,' she went on as if nothing was happening.

'Which Blake is that?' he asked her, continuing to stroke. 'Not old "Tyger, Tyger" Blake?'

'Yes,' she said. 'The same.'

'Really? Old "Paschal lamb" Blake. I didn't know he drew. Dear me, how interesting. Did you know that your little pink feet are positively indecent?'

He pushed her so that she fell over, and she went down curled, all-of-a-piece, where an adult would have sprawled awkwardly. Lying on her back with her legs still crooked and her feet still folded, like hands, one on top of the other, and her dark eyes fixed unwaveringly on him, she reminded him of some kind of animal.

'You look like a hedgehog. Or an armadillo,' he said. 'Or even a woodlouse. Curled up defensively. Impossible to straighten out.' He put his left hand to her throat and with his right hand pushed her knees down to straighten them. Her eyes glinted, and just as he exerted his full force she relaxed suddenly so that he was thrown off balance and sprawled across her.

She laughed silently, and he smiled back and said, 'That's all very well, but you see you've sealed your own fate, because now I've got you where you can't move.' And he wriggled himself round so that he was lying almost on top of her, with both his hands at her throat, high up under her jaw. 'Now, what are you going to do?'

'Nothing,' she said, with what would have been a shrug if she had been in any position to shrug. She was still smiling, and he dipped his head and kissed the corners of the smile and then moved inwards, working his way into her mouth. Her left arm, which was the only part of her free to move, came up and round him, her fingers bracing at the back of his shoulder.

'What are you doing?'

Had he found himself in the path of an oncoming car, Peter could scarcely have moved more quickly. He must also have thought quickly, for while Julia was still only just registering that it was Michael who had asked the question, Peter was swooping down on the pyjama-clad figure in the doorway, lifting him up almost to the ceiling in a way calculated to blow minor musings right out of a child's head. Michael squeaked satisfactorily and Peter laughed jovially, and Julia had time to arrange her features into an expression suitable to a childish romp.

'I'll tell you what we were doing,' Peter boomed, grounding Michael only long enough to grab him by the legs and lift him again, upside down this time.

Romps of this sort were not infrequent occurrences, and Michael used his hands to climb up his father's leg until his head was, if not the right way up, at least horizontal, and said remorselessly, 'Well, tell me then.'

'I will tell you,' Peter said, playing for time. Julia was standing by the sofa, half-laughing, half-frightened, and Peter shook Michael vertical again, exchanged one leg for an arm, swung him round once and threw him at Julia, knocking her backwards on to the sofa with Michael across her lap.

'Ow,' said Michael, simultaneously with an 'Oof' from Julia.

Peter surveyed them with his hands on his hips and said, 'I was just telling Julia that she can come with us on Sunday.'

'Where on Sunday?' Michael demanded, righting himself with a scramble.

'To Grandpa's,' Peter said, thanking his stars that he had not already told the boy about the treat.

'What, where Mummy's gone?' Michael asked.

'No, dimwit,' Peter said, rolling his eyes in horror at the thought, 'to Grandpa's in Suffolk.'

'Goodee,' Michael said happily. 'I like Suffolk.'

'I'm glad you do. I like Suffolk too. So I hope you'll be good between now and then so that I don't have to cancel the trip.'

'And Julia can come too?' Michael said, diplomatically glossing over that aspect of it.

'Yes, I don't see why not – if she's good.'

He glanced at her, enjoying her expression of puzzlement.

'You'll like it at Grandpa's,' Michael told her earnestly. 'There's horses and dogs and a parrot, and super cakes—'

'All right, my son,' Peter interrupted before he could get into full spate. 'Now, how about a spot of shut-eye for you? Come on, I'll take you up.'

'Coley-buckie?' Michael asked cunningly.

'Just this once then, you spiv.' He presented his back and Michael half-jumped, half-scrambled up. His father hitched him into place and said, 'Don't hold on by my hair, please. I haven't enough spare for you to pull it out.'

'All right,' Michael said agreeably, taking hold of an ear instead. 'What's a spiv?'

'Ouch. Sometimes you go too far. A spiv is a wide boy. Open the door, Julia.'

'What's a wide boy?' Michael persisted.

Julia opened the door and held it open, and Peter inched through. 'Duck,' he commanded, and Michael ducked under the lintel, and Peter touched her hand that rested on the doorknob as he went through. She smiled at him, and watched his painful progress up the stairs while the imbecile conversation drifted back to her.

'What *is* a wide boy, Daddy?'

'A boy who eats too many super cakes when he goes to Grandpa's for tea. He gets wider and wider until he finally bursts. Stop holding on to the banisters, muttonhead, you'll pull me over backwards.'

'I'm helping you climb up.'

'I don't need any help. I'm not that old . . .'

Julia picked up her sketching block and the book from the floor and put them on the chair by the door, ready for when she went home. She had a scraped-out kind of feeling, which she always got when she had been watching Peter playing with either of his children. When she saw him with them, she loved him almost unbearably. It was the same when, on rare occasions, she went to watch him play, at such of the rehearsals as were open to members of the public. It seemed that to watch him perform in any sphere that did not involve her, heightened her awareness of him. She was excited, for that reason, about the visit he had mentioned to his parents' house. That would add another dimension, another aspect of him to love. She had fallen in love, in the first place, with a picture; the reality made her feel as if she were breathing pure oxygen.

When Peter came back in she was standing almost as he had left her, but now her cheeks were pink and her eyes bright as if she had been out in the cold air.

'I think he'll stay put this time,' he said, 'but in case he doesn't . . .' He locked the door, and then turned back to look at her again. 'Come here,' he said. She came obediently and stood before him. 'You look excited. Is that because of the trip on Sunday?'

'Mm. I am excited, and . . .'

'And what?'

'Scared.'

'Why are you scared?' He usually found that this peremptory style of questioning would make her answer in spite of herself, but not this time. She was scared of what might be said, of their illicit relationship being discovered; but because she would never discuss that aspect of things with him – mainly through fear of his reaction – she would not now tell him what scared her. Instead she merely looked at him, her eyes unwavering. She was never sure of him, but being afraid of him made no difference. She was like an animal, drawn to him in spite of herself, obedient first, afraid second.

'I hadn't finished kissing you,' he said, his voice coming out strangely. He ached for her and her small body, but he was not afraid of that desire. What made him nervous was the upsurge of tenderness for her which accompanied every erection, and which made him put out his hand and touch her head or face as gingerly as if she were a soap-bubble. 'Come and kiss me, hedgehog,' he said, holding his arms away from

108

his sides to make himself look vulnerable and she came up close and leaned her body confidingly against him.

'What funny things you call me,' she said. 'Hedgehog and owl and woodlouse. All animals.'

She kissed him, parting his mouth with her tongue in a way that melted his guts. She did it to him because it was what he did to her; it was utterly innocent. Every gesture of passion she had learnt from him. Every gesture, that is, but one, and that was biting him. She did it now, laying her teeth against his cheek and closing them just enough for him to feel the pressure – as if she were saying, I could hurt you very much if I wished, but I don't wish. He drew his face away from her teeth and kissed her mouth to occupy it; so very small and soft, as if there were no teeth inside, nothing but softness and smoothness.

His hands were inside her T-shirt, having found their own way from experience. 'You're no hedgehog here,' he said running his hands up the smooth length of her body from her waist. 'You're a weasel.'

Her hands were sliding into the waistband of his trousers, and his intestines were pure liquid. 'And you're a stoat,' she said, and he thought how singularly appropriate that was.

'Julia, my mother,' Peter said.

'How do you do,' said Mrs Kane kindly, as to a child, holding out her hand. Julia stopped herself saying 'Very well thank you,' shook the hand and said how do you do in reply. Mrs Kane was a Scotswoman of the queenly type. Peter, Julia could see, had inherited her luminously clear skin and heavy-lidded, bright blue eyes. This was so interesting that Julia went on looking for further resemblances, forgetting that she herself was also under scrutiny.

'Daddy will be down in just a moment,' Mrs Kane went on, 'and then we shall have lunch. And – ah, here he is!' Julia turned to follow the direction of Mrs Kane's gaze and saw entering not Peter's father as she expected but a young man, only a year or two older than herself, whom she could never have expected.

'Oh, Julia, this is my brother Rowland – my *younger*

109

brother,' Peter said, with a kind of wry emphasis that she did not understand. Not that she was trying to, for she was looking at Rowland with what bordered on astonishment. She had not thought there could be two people in the world who looked like Peter, but Rowland looked so like him you could not have missed the resemblance even had you met him out of context. The colouring, the features, the expression – all were shiveringly similar; but in Rowland the fraction of an inch here and there of tweaking by nature of the basic mix had made him devastatingly handsome, where Peter was not.

'Hullo,' Rowland said jauntily, advancing across the room to shake her hand and stand looking down at her with a kind of impudent charm. 'Who're you? Oh, no, of course, I remember, you're Thingummy, Michael's new big sister. How nice of you to come! You must let me show you around after lunch.'

'You'll have to excuse Rowland,' Peter said from behind her. 'He's rather excitable.'

'No, no,' Rowland protested. 'I'm serious. It's jolly nice of you to bring her along to brighten my day, Peter old man. I appreciate it. Come along – Julia, isn't it? – you must let me take you in to lunch. Don't worry about the "auld yins" – they can follow on at leisure.'

Even through her astonishment that anyone as divinely handsome as Rowland Kane could exist, she could appreciate that he was teasing Peter in some unsubtle way, but that was as far as she got. She spoke very little during the meal, which was served directly Peter's father came down; content to listen, and to look from face to face, tracing the family resemblances; from face to face, but mostly at Rowland. In him, Peter's idiosyncratic features were perfectly shaped and perfectly in harmony with one another. He had the same clear skin, but with a touch of colour over the high cheekbone; the same smooth black hair, but thicker and with more spring to it; the same eyes, but with, instead of the languid cynicism, a young alertness; the same mouth, but more symmetrical, fuller, and lacking the up-one-side twist when he smiled.

Here, then, was the paradigm of Peter's beauty, six or seven years younger, and unmarried – Julia would not have been normal if she had not allowed that thought to pass, however briefly, through her mind. And he was doing his best to entertain her, as if he really wanted her to enjoy herself. After lunch – a heavenly stew, was there no meat rationing in the country? – everyone retired to the drawing room. Rowland sat still only long enough to see a conversation start between Peter and their father, and then said, 'How about Michael and me showing you round the estate?'

'I want to play with the train,' Michael said. They both looked towards Peter, who appeared to be paying his father only perfunctory attention.

He said, 'I more or less promised Julia a ride.'

'Well, that's all right, dear,' his mother said capably. 'I'll take Michael up to the playroom, and Rowland can take Julia for a ride and show her the farm, and you and Daddy can have your talk in peace and quiet.'

Peter opened his mouth as if to object, and then met Julia's eyes, and shut it again. He gave the ghost of a shrug and said, 'What have you got for her to ride?'

'Can Julia ride?' his father asked of Peter. He had not yet spoken to Julia except to say how do you do, but Julia was still enough of a child not to expect grown-ups to notice her particularly, and had not minded.

'Well enough,' Peter said, his eyes still on Julia.

'I'll take Tarquin, and she can have Taggart,' Rowland said. 'That okay, Dad?'

'Yes, yes, of course. Ride round by the church. I'm sure she'd be interested to see it. It has a very fine mediaeval screen.'

'We will if we've time. Have you got some trousers, Julia?'

'In the car,' she said, turning again to Peter.

'It's open,' he said. She nodded and went out to fetch them, feeling Peter's eyes on her, but missing his question to Rowland.

'Which way are you going?'

'Up to Beacon Hill, I thought, and then back by the pack bridge.'

Peter appeared to digest this in silence for a moment and then said, 'Take care, won't you,' and the two brothers stared at each other, one defiant, one angry, until Rowland smiled, said 'Okay,' and turned away.

Julia was glad to be out. Not only did she love riding with a passion that was never likely, because of her geographical and financial situation, to be satisfied, but she had found the atmosphere in the house tense, and had been made nervous by Peter's mother, who was so gracious and dignified, and possessed such very penetrating eyes. The father she didn't mind, because he had virtually ignored her, which was comfortable; but she thought it would be fun to chat to Rowland, who was just like Peter but not so awe-inspiring. Not that they did much chatting at first, for riding took all her attention, and what little she could spare was turned towards the countryside and to the points of interest that Rowland was showing her.

Taggart was a liver-chestnut mare who, Rowland explained, had been Peter's but now belonged to him. 'She goes better for me than for Peter – but then Peter isn't much of a rider. He has good hands but poor legs.' He looked at her appraisingly. 'You ride rather like him yourself. You look good on a horse, but you've no seat to speak of. Where did you learn?'

'At a riding school,' she said. 'I helped take care of the ponies in exchange for rides.'

'That explains it, then. Never had a horse of your own? No, and of course you can't develop a seat unless you ride regularly. That's what was wrong with Peter – too many other interests. Tarquin is my father's horse. He still hunts twice a week in the season. Peter used to hunt, but I think it was the society he liked rather than the sport. I always got the impression that if the meet had lasted all day and never got mounted Peter would have been best pleased.'

In this way they walked and trotted through the lightly wooded lanes, where the leaves were just beginning to colour and turn, and across stubble fields, until they broke clear of the trees and saw a small, pudding-shaped hill ahead of them. Rowland broke off a comment on Peter's school days to say, 'That's Beacon Hill – there's a good view from the top. It's safe to canter along here. Come on!'

The two horses were apparently accustomed to a run at this

point for they were snatching at the bit before he had finished speaking, and without any aid from Julia her mount sprang forward into a canter to race with the bigger Tarquin. Julia clung on, bouncing unprofessionally until she got her balance again, and prayed that Taggart would not start bucking. The rising ground slowed them, however, and they finished the hill at a walk. At the top they dismounted and walked round the flat summit of the mound looking at the view, while Rowland gave a running commentary interspersed with miscellaneous information about Peter.

'You're supposed to be able to see four counties from here, but I've no idea which four. I suppose that's why they chose it.'

'Who chose it?'

'The Anglo-Saxons or early Britons or whatever. It's a beacon hill. They lit signal fires to pass messages down the coast when there were sea-raids. All the land on that side used to belong to our family years ago.'

'What – as far as the eye can see?' Julia asked.

He glanced at her to see if she was mocking him, but she seemed quite innocent. 'Not quite,' he said. 'Up to the end of the ploughland that way, and to the river that way. All that land beyond the house used to be the park, but it was sold off years ago for agriculture. Now we just have the one farm. You can see the farmhouse over there, look.'

Julia gazed, entranced. This was all quite foreign to her, like something out of an eighteenth-century novel. She had known, obviously, that Peter's background was different from hers, but she had never imagined how different.

'And will all this belong to Peter one day?'

'Oh, I shouldn't think so. I hardly think old Peter would want to farm. Besides, he's got his career – he's provided for, if you like.'

'I thought, perhaps, that being the eldest son—'

'Oh, come on, the old man isn't as feudal as all that. I mean, I know he looks pretty ancient, but . . .' He turned his amused gaze on Julia, and she coloured. 'You've been reading too many novels.' She said nothing, looking down, and he said, 'That colour suits you, you know,' leaving her to

113

wonder if he meant the blush or the shirt. 'Let's sit down for a while.

They sat on the grass at the edge of the hill and held the reins loosely while the horses cropped the short turf behind them. After a brief silence, Rowland said, looking out over the misty blue view, 'No, if you're after the estate, you've attached yourself to the wrong brother. All this will probably come to me in a few years' time. The old man will have to make it over to me in good time, or the whole thing will get swallowed up in death duties, and that would be, to put it mildly, a shame. So now you know.' He turned to look at her. 'Are you going to switch your allegiance to me?'

She looked surprised, and began to say 'What are you talking about', but before she could finish the sentence he had flung an arm round her shoulders, pulled her to him, and kissed her.

The startled horses snorted and tugged as Julia struggled for a moment, and then merely stood watching with their ears pricked as she remained still in Rowland's grasp, her hands taken up with keeping her balance. She stopped struggling because she was in too weak a position to have any effect on him, but she had not given in – he kissed a face as unresponsive as cardboard. At last he let her go and she struggled upright again and stared at him, too puzzled to be much angry.

'Sorry about that,' he said lightly. 'Just a little experiment of my own. I wanted to see how the land lay.'

'What do you mean?' she asked. She felt she ought to take grave exception to his behaviour, but he was so at ease and matter-of-fact that it seemed inappropriate.

'You're having an affair with my brother and I wanted to see who was the instigator – how much of it was you. And now I know.' He smiled in a self-satisfied way. 'Whatever he does to you, you aren't in on it, that much is obvious. So, how did you come to get involved with him?'

She wasn't sure if he was musing to himself or asking her a question, and while she hesitated he said, 'I imagine you don't mean to deny that you are having an affair?'

'I – I don't know,' she said, still much puzzled, and seeing his derisive look she added, 'I don't mean that, I mean I don't know what you'd call it. How did you know, anyway?'

114

'The looks between you would melt rock.'

She looked so anxious that he laughed.

'Oh, don't worry. You've been the soul of discretion, really. It's just that I know my brother very well. But what's in it for you?'

'I don't know.'

'I see you don't. What a confused young lady you are. Why don't you stop? You'll get found out in the end, you know.'

'I don't see why,' Julia protested with something like spirit.

'Well, I do. You can't keep it concealed for ever – law of averages. And even if you could, Peter won't. He'll force a reckoning one day. He hates a status quo. Besides . . .'

He hesitated long enough for Julia to prompt him, 'Besides what?'

'I don't know if it will make you feel any better, but Peter's very fond of you.' There was a very long silence as Julia digested that, and at last Rowland said, curiously, 'That surprised you, I wonder why? You are an odd girl. Didn't you know?'

'It never occurred to me,' she said, and then, shyly, 'How do you know he is?'

'As I told you, I know my brother. His eyes follow you around the room. He's got a kind of hungry look when he looks at you. That's what will give him away, you know, even if nothing else does.' He stood up abruptly and pulled Tarquin's reins over the horse's head. 'Come on, let's ride.'

'If I were you, I should get away from him,' Rowland said later, when they were walking side by side along the road home. 'When the trouble comes, it'll be pretty beastly. I can't see old Joyce giving up her breadwinner without a fight. Remarkable character, is Joyce,' he went on musingly. 'She's got everything sewn up. I don't think she loves Peter one jot more than he loves her, but she certainly knows what makes him tick. I've every admiration for her.'

'Yes,' Julia agreed.

'So if anyone's going to go to the wall when the crash comes, it's more than likely going to be you. Why don't you get out now while the getting's good?'

'I tried,' she began.

'Not very hard, I suspect.'

'No, not very hard. I didn't want to. I have no other friends. I can talk to Peter, you see.'

'I think I do. You did a trade – sex for conversation. That explains a lot. However, there are other conversationalists in the sea. Me, for instance.'

He smiled to show he wasn't serious. She tried to visualise her life without Peter, but having had no practice she could not do it with any conviction.

'He's selfish, you know,' Rowland went on. 'If it came to it he'd sacrifice you to save himself.' Julia shrugged. 'I can see there is nothing bad I can tell you about him. Well, I'm sorry. No hard feelings?'

'No. I think you were trying to help me.'

'Don't sound so surprised about it. Has no one ever been kind to you in all your life? I'm really sorry for you. You don't seem to get much fun out of it all.'

'It isn't like that,' Julia said quickly. 'It's just the lies, the hole-and-corner business I hate. I just wish it could all be above board and open. And besides . . .'

'Nice honest sentiments. And besides what?'

'I love him.'

'So I imagined.'

'You were gone quite a time with Rowland, weren't you?' Peter said conversationally as he drove home that evening. 'What were you doing all that time?'

'Talking, mostly.'

'About what?'

'You, mostly,' she said, smiling.

Peter did not seem to be amused. 'He was trying to put you off me, eh?'

'He told me things about your childhood.'

'Such as?'

'He said he was a better rider than you. Is that true?'

'I suppose so. I never went in for it as much as he did. He was the country boy. What did you think of him then?'

'Rowland?'

116

'Of course Rowland.'

'I thought he was nice.'

'He's very good looking isn't he?'

'I suppose so.'

'Only suppose?'

'Well, of course he's good looking. He's very handsome in fact.'

'Better looking than me, blast him.'

'Much better,' Julia said serenely, looking out of the window at the lights dashing past.

'Where did he take you?'

'Up to the beacon hill. We sat there for a while admiring the view, and he showed me how much belongs to your family. He said it would probably be given to him in a few years' time. I suppose that would make him very rich?'

'Adequately,' Peter said, seeming amused by the question. 'So he told you what his prospects were, eh? What was he doing, proposing to you?'

The turn of the conversation would have surprised Julia had she not had the talk with Rowland; he had given her enough new food for thought to be able to say quite calmly, 'The parrot was beautiful too, but I'm not in love with it.'

After a moment Peter laughed, and under cover of the darkness reached out and laid his hand on her leg.

'I can't tell you how glad I am to hear it.'

Seven

The blow, when it fell, fell swiftly. Julia went round to the Kanes' house the next day and found the side door, unusually, locked. She went back to the front door and knocked. It was opened by Joyce.

'Oh,' said Julia, surprised. 'It's you.'

'Yes. Surprised, aren't you? Didn't expect me back so soon?'

'Well, no,' Julia began. She had stepped past Joyce automatically into the hall, and Joyce shut the door behind her so violently that Julia stopped short and turned to her.

'No, of course you didn't. I'm sure you're disappointed too, aren't you?' Joyce was standing with her back to the door. She looked pale and, strangely, gave the appearance of being dishevelled, though Julia could not immediately see why. She was also glaring with a fury that belatedly aroused Julia's fear.

'No, of course not,' she said feebly.

'Don't trouble yourself to lie to me. Just answer me one thing – how long has this been going on?'

Julia felt the blood drain from her face as the realisation that she was caught hit her with an almost physical impact, like a blow to the solar plexus. It was as if she had heard the cage door clang shut behind her. She made one vague, escaping movement of her head, and then froze. She whispered, 'I don't—'

Joyce cut in impatiently. 'I said, don't bother to lie. I know what you did with my husband on Friday – when I was barely out of the house. You couldn't wait, could you? And in my house, you cold-blooded little slut, in my house!'

The language, from Joyce, was as shocking as the anger.

Julia could only stammer, 'But – I didn't – it wasn't like that.'

'I know what it was like,' Joyce shouted, incensed by the implied denial. 'And do you know *how* I know? I'll tell you – my son told me! Does that surprise you? You thought he was too young to know what was going on, didn't you? But he wasn't, he understood all right, and he came and told me.' Her voice cracked, and she went on waveringly, 'I suppose I can understand you falling for him – God knows you aren't the first – but to do it in my house, and in front of my children! To think I trusted you with them! How could you expose them to it? How could you?'

She made a hoarse sound like a sob, and turned her face away and hit the jamb of the door with her fist, angry and frustrated with herself for being so close to crying when she had meant only to be icily scathing. She had been betrayed – and by this girl whom she had liked and trusted. She had thought Julia was hers, and all the time she was Peter's. Behind her back! Betraying her behind her back!

Julia, standing rigid with shame and terror, made one movement towards the other woman, instinctively wanting to comfort her, before realising that she could not touch her, nor even speak to her. Any word or gesture on her part would be further injury. She could only stand and watch, and wait for whatever else was going to have to come to her.

Joyce recovered enough to speak again. 'My little boy – to see that, at his age – do you know what it could do to him? But I don't suppose you care about that. You don't mind who suffers. You don't care if you break up a marriage, and leave two little boys fatherless. All you can think of is yourself, you selfish little bitch! God, and I trusted you. What a fool! To think I left you alone with my children all those times! I thought you were really fond of them. I suppose you've been doing this all along, sneaking in behind my back, using those two poor innocent children as a blind. Well? Haven't you got anything to say?'

Julia shook her head, and then added hopelessly, 'I'm sorry.'

'Sorry!' Joyce's mirthless laugh was horrible, distorted like

119

her face. 'How dare you say you're sorry! You come sneaking in here, worm your way into my confidence, and all the time you're carrying on with my husband – lying on the carpet, for God's sake!' Her rage burst again like a fountain of sparks at the thought. 'You did it lying on the carpet! What kind of a person are you? You must be sick in the head, that's all I can think. You're like a – like a bitch on heat! How many others are there? I should feel sorry for you, really. There's a name for people like you, people who can't control themselves.'

Julia closed her eyes as if she'd been slapped. The ugliness was worse than anything, and despite herself tears began to seep out from under her eyelids. She had not wanted to cry, feeling she had no right, but the low, sick, moaning feeling in her soul left her with no other resort.

Joyce seemed to have stopped herself with her own violence. When she spoke again her voice was low, glutted with tears.

'He won't marry you, so don't think it. You aren't the first, you know. If he married every girl he had sex with, he'd have as many wives as Solomon. He doesn't care about them – they're just a bit on the side to him. You're no different. He married *me*. I'm the one he chose. You're just a passing fancy. He'll have forgotten you by tomorrow.'

Julia saw that she was reassuring herself, that her anger had passed and it was fear and grief that moved her now. Joyce wanted to believe that there had only been the one occasion, and Julia would gladly have lied to her on that score had she not been afraid to speak. She didn't want to hear her own voice – she felt that the sound of it might sicken her, and enrage Joyce.

'But how could you do it, that's what I want to know.' Joyce's voice was plaintive now, and the naked hurt in her face was hard to look at. Her pain was harder to bear than her anger. 'I thought so well of you – you seemed such a nice girl, and the boys loved you. How could you do it to us? Did you really hate us so much? What did we ever do to you to make you hate us so much?'

'I didn't, I didn't hate you,' Julia broke in passionately. 'I never meant to hurt you – or the children. I love them. It just – sort of – happened. I couldn't seem to help it.'

She wanted to tell Joyce how it had happened, and had to restrain her tongue; for to explain, to justify, to tell her that all along she had hated that part of it, the betrayal and the lying, to allow herself to be run away with by the longing to be exonerated, would mean telling Joyce the whole story, including how long it had been going on, and that would hurt Joyce worse than anything.

She stopped short, and Joyce, who might have forgiven a spontaneous outburst of regret or a confession of guilt, was repelled by what looked to her like too much self-assurance. When she spoke again, her voice was cold and contemptuous.

'If you have so little self-control, I suggest you seek medical help, before you get yourself into even worse trouble. In fact, I shall tell your mother that I recommend she has you examined by a psychiatrist.'

'My mother?' Julia turned pale all over again.

'Yes, your mother. I'm going to make sure someone keeps an eye on you from now on. You're a danger and a nuisance. And I hope your father beats you black and blue. I'd like to do it myself.'

At that moment the front door opened, almost hitting Joyce who was still standing in front of it. Peter came in. 'What's going on?' he asked sharply, and when he saw Julia a look compounded of consternation and relief passed across his face. 'Oh, there you are. I was looking for you.' He glanced at Joyce, taking in the tear-stains and anger, and then said to Julia, 'What's she been saying?'

'What do you mean, "she"? Don't talk about me as if I wasn't here,' Joyce said, her rage boiling up again at the sight of him.

'She said she was going to tell my mother,' Julia whispered. She seemed to be trying to shrink herself into as small a space as possible. Everything she had felt during the confrontation with Joyce was flooded out by fear now that Peter had arrived, for the air between the husband and wife seemed to crackle like static, and she dreaded what they might say or do to each other.

'Like hell she will,' Peter growled, and turning on Joyce,

'Anything you've got to say, you can say to me. You can leave her, and her family, and anyone else, out of it.'

'Of course you jump to her defence, don't you,' Joyce sneered at him. 'The poor sensitive little soul mustn't be upset, must she? You weren't so worried about upsetting your own son, were you, when you were rolling on the carpet with your whore, right in front of his eyes? Oh no, it doesn't matter if he gets mentally damaged from seeing the kind of thing his father gets up to while his mother's away, but dear little Julia mustn't be upset, must she?'

'Shut up,' Peter said roughly to her. 'This is between you and me, it's nothing to do with her. Julia, you'd better go.'

'Oh no you don't,' Joyce interposed, making a movement to get between Julia and the door. Peter grabbed at Joyce and managed to catch her arm. 'Let me go. Don't you dare lay your hands on me! I'm not one of your Saturday night tarts. Let me *go*!'

'Nor is she,' Peter said, shaking Joyce furiously. She struck out at him, and Julia drew in her breath in terror, and then Peter flung Joyce away from him so that she staggered back against the hall table. She began to weep, helpless with anger and frustration, and Julia, seeing the doorway momentarily clear, made for it, white-faced.

'Let me get out,' she said, but Peter now caught her by the arms, as strongly but with a gentler intention than he had caught Joyce.

'Where are you going?'

'I don't know. Just let me get out.'

But Peter wanted to know what was happening before anyone escaped him. Still holding Julia he looked across at Joyce and said, 'If you tell her mother, there'll be hell to pay.'

'Let her pay it. She deserves everything she gets.'

'Take it out on me, not her.'

'She's just as guilty as you. I'm going to tell her mother *and* her father.'

'They'll turn me out,' Julia said.

'I hope they do,' Joyce said viciously. 'Do you think I want you living in the same street?' She turned back to Peter. 'I don't want her anywhere near us. I don't want you sniffing round her gate like a dog whenever you feel randy.'

Peter felt the impact of the words run through Julia's body, and he held her tighter, defensively. He did not care what this woman thought or felt, he only wanted peace and quiet and a re-establishment of the status quo which gave him his freedom. But the ugliness of Joyce's anger repelled him and he struck back thoughtlessly.

'If she goes away, there'll be nothing for me to stay for, will there?'

There was a silence in which the breathing of all three of them was audible; and then Joyce said fearfully, 'What do you mean? You don't care about her . . . ?'

'Did you think that was the first time then?' Peter said. Slowly, cruelly, he cut away her defences. 'You were easy to fool, weren't you? It's been going on all the time – *all the time*, d'you understand? From the beginning. We've been lovers from the beginning.'

'No,' Julia moaned in soft desperation. She tried to wriggle herself free, and finding his grip too firm she whimpered. He shook her to quiet her.

Joyce was silent, her eyes going from Peter to Julia, her lips moving as if she was beginning many sentences and changing her mind. In the end she looked at Julia, and said only, 'He won't marry you. I told you he won't marry you.'

Shaken and sick and desperate Julia made one last effort, twisted out of Peter's grasp, dodged his outflung hand, scrabbled at the door and then was out and running, deaf and blind to everything, wanting only to put distance between her and that house.

A long time later, Julia lay in bed in the spare room at home, feeling scoured out with grief and shock and shame. She had been sent to the spare room as an extra punishment, as being unfit to share a bedroom with her sister any more. The spare-room bed was narrow and very hard, the mattress old and flocked into lumps. The room smelled cold and unused, and the curtains did not quite meet, so the yellow lamplight from the street lay in a vertical slice down the wall. Occasionally a car would motor past, the glow from its headlamps appearing and disappearing as its engine noise first rose and then died away.

The spare room was over the sitting room, and in the silence of the evening Julia could hear her parents talking – arguing, she supposed, over what was to be done with or to her. She had heard the beginnings of the discussion before she went to bed; that it went on for so long proved how adamant her mother was, for usually her father's word was law. But she evidently felt sufficiently exercised about the present trouble to hold out for her own way.

They did not argue as Julia had heard the Kanes argue in earlier, happier times, with a direct and energetic batting of words back and forth, like table tennis: crack, whizz, and an instant leap of the opposing mind to intercept and refute the thought. This was much more intermittent. From below, rising muffled through the floorboards, she would hear a murmur, and then a long silence, and then another murmur, the sounds too low for her to tell which voice was which. It seemed both effortful and torpid, and oddly indirect. She thought of one of those games you play on the beach, throwing a very large, light ball to one another. It takes all your force to launch it, and yet it floats so slowly, and half the time falls short or drifts off in the wrong direction.

In her state of shock she felt light, unsubstantial, as though she might float off the surface of the earth. The cloistered silence of her life at home, the dreamlike delight of her secret life with Peter, had both been shattered in the same moment, and what was left? Real life, she suspected, was going to claim her, and she was afraid it would prove harder and uglier than anything she had yet experienced. Often before in her life she had thought of the time when she might get away and be free to shape her own days; but now she was frightened of the future, too frightened to feel any anticipatory pleasure. She could not go back; she did not want to go forward. She could only wish, pointlessly, that things had been different.

She lay in her narrow bed listening to the distant murmurs of her fate being decided, and felt cold, and alone. She could not even talk to Sylvia, for what little comfort that would have been. She wished, not for the first time, that her other sister Lydia had not died, for perhaps she would have been on her side, would have been someone to talk to, someone to understand her.

'I cannot understand you at all,' said her father coldly. 'You have committed an act which must be viewed with abhorrence by all right-thinking people. Not only that, but you have betrayed the trust of someone who has shown you nothing but kindness, and exposed two small children, who were in your care, to great harm. You must have known that what you were doing was wrong, yet that does not seem to have placed any check on you. It is as if you are without any moral sense at all. To behave so – a misdemeanour of this particular sort – it leaves me speechless! It is quite literally beyond my comprehension that such a thing could ever have occurred to you.'

Julia, feeling an answer was required, began to speak, but was stopped by her father's raised hand.

'Do not trouble to justify yourself. As I have said, I cannot understand what could bring you to do such a thing in the first place, and I am not interested to know. Though abhorrent to me, I do not view your act of fornication with this man as being of any lasting importance in the great scheme of things – though it seems to be the point most dwelt upon both by your mother and Mrs Kane – but the deceit and dishonesty you have displayed towards all of us show a deplorable want of character. You have caused a great deal of trouble and distress to a number of people, and I agree with your mother that it would be an embarrassment for everyone concerned if you were to continue to live here.'

Julia stood up straight in front of him – her posture in the past two days had become as rigidly upright as a guardsman's – and only half listened. She had heard more words on the subject than she could possibly remember, even if she had wanted to, and it was a relief, after the dreadful confrontation with the Kanes, the hullabaloo between Joyce and her mother, and all the things her mother had scarcely stopped saying to her since, to listen to her father's quiet, monotonous voice putting her sin into his own perspective.

He sat with his pen in his hand, shoulders hunched, not looking at her, so grey and faded and still that she could almost imagine there was a fine film of dust all over him. By this point in the denouement, from sheer reaction, Julia had decided that there was nothing so very terrible in what she had done, that it was all a fuss about nothing. This position was nothing more than a way to get through it, to bear it all; but her father's emotionless voice was almost a confirmation of it. He looked up at her, his eyes flat, like lead coins in the wrinkled sockets; looked at her utterly without interest. She was interrupting his work, and he spoke to her only because if he did not he would not be allowed to carry on with it in peace. He doesn't care, she thought, he doesn't care at all. This means absolutely nothing to him.

'While I agree with your mother that you should go away, I cannot agree with her rather extreme demand that you be turned out forthwith without a penny. You are in any case going to college in a few weeks' time.' Julia had won a bursary to a famous art school. 'You had better take up lodgings near the college itself. You may find that the college authorities can help you find rooms, and while I urge you to move out as soon as you possibly can, you may nevertheless stay here until you have accommodation of a suitable nature.'

'Yes,' Julia said, feeling that something was necessary. 'Thank you.'

'If any expenses are incurred in your move, I will supply them. Once you are at college, you should with care be able to live on your bursary and will not in any case need financial support from me.'

'Yes,' Julia said again. 'So you couldn't have cut me off without a penny anyway.'

It didn't sound either humorous or defiant – her voice was tired and flat – and her father did not react to it.

'I think that is all,' he said, looking away from her again. 'It would be best if you begin looking for a place immediately, and stay out of the house as much as possible.'

'Keep out of mother's way,' Julia translated.

'It would be advisable.'

'Yes. All right.' Seeing that he had nothing more to say, she turned and walked to the door. She glanced back, and he was already bent to his books again, looking shrunken and grey and so familiar that a wave of some kind of emotion swept over her. He was her father, and once she left here, left him, left home, she would be a child no more; no one would be responsible for her; she would be really alone. She wanted to cry out to him; she checked an impulse to run back to him and – and what? Hug him? Shake him? She hardly knew. In any case it wouldn't do. He would only have rebuffed her. She would keep her dignity, if nothing else. She pushed the feelings down and cleared her throat.

'I'm sorry,' she said. He did not look up, nor give any sign of having heard, and she went out and shut the study door behind her.

She went to an agency near the college later that day, and, for a fee, they found her a bed-sitting room in Shepherd's Bush, on the Uxbridge Road. It was a small room with a large single bed, a wardrobe, chest of drawers, chair and table. There was a sink in the corner with an Ascot water heater, and beside it on a sort of tin draining board there was a gas ring. Down half a flight of stairs was the communal bathroom and toilet. The rent, she was told, included service. What, she asked the rather slatternly-looking housekeeper, was service? It meant clean sheets once a week, and your rubbish bin emptied and floor hoovered daily.

She paid her first week's rent in advance, received her rent book and two keys, one for the house door and one for her room door, and went back home. That evening, helped by Sylvia, she sorted through her belongings to see what she could throw away and what she needed to keep. She packed her clothes, books, paints, and various odds and ends into three suitcases and the next day, again with Sylvia's help, she transported them across London to her new home. Sylvia's attitude was torn between envy of Julia's leaving home and setting up on her own, and disapproval of her having been caught out in what she had always regarded as a stupid and pointless sin. Being in

127

digs would mean Julia could do as she pleased; but the room was not so much of a muchness, and hardly worth exchanging her virtue for. No one would ever marry her now – as Sylvia had told her without mincing words – and she would inevitably sink further and further into degradation. But she was her sister, after all, and when they finally parted she hugged her and said, rather hopelessly, that she hoped she would be happy.

Black reaction set in at the end of that first day away from home, when Julia prepared to go to her strange bed with the knowledge that now she was really on her own. Of course, other young people left home – went away to university, for instance, or to be apprenticed or articled in another town. But this was rather different. Little as she had ever shared with her parents, they were all she had known, and there was a deep, unspoken but bitterly felt, pain at their rejection. Lost, bewildered, she lay in her bed unable to sleep, the slow tears seeping sideways from her eyes as she stared up at the ceiling thinking, thinking; round and round in a loop she could not escape. She had never been on her own before. How would she manage? What would she do when emergencies arose? No one to turn to now, no one to ask – *she* would have to find the answers. Life seemed to stretch before her in all directions, a vast empty plain, a desert across which she would have to trek alone, finding her own water. It was frightening. She would always be alone now. Always. She rolled on to her side and wept bitterly.

For days she wandered almost in a stupor, miserable, apprehensive, lonely. She had never had friends, had been used to being her own company, but that had been with a background of a family, however undemonstrative, of a place where she belonged. She had had someone to speak to, even if they weren't interested in what she said. Now she had no one. She missed Sylvia, missed the ugly little room they had shared. She missed Peter, dreadfully; she missed Joyce and the boys, but she never let herself think about them. It was too painful. She shut everything about them away in a compartment of her mind, and its locked door haunted the edge of her thoughts as the door of Bluebeard's closet must have haunted the corner of his wife's vision. Now she understood the paradox of being constantly aware of the one thing one must not think about.

But as weeks passed, she adjusted to her new surroundings and altered expectations, as a walker adjusts to the weight of a burden, and she found that it was possible to be happy. All creatures love freedom, and for that reason alone she would have become reconciled. Her little room, quite as shabby and dowdy as anything in her parents' house, became familiar and, as her one refuge from the vastness of the rest of the world, dear. It was compact and comfortable, it held all she needed except for the bathroom. From its security she began to explore outwards.

There was pleasure in finding which shops were best for what, in planning and cooking her own meals, eating what she liked and when she liked, sitting up as late as she liked, or getting into bed early with a book and reading until she fell asleep. She made friends with the local greengrocer and the man in David Greig's, and tried some of the new and unexpected foods that were beginning to come on to the market – capsicums and Chinese gooseberries, French garlic sausage and Dutch Edam. She found the best cafe along the road for Sunday dinner, and where the fish and chips were cheapest and best, and, with huge daring, had her first meal in a Chinese restaurant. One evening when she couldn't sleep she discovered the delights of the all-night coffee-stand at the end of the Market where one could enjoy tea and a sausage sandwich in the company of the lorry drivers who stopped there for a break during the night. They smiled at her cheerfully, but did not bother her with conversation, which she found comforting. A pleasant acceptance was all she wanted from them, and when they looked kindly and parted ranks silently to let her through to the counter, she was grateful and felt that they were the best of men.

She found cinemas within easy reach – so many of them that she could have gone to a different one every night of the week if she had had the money. She was fifteen minutes from Oxford Circus, twenty minutes from Piccadilly Circus. The whole of London, with all its riches, was at her feet, she realised. One day, when she had funds, she would take a seat at the banquet.

She began to think more positively of life – life after college, when she would earn a living and be free to enjoy freedom.

College began, and that was a joy. She loved the work and found that she could do it easily and well, her talents sprouting like bulbs that have been kept in the dark. The other students mostly seemed very nice, and one or two tried tentatively to strike up a friendship with her. She held aloof at first, partly through shyness, partly from a vague feeling of unworthiness, an unformed reluctance to contaminate them with her own sinfulness. But gradually she learnt their names and faces, exchanged comments on the teachers and the work, and thence on the world in general. She discovered that they liked her; some even admired her, thinking her more sophisticated than they were. Her reserve came across to them as wisdom, and surprisingly often people would ask her for information or advice as though she were older than them. It was not long before she had a 'crowd' with whom she 'hung around'. They walked and talked together between classes, even went for coffee together, and occasionally to the cinema.

Because she had come from such a frugal background, and because she could cook a little, she found that she could live on her grant and even have enough left over for the occasional treat. In a junk shop she found a very second-hand gramophone, and she began a collection of records. The old-fashioned needle did not do them any good, but they were second-hand too, from a stall in the market. The hissing, the click of surface scars, the tinny quality of the reproduction through the horn, she soon got used to. Through them the music surged into her brain as though by-passing the aural dimension. It was a bliss beyond any other to listen to music whenever she wanted, to desire it and choose it without reference to anyone else.

So she settled into her new life, and the contrast between all this lovely freedom and the misery that had gone before, and the apprehension and secret doubts that had gone before that, was such that most of the time she felt herself content, almost completely happy.

She had not seen Peter since the showdown in the hallway. She did not really expect ever to see him again. Their secret

130

affair had been discovered and was over. Joyce knew, there had been a reckoning, and now he was Joyce's entirely, her husband chastened and brought back to rectitude. In her innocence, Julia had not known or ever imagined that what he did with her he had done before with others. She saw herself as the sole aberration of a faithful husband, and her guilt was so much the greater. With her present freedom and plentiful spare time she could have sought him out, found out where he was playing and gone to a rehearsal or concert, but it never occurred to her to do so. She had never had a very high view of her claims on him, and did not suppose, even if he had wanted to see her again, that he would risk the trouble it would involve. They had sinned, and been punished, and that was that. She thought that he would consider the episode closed, and so she did.

Oddly enough, it was not the lack of male friends that changed her mind, but the acquiring of them. From the beginning, some of the male students at college looked at her with what was plainly admiration. She accepted their advances as ordinary friendship: when they bought her coffee in the recess (she had learned to drink it now), or arranged to meet her in the refectory at lunchtime, or made sure of sitting next to her in class, she thought they were just being kind. She accepted their compliments on her physical attractiveness as pleasantries, and laughed when they asked her out in the evening. For her, all sexual feeling and thought was bound up with Peter, and in some crazy, unthought-out way she assumed they must know or at least feel that too.

The situation could not last, however. One particular young man, Graham, was more persevering and took Julia out several times. He thought her avoidance of physical contact was a kind of natural modesty, not, of course, realising that it was simply because she liked him as a friend and was not aware of any more fundamental attraction. One evening, he took her to see the picture at the Essoldo at Shepherd's Bush Green, and when, since it was so close to home, she invited him up to her bedsit for coffee afterwards, he thought his patience had been rewarded.

She made the coffee and they drank it and talked about the

131

film, and then in a sudden awkward pause the boy crossed the room and sat down beside her on the bed. She looked at him with some surprise, for he seemed to be breathing hard and staring at her in a peculiar way. She opened her mouth to speak and he said her name in a strangled kind of voice, and put his arm round her, pulling her towards him uncertainly.

He wants me to kiss him, she thought. She remembered the time Rowland had kissed her; but this one doesn't seem to know what to do, she thought. She didn't particularly want to kiss him, but he was nice looking and she enjoyed his company, and she thought it was little enough to do for anyone, so she leaned towards him obediently and closed her eyes. It wasn't pleasant, for his face was much softer than Peter's, and his mouth seemed sloppy and wet, and she didn't like the smell of him. But she endured it for the sake of friendship.

But to her surprise he got terribly excited, kissed her harder, pressing his teeth against her and hurting her lips. Then he began to fumble with her buttons, and she was shocked.

'Hey,' she protested, pulling away. He took no notice, went on trying to get inside her blouse. 'Stop it. Don't do that,' she cried, struggling and pushing at his hands.

He stopped and stared at her. 'What do you mean, don't do that?'

'I mean, don't do that. What on earth are you thinking of?'

That must have been obvious even to her. He did not answer the question, but asked instead, 'Well, what did you invite me up here for?'

'Coffee,' she said simply. 'What did you think?'

'Are you being funny?'

'No, of course not.'

She was beginning to be upset now. There was some social code she had offended against – again. Guilt rose alongside affront and diluted it, making her feel nervous and unsure of her ground. If it *were* her fault, she would have no right to be offended.

'Well, why did you kiss me, then?' he demanded, as if it were the unanswerable argument.

'I thought you wanted me to.'

132

'Yes, but . . .' He stopped, confused by her apparent sincerity. What the hell was she playing at? 'I don't know what you're talking about. Are you crazy? Look, we went out together. You asked me up here. You encouraged me.'

'Encouraged you?'

He lost his temper at that point, deciding that she was making fun of him. 'I'm off,' he said. 'But I'll tell you one thing – if you carry on with that game, you'll get yourself into trouble. Men don't like being led on like that, and made fools of. You'll get yourself a name as a prick teaser.'

He left Julia in tears, hurt by the coarseness of his language, not really understanding where it had all gone wrong. She learnt, of course. She learnt that there were social rules to be obeyed, and tried to keep by them. She did not ask young men up to her room alone, and she did not allow them to kiss her; in fact, she tried after that to keep them at an extra distance, just in case. But it all seemed a dismal business, and so different from the friendship she had shared with Peter. She was used to being at ease and natural in a man's company, in doing and saying whatever she wanted, and sometimes she forgot to be aloof. It made her seem forward to the young men who were used to girls who conformed to a strict pattern of behaviour she had never had to learn. They misunderstood, and called her that bad name, and it muted her happiness.

It was after one of these unfortunate misunderstandings with a boy at college that she found herself thinking about Peter with a kind of wistful longing. With Peter she had always been able to be say what she thought, knowing that it would not be misconstrued. With him she could discuss things, ask when she wanted to know, speak her mind when she had an opinion. When they were alone together, there had never been any stress of guarding her tongue, or her body for that matter. He had taught her how to speak through her body, and now it seemed she must for ever more be dumb.

Having once been let out of the locked cupboard, the thought of him stretched and made itself at home in her mind. She lingered over thoughts of him by day, dreamt of him at night, and at last began to imagine how she might see him again. Gradually a plan shaped itself in her mind. She would arrive casually at rehearsal one day, and sit in the back where it was dark, until they stopped for their coffee break. Then she would walk slowly down towards the platform, and he would look up and see her, and – well, after that she didn't know. She would take his cue and behave accordingly. If he wasn't glad to see her, she could just go without ever speaking to him. But if he *was* glad . . . She planned what to wear, how to do her hair, what expression to have on her face, and then she laughed at herself, a pleased, excited laugh.

She knew they would be rehearsing at the Festival Hall on Tuesday week, and on Tuesdays she had private study in the mornings, and only one class in the afternoon, which she could miss if things worked out. And in the end, none of it happened the way she had imagined. She arrived at the hall ten minutes before the start of the rehearsal, and as she stood at the kerb waiting to cross the road to the hall entrance, the approaching car stopped a little ahead of her and Peter got out, obviously being dropped off by a friend. It was like something on a film, his glance at her, his double-take, and then the two of them slowly walking towards each other, their eyes fixed on each other's face, afraid to be the first to smile.

'Hello,' he said, when they were standing a few inches apart. 'What are you doing here?'

'I had the day off, so I thought I'd come to rehearsal,' she said. They scrutinised each other. 'You've had your hair cut,' she said at last.

'Have I?' he said foolishly, putting his hand up vaguely to his head. 'You're looking well.'

'I am well,' she said. It sounded too emphatic. Her voice was doing silly things, because all of a sudden she didn't know where she was with him. Was he pleased to see her? His voice sounded cool and non-committal, but his eyes seemed to be devouring her. Why didn't he touch her? She glanced around to see if there were anyone looking whose gaze he might be wanting to avoid, but they were alone in the street.

'Peter,' she said, putting out a tentative hand to his coat-sleeve. He looked down at her hand as if in surprise, and she withdrew it hastily. 'Aren't you pleased to see me?'

'Why did you come here?' he asked her.

'To hear the music and to see you,' she said. 'Shouldn't I have?'

His anxious face relaxed suddenly, and he smiled, turning her heart to water. 'I didn't want you to. I hoped you were well out of it – I hoped you'd settled down somewhere on your own and were happy. For your sake, I mean.'

She smiled now also. 'I did. I have a dear little bedsitter all of my own, and I'm going to art school, and I have a grant and look after myself and everything.'

'And you're happy?'

'Do I look happy?'

'Yes, very,' he said, and his voice was peculiar, as if he was surprised or disappointed.

'Well, I am happy – now.'

He didn't answer her, and she felt suddenly afraid that she shouldn't have said that. But, she thought impatiently, why not?

'What's the matter,' she said again, 'aren't you pleased to see me?'

'Always pleased to see you,' he said with a large and jovial gallantry which was entirely false. 'Must go in now and get warmed up. Ferguson hates us to be late.'

Julia was now completely puzzled.

'All right,' she said, falling in beside him as he crossed the road, his fiddle case defensively between them.

'You're coming in?'

'Should I not?'

He sighed suddenly, and his tense shoulders relaxed in what looked like resignation. 'I'll talk to you in the interval.'

They went up in the lift together in silence, and parted ways when they got out, he to the dressing rooms and she to the auditorium to take a seat. She watched the musicians wander out and take up their places and begin to practise the parts that they found trickiest, breaking off now and then to chat to their neighbours. One of the bass players was reading a newspaper, oblivious to everything; the second trumpet was showing photographs one by one with voluble explanations to the first trumpet, the second trombone, and the

135

tympanist. A back-desk cellist was apparently writing a letter, referring frequently to a piece of paper propped up against his music; four first violins were smoking and having a leisurely conversation about – judging from their gestures – football. They looked nothing like an orchestra, Julia thought; with a few exceptions they looked so scruffy you wouldn't want them in your house. Genius takes strange shapes.

Then the leader, Peter, and the conductor came out together and mounted the platform, and the buzz of conversation dwindled away. Julia saw, to her surprise and pleasure, that Peter had been promoted and now occupied the principal's seat, next to the leader. It must have happened in the past few weeks, and it represented quite a step up. Why hadn't he told her, she wondered – but then, he hadn't told her anything in those few odd minutes outside the hall. Perhaps he had wanted to surprise her. The conductor tapped the front of the rostrum with his baton for silence, and the rehearsal began.

She had no chance to speak to him in the break, for the violins were kept back. They were playing Mahler's first symphony, and Ferguson, the conductor, wanted the violins alone during the break to go over the difficult opening and one or two other bits. Julia went into the bar and got herself coffee and waited for Peter, but when the other first violins came dashing through to grab a quick cup before the rehearsal continued, Peter did not appear, and when she followed the men back into the auditorium she saw Peter standing on the far side in conversation with Ferguson, John Collins, the leader, and another man who was pointing out something in a score and looking earnestly at the other three as if begging them to believe him.

He had got collared, then, she thought. She would just have to wait until after the rehearsal. Better in a way, no need to break off for anything. She became wrapped once more in the music.

Rehearsal broke at one, and there was the usual reaction, half the musicians bolting off the platform like kids let out from school, and the other half packing up at their leisure and talking among themselves. Julia sat quietly watching

Peter, waiting for him to move before she would stand up, for she didn't want to be conspicuously waiting for him. He, however, came down off the platform with his instrument and jacket and disappeared into the dressing rooms, leaving her to wonder where she was to meet him. She waited where she was for a while, and then, worried that she might be in the wrong place, she walked down and went backstage to wait by the lift.

Time went on. People passed her, some taking the lift, some the stairs, some smiling pleasantly at her, some staring rather rudely. The crowds thinned out, and she wondered suddenly if he was waiting out on the street for her. The lift doors opened again, and this time she got in and travelled down to the street level with the others, feeling more and more foolish.

Out on the street she waited again, walking up and down slowly. No one was coming out of the hall now. It was twenty to two. He must have gone; she must have missed him: misunderstood his intentions, been in the wrong place; anyway, got it wrong, wrong, stupid, wrong. Tears of frustration gathered behind her eyes; she turned away to head for the station, and as she did so she caught a glimpse out of the corner of her eye of a dark figure coming out from the side exit.

'I thought you'd gone,' he said when he reached her. Her smile drooped and disappeared at his lack of one, but he walked on, apparently expecting her to accompany him, so she fell in beside him, much puzzled. 'Where are you off to now?' he asked after a moment.

Earlier she might have said home, but now she said cautiously, 'Nowhere in particular. Where're you?'

'To the station,' he said.

'Where's your car?' she asked. A safe, neutral question.

'It's in the garage, being serviced. I'm training it today.' They walked on a bit and then he said abruptly, 'Do you want to have some lunch?'

Her heart lifted. 'Yes, please,' she said. 'Look, why don't we go back to my place. I've got food in, and it isn't too far.'

137

'Okay,' he said, and she thought he sighed in a resigned way.

They travelled in silence at first, Julia's attempt to open a discussion of the music meeting with a stone wall, but when they had changed on to the central line he seemed more relaxed, and she tried again.

'I see you've been promoted. I'm awfully pleased for you. It's quite a step forward, isn't it?'

He looked at her searchingly. 'Yes,' he said with an effort, 'yes it is. Collins is leaving, and I think they'll offer me his position.'

'But that's terrific,' she said. 'How terribly exciting! Why didn't you tell me at once?'

He shook his head as though she were distracting him. 'Listen, Julia, listen.' He took her hand, and she saw there was something he was determined to say.

She didn't think she would want to hear it, but she said obediently, 'Yes, I'm listening.'

'Joyce wants a divorce.'

She was shocked. Divorce, a huge and bristling word for an unthinkable, appalling thing. 'Because of me?' she asked at last, timidly.

He didn't answer directly. 'I thought it would all blow over. It has before. But it was different this time. A cumulation of a lot of things – I won't go into it. But anyway, she's determined, and there doesn't seem anything I can do to change her mind. God knows, I've tried. The thing is, if I contest it, she will have to produce evidence. Michael was the only witness, and he can't testify. If I don't contest it, I will have to provide her with evidence – you know the kind of thing: the hotel room and the private detective. It's crummy. I don't know what to do.'

'Is that why you didn't want me there this morning, in case there was a detective watching?' Julia asked.

'No, no,' he said impatiently. 'Where d'you get silly ideas like that? No, I didn't want you to come back and get mixed up in it. I can only mean trouble for you. I hoped you'd got yourself settled in with a crowd of your own age and interests. I've been selfish all along, I know that now, never thinking what was going to happen to you. But I do care about you. I want you to have a normal happy life, away from me. I'm ten years older than you. You should meet people your own age, get a boyfriend, get married. That's why I didn't want to see you today.'

Julia smiled, mainly with relief. 'But that's all wrong,' she said. 'I am with a crowd my own age now, but they aren't of my own interests. I have nothing in common with them. And as for boyfriends – well, I'm afraid it's too late for that now. I've gone past boyfriends.'

'What are you talking about?' he asked, surprised.

She told him the story of Graham et al. 'I'm just not interested in them that way. I don't want to do that sort of thing with anyone else.' She had almost said, with anyone but you, but at the last minute thought it sounded too presumptuous, too demanding.

He looked grave. 'You can't generalise on the basis of so little experience. Just because one or two boys misunderstand you, you can't write it all off as hopeless.'

'It isn't only that,' Julia said. 'I don't understand them either.'

They got off the train and headed for her bedsit, threading through the midday shoppers without speaking. Peter stopped as they passed an off-licence and bought a couple of bottles of pale ale, and in a few minutes they were at the door of the house, waiting while Julia found her key.

'So this is where you live,' Peter said, squinting up at the sooty building. 'It doesn't look very salubrious.'

'It's all right inside,' she said, opening the door. 'And it's absolutely private.'

The house was silent and deserted, not even the housekeeper about. They crept upstairs and Julia let them in to her room and closed the door with a sigh of relief at shutting out the world.

'Well,' she said, 'here we are.' She took off her coat and turned to face Peter. He put down his fiddle case carefully in the corner, set the beer bottles on the table, and looked at her quizzically. We can stand here staring at each other for ever, she thought, and crossed the room to him, put her arms round him, and felt his, belatedly, round her.

'Oh Julia,' he sighed, 'I shouldn't do this.'

'Why not?' she said simply. 'I want you to.' She pressed against him, feeling the huge, unspeakable relief of being back where she wanted to be, where she felt right, where she belonged. She said, 'You want to. And I can think of no one it can conceivably harm right now.'

He kissed her briefly, looked into her eyes. 'You used to be so shy.'

'I used to be in very different circumstances. I'm free now.'

'I want you to stay free.'

'Free to be with you?'

'That wasn't what I meant.'

'Are you and Joyce going to divorce?'

'There doesn't seem to be any alternative. She means to divorce me.'

'Then you can make love to me with a clear conscience. It can't hurt anyone.'

'Damn you.'

'I expect I will be,' she smiled, laying her face against his chest.

They undressed and lay on the bed, and finding him still uncertain Julia took command, kissed him and stroked him and made love to him, and was stunned by the quality of his response and the quantity of her pleasure and joy. When they lay breathless together afterwards, and he stroked her head that lay on his shoulder, she whispered to him, 'What's happened? It was never like this before.'

'It wasn't,' he agreed. 'I never knew all that time that you disliked it so much.'

'Not disliked,' she protested. 'But I was never at ease. I never felt safe or private.'

'You never enjoyed it, then.'

'I did. But it's different now,' she answered. Now it was even more important. She felt she had tapped straight into the main power cable of life. 'Did you like it?'

'How can you ask, simpleton?'

'Can we go on then? It isn't all finished?'

He didn't answer for a moment. She lifted her head to look

at him, and he was grave, as if he saw all the problems he would ever have lined up before him. He said, with difficulty, because he had never spoken of his feelings for her before, 'I don't think it will ever be all finished.'

She kissed his mouth, and laid her cheek against his, and they lay still like that for a long time.

Eight

In real life, things are never resolved neatly at the end of a chapter, and a new page turned. Nothing was decided during that long afternoon when they lay on the bed in Julia's room, drinking bottled beer and talking; but some things were at least made clearer, and Peter was pushed farther along the road to making a decision.

It was not true, as Rowland had said, that Peter hated a status quo – that depended entirely on the status. It was also not true that Joyce wanted a divorce. After Julia had made her precipitous exit from the district, Joyce had expected life to resume a more or less normal pattern. There would have been a period of coldness while Peter served out his punishment and she got over the shock and hurt, but she had planned the stages of her forgiveness of Peter and the steps in their return to intimacy, and would have put the plan into effect if it had not been that Peter, inexplicably, refused to play.

She believed that the Julia episode had been a one-weekend stand, and when he insisted otherwise it put her in a difficult position. If he was telling the truth, she could hardly forgive him on the same basis; and if he was lying, then it must be with malicious intent, and the same thing applied. Not only that, but he had put James in to sleep with Michael and was sleeping himself in James's room, which made things very awkward and upset the children. She told the boys that Daddy had to sleep alone because he was in quarantine, but Michael at any rate did not believe it and was showing signs already of developing the emotional damage that Joyce had predicted for him. Peter suggested, rather coldly, that she should go back to her parents' house (from whence she had returned rather hurriedly as James was proving detrimental to her father's recovery) and take the children with her, ostensibly for a holiday. She had refused, feeling that she would not be able to maintain normal behaviour under her mother's eye, and also not wishing to be going away from home with nothing settled.

Peter's position was easier in one respect, for his job meant that he was away from home most of the time, and it was quite easy for him to avoid contact with either Joyce or the boys if he wanted. On the other hand, this promotion business had come up, and it was important for him to be performing at his best for the next few weeks, as he had a rival for the leader's position in a very bright young man from one of the provincial orchestras. Also, divorce would not make good reading at this stage of his career.

Secondly, he discovered that since Julia had gone away he had little to interest him in Spenser Road. Even for the sake of appearances he could not bring himself, at least not yet, to resume normal relations with Joyce. On the other hand, divorce would be distressful and complicated, and would be dreadful for the children. He loved the boys, wanted the best for them; did not want to figure in their eyes as a villain.

So he would have been quite content to leave things be for the present, if not for ever, to muddle along without coming to any uncomfortable sticking point. But Joyce seemed to be in the grip of a determination to 'have things out'. It was not surprising – though Peter could not see this – for she was, under the current arrangement, neither one thing nor the other. She had to maintain a home for Peter, but there was no contact between them, and she was without the benefit of his society: she was no more than an unpaid housekeeper. Furthermore, she had nothing in particular to occupy her mind with, and was therefore more inclined to brood over the situation. She also had to cope with the children, and parry their awkward questions.

All this meant that she was not as eager as Peter to avoid further confrontation, and having waited up in vain for him for some nights, managed to catch him late one evening in a foul mood, had a row and, driven to it by hurt pride, told him she wanted a divorce.

'You can have a divorce, for all I care,' Peter retorted

inelegantly. 'I'd just like to know how you're going to go about it, though.'

'You've given me grounds enough,' Joyce snapped.

'Where's your evidence? I can't see you hauling the boy into the witness box.'

There was a brief silence while they both digested the impossibility of using Michael as a witness, and then Joyce said, with rather less assurance, 'Well, you could provide me with evidence.'

'What? Check in to a hotel in Brighton with a platinum blonde? Allow myself to be surprised at the door with my trousers undone, by a seedy bloke in a raincoat? No thank you very much.'

'It wouldn't hurt you.'

'No, but I tell you what would, my girl. You'd get the kids, the sympathy, and the alimony, and I'd get all the fingers pointed at me as the guilty party.'

'Well, you *are* the guilty party,' Joyce said, with more justice than tact.

'Prove it, then,' he retorted.

And so it went on all through the uneasy truce; until he met up with Julia again.

She was changed, so changed; now he was able to see just how repressive her home background had been. She was lively, talkative, uninhibited, utterly charming. He had gone home with her with the utmost reluctance that day, had succumbed with a kind of helpless groan to her physical advances, and had found that Julia safe from being overlooked, in her own home, was quite a different person to make love with from Julia on somebody else's living-room carpet. He wanted her almost agonisingly badly. His feelings of guilt might have stopped him from doing anything about that, but he found that she wanted him too, and allowed himself to believe she took no harm from association with him.

At first infrequently and reluctantly, and then more and more often, he visited her, or met her in town. Her company was stimulating and original, and he found himself becoming more and more involved with her. Her bed-sitting room seemed more homelike than home. Out of this new equilibrium he behaved better towards Joyce, and discussed the problem with her instead of having quarrels over it. She might have withdrawn the demand for a divorce had he shown any desire for a reconciliation, but though more considerate and gentle, he was less *there* than he had been even when quarrelling; he was a polite and detached stranger. He now spoke of their divorcing as a decided thing, and at length she agreed to consult a solicitor in a preliminary sort of way.

'You know the basic problem over the divorce?' Peter asked, propping his head up with his hands to look at her.

'Yes,' Julia said. She was sitting, cross-legged and naked, on the end of the bed where a band of sunlight from the window fell, holding his feet. They had just been making love, and she looked plushy and warm and cared-for, closing her eyes against the sunlight like a basking cat. Her hair was ruffled up around her face, and her mouth slightly smiling.

'Well, it appears there is another way to go about it, that would avoid the pitfalls.' He paused, and she lifted one of his feet and kissed the sole of it, and prompted him,

'There is?'

'The trouble is, it would involve you.' She was rocking backwards and forwards slightly like a mandarin, and he asked rather sharply, 'Are you listening to me?'

'Yes,' she said equably. 'You're speaking very slowly and with lots of annoying pauses, but I'm listening.'

He relaxed into a smile, and said, 'All right – this is it. If she cites me for adultery – horrid word – with you, and you and I both give a signed statement admitting it, with dates and so on, and I don't contest the action, it can go through without any hullabaloo and probably with no publicity. The thing is, I hate to drag you into it all.'

'I seem to be rather in already, don't I?'

'Yes, but the divorce is really nothing to do with you. I mean, it's a settlement between me and Joyce, and it's a bit much to expect you to allow your name to be dragged through the mud for our sakes.'

'Would it be just the name?' she asked. 'Or would I have to appear in court?'

145

'Oh no, that would be the point of the statements. In fact, if we can agree on alimony and division of the goods and so on, I won't need to appear in court either. It will be all Joyce's show.'

'And how do we go about making these statements?' she asked.

He looked at her, narrowing his eyes against the sun. 'Dash it all,' he exclaimed, 'I don't believe you care about anything! Aren't you even going to swear at me a bit for daring to ask you?'

'No,' she said, kissing his foot again. 'Why should I care? I don't believe for a moment that the matter will be made public – why should it indeed? – and even if it was, I have no reputation to lose. And if I had, it would only serve me right for what I did. After all –' she opened her eyes and fixed him with a disconcertingly frank stare – 'it *was* adultery, you know.'

'I know,' he groaned, rolling over on to his side to make room for her to lie down beside him. 'That's the devil of it. And it still is, technically, because I'm still living with her, though, naturally, we sleep apart.'

'You don't think she'd have you followed or anything, without telling you?' Julia asked suddenly, sitting up as if to look out of the window.

He pulled her back down and kissed her firmly. 'Good Lord no! Joyce wouldn't do that – she's very fair and above board.'

'What about hell hath no fury? Anyone can change if they're peeved.'

'Peeved? What a beautifully inappropriate word! But I still don't think Joyce would do a thing like that. In fact, I know she wouldn't. She isn't sneaky.'

'How does she feel about the divorce? Is she happy about it?'

'You'd hardly expect her to be turning somersaults,' Peter said. He ran his hand over her breast and caught the nipple between his finger and thumb, and she grunted and arched up in reaction.

'Stop trying to distract me. You know what I mean – is she

146

all out to get rid of you? Is it pistols at dawn, poison for two in the library? What does she feel about it?'

'I think she just wants to get it all over with. She wants to see the back of me,' Peter said through a mouthful of breast. Julia doubled up round him, lifting from the hips, and they spoke no more for a while.

'So,' he said eventually, 'I can tell her you agree to sign along the dotted line, then?'

'Mm-hm,' Julia agreed drowsily. 'What happens then?'

'Well, apparently we arrange for some clerk of the court or inspector or something of that sort to come and interview us and make the statements – oh, and before that, I'll have to move out of Spenser Road, of course. Find myself some kind of pigeonhole for the time being. A bedsitter, I suppose – the cheaper the better. It might not be so bad, now I've seen yours.'

'What do you mean, now you've seen mine?' she asked, still with her eyes closed.

'Well, I always thought bedsitters were ghastly little holes overlooked by a granite-faced landlady who watched you in and out and read your mail. But I like the privacy of yours, and the compactness.'

'Novelty, that's all it is,' she said. 'You're enjoying slumming it.' Her eyes opened. 'If you like this so much, there's another on the floor above that's empty at the moment. Why don't you take it?'

'It's an idea,' he admitted grudgingly. He wasn't sure he wanted to be under Julia's eye all the time, any more than under Joyce's.

'Of course it's an idea,' she said sharply, sitting up and swinging her legs over the edge of the bed. 'You needn't think I'll be a nuisance. You don't have to live in my pocket just because we share a front door.'

'Ach, now you're peeved,' he said, catching at her hand as she stood up. 'You really shouldn't read my mind like that, it's indecent.'

She smiled at him, but pulled her hand away anyway. 'I have to wash,' she said. She went over to the sink and turned on the water, and looked back over her shoulder to say, 'I'm

147

not peeved. I mean it. Besides, you know, I might not want you in my pocket. There's always the possibility I might want to invite someone up here myself.'

'Like hell you will,' Peter said, jumping up from the bed and crossing to her in two strides. He caught her by the shoulders and swung her round, and she was laughing at him with her mouth pinched closed and her eyes shiny. 'If I catch any more of those hairy art students hanging round your door I'll knock their blocks off.'

'Dear me,' she said demurely, 'what a ferocious, manly kind of person you are.'

He took her throat in a half-fierce, half-affectionate grip and pulled her up to kiss her mouth, but she flicked her head aside and bit his cheek, hard enough to make him yelp and let her go, and they looked at each other and laughed.

'You,' he said, 'always did plague me.'

'That's because you try to bully me. There's only one thing you'll never be able to make me do, and that's anything I don't want to.'

'I begin to believe you,' he said.

Peter did move into the bedsitter on the floor above, though without telling Joyce that Julia lived there too, for he did not want to hurt her pride more than was necessary. About three weeks later the interview with the inspector, by the name of McPherson, took place in Peter's room. He was a tall, heavily built man in his fifties, and he made hard work of the stairs up to the third floor. His dark-jowled face reddened alarmingly, and he had to sit for a few moments to catch his breath before he began.

Julia observed him in silent apprehension as he searched out his notebook, a pad of headed sheets for the statements, his fountain pen. It felt like waiting at her father's study door all over again. Then he looked up, catching her eye on him, and said, 'Is it all right with you if I sit at the table? Something to rest on while I write.'

'I'll sit on the bed,' Julia said, vacating the chair in his favour. Peter lit a cigarette and leaned on the mantelpiece in a most unnatural pose.

'Right, now,' McPherson began, 'I'll start with you, madam, if you don't mind. I'll just ask you questions, and I'll write your answers down in statement form, and then I'll ask you to read and sign it.' His attitude was stern but kindly – like a doctor with bad news to impart, Julia thought. 'And of course, it will be the same statement for you, sir, only the other way round, if you understand me.' Peter nodded. 'Now, your full name is?'

'Julia Maitland Jacobs,' she replied.

'Is that with a hyphen?'

'No, Maitland is a Christian name.'

'I see. Address?' She gave it. 'How and when did you first meet Mr Kane?'

'I answered an advertisement for a babysitter and went along to his house. That would be some time in May, 1953.'

'And did sexual intercourse take place on that occasion?' McPherson asked without taking his eyes off the paper.

It sounded so horrible – 'sexual intercourse' – and to have to talk about it to a stranger made her realise for the first time what she was involved in. Talk of the divorce had not impinged on her until then, for it was a word with meaning but no reference. Now she was face to face with it in all its ugly necessity. 'Dragged through the courts', she thought; and 'dragged through the mud'. Yes a person, a reputation, might well be left bedraggled – and would a love affair survive being described as 'sexual intercourse taking place'?

She felt her cheeks burning, but she tried to speak normally and not show her embarrassment. 'No. He wasn't alone.'

'Not alone?

Julia swallowed. 'His wife was there too – and the children.'

'I see. When did sexual intercourse first take place?'

'The following summer – in August.'

'August 1954? And how did it come about?'

Peter walked up and down the room, smoking his cigarette restlessly, while Julia answered the remorseless catechism quietly and factually. From time to time he glanced at them sitting opposite each other and laying out the body of the affair so unemotionally as if they were both professional undertakers.

149

What he accepted in McPherson irritated him in Julia. She had no right to be so composed – damn it, she was not even ruffled. Did she have no feminine modesty, no natural shame?

He made some kind of a noise, and she turned her head to look at him, without pausing in her answer, and gave him a look so quelling that he paused in his prowling and then relapsed against the mantelpiece again, scowling darkly.

'Right,' said McPherson at last, 'that seems to cover it. If you'd just like to read this over, madam, and see it's all correct, and I'll write out the other one for you, sir.'

He ducked his head again and began beavering away, verifying his facts as he went from the carbon copy of the statement he had kept back. Peter walked over and stood behind Julia to read it over her shoulder. 'I first met the said Peter Kane in May 1953 when I answered his advertisement for a babysitter.' And so on. They finished reading it and Peter resumed his prowling while Julia sat politely holding the paper and waiting for McPherson to finish with the other statement.

'There. Would you like to read this over, sir, and I'd like you to sign yours, madam, and I'll witness it.'

Peter took the paper from him reluctantly, as if it would implicate him more than he already was. It was the same as Julia's, but with the names reversed, so to speak. 'I first met the said Julia Maitland Jacobs . . .' Where in God's name did she get this Maitland business from, he thought irritably. He read it through hastily and gave it back, signed it, watched McPherson witness the signature, and then felt vaguely surprised when he stood up and took up his hat.

'Is that all?' he asked.

'Yes, thank you sir, that's all we need. For the present anyway. The solicitors will be in touch with you in due course.'

'Aren't you from the solicitors, then?' Julia asked him.

'Oh no, madam. I'm an officer of the court.'

'Ah, that explains it,' Julia said.

'Explains what?'

'Why you're not wearing a mac.'

McPherson looked surprised, not knowing whether she was

serious or not. Peter gave her a quelling look and intervened quickly. 'So what happens now?'

'You'll be receiving a notification of the date of the hearing, but I imagine you'll be hearing from the solicitors before that to arrange settlements.'

'I see. Well, thank you very much, Mr McPherson. I'll see you out.'

Peter came back up to find Julia making tea with apparent unconcern. 'Well, you were very cool, I must say,' he said on the tail end of his irritation with the whole business.

She looked up, and he saw she was not as unmoved as he had thought. There was a look of strain about her eyes but she said calmly, 'It was the only way. It wouldn't have done any good for me to tremble and cry, would it?'

'Did you want to tremble and cry? It might have done me some good to see it. And McPherson might not have gone away with the idea that you are a hardened sinner.'

'Do you care what he thinks?'

'I should have thought you would have. Didn't you find it all a little intrusive?'

She sighed. 'Have you ever had a medical examination of what nurses used to call "your privates"? The doctor's absolutely cold and clinical about it, and the only way to save your sensitive soul is to be the same. If you allow yourself to get embarrassed or upset, or even personal, you risk never being able to undress again, except in the dark under a dressing gown.' She looked at him, a little bleakly. 'So you look down, and you prod at it with the rest of the scientists.'

'Hmm. But he made it all sound so sordid.'

'That's the point, don't you see?' Julia broke in anxiously. 'Be impersonal about it. It's a story in a magazine. What happens between you and me is what happens in our minds. That's not sordid. Though,' she added with a sudden smile, 'only you can tell if it's all sunshine and flowers, or red, red passion.'

'You're right,' he said. He walked over to her, disengaged her hand from the teapot and pulled her against him in an affectionate embrace. 'I don't know how you do it.'

'What?' she asked, muffled.

'Read my mind. And then argue me out of it. You're a very odd person.'

'That's what Rowland said,' she replied, and he pushed her away abruptly.

'It's like cuddling a scorpion. Come on, I want to get out for a while. Turn off that kettle, and get changed. We'll drive out into the country, with the windows down, and find a hotel to have dinner in. Four courses and a bottle of wine. And then we'll come home and go to bed and talk and love until we fall asleep.'

'D'you mean,' she asked slowly, 'that you'll spend the night with me?'

'Yes, why not?' he said.

'Oh boy!' Her eyes shone, and he raised a quizzical eyebrow. 'I've had an ambition to sleep with you for as long as I can remember. I mean, really sleep with you.'

He grinned sheepishly, all up one side. 'You're easily pleased,' he said. 'I might snore, you know.'

'So might I. Besides, I'd never hear you for the noise—'

'Of the lorries. And ditto. Come on then. I know a place near Windsor, on the river.'

'Yippee,' she said.

They drank more wine than was wise, and Peter drove home in a very antisocial manner and didn't feel at all like a sexual romp on arriving back at the house.

'*Chez nous*,' he said facetiously as Julia unlocked the house door.

'I always thought that "*Chez Nous*" on people's front gates was French for "Shady Nook" on other people's front gates.'

'Idiot,' he said, draping an arm over her shoulder. They climbed the stairs slowly, side by side, which was not easy on a stairway as narrow as that, to Julia's room, which had the bigger bed.

Julia undressed by the light of the street lamp outside in the street, watching Peter as he moved about aimlessly and finally fetched up in front of the wardrobe mirror, staring at his reflection gloomily.

'"O rose,"' she suggested, '"thou art sick!"'

152

He turned. She had just taken off the last of her garments, and she gleamed like a phantom in the sulphurous
light, slender pearly body, silvery hair in a long bob, like a
Pre-Raphaelite angel.

'*"Non Angli"*,' he murmured, '"*sed Angeli.*"'

'Pardon?'

He crossed to her and laid his hands on her shoulders, and
ran them down her arms until he could pick up her hands. She
stood straight in front of him, unperturbed by her nakedness.
He was not a tall man, but she was small by comparison with
him, and it excited him, for what reason he could not tell.

'You are the rose.' He chafed her hands softly. The light
came from the side and behind her, and her face was mostly
in shadow with only a curve here and there picked out, and
the half-hidden glitter of an eye. 'And I have found out your
bed of crimson joy. What an image-maker Blake was – I think
he knew you. There you stand, white and closed and complete
as a sarcophagus, and inside, rich and warm and flowing and
crimson. All hidden, so that it has to be found out; found out.
And have I the key that will unlock you?' His fingers traced the
lines of her body, curve and reversed curve, white and cool as
marble but starting into warmth wherever he touched her.

'I'm afraid every time I come into you that I will somehow
destroy you – like breaking a bubble – only you're not brittle.
Perhaps you'll just melt away. Can a citadel melt away?'

'If it was a cloud-castle it might,' she said. 'Or a mirage.'

'Oh, you're not a mirage. I can't describe what it is, but just
seeing you isn't enough, or touching you – I have to be in you.
It's like aching, only worse; and yet until I am in you I am
afraid.' He stroked her hair. She began to undo his buttons,
and he paid no attention, but went on stroking her and looking
at her in that troubled way. 'And in you, it is dark and secret,
and – I can never get near enough. As if there's some place in
the centre, some core that if I could get to, I could stay. And
I can't reach it, I can't get there.'

He pushed her hands away and took off his clothes with
his usual abrupt movements. She lay down on the bed and
watched him, and when he was naked held out her arms
to him. He lay down beside her and held her and kissed

153

her face and hair, breathing as though he was drowning in her.

She only half-understood him, understood without words, with the feeling part of herself. She knew it was difficult for him, as it was not for her. Her need of him was simple and absolute, the starting-point of everything else, where she seemed to be a sort of ending for him. 'You needn't be afraid,' she said at last. 'You won't hurt me.'

'I know. You're indestructible. You are more likely to destroy me. You seem to walk in and out of my brain as if you lived there, but I can never get anywhere near you.'

'Not true,' she said. 'My brain isn't separate from yours. If I walk in and out of you, it's only because you seem so like me I feel at home.'

'I must be very drunk,' Peter said slowly, 'to talk such nonsense with you. You know, I hardly know you're here.' He slid across her and she seemed to move and part in front of him like water so that her movement was part of his, and he went into her, and drew her on to him like a garment, and it was he that was dissolving, drowning without a struggle like a fly in honey. She seemed to lap him, drawing him on, effortlessly, buoyantly, into a crimson darkness.

When he woke it was morning, and he couldn't remember being asleep. He turned his head and Julia was looking at him.

'What?' he said.

'You fell asleep in me.'

He digested the information, and gave a little snort. 'In *corpus dilecti*, your delectable body. So much for romance. I'm sorry. That wasn't much of a first night for you, was it? Have I spoilt the realisation of your ambition?'

She smiled. Her eyes were like a monkey's – dark, bright and ancient. Or a snake's.

'There'll be others,' she said.

'But not first nights.'

'Why not? Every night can be a first night. It's all a matter of intent.'

October, 1956

Peter looked up during a ten-bar rest, his eye caught by a slight movement at the back of the hall, and saw Julia taking a seat in the back row but four, her usual place. He smiled, not that she could have seen a smile at that distance and with only half the lights on, but it was a sort of smile of relief that she was there. Tom Streeter, who had moved up the ranks with him and now had the principal's chair, caught the direction of his look and grinned, and would have no doubt said something had there been time.

She was a familiar sight by now, and she occasioned no comment when she sat quietly through rehearsals and recording sessions. She got on well with most people, and most of the musicians liked her, would chat pleasantly when the occasion arose. Knowing each others' conversation only too well, the members of the orchestra were always glad to have someone new to talk to, especially someone who identified so closely with their interests. Peter never knew if she had a fantastic ear, or if she was a fantastic liar, but let anyone ask her how he, individually, had played, and she could give an answer. However, she was intelligent and he knew she was a quick learner from the way she picked up things from him, so it did not really surprise him to see her, while he was otherwise occupied, discussing technicalities with the clarinet section, or debating the relative merits of different pins with a pair of cellists.

Now in her second year at college, she had more free time than ever, and she spent most of it with him, or to be more accurate, with the orchestra. They had been living together for eight months. After some weeks of living in the same house they had decided it was wasteful to pay two rents and had taken a double bed-sitting room that had fallen vacant in the house next door. It had worked very well so far. She managed to do what housework needed doing without making any song and dance about it; they knew how to leave each other alone when either wanted to read or think quietly; and he could have her every night and day, whenever he wanted her.

It was good to have her with him while he played, too, for it kept a kind of continuity for him which he would have missed otherwise, now he was busier and less often at home than ever. When the orchestra went away, she went too. She was a true companion to him, and he knew quite a few of the other players were envious of him – and that was not only because Julia was lovely looking. He had at first been rather ill at ease to see her get on so well with so many men, but any attempt on his part to restrict her sociability made her droop miserably in a corner with a shame he had no right to put on her. For that reason he left her alone, and, true enough, the others did not seem to advance any further in familiarity with her than a certain point.

They broke for coffee, after which they would be rehearsing a new piece by Tippett. Ferguson, who was now their principal conductor, called to him as he stood up, 'Oh, Peter, don't dash off for a minute, will you,' and resumed his conversation with the principal cello, holding one hand out to Peter all the while as if any move on Peter's part would be forcibly restrained.

Fretting to get off and get a cup of coffee, for he had had no breakfast, he had to wait where he was until Ferguson got through whatever was bothering Jimmy Tufnell so much. He saw Julia walking down the steps towards the door that led to the bar, where the coffee was served. She looked across at him, raised her eyebrows. He waved perfunctorily to show that he had to stay put for the time being, and she gave a charming shrug and carried on down. He admired her impersonally: her shape, the way she managed the awkwardly-distanced steps, the way she dressed – now he was partly financing her she could afford to indulge her taste for well-tailored clothes a little more often – and watched her being neatly intercepted and carried off by the two trumpets who descended from the platform to arrive by the exit at the same time as her. They talked for a moment, the two dark heads bent conspiratorially over her fair one; they paused and all looked across at him, back at each other, and then Julia lifted her hands in a funny little gesture of resignation and they went out together.

Bringing his attention back to the platform, he found

Ferguson looking at him with a wry smile. 'Happens all the time, doesn't it?' he said pleasantly.

Peter shrugged. 'I don't blame them,' he said.

'Nor do I. But you're a brave man to bring her all the same,' Ferguson said.

'Oh, I don't bring her,' Peter laughed. 'Like Lulu in the song, she comes by herself.'

When he finally got down to the bar Julia was at the far side of a crowd, and he was annoyed. He hadn't seen her for nearly two days, for the orchestra had gone down to Portsmouth for one night, and Julia had decided not to come with him since she had some work to finish for a class. Peter had stayed the night in Pompey, and had come to the rehearsal straight from there, to find a letter waiting for him, forwarded from Spenser Road.

He squeezed his way through, to find Julia, feet well planted, arguing passionately over whether a certain five notes on the trumpet in the Mussorgsky *Pictures* should be played with or without vibrato. She and the first trumpet seemed to be anti, and the second trumpet and one of the clarinets pro.

As Peter arrived the clarinet seemed to tire of the whole thing, for he said peaceably, 'Well, I don't see that it really matters all that much anyway.'

'But of course it matters,' Julia exclaimed. 'That's like saying it doesn't matter if a picture's done in oils or in line and wash!'

'Well, does that matter?' the clarinet persisted. Everyone laughed, and someone said, 'Get out of that, Ju.'

She laughed and ran her hand through her hair in a distracted way. 'I wish I'd never started this,' she said. 'Well, look, after all, what's the difference between a Vernon Ward and a Stubbs? Or between MGM scores and some of the better-known programme music?'

'Beats me,' someone said.

'Damn little, if you ask me,' someone else said, and there was laughter.

'It's only atmosphere, certainly as far as nine-tenths of the audience goes, and even then it's only a handful of notes that make the difference. If you put vibrato on those five notes you might as well go and play the organ down at the local cinema, because you turn the piece into a sentimental ballad.'

Several people broke in at that point, one of them the second trumpet who said, 'But surely what the audience thinks isn't important?' Which threatened to start a whole new uproar, and Peter decided the moment had come to intervene.

'Excuse me, but could I have my woman back?' he said loudly, parting the last two people between him and the centre of the crowd.

'Whoops! Look out boys, papa's here,' said one of the trombones, and the first trumpet patted Julia's shoulder fondly and said, 'Run along now. HMV, you know.'

Julia smiled amiably, and as the crowd dispersed she led the way to the corner table which was always empty because it was awkwardly placed for getting in and out, and therefore was private. Peter sat down opposite her, shifted his seat so as to block her view of the rest of the bar, and then said, 'How do you do it?'

'It just happens,' she smiled, spreading her hands. 'I'm just alleviating their boredom. Did you have a good night?'

'The concert went well.'

'How was the hotel?'

'Shabby but clean – the breakfast was good, but I didn't have time to get any.'

'Then how do you know it was good?'

'I saw it being served as I checked out. Let me finish your coffee.'

'Shall I get you one?'

'No time, just give me yours.' She pushed the cup over and he sipped it gratefully.

'I thought,' she said casually, 'that we might go out for a meal tonight – in celebration.'

'No, I have to go and see Joyce,' he said quickly. 'Celebration of what?'

Her smile had drooped a little at the mention of Joyce, but she hitched it back up again and said, 'Nothing really. Why do you have to see her?'

'That's what I've been trying to get hold of you to tell you, only what with Ferguson on the one hand and the

158

brass section on the other, I don't seem to be able to get near you.'

'All right,' she said reasonably, 'you're near me now, so what did you want to tell me?'

'I had a letter waiting for me when I got here – the decree nisi. They'd sent my copy to Spenser Road by mistake, and Joyce sent it to me via the orchestra, with a note asking me to go and see her.'

'What does she want to see you about?' Julia asked.

Peter scowled. 'How the devil should I know what she wants to see me about? She didn't say.'

Julia saw that he was likely to savage her if she stepped on his sore paw, and on the subject of Joyce or the boys he nearly always seemed to have four of them, so she tried to be tactful. 'What time will you be back, then?' and seeing him open his mouth to snap at her again, she added quickly, 'I only ask so I know whether to have any food for you when you come back – honest!'

He smiled reluctantly at her, and said more reasonably, 'I don't know what time I'll be back, but I should think late. Joyce will probably feed me, so don't worry about that.' Now it was his turn to be conciliating, for he knew that she would not like the idea of his eating there. 'I expect she just wants to talk things out. It's a big thing for her, you know, and it leaves her with quite a responsibility.'

'Yes,' Julia said inadequately.

There was a pause. Peter went on, 'What did you want to celebrate, anyway?'

'Oh, it doesn't matter, honestly.'

'But what?' he insisted.

She smiled hazily. 'It's Thursday. I wanted to celebrate Thursday.'

Peter reached a hand across the table and hers moved to meet it. 'You funny creature. Maybe we could celebrate Friday?'

She moved her head impatiently. 'It doesn't signify. Listen, they're calling you. You'd better go.' She stood up and followed him out as far as the lift, and then she stopped, and touched his arm. 'Give my love to the children – metaphorically speaking, that is.'

'Are you going? Aren't you staying for the Tippett?'

'No, I have to do some work. I can hear it tomorrow at the final rehearsal, can't I?'

'Well, yes, I suppose so,' he began.

She smiled quickly. 'Okay then. I'll see you later. I want to go into college and finish something.'

'All right then,' he said, puzzled, and watched her walk quickly away and down the stairs. She was hurt, he thought, that he was going to see Joyce in preference to this mysterious celebration, and was going off in a huff. His lips set tighter. He wasn't going to put up with that sort of thing. She'd have to learn that his time was his own, to spend where he wanted.

'Peter! Come on, laddie, everyone's waiting. Whad'ya want, an engraved invitation?' someone called to him in an agitated voice, and he spun round and hurried out on to the platform, to a derisive slow handclap.

Julia stayed late at college because she didn't like to come home to an empty house, but she had to leave in the end because the refectory closed at six and she was driven back by hunger. She let herself in, switched on the light, and glanced round, registering automatically the things that needed doing to make the place tidy.

'Do those first,' she said aloud. 'Nicer to eat in a tidy room.'

It didn't take long. She made the bed, for she had learnt that, in a bedsitter, if the bed was made it went a very long way to making the rest of the room look tidy too. She pulled up the bedspread gingerly, for it was candlewick, and although she had it on the bed inside out, it still made her shudder. She loathed candlewick. It did to her what peach skin, or a fingernail down a blackboard, did to other people. When she was a child her mother had bought matching candlewick bedspreads for her and Sylvia, and Julia had cried for a week every time she was put to bed. Then she had patiently night by night pulled the threads out of it, one by one until it was bald. Her mother was livid, but she could sleep again.

The one on the bed here hadn't too much pile. As her mother would say, candlewick isn't what it used to be in my young day

160

– and thank God for that, Julia added devoutly. Looking round again, she took two empty cups across to the sink and rinsed them, restored the books and records to symmetrical piles, and picked up some clothes and took them over to the big wardrobe in the corner. Opening it she got a familiar thrill from seeing Peter's clothes hanging up with hers – how immoral! Like our undies twirling round and round together at the launderette. She smoothed his dress coat with her fingertips and tutted at a stain on his cummerbund. He ought to wear a black one if he couldn't be more careful than that with beer.

She closed the wardrobe door, twiddling the faulty lock until it caught, and smiled at herself in the mirror, and then turned sideways on to inspect her profile. So that's what happens to all those massive Victorian wardrobes that people throw out when they go all contemporary – they end up in bedsitters. Where do wardrobes go when they die? I must have another shot at a self-portrait, she thought, and was immediately sidetracked to the thought of the portrait of Peter that she was doing for his birthday. She felt excited. It was good, she thought. She had been doing sketches in various media of Peter since she first met him, and now at last her skill seemed to be catching up with her desire. Whenever she sat before the canvas and lifted the brush, she felt the wonderful sensation of rightness, of knowing that when the brush touched the canvas, the mark she would leave would be what she meant.

Still thinking of Peter she danced a few steps, humming softly, kicked some dust mice dishonourably back under the wardrobe, whence they had been wafted by the draught as she opened the door, and danced across the room to the gas ring to boil herself some eggs. Food in conjunction with Peter made her think of his being with Joyce, and her elation ebbed. She didn't like to think of them together. She had seen them together too often, and could imagine it too easily.

What did they talk about? How much did they say to each other of everything? Joyce had shared so much of his life, and she, Julia, had shared so little – this was what she was jealous of, the mental intimacy. She didn't imagine that Peter touched or kissed Joyce – it might almost have been better if that was what he went there for.

And why, why, did she have to feed him? That was terribly intimate. She saw, too clearly, the kitchen, saw him standing in the doorway watching while Joyce bustled about preparing things, saw them in the dining room sitting down across the table from each other and felt, vicariously, the dreadful familiarity of the action. He would speak to her, then at least, in his ordinary voice, his everyday, matter-of-fact voice that he used to say ordinary everyday things to Julia. Joyce would know what things he liked best to eat and how he liked things cooked. And they had the children! They would talk about the children, and look at each other, and know that the children were part of them both, part of Peter's body that came out of Joyce's. It was horrible to think about.

Worst of all, Julia thought, resting her face against the window to cool her hot cheeks, was the inevitability, like death: for nothing, now, absolutely nothing, could make that intimacy not to be. If Peter never saw Joyce or the children again, if they should all die now, right this minute, there would still have been that intimacy between them, it would still have existed, and to that extent Julia would never be able to be near him. Those years could not be wiped out or rewritten.

That was why, of course, you could never go back. People of her age talked a lot about brief passions, saying that you could have a whole love affair in one night – it was a regular topic among girls in the refectory. They said that it was the quality of the love that counted, not the quantity; but it was not so – the length of time was more important. Ten years of living together, even without perfect understanding, made more of a mark than one night of perfect love and passion. We measure our love by the yard, she thought; when we are habits to each other, we are safe. But to that extent, he could never go back to Joyce, because if he tried to live with her again, Julia would come between him and his sleep, as Joyce sometimes did now. He had lived with her: he would never forget her.

I shouldn't be jealous, Julia told herself, lifting the eggs out of the water and rolling them on to a plate. Everyone has the years before they meet someone that they can never know about – and I wouldn't want to be Joyce. She tried to imagine what Joyce must be feeling, and failed utterly.

Joyce, apparently, wanted to divorce Peter, and she couldn't imagine ever wanting to do that. And, she whispered, he will come home to me tonight, and Joyce will have to sleep alone again. Julia imagined her turning over in bed and reaching out a hand to encounter only empty space. If I were her, she thought practically, I'd get myself a single bed. Or swap with Michael.

The food made her feel more substantial, and when she had washed up the few utensils, she went and had a bath for the sheer pleasure of it, smoothed herself with scented talc, and then got into bed with a book.

Peter arrived home late, tired and despondent from the evening with Joyce. She had not been unpleasant to him, and he hated that. He would rather see her fight than try to chatter lightly to him in that pathetic way when anyone could see that she was as miserable as sin. The children had stayed up past their bedtime to see him, and James had been sulky and refused to speak to him, while Michael had been overexcited and had got sillier and ruder until Peter lost his temper and Joyce had to intervene before he slapped the boy. Then she had taken them up to bed, and they had had supper, and she had sat across the table from him, chattering nervously like a debutante on her first date.

When he had got up to go, the veneer had cracked a little, and he saw that she was on the point of asking him to stay.

'This house is too big for you,' he had said bluntly. 'Why don't you get something smaller? You wouldn't be so lonely in a smaller place.'

'Who said I was lonely?' she protested with bravado. They looked at each other hopelessly for a moment, and then Joyce shrugged. 'It doesn't matter.'

He touched her hand; all the kindness he could offer. 'We're strangers to each other,' he said. And then he went.

He felt like a stranger to himself: homeless. The thought of the bedsitter was not like home, and he could imagine what would be waiting for him – Julia, resentful and tearful, or aloof and petulant. When he reached the house and saw the light still on, his spirits sank still further, but he braced himself and determined that whatever she said, he wouldn't have a row tonight. By God, if he had to knock her out, he wouldn't have a row tonight.

He opened the door of the room, and saw that it was the bedside lamp that was on, not the main light. Julia was propped up in bed, her head tilted over, asleep, and a book, drooping from her fingers, showed how she had spent her evening.

He closed the door quietly, put off his coat, and walked over to the bed to look down at her. Her sleeping face was a curve in the lake of hair, a curve made of curves, as if she was smiling in her sleep. She looked so content that all his unhappiness drained from him, leaving only tiredness. He wanted to be bed beside her, asleep.

He took off his clothes and came back to the bed and carefully lifted the book from her fingers, but despite his care her hand fluttered for it, and she stirred and straightened under the covers. Her eyes opened, against a tremendous drag it seemed, and she smiled a little more and murmured 'Hello darling' out of the depths of a blissful languor. Peter sat down on the edge of the bed abruptly, and gathered in her sleepy soft length, trying to hold her up and hug her all in the one movement. He felt as if he wanted to cry, but tears wouldn't come so easily. Then, just as suddenly, he thought how unfair it was to wake her; he switched off the light, slid in beside her, felt her body curl automatically round his, and fell into an exhausted, dreamless sleep.

They slept spoonwise, with him fitted in behind her – or, as Julia put it, 'on my back like a monkey'. Peter woke from the beautifully thorough sleep feeling marvellous, and began to kiss as much of Julia as he could reach. She stirred and woke, rolled over to face him, and opened her mouth to be kissed.

'Hello darling,' she said.

'That's what you said last night,' he told her.

'You must have been late,' she murmured. 'I don't even remember your coming in.'

'Well, in that case, I'll do it again,' he said, suiting the action to the words.

'The nice thing about you,' she said later, 'is that you're so delightfully vulgar.'

'The nice thing about you,' he said, kissing the end of her nose and sitting up, 'is that you wake up in a good temper.'

Julia just managed to stop herself saying, why, didn't Joyce? and said instead, 'Shall I come with you this morning?'

'To rehearsal? I thought you were going to anyway?'

'Only if you like. I shouldn't want to outstay my welcome.'

'Ass. What will you wear?' He jumped out of bed and reached for his dressing gown, adding, 'The trouble with this place is that you have to get dressed to go to the bathroom. The sooner we get a place of our own the better.'

'Wait until you're a famous soloist, laddie, then you'll be able to afford a toilet. And hurry up, I want to go.'

She got up and went to the wardrobe to choose something to wear, feeling the pleasurable shock his words had given her. 'A place of our own'. A flat, possibly? It had such a lovely sound of permanence to it, as if he meant to stay with her for good. She had never dared expect that, and tried not to now, but it was a lovely thing to have said to you first thing in the morning. It made her feel like wearing her canary-yellow dress.

'Oh, you're wearing that, are you?' he said as he came back in. 'You must be feeling happy.'

'I am. Don't I look it?'

'You certainly do,' he said, clearing his throat. 'We'd better hurry, or we'll be late. What do you want for breakfast?'

'There's only eggs. I'll do them while you shave.'

'Who said I was going to shave?'

'If you don't, I won't take you out to lunch.'

'I'm already shaving.'

In the car she sat beside him, one foot tucked under her in her favourite position, her long bob of hair swinging about as she turned her head to look at everything.

'Don't you ever get tired?' he asked her.

'Of what?' The hair swung again, parting round her face.

'Of smiling all the time. You look like a bushbaby.'

'Do I smile all the time? Well –' she put her hand up to feel her mouth – 'perhaps I do. Do bushbabies smile?'

165

'There was a full stop between the two sentences. They had nothing to do with each other.'

'"The crocuses are out, and your father is in a filthy temper",' Julia said.

'What?'

'Quotation. I do miss Sylvia sometimes. At least she read the same books as me.'

'I used to feel that way about Rowland, until puberty hit me, and my interests changed drastically.'

'It must have been awful,' Julia said gravely. 'I shudder when I think of the frightful things boys have to go through to get to be men. It's a wonder any of them grow up sane.'

'What about girls?'

'I can't speak for other girls, only for me.'

'And what about you?'

'Oh, I didn't grow naturally in a hedgerow. I was forced, in a greenhouse.'

Peter burst out laughing. 'That sounds like the title of one of these modern books – you know, *Frank Confessions*. She was only a gardener's daughter—'

'You should know, you were the head gardener.'

Well, he thought, I asked for that. He drove fast along the Embankment, wondering, not for the first time, what her life would have been like if he had never met her. Safe? Dull? Worse, in some ways, of course, hemmed in on all sides, but in the end she would have struck her own bargain: she was too intelligent to beat her wings against insuperable bars. All the same, it was a responsibility. In some ways she was younger than her nineteen years. He didn't doubt that if he wanted to go away and leave her, she could look after herself, but he doubted his ability to want to, and that was the problem.

She was on top form at the hall, laughing and talking to everyone, and her particular exuberance must even have attracted Ferguson's attention, for during the Tippet he jumped down off the platform and asked if she would go up to the back of the hall and tell him if she could hear the basses. Normally he would have sent one of the players, or else asked Peter to conduct while he himself went back to listen. Too much attention altogether, Peter thought; he was glad when the

166

rehearsal was over and he could whisk her away for lunch, to a restaurant behind the Strand.

They ordered steak and kidney pudding, which was one of the specialities of the house, and followed it up with apple pie. 'Pie and pudding, shocking diet.' Julia talked most of the time, and seeing she was in a voluble mood he just relaxed and let her entertain him. She could keep him laughing when she was in that mood, and he was amused to see other heads turning to look at her. With her yellow dress and her happy face she had the same sort of impact as the first daffodils after a particularly grey winter.

'Well,' she said when the waiter had removed their pudding plates and they were waiting for coffee, 'that's what I call a celebration.'

'What, the lunch? We're still celebrating then? And is it still Thursday?'

'Uh-huh. Do you want to know the occasion?'

'You're looking uncommonly pleased about *some*thing today, at any rate.'

'I'm pregnant,' she said.

He stared at her, his mouth a little open, and could think of no single word to say. The waiter delivered their coffee, and as he retreated Peter said, 'Pregnant? You're going to have a baby?'

'The one usually follows the other,' she said, and then, cocking her head a little on one side, 'Aren't you pleased?'

'I don't know what I am yet,' he said, 'apart from astonished.' Dismayed, shocked, he hadn't got over those yet. Dear God, this was a complication.

'Well, I don't see why you should be astonished,' she said reasonably. 'You were there at the time.' Luckily it seemed she was so cock-a-hoop that his failure to say the right things had not yet disturbed her.

'Yes, but I mean when? Where? Why now all of a sudden and not before?'

'*I* don't know,' she said laughing. 'Ask yourself those questions. You did it.'

The man at the next table was eavesdropping shamelessly, his mouth open to show a wad of half-masticated peas. Peter shielded his eyes from the sight and said urgently, 'Listen Julia, seriously, are you sure?'

'Certainly I'm sure. I waited to tell you until I was.'

'When is it to be?'

'The middle of March is what I'm told, and you can count up to nine, in either direction, as well as I can, so work it out for yourself.'

He was already counting. 'I don't understand it,' he muttered.

'You are sceptical,' she said.

Now he saw that the smile was beginning to fade a little. He tried to clear his head and concentrate on her, think how happy she had been about it, how . . .

'My God, you must have known about it last night.'

'Of course I did.' She sounded puzzled.

'And that's why you wanted to – but you didn't say anything?'

'It would have been rather a dirty trick, wouldn't it,' she said.

To have told him that then would have virtually forced him not to go and see Joyce. She had been too honest not to lie when he asked her why she wanted to celebrate. 'What a good girl you are,' he said. The idea was beginning to sink in at last, that she was pregnant. A silly kind of smirk began to creep up one side of his mouth. He felt a surge of affection, quickly followed by a surge of desire. 'Drink up your coffee, I want to take you home. Quickly.'

She stood up, laughing, ready to do anything, just as the fancy took him. He paid the bill, and then headed for the car, catching her hand and walking so fast that she had to hop-skip-and-jump to keep up with him. His brain was racing now, working things out in their proper order, the realisation coming over him in waves. During one of them, just as they reached the car, he stopped and spun her to face him, and hugged her.

'Then you are pleased,' she said when he let her go again.

'Pleased? Of course I'm pleased. I'm – delirious!' He wound his arm round her waist and pulled the car keys from his pocket to let her in. 'I'm taking you home now to make love to you,

168

you glorious fertile creature. And we're going to look for a flat
– nothing large, nothing fancy –' he made vague sketches in
the air, shut her into the car and darted round to his side – 'but
enough for two – three,' he corrected himself just before her.

'And I'll tell you another thing,' he said as he drove off,
'now the nisi is through this whole business should be over
by Christmas at the latest.'

'And I'll tell you another thing,' he said as he swung the
car round Parliament Square, 'I am going to do solo work. It's
going to *happen*, Julia.'

She smiled serenely. She would believe anything that was
told her just then. Oddly enough, he didn't mention marriage,
and, more oddly, it never even crossed her mind as a possible
subject for discussion.

Nine

'This is it,' Peter said, stopping the car halfway down the mews.

'Which?' Sylvia asked, poking her head out of the window.

'All I know is it's number three,' Julia said.

Sylvia jumped out of the back door of the car exuberantly, saying, 'Yes, that's it, with the green door, Jule, look.'

'I just hope you're going to like it,' Peter said, opening the other door of the car and helping Julia out. She looked around her at the cobbled mews with its whitewashed buildings and green-painted window boxes. All the doors were painted a different colour; number three was dark green, but obviously old, shabby against the brightness of its neighbours.

'The first thing we'll have to do is paint the door,' she said.

Peter gave her an amused look. 'Highly important first thing,' he said.

'Well, it is,' she protested. 'Your front door is the first thing you see when you come home from a hard day's work. It ought to look welcoming.' Peter was not disposed to argue about this and went round the back to open the boot and get the luggage out.

'You've got a window box,' Sylvia observed, 'but nothing in it.'

'That can be remedied for the summer,' Julia said. 'A few geraniums, and some alyssum and lobelia—'

'The way you say it, alyssum-and-lobelia sounds like one plant,' Peter said.

'It very nearly is. Look at municipal parks. Always A and L, with salvias in the middle. Red, white and blue. It's the patriotic way.'

170

'Are you going to stand there talking nonsense all day?' Sylvia complained.

'Here, you take the keys and open the door,' Peter intervened, holding out the bunch to Julia, 'while Sylvia and I do the cases.'

'Which key is it?'

'The one that's on the separate ring – the big key. No, not that door, clot, that's the garage. The small door.'

The door opened straight on to the stairs: narrow, wooden, steep.

'We'll have to get a gate put across the top when the baby comes,' Julia said. She began to climb the stairs, slowly and rather laboriously, for she was large with child and there was no handrail. Her hand, pressed for balance against the wooden stripping on the wall, caught a splinter and she said 'Ouch!' and used the other hand. Peter came up behind her, the suitcases banging and scraping at either side of him, and Sylvia appeared in his shadow with two bundles of books.

'Buck up, Julia, do!' Sylvia called peevishly.

'There's no buck left in me,' she answered. 'The baby took it all.'

Julia stopped at the top of the stairs, for the passage led off to right and left, and she did not know which way to choose, so Peter pushed passed her and led her into the kitchen where he dumped the cases heavily on the floor.

'Needs painting,' he said tersely, for he had not got his breath.

'Don't the chairs and dresser look lovely against the tiles? And I'm glad you chose the yellow curtains, now I see them up. However did they get the furniture up those stairs?'

'With difficulty,' Peter said. 'I had to give them enormous tips, and even then I thought they'd give them back and go home when they saw the piano.'

'They should have been grateful it was an upright,' Julia said indignantly. 'Suppose you'd been a pianist and not a violinist?'

'Where d'you want these books put, Ju?' inquired Sylvia from the doorway. Peter and Julia exchanged a smile.

171

'If you abbreviate her name any more, you'll choke your-self,' Peter said. 'I refuse to be married to a glottal stop, forbye.'

'For what?' Sylvia said.

'For Julia. Do you want to have a quick look round before we bring the rest of the stuff up?' Peter asked.

'Oh, certainly. I want to approve your taste.' Julia had not seen anything yet, for she had had to go into hospital for observation for a month, and Peter had chosen the flat and the furniture with no more than a guide from Julia by means of a catalogue as to what kind of things she preferred.

The bathroom was at the other end of the long passage, its door facing the kitchen door, and between them were the doors to the bedroom, the living room and a spare room.

'The music room,' Peter said. It was empty at present except for a music stand, a chair, a very battered wooden table, and a tea chest full of music and books.

'The nursery,' Julia countered firmly. 'You can practise in the living room like everybody else. Where on earth did you get the table?'

'Where, or why?'

'It was already here,' Sylvia offered. 'The only thing they left behind. I wonder why? Perhaps it's stained with the evidence of a crime, blood or acid or something.'

'Not to notice,' Peter said, peering at it. 'Only a quantity of ink and some very bored-looking carvings. Ye olde home-work table, I deduce, left behind because of its unpleasant associations.'

'Come and look at the living room, Julia, it's super,' Sylvia said, losing interest in the mystery of the table and pulling at her sister's hand as if she was quite ten years younger than she was. Julia followed, wondering whether she would be surprised, and if so, whether pleasantly or unpleasantly. This would be her first chance of seeing Peter's taste let loose. In his previous home, his wife had apparently chosen everything; and since he left that he had lived with Julia in already-furnished rooms. She felt just a touch of trepidation, in case he should turn out to have a morbid passion for pokerwork, or anything similarly unbearable.

172

The room was surprising, but only because Julia would never have imagined anyone duplicating her taste so exactly. It was plain almost to the point of starkness, and then rescued by the richness of the colours. The walls were distempered plain white. The square carpet in the centre of the floor was Chinese, predominantly white, which showed up attractively against the dark varnished boards, and patterned with a deep blue, darker than royal. The curtains were a similarly dark blue, and floor length, in accordance with the fashion that was coming in. On either side of the fire was an old-fashioned wing-back chair, obviously old, but freshly covered with a crimson cloth. Against the opposite wall a huge leather chesterfield, which looked as though it had come out of someone's library, glowed richly dark with age, with cushions of dark blue and crimson propped in its corners. Between the fireplace and the window, the wall was shelved to the ceiling, and someone had already started putting the books up. Between the fireplace and the wall on the other side was a mahogany chest, bow-fronted, brass-handled, bearing only a red-and-white majolica vase that needed flowers. On the wall between the two windows, and directly opposite the door, was a print of the detail of Adam's head from *The Creation*, in black and white, stunning against the white wall. And that was all.

Julia stood at the door and looked, and Peter behind her could hear her soft rapid breathing of pleasure. He didn't ask, and she didn't answer, but after a moment she went and sat down in one of the armchairs so that her back was to him.

'It looks really modern and rich, like someone's Hollywood Home,' Sylvia said, walking over to the windows and fingering the curtains lovingly. 'You know the kind of thing I mean. It always seems odd that when you get very rich, you have your rooms as bare as possible. You'd think it would be the other way round, wouldn't you?'

While she filled their silence for them, Peter went across to Julia's chair and looked down at her. Her eyes were fixed on the window, and in the thin last-of-winter light she looked pale and tired; there were tears on her cheeks. He touched her hand as it rested on the arm of the chair, and she looked up at him, and saw his anxiety, and smiled.

'Why do you cry?' he asked her softly.

'I'm happy,' she said. 'Peter, it's just so perfect. If I could have furnished it myself without reference to anyone, it would have been just like this. It's rather frightening to be so alike.'

'Nonsense,' he said robustly. 'Why shouldn't we have similar tastes? You learnt from me.'

'You're looking a bit worn, Jule. Shall we have some tea or something? I could make it,' Sylvia said, eager to help.

'Oh, that's good of you. Thank you. Yes, let's have tea – and crumpets or toast and jam or something equally cheering.'

'Good idea,' Peter said, putting an approving hand on Sylvia's shoulder. It disturbed him a little, because it felt so much like Julia's through the wool of her blue jersey, and he made himself leave his hand there rather than snatch it away as he wanted to and draw attention to himself. 'You go and put the kettle on, while I get the rest of the things up out of the car, and then I'll come and help you make the toast.'

'And what must I do?' Julia asked.

'You must rest, put your feet up.' He came back to her as Sylvia went out. She reached up and took his hand and he squeezed hers comfortingly. 'Are you warm enough? I'll make the fire up later on, but I want to get the bits in before it gets dark.

'I'm all right.'

'Do you want a blanket round you?'

'I'm all right. I'm warm.'

'Is the boy behaving himself?'

'It's a girl!' she said, and he grinned to see the light of battle revive in her eyes.

'That's better. As long as you're fighting, you're still alive. Even if you are wrong. I can tell, you know.'

'You should be able to,' she agreed. 'But this time it's a girl. This one's mine, and it's different from any other one you've had, and it's a girl.'

'*Touché*!' he laughed. 'I'll come back to that later. You look good when you get a bit of combative colour in your cheeks.'

'Aye, we're dead but we won't lie down,' she said.

'Be back in a minute.'

He was gone, and Julia relaxed back into the chair and watched the frail light fading from the two windows. She was home at last, she thought, and she must never let any bad thought enter here to alienate her. There had been one point during the settlement with Joyce when she thought she would get half of the Kane conjugal furniture to live with, and though she would not have made any fuss, she had dreaded the thought. Acting on Peter's suggestion, Joyce had sold the big house in Spenser Road and bought a smaller town house in Shaftesbury so that she could be near her own people, and the children could grow up away from London. The new house had needed far less furniture, and the surplus was to have come to Peter to furnish his new home.

Then at a later discussion it was decided that they would sell the surplus stuff and split the proceeds. Julia did not know how much the sale raised, but Peter intimated without actually saying so that his share had been enough to furnish and partially redecorate this flat, and she had breathed again, too relieved to be more curious. According to Peter, all the negotiations had been very civilised, and there had only been one bad meeting between Peter and Joyce. That was when he had deemed it necessary to tell her that Julia was pregnant. The reason for telling her was to get her to agree to a more reasonable alimony settlement, for though Joyce would have the children to keep, she would have no capital expenses, since the house and all furnishings were being provided, and she had quite a decent income of her own; while Peter had only his fees, which fluctuated greatly, and had, as well as all the usual expenses, a large insurance to pay for.

'But you've always had those,' Joyce said rigidly. 'I can't see how that girl getting pregnant can make any difference. You aren't bound to pay her anything are you?'

'She's entitled to claim maintenance from me,' he said, trying to keep emotions out of it; but the one thing that could infuriate Joyce was the mention of Julia, however indirect.

'Oh, it is your baby then?'

'Of course it's mine, Joyce,' Peter ground out. 'Don't try to be funny.'

'I don't think it's funny in the least, when you try to cut down my alimony simply because you think you're going to have to pay maintenance for a bastard. Why should I suffer?'

'But you won't suffer,' he said, still trying to be reasonable. 'You'll have plenty to live on.'

'My own money,' she said. 'My own personal money.'

'Well, damn it all, this is my own personal money we're gaily splitting up! I suppose you haven't thought of that?'

'I'm entitled to your financial support,' she said stiffly. 'I am your wife, after all.'

'Barely,' he said, losing his temper, 'and not any longer than I can help it.'

'You needn't take that tone with me. Remember it's me that's divorcing you – for adultery, in case you've forgotten! And you have the cheek to ask me to give up my income so you can finance your slut?'

'Shut up,' he said fiercely. 'When you talk like that I want to hit you! She doesn't run you down, never, she never speaks about you with anything but respect; you damn well show her the same respect.'

'Her? She should show me respect. I'm your wife. I'm a decent married woman. And what's she?'

'You *were* my wife,' Peter said savagely. 'She *will* be my wife. That's the difference.'

There was a pause. Joyce's eyes grew wider with a mixture of shock and disbelief. 'You won't – you wouldn't *marry* her? Not really?'

'Why not?' Peter asked. He was calm again, now that he had the upper hand. 'Why shouldn't I? What did you think I was going to do?'

That was not an answerable question, for while both of them knew that marrying Julia had never been one of his reasons for wanting the divorce from Joyce, it had never been stated. Moreover, neither of them was any longer too sure of the real reasons behind the whole thing. It had grown like a river, and gathered up so much silt and rubbish in its course that you could no longer see the bottom.

'I don't believe it,' Joyce said firmly at last. 'She may be pregnant, but that's no reason for marrying her. You wouldn't do it.'

Peter merely smiled.

Julia did not know all of this, of course. He had told her expurgated sections of it at various times, and she had pieced together a version of her own. The fact that did arise out of it was that a few days after this Peter had woken her in the night to tell her that they were going to be married, as soon as he was 'single again' as he put it.

The decree absolute had come through just before Christmas, and Peter had taken her and two friends – Tom Streeter and Martin Newman, who had, incidentally, found them the mews flat – for a drink to celebrate, in a pub in the alleyway behind Holborn station. Julia remembered it particularly because it had been the only part of Christmas she enjoyed, coming in from the snowy street to the warm, brightly lit pub: the paper streamers and the jollity, the two best friends so very pleasant and intimate and kind, and Peter in a mood of rare hilarity. A couple of days later he had gone away. He said he had to spend a little time at Christmas with the boys because it was their first Christmas away from him. Also, he said, there were things he had to discuss with Joyce.

'But surely you could discuss them over the phone – or by letter,' Julia had said, protesting for the first and last time. She hated the thought of his being with Joyce. She wondered why he wanted to be – could he be still in love with her?

'No, I can't,' he said shortly. 'And besides, I've told you, I want to see the boys.'

The boys were always the clinching argument. Her rebellion had subsided. Telling herself she had no claim over him anyway, she had not mentioned it again. She had been at an awkward stage of her pregnancy, and felt dispirited and ungainly. She had spent Christmas alone in their bed-sitting room feeling that the end of everything had come and wishing she was dead. When Peter had phoned her up from a call box on Christmas Day and told her that he was fed up to the teeth with the in-laws and Joyce and the children and Christmas and everything, and that he was coming home the next day and would be with her by early afternoon, she had not felt any triumph, nor even pleasure.

Peter had kept his word and arranged the marriage for the

earliest possible date, which was the twenty-third of January, at Caxton Hall. Newman had been Peter's witness – Streeter couldn't get the same time off as Peter – and Julia had asked Sylvia. She had been forbidden to attend by their parents, but she had come anyway. Since the wedding was on a weekday, there was no reason for the parents to know where she was.

Julia's reactions to her wedding were minimal. It had never been offered to her as any kind of prize. Peter's proposal, if you could call it that, had been factual and businesslike. He offered her no reasons, spoke no romantic words. She thought at first that he was marrying her so that the baby should not be illegitimate, but later she changed her view. Had she been asked, she probably would have consented, partly because of the baby, and mainly because she loved him too much to refuse, but she was not asked – she was told, so the matter never arose.

Julia wore a navy-blue dress, a camel-coloured coat, and a navy-blue beret. She and Peter arrived in Peter's car at ten to eleven; Sylvia walked from St James's tube station and arrived one minute later. Newman arrived in a taxi at three minutes past having been held up by the traffic. At twenty past eleven they were on the steps again, and Julia clutched at her beret to stop it blowing away with a hand that felt very peculiar and very heavy under the burden of a narrow eighteen-carat gold ring.

'What do we do now?' Sylvia asked. 'Do you go away, or what?'

Newman glanced at his watch. 'I have to be at a session at twelve thirty, but there's time for a drink, if you like?'

'I'm very hungry,' Julia said. Peter looked at her, and saw that she was pale and pinched-looking in the gritty wind.

'We can get some bread and cheese in the pub,' he said. 'Come on, let's at least get out of this wind. Are you coming, Sylvia?'

'Yes, just for one. Then I really should get back too.'

They went into a pub called The Albert on the corner of the next street and ordered bread and cheese and beer, cider for Sylvia, and orange juice for Julia.

'Well,' said Martin, lifting his glass, 'here's to long life and happiness for you both.'

'Here here. Cheers!' said Sylvia.

'Thanks,' Peter said. 'Add a bit of health and wealth to that as well, eh?'

'And here's to the new Mrs Kane,' Newman went on, lifting his glass again.

Peter and Julia looked at each other, startled. 'Do you know,' he said, speaking for them both, 'I hadn't thought of that aspect of it. I suppose you are Mrs Kane. What does it feel like?'

Julia looked a little strange. 'I haven't had a chance to tell yet. This feels funny, though. My hand feels heavy.' And she held out her left hand to show them. The ring looked so small and thin and cheap that Peter was struck with a kind of shame, and his heart went out to Julia. She was very young, and most girls dream of their wedding, so he was told. She must be very disappointed with this.

'I'll buy you a better one as soon as we have the cash to hand,' he said, taking her hand and covering the ring with a squeeze.

Her eyes met his candidly. 'Oh, no, I couldn't have another one. This one is mine for good now.'

'Congratulations, Peter,' laughed Newman. 'You've acquired yourself a wife of simple tastes.'

'A wife. Yes,' he said musingly, looking at Julia. Then a new thought struck him. 'And a sister-in-law.' And the idea seemed to amuse him, for he repeated it several times, and laughed heartily, somewhat to Sylvia's confusion.

And shortly after that Julia had got kidney trouble and had been whisked off to hospital, firstly for treatment, and then for what they called 'bed rest', which meant that she was not allowed to get up for anything, not even to go to the toilet, though she felt all right after the first few days.

And then Peter had come to take her home, really home at last. She had had no experience yet of being married, and in a way she was glad, for it meant that the marriage would start properly here, just as if he had brought her home from the church, instead of the hospital, and carried her over the threshold.

The room was growing dark, but she had already impressed

every detail of it so firmly and lovingly on her mind that she did not notice. Her back was aching, and she tried, heavily, to lift herself up and back in the armchair to get more support. The baby turned a little inside her, and then kicked hard, petulantly, against her belly. 'Sorry,' she said, and sat still.

She was afraid; a low, slow undercurrent of fear was like an accompaniment to her days, noticed only intermittently, like the hum of a generator. She felt trapped, for there was nothing now that she could do to avoid what was to come. She was committed to the birth as firmly as was the baby; and it was something she was going to have to do alone. She did not tell Peter of the fear, because she could not share any part of the experience with him, and the fear was part of it. It was like being walled up alive, being unable to tell him, and she noticed now how much she shared with him – noticed by sheer contrast. She was going to have to do it without any help from him, her first independent act.

They came to fetch her into the kitchen for tea. 'Sitting here in the dark!' Sylvia exclaimed kindly. 'Can you manage to get up? Shall I help you? We've got crumpets, all hot and buttery, and then Peter's going to light the fire.'

She let Sylvia mother her, because it apparently pleased Sylvia to be motherly, but she didn't need it. She felt alone and isolated, and her fear, because it could not be shared with anyone else, could not be appeased by anyone else. Peter looked up at her sharply as she came in slowly on Sylvia's arm, and he seemed a long way away from her, and very strange, as if she had not seen him for years and years.

But the fire was lovely. Peter got it going in record time, and Sylvia helped Julia back gently to her chair beside it, and fetched cushions to wedge between her and the chair-back, and then sat on a cushion on the floor between the two armchairs and gazed at the flames.

'It *is* lovely,' she said contentedly. 'We never had a fire at home, did we Julia? It always seems so special.'

'Oddly enough, that was one of the first things I ever knew about you,' Peter said, smiling, 'that you didn't have a fire at home.' Sylvia looked at Julia and then up at him, turning her head round over her shoulder. Peter looked down at them

180

both, caught suddenly by the similarity of their features, which was hardly ever apparent to him, for the superficial differences of colouring disguised all else. But here in the gloaming, in the flickering light from the fire, Sylvia's narrow, startlingly pretty face, framed in the long dark curls, and Julia's broader fairer face, not pretty at all, but very beautiful, were one, from one stock, and which of those distressingly dull parents had been responsible for them? Perhaps, he thought, toying with the idea, they were both changelings; or perhaps the mother had been very different in her youth.

'I know what we shall have now,' he said. 'A glass of sherry.'

'Oh yes,' said Sylvia.

'Not for me, darling,' Julia said automatically. She had not touched any alcohol since she discovered she was pregnant.

'I think you should,' said Peter. 'It can't possibly hurt the baby now, and it would do you good. You're looking worn out and uncomfortable.'

'Yes, I think you should, Julia. It would make you sleep.'

Julia smiled wearily at them both. As if anyone could sleep when they were this shape! 'All right,' she said.

'And then I'll have to go, I'm afraid,' Sylvia said.

'I'll run you home,' Peter said – surprisingly, for he was very mean about giving lifts generally.

'Oh no,' Sylvia said. 'Really, I'll go on the train. It'd be quicker actually, there's so much traffic about. I can get the Piccadilly line right through.'

'I'll walk you to the station, then,' Peter said, evidently so much relieved that Julia laughed, and he looked at her, surprised.

When Peter came back from the station, Julia was still only halfway down her glass of sherry. He thought she did not really want it, but was drinking it to please him. She didn't look at him as he came in, and he sat down opposite her and waited for her attention, and then finally asked, 'Are you in pain?'

'No,' she said.

'What's wrong then?'

'Just tired,' she said. 'You know how it is.'

Did he know? He was as experienced in pregnancy as a

man could be, but he knew little about it, because he had always deliberately cut himself off from his pregnant wives. He remembered that Joyce had gone through all the textbook stages of nausea, dizziness, fads and fancies, backache, cramp, irritability, but he remembered them only as facts. He had dissociated himself so firmly from any suffering on her part that she might have come by Michael and James by spontaneous cell division. And Julia, too, had gone through the same miseries, and even through a month in hospital (why, incidentally? The hospital was going through a fashion for not telling the patient anything, and he only knew that Julia had had some kidney trouble; not even how serious it was, though that bed rest business had unnerved him, suggesting as it did that she might slip the child). But Julia had spoken less about her condition, and so he had assumed – happily – that she was less troubled by pregnancy than Joyce had been.

But now he looked at her more closely he could see that she was worn out; she seemed almost at the end of her tether, and suddenly not like a child any more. When she looked at him her eyes seemed to reach back into her head long distances. He felt as if he were seeing her through the wrong end of a telescope. Her distance from him frightened him, and made him angry. Was it for this that he had destroyed his marriage, cast off wife and children, uprooted himself to begin a new and perilous life as a divorcé? Not to be ignored by her, not to be kept at a distance. The least she could do, after all his sacrifice, was take heed of him.

'You're shutting me out!' he exclaimed suddenly. He got out of his chair and on to his knees, getting between the fire and her to drag her attention back from the movement of the flames. *Look at me! Be here, with me; you are my wife, I married you, you must not be gone from me in this way.* He wanted to take both her hands, but seizing the left he saw the glass of sherry still held in the right – the sherry she drank to humour him. He grabbed the hand anyway; the sherry spilt a little and she looked at him in mild surprise.

'Put it down,' he said, and when she did not immediately move to obey him, he took the glass away and put it down on the hearth so roughly that it broke.

182

'Don't,' she exclaimed sharply, as if the sound or the movement hurt her, and she made an automatic gesture towards the broken pieces, but he restrained her with a little shake, and then lifted her hand to his mouth and licked off the spilt wine. She struggled to free herself, and he held her more tightly until he knew he was hurting her wrists. He wanted to hurt her – not badly, but enough to make her attend him. He met her eyes, and saw her expression change, and she stopped struggling and he felt her fingers uncurl.

Slowly, very hesitantly, he released his grip on her wrists, and as he moved his hands away, hers opened like flowers and reached forward for his face, so slowly that when the tips of her fingers finally touched his skin he shuddered. Her hands curled onwards, closing round his face so that it was cupped. He shut his eyes and his nostrils arched, dragging in breath as though he had been running, while the hands closed inexorably. Her great weight moved forward too, and he felt her pull herself out of the chair and kneel down in front of him so that she was on his level, still holding his head in a grip as firm, though not as fierce, as his had been.

He could not open his eyes. He was in the clutch of an unreasoning fear, panic fear perhaps, and he breathed through clenched teeth and felt the warmth of her breath as she leaned closer to him. He did not know what she was going to do. Her mouth touched his, very lightly, and with the point of a stiff tongue she began to prize apart his lips and teeth, kissing him as though he were a girl, and she the man. He yielded to her inch by inch, letting his lips part and feeling her tongue penetrate, feeling it hot and obtrusive in the wet hollow of his mouth. He breathed around her as best he could, unable to move, but writhing in every nerve end, as if he were impaled, like some small animal on a spear, on the point of her tongue.

The desire to yield forced its way uppermost in him, and now he was opening under her mouth, snatching breaths, and not noticing her hands moving from his face to his neck, closing tighter, beginning to press down and forward. He put his hands up to her body to steady his balance, and at last opened his eyes as her mouth was withdrawn suddenly from his, and the hands tightened convulsively.

The fear that had dissipated surged up again. Forgetting that he was twice as strong as her, that she was weak and vulnerable in her pregnancy; seeing only her moveless face too close to his and feeling the air being cut off from his lungs. Blackness began to rush before his eyes, and he lifted his hands and made a small sound of protest.

She let him go, so suddenly that he almost fell, and sat back on her heels, hanging her head as if exhausted. He rubbed his neck vaguely, his eyes fixed on her. 'It would be so easy, so easy,' she muttered, and then gave a little moan, like a child about to cry. 'One day, one day, one day I will.'

'Why? Why should you want to kill me?' he asked. It came out as a croak.

She looked up at him fiercely. 'Because – you – oh! How can I explain? Because I am less me than you, because sometimes I can't bear your existence outside of me, because the more you are, the less I am myself, because I am – a stump!'

The word sounded so odd, even despite the tone of her voice, that he laughed. She gave him a bitter look, and then put her hands up and felt her face, as if she wanted to make sure that she was the same.

'What's the matter?' he asked.

'I am afraid,' she said. She saw he did not understand, and said, 'Give me your hands – quick!'

He held them out, and she snatched them and laid them against her great belly, and he felt the long struggling ripple under her taut skin of the child moving.

'There,' she said, 'you feel that. No! Keep your hands there. Feel it. Something alive inside me. Feel it. You did that to me. You trapped that thing inside me. Know it. You must know it and feel it and suffer it with me. That is you and me in there, something wriggling that we made, both of us, it's inside both of us and it wants to get out. You have it inside you. Feel my fear. It wants to get out.'

Her eyes strained into his as she held his hands on her, and he felt his stomach turn over coldly. The baby moved again, and then kicked, and it was like a drum skin being struck.

'You say I am shutting you out?' she said fiercely. 'You shut yourself out, but now I don't let you. Can you feel the way I am feeling? Are you afraid?' He opened his mouth to speak, and she shook him. 'Be me.'

She let him go at last, and he put his arms round her shoulders and held himself against her wordlessly, cheek to cheek, and the child kicked against his stomach as though her flesh were not between him and his son.

The bus did not stop right against the pavement, and she had to step down from the platform into the road, a step slightly longer than she had expected. It jolted her, and she felt something jar inside her as if dislodged; she stood still for a moment in the road, waiting to see if anything were going to happen.

'You all right love?' the conductress asked behind her.

'Oh, yes, I'm all right, thanks,' she said, and stepped up on to the pavement and began to walk the last few hundred yards home. She walked carefully, as though her bulging body was a sack of eggs. It was hard to climb the stairs, though easier than going down them – easier to balance. When she reached the top she went into the kitchen and sat down on a hard chair to rest for a moment before putting the kettle on.

When Peter came home at four o'clock she had gone to bed. The backache to which she was long accustomed had changed into a pain by such imperceptible degrees that she had only just begun to acknowledge that it was a pain. He found her lying on the far side of the bed, on her side, with the space between her back and the wall stuffed with cushions, and another under the hump of the child to support it.

'What is it?' he asked anxiously. She held out a hand to him and he took it and stroked it, sitting on the edge of the bed beside her.

'I have a pain,' she said.

'Where, darling? Are you in labour?'

'I don't know. I don't think so,' she said. 'It's a pain in my back, a continuous pain, like a toothache, not spasms or contractions.'

'It doesn't sound like labour,' he said doubtfully. 'Shall I call the doctor?'

'No,' she said. 'No, don't do that. It isn't too bad. Just a backache. It'll go away in a while.'

185

'Can I get you anything? An aspirin?'

'Yes, I'll take an aspirin,' she said, and the eagerness of her voice gave her away. He brought her aspirin and tea, offered her food, but she said she couldn't eat. 'You'd better get on with your practice,' she said. 'It'll be better now I've taken that pill. I'll be better soon.'

But she wasn't. The night seemed endless for, though she kept very still and made no sound, he knew she wasn't asleep, and he dozed fitfully, waking to the knowledge of her pain, and longing for daybreak as only those in pain can long. When it began to grow light he got up and made tea and brought her some, with some more aspirin. He offered again to call the doctor, but she refused him. It was only a backache, she said, you couldn't call in the doctor for a backache.

'Well, I'm not going in today. I'll call them and say you're ill. I'm going to stay with you.' She neither agreed nor disagreed, but he thought she was glad. The morning dragged on. She lay still on the bed, on her side, with one leg drawn up to support her belly. She would not read, and she neither spoke nor moved, as if afraid of jogging some hideous wound. Her eyes followed him as he moved around; the delicate skin round them looked bruised, and her face was drawn.

At lunchtime his patience ended. 'I'm going to take you into the hospital,' he said. 'You can't go on like this hour after hour.'

She said nothing, but she closed her eyes as if squeezing back tears of relief.

'Can you get dressed and get in the car, or shall I call an ambulance?'

'I'll get up,' she said.

Halfway to the hospital she said, 'I feel sick.'

He speeded up. 'You've nothing to be sick with,' he said. 'You haven't eaten all day. Perhaps that's why you feel sick. What did you eat yesterday?'

'I don't remember,' she said. He decided that meant she had eaten nothing, and was about to push the matter when he caught sight of her face in the mirror and closed his mouth again, inching his foot further down on the accelerator.

186

In the clinic he told the attending sister about the pain, while Julia drooped beside him, supported by his arm.

'When is she due?' the sister asked. She looked as if she had a dozen false alarms a day to deal with and was prepared to deal firmly with time-wasters.

'Next week. Next Wednesday,' Peter told her. Julia's hand closed over his momentarily and he felt her pain sharpen.

'How frequently do the pains come?' the sister asked her.

'One pain – all the time. Continuously.'

'And you've had that same pain since yesterday?' the sister asked incredulously.

Julia turned agonised eyes to Peter and, for once clairvoyant, he said, 'She's going to be sick. A basin—'

The sister moved to that command, scooting across the room and snatching up a chrome instrument bowl from the admission desk. Julia's hands went out for it, and she vomited into it violently, but brought up nothing but a little liquid. Peter held her body firmly while she heaved, vomiting dry until the fit had passed.

'I'll get a doctor to examine her,' the sister said. 'Take her into the cubicle there and get her on the couch.' And she moved away quickly, taking the bowl with her.

'Convinced at last,' Peter said lightly. 'Come on then, darling, up on the couch.'

He was sent outside into the waiting room while the doctor made his examination, and he heard Julia groan once, and another time heard her vomiting, dry retches ending in a cough – she had nothing more to bring up. At last the doctor came out, looked around for him, and gave him a professional kind of smile.

'Yes, Mr Kane, your wife's in labour all right.' (*My wife!*) 'When did the pains begin?'

'Some time yesterday. I came home about four, and she was in pain then.'

'I see. That's what she said. Well, we'll get her up into the labour ward in a few minutes. You can go in and speak to her until the chair arrives.'

Julia was lying on her back, but she turned over to her side as he came in. She looked different; still in pain, but no longer

187

afraid; more relaxed; and at the same moment he realised it was because she had given up the responsibility for herself, yielded herself into other hands. He felt himself put back at a distance from her. Now the hospital would take her body and do what they liked with it, and she would submit, and from then on he would be an intruder, a barely tolerated outsider.

As she submitted to them, she thrust him away. Bear my pain, she had said to him; he would say to her, bear my loneliness. He wanted to make contact with her, real intimate contact, so that she would stay with him, whatever they did with her body – yet what right had he to take away the relief she was feeling now? What right to intensify her suffering for his own comfort? Perhaps that's what she meant by 'bear my pain' – be lonely so that I may be safe; stay awake so that I can sleep in safety. He took her hand and smiled, comfortingly, undemandingly, and she smiled back with relief, and sighed, and closed her eyes.

In a little while the chair was brought and they helped her into it. She reached for his hand again, anxiously, and he squeezed hers and smiled again, the same sort of smile, and said, 'See you later!'

He saw her mouth change shape, and her face sag, ugly with relief, letting go at last to the pain and weariness. The porter wheeled her away and through the swing doors at the end, and as the doors slapped shut behind them, leaving Peter alone in the waiting room, he felt the full weight of solitude for the first time in his life, the loneliness of responsibility which was his payment, as the loneliness of pain was hers.

He went home, and did what few things there had to be done, and then, restless, looked around the flat with aversion. He could not be still, and prowled around from room to room, afraid to go out, as he wanted to, in case the phone should ring. The thought of Julia was with him constantly but she was no longer Julia to him; not even *my wife*; she was the part of them that was suffering, and her pain was his. Drawn outside himself for the first time, he was more than himself; and being so much more than himself, there was more of everything: more awareness, more feeling, more pain. He felt as though he had been thinking all his life with gloves on, and had at last taken them off. He was hypersensitive to everything as if there were nothing between his nerve endings and the outer air.

He telephoned. The girl on the switchboard began to recognise his voice. No, there was no change. No, he could not see her. No, there was no point in his coming in. No, there was no cause for alarm.

It was an effort to prise each scrap out of them. They didn't want to tell him anything, but as night came and nothing had happened they began, reluctantly, to let shreds go to his importunate tugging. There were complications. The baby was in the wrong position. No, there was no immediate danger. No, he could not see her.

He sat in a chair by the telephone, for they had promised to call him the moment anything happened. He dozed off and woke every time as his head rolled over and he jerked himself upright. It was very cold. He fetched a blanket from the bed and a chair from the kitchen, put his feet up on its seat, and wrapped the blanket round him. Both Joyce's children had been born during the day, while he was at work, by some esoteric female process that he did not associate with childbirth. She had gone through pregnancy all right, but in the end he had gone off to work in a normal way and come home at night a father. All very orderly and civilised.

He woke at dawn, stiff and cold, eyed the telephone with disfavour, and hobbled into the kitchen to make tea and toast before telephoning. The real, vivid image of Julia had retreated in his brain, and he could not draw it up with any freshness, though there was still the same gnawing worry to reassure him that he had not lost the ground he had gained. Having finished the tea and toast, he went back to the telephone and made his call. Reluctantly they admitted that there was a further complication: it was a dry birth. He slammed the phone down and headed for the door, the pain beginning again, and sharper now as he read between the lines. He had to be there.

They wouldn't let him see her, but they answered his questions, albeit unwillingly, asserting once again that there was no immediate danger, from which he now inferred that

189

danger was not far off. If the worst came to the worst, they would do a Caesarean, but they wanted to avoid that if possible, they said, which was why they were leaving it to the last possible minute. The main trouble was that she was very debilitated, as was natural after such a long labour, and without nourishment. They had her on a drip feed now.

'Why can't I see her?' he asked again.

'It would do her no good, and it would only upset you,' was the answer.

Did she look so dreadful then? A new thought struck him. 'Do you mean she wouldn't recognise me?'

The young houseman looked impatient, as if he wanted tell him just what he meant, and then he said shortly, 'It always looks worse than it is. We'll keep you informed.' And he swung on his heel and went away, swinging his stethoscope in an irritable way.

Peter sat down again and put his head in his hands. Did he want to know the worst? One is always tempted to think so, but what if the worst turns out to be worse than the worst one could think of? Maybe that's what the doctor meant. Sometimes a thing can be wounded so badly that it cannot live, though no vital part is destroyed. They said that the pain of childbirth is forgotten as soon as it is over. If she forgot it, and he never knew it, they would be as one in this thing. But if he saw it and could not forget it, as she did, he would be held apart from her for ever by that memory. Or was that merely a rationalisation of his cowardice?

Well, if it was, it needed to be admitted. I don't want to see her suffering. Let this be my contribution, the agony of helplessness, the agony of *not* bearing the pain. I would suffer for her if I could, and then she would feel the pain of being whole while I was torn apart. If she should die, mine would be the worst part. If she should die? The new agony seized him and drowned the old one briefly until he shook it away. She won't die. She can't die. We can't die, she and I.

A nurse, new on duty, approached him with a friendly enquiring smile.

'Mr Kane? They've just rung through to say that they've taken your wife up to the delivery room.'

'Does that mean . . . ?' he began, making to stand.

'It shouldn't be long now,' she said, smiling encouragingly. She did not know the saga, and was touched that he should look so drawn and worried over his wife. They were mostly nervous over their first child, but this one looked as though he was really suffering. 'We'll let you know as soon as there's any news.' She pressed her hand on his shoulder and he sat again, obediently. She was very young. 'Is this your first?' she asked. He looked up at her as if he had just noticed her presence. Her face was clean and plain as if she had just put it on fresh that morning.

'It's *our* first,' he said, and, not knowing what he meant by that, she was touched again.

'Don't you worry,' she said, 'it'll all be over soon.'

And in the setting of the long wait, it did seem soon, it seemed like only five minutes before the nurse was back again, beaming at him with the assurance of one who never had any doubt of the outcome.

'It's a boy, Mr Kane. They're both all right.'

The news did not make an immediate impression, for he had waited too long for it. It struck him as odd that she should have said 'they're both all right' instead of the usual formula of 'they're both fine'. How much of a struggle had there been, then?

He asked, automatically, 'Can I see her?' expecting, out of habit, to be refused, but she said, 'Yes, in a little while. They're just washing baby and making him look pretty, and then you can go up and see them both for a minute.'

'Why only a minute?' his anxiety asked her.

'Well, they will have given her a sedative, and she'll be going off to sleep. But you can see her for a minute. Someone will come and fetch you.'

She went away, and Peter stood up again and walked about the room to restore his circulation. The blood seemed to be flowing round his brain again, too, after long stagnation. 'It's a boy, Mr Kane', the time-honoured words. They had a boy. That formless lump on the front of Julia, like a badly-packed haversack, was a boy after all. Julia had protested girl all along, but she had not really believed it. They were all right, she was all right. He walked rapidly round the room impatient for the guide to fetch him.

An older nurse this time, comfortable and Irish, came in and said, 'If you'd like to come this way, now, sir, you can come and see your wife.' He smiled, thinking always *your wife*; like fetching a dog from kennels, *your dog*; never the name. They went up in the lift to the third floor, and the nurse made cosy conversation to which Peter did not attend. He felt as if the top of his head might blow off with excitement and impatience.

The post-natal wards were divided into rooms containing four beds each, so he was spared the horrors of an open ward, though he did pass several women, huge in dressing gowns as if they were still pregnant, hobbling slowly down the long passage, and he winced in sympathy. Like being saddle-sore, only a million times worse, he supposed.

'Your wife's in the end room, now,' the nurse said, 'on her own just at the moment. You can have a few minutes with her.'

It was tea time, and ward maids were pushing trolleys along and carrying trays into rooms with cheerful greetings. The nurse opened the door of the end room and held it for him to go in, and closed it behind him.

Julia lay on her back in the bed, looking so flattened, so utterly steamrollered that she barely made a shape under the white coverlet. A nurse stood by the bed taking her pulse. A white bundle was resting in the hollow of her shoulder, and as he came in Julia turned her face against it and looked at him across it.

'Hello,' he said, and it came out as a whisper. He had never seen anyone look so utterly exhausted. She did not smile or speak. Her hands rested on the flatness outside the covers. She looked as though she would never move again.

There was a chair beside the bed, and he crossed to it and pulled it out and sat down, staring at her, at her eyes which looked black without light, empty black. He picked up the hand that the nurse was not using, and held it. It felt warm and limp, like a dead pheasant, and did not return his pressure.

'She's been given a sedative,' the nurse volunteered. 'She

192

needs sleep now more than anything, so we'll have to ask you to leave in a minute. Have you seen the baby?'

He made no reply, and the nurse replaced the limp hand on the cover and picked up the white bundle and walked round the bed to him, stooped over him and plucked back the edge of the shawl to show him the baby's face.

It hit him in the pit of the stomach to see the baby for the first time. What had been unknown, a mere inconvenience in the bed between him and Julia, was now a person, a separate, living, individual. The three of them. Someone you had lived with for nine months and did not recognise, someone who would be with you for the rest of your lives, who could not now be undone, who would be alive as surely and individually as you were alive. There could no longer be, there could never again be, just the two of them: birth was as irrevocable as death.

He turned the white wool back from the small crumpled face. The baby slept fast, sealed in like a hermit crab, not to be woken after the long ordeal of birth. He had forgotten how tiny new babies were. It hardly seemed possible that anything could be so small and live.

'He's a fine boy,' the nurse said, as if hearing his thoughts; or maybe she was merely disconcerted by the long silence. Peter would have touched the baby's hand for the joy of making contact, the first starfish touch that makes the heart move, but he was wrapped up securely with his hands hidden inside the shawl. He. Not just the baby, but he. His son. The love yearned in him for his son.

'I'm taking him away now to sleep in his cot in the nursery,' the nurse said, more for Julia's sake than Peter's. 'And you must sleep too, Mrs Kane. You'd better say goodbye for the present,' she added to Peter, and withdrew leaving them alone for a moment.

He would have thought she was asleep already, except that her eyes were open – wide open in fact, the lids rolled so far back they might have been drawn up and pinned like roller blinds.

'How are you feeling?' he asked softly. The dead black eyes stared motionlessly from far back in the head. There was no glint of light from them. Surely she *was* sleeping, sleeping with her eyes open? Not dead? A panicky thought, thrust away. Of course not dead. He would know if she were dead. She was exhausted. He smiled at her and pressed her hand, and then at last he saw her lips move.

'What?' He leaned over her to hear, for she only whispered. Her lips looked dry and cracked. She licked them feebly and tried again.

'We made it,' she said. He saw now that she did look at him. Relief and love and a strange kind of sorrow came over him in waves of weakness, and he laid his head down by hers, and kissed her cheek, and laid his cheek against it.

'Oh Julia, I do love you,' he said. Julia's eyes closed, and her hand grew a shape in his. The Irish nurse came back in.

'Come along, now, Mr Kane. We'll have to let your wife get some sleep,' she said gently. 'You can come back and see her again tomorrow.' He stood up reluctantly. 'There, look, she's already asleep.'

Peter let go of her hand, and it straightened slowly, like the dent coming out of a cushion.

Ten

The baby's eyes were neither black nor blue – the colour of a rook. His hair was thick and black, with a sheen of silver hairs over the top, so that the effect was of a piece of Carolean silver-plated furniture from which the plating was wearing off. Julia had always expected the baby to be pink and gold and smiling in the fairy story tradition, and this dark stranger was something of a shock to her. He was the unknown quantity, and she treated him with a polite deference as if he might turn and savage her, until it began to dawn on her that this was *her son*, with all the emotive associations of those two words, and then the excitement of the thought of beginning to know him drove out every other feeling.

Peter was at home with him from the start. Fatherhood was not new to him, of course, and he knew how a baby was to be picked up and held, and how it functioned, and even, roughly, what it was going to do, and while Julia was still nervous about touching him at all, Peter was handling him with calm assurance. Julia was not sure how she felt about this reminder that her firstborn was only Peter's thirdborn, and had his delight in the child not been so patent she might even have been jealous.

She stayed in hospital for two weeks after the birth, during which time Sylvia was often at the mews flat – not so much from any necessity of looking after Peter, for indeed he was hardly ever there, spending every spare minute at the hospital with his newly discovered wife and child, but so that the place would be habitable when Julia finally came home. Julia wondered a little at Sylvia's volunteering for dull household duties like dusting and washing-up, but Peter told her he thought it had the attraction of novelty, 'like playing house'.

Though she was over twenty-one now, Sylvia still lived at home, not having quite plucked up the courage? – impetus? – to strike out on her own. Life in Milton Street had always been more comfortable for her, as her mother's favourite.

Peter spent his days in a frenzy of activity, cramming the space between his normal commitments with auditions and interviews, besides visiting Julia. For some time he had been intending to 'go solo'. He had played solo parts with his own orchestra on several occasions, and had had some outside work with a string quartet, but now his effusion of joy drove him forward with the energy necessary to all would-be soloists, and he pursued engagements and harassed agents tirelessly.

He had never been so happy. The top part of his mind bubbled continuously with the thought of *the three of them*, while underneath, layered with his present occupations and his driving ambition, was all the happiness of the growing relationship. The intense but intangible notion he had had of Julia had dispelled like mist. She was solid and real – vividly, hypersensitively real to him now. He was beginning to understand his various needs of her. He had married her in the first place out of a mixture of perversity, affection, pity, and lust, and it seemed now that his impulse had been more right than he had intended.

Julia, better than anyone, knew how little he had intended when he had left Joyce and come to her. She had observed him poised, so to speak, like a runner, ready to take off at any moment, drawing his security from the fact that nothing bound him. And she felt that it was not the marriage service which had changed that, nor even, really, her pregnancy. The change had happened inside Peter, and what delicate trigger had set it off she did not know. But now he came every day to visit her, telling her about his pursuit of bookings and his successes, his plans for their future, what they would do when she came home, how they would bring up the child. He had taken off his spiked shoes, and had ranged himself at her side, ready to keep and defend her like any normal husband.

'We'll do everything properly,' he said to her, holding her hand as she lay propped on the pillows. 'We'll take him to the park on sunny days, and take him to see his grandparents on

196

Sundays, and bore our friends with accounts of his teething progress – we'll even start a photograph album.'

Julia laughed. 'I'll bet you're already thinking of teaching him to play cricket.'

'As soon as he can hold a bat,' Peter assured her solemnly. 'Laugh again like that! You've no idea how beautiful you are when you laugh.'

'Tell me about the music room – what you've done to it.'

'Nursery,' he corrected her. 'Nothing more since yesterday, but Sylvia and I are going to paint the nursing chair and the chest of drawers tonight if I remember to get the paint on my way home.'

'How is it I always miss the decorating and moving in?' Julia sighed. 'It's nice to come back and find everything ready, but—'

'That's how things should be for you,' he interrupted. 'And will be. No more troubles from now on, my darling. I'm going to be famous, and rich—'

'In that order?'

'And you're going to have nothing to do but bring up our children and do your painting and love me.'

'You call that nothing? I call that everything.'

They called the baby Nathan. There was no problem over the choice – Julia said she had a fancy for the name, and Peter agreed that it went well with Kane, and so the matter was settled. Just plain Nathan – no middle name, to Julia's unspoken relief, for she had learnt of the older boys, during her time as their sitter, that their names were Michael Swinburne Markham (Joyce's maiden name) and James Alexander Ferguson (Peter's mother's maiden name), both of which seemed to her pretty hard to live with.

They named the baby Nathan, and registered him, but he was hardly ever called by his name, for they referred to him more often than not as The Boy, and thence merely Boy. They did not have him christened, and it was this circumstance that caused the final breach between them and Peter's parents which was never properly healed. Even for people with little use for the church, christening was still very much the rule, departure from which was socially frowned upon. And Peter's parents were Roman Catholics. His mother was a Glaswegian Catholic of very firm persuasion. Colonel Kane, by virtue of his mother, who was a Howard, was a member of one of the oldest High Catholic families in England, which had stood firm by the faith even during the Tudor persecutions, so it was a matter of great import on several fronts. Peter and Rowland had been brought up as Roman Catholics, though in those post-Vatican II days they had felt almost entitled to take their hereditary faith lightly. You couldn't argue with the Holy Father, could you?

But the senior Kanes had been horribly shocked when Peter had divorced his wife, shocked again when he married Julia; and they were especially hurt to reflect that he had brought her to visit them while she was secretly his mistress, feeling that he had tricked them into helping to deceive Joyce. Peter had not taken Julia to visit them since that first time, and had not tested their resolve since his marriage to Julia by suggesting that they should receive her. However, when the news had reached them of Julia's pregnancy, there had been some indications of a softening of their attitude. Peter's father, seeing everything from a man's point of view, was more inclined to accept a fait accompli and make the best of things; Mrs Kane felt that the baby at least was blameless of its parents' faults and should be given as good a start in life as its unfortunate conception would allow.

But Peter's refusal to have the child baptised broke the camel's back, and Mrs Kane determined never to receive Peter's mistress – so she thought of Julia, for since, in her eyes, there was no such thing as divorce, Peter was still married to Joyce and could not therefore be married to Julia – into her house. The Colonel, after a long telephone call during which he tried every persuasion he knew to change Peter's mind, lost his temper and said something unforgivable.

Julia had been brought up without benefit of religion – though she had been christened in the usual way in the Church of England – and to her religion was a matter of complete indifference. Not being able to see any importance in the matter, she was inclined, for the sake of peace and to save a breach with Peter's family, to have Nathan christened and be done with it, and she was rather startled at Peter's vehemence in refusing to consider it.

'But Peter,' she said at the end of a tirade, 'what harm can it do? Just to go through the ceremony, to keep your parents happy? It can't hurt the boy.'

'Look, Julia,' Peter said patiently, 'I know I haven't been much of a success up to now in being a father, but I'm determined that Boy will be given the very best we can do for him, the best start in life we can manage – and that includes not being handicapped by the burden of Catholicism, as I was.'

'I can't see that it's so much of a burden to you,' Julia said. 'You seem to do pretty much as you like.'

'But at a cost. I have to fight for my freedom all the time.'

'Freedom from the church? I don't believe it. There are more important things in life than religion.'

'That's exactly what a Catholic can't think, don't you see? I don't want my boy ruled by fear and superstition. I want him to do things because he believes them intellectually, because he's worked them out himself from experience – his own, and other people's. I want his mind to be free. I want there to be nothing he can't think, if he wants to.'

'Yes, I see,' Julia said. 'I agree with you about freedom. I'm not suggesting for a moment that we bring him up as a Catholic. All I say is, what harm is there in humouring your people and just having him baptised?'

Peter regarded her for a moment as if despairing of ever making her understand, and at last he said, 'That would be immoral.'

'What?' Julia asked in surprise.

'It would be immoral to put him through the form of service when we did not believe it ourselves.'

Julia turned her head a little to hide a smile, and failed.

'Why are you smiling?' Peter asked.

'You're such a strange mixture of a man,' she said. 'You break every rule in the book, and then baulk at some tiny thing most people wouldn't even notice. You're a peculiar kind of rebel.'

'Rebel?'

'Rebel Catholic.'

'But I'm not, don't you see? That's the whole point. You talk of my breaking the rules, but they aren't my rules. To them, my living with you is a sin, it's immoral – but not to me. To me, the immoral thing was living with Joyce, because it was all *wrong*. Nothing I can do with you can possibly be immoral – unless it were something to hurt you – because I love you.'

'A convenient philosophy,' she said, but she smiled as she said it.

'You know that I love you, don't you?' he asked, taking her hand.

'Yes,' she said, all her pleasure in it on her face.

'Do you ever wonder why?' he asked, curious.

'Of course. Anyone who was ever in love wondered that at one time or another.'

'And you never ask me?' She shook her head. 'Why?'

'Perhaps because I don't think you could tell me. Perhaps because I don't really want to hear the answer, in case it's the wrong one.' She paused. 'Perhaps because I know.'

'What is it, then?'

'What you just said about being with Joyce being all wrong. I think you love me because it's all right. No – don't tell me if I'm right or wrong. I'd sooner not know. You see,' she added honestly, 'that was the real answer.'

'Now it's my turn to ask you why you love me – if you do – and for you to sum it all up in one neat, utterly memorable phrase, the way they do in books. Like one of those competitions where you have to complete the caption in not more than twelve words – "I love you because dot dot dot". But you've never even said that you do love me. You've never said it, did you know that?'

'Do I need to say it?'

'That's pure evasion.'

'So's that.'

'All right – yes, perhaps you do. Perhaps everyone needs to hear it now and then. More than now and then – often. Why *do* you love me?'

'I don't know. I don't know. I don't know. I used to ask myself that. Now I don't any more. Birds don't sing because they're happy, or for any other reason – it's just a thing birds do. There's no reason for me either. I love you, that's all.'

'You said it.'

'Not very graciously. Shall I do it again?' She moved closer to him, looking up at him solemnly so that for a moment he had a fleeting vision of her at fifteen with long plaits. 'I love you, Peter. With every part of me that knows anything, with every breath I breathe. Not in any way I can distinguish, but with my whole life. I can't tell loving you from being alive. It seems to me the same thing.'

He didn't know how to bear it. He drew her against him and rested his cheek on her hair, and closed his eyes against tears, and said nothing, not knowing anything that would say more than that, except, eventually, 'Be near me.'

'I am.'

July 1959

Julia parked the car in the Festival Hall lot, got out and locked the door, and went back to let Boy out. He was so obviously glad to be let loose again that she felt rather sad to have to put his reins on, but with so much traffic around she did not trust herself to be quick enough to grab him if he ran in the wrong direction.

'Come, Boy, we're going to see Daddy,' she said. She slipped the car keys into the pocket of her jeans, pulled on her reefer, and allowed herself to be towed forward by her son. 'It's a bit like taking a dog for a walk,' she said conversationally, but Boy ignored her, concentrating on his legs. He had discovered that, when walking in his reins, if he leaned as far forward as he could his mother took his weight, which left him free to move his legs twice as fast. He had not yet learnt that it didn't get him anywhere.

'Hello, Mrs Kane,' the gate attendant said affably. 'Hello, young feller. Where are you off to in such a hurry?'

'Go see Daddy,' Nathan told him.

'Going to see your Daddy up on the stage, are you?' the attendant went on in the high-pitched, lunatic voice that most adults reserved for very small children. 'What does your Daddy do then?' He winked at Julia in a conspiratorial way, and she smiled weakly. All the attendants in the hall knew her, and though her small local fame pleased her in some ways, she also at times found it wearing.

'My Daddy plays the fiddle,' Nathan said, fiercely, as if someone had denied it.

'And I bet you think he's the best fiddler in the world,' the attendant smiled indulgently.

'He is the best in the world,' Julia said firmly. 'Come, Boy. We must be off. Cheerio.'

'Cheerio. Bye bye, son. Likes music, does he?' But Julia was not to be beguiled into conversation, and pretending not to hear she bolted for the lift. Rehearsal had just broken, and when she reached the orchestra level she walked into such a mêlée that she snatched Boy up, despite his protests and his huge weight, and carried him on her hip, threading her way between the musicians. This was the orchestra Peter had led, and with which he was now playing as a soloist, so most of the men knew her and greeted her cheerfully with an intimacy that had nothing to do with her being Peter Kane's wife.

'Hello, Julia. Come to hear us play?' This was Tom Streeter, still principal under the new leader. 'You aren't a Mahler fan, are you?'

'Certainly not,' she said, laughing. 'Who is? Seen Peter?'

'Peter Who? Dash it, I thought you'd come to see me. Don't say you're still a fan of his. Listen,' catching her free hand and drawing it under his arm confidentially, 'never mind old Peter. Come on with me and let me buy you a coffee, and we'll talk about something more interesting.'

'Don't you do it, Julia,' said another old friend *en passant*. 'He says that to all the girls.'

'Go see Daddy,' Nathan said firmly at that moment, not seeing the point of all this delay.

'The voice of conscience,' Tom groaned, releasing her hand. 'Peter's out front talking to Boult – or was when I came off. Are you coming in later?' he asked, meaning into the coffee room.

'No, I'm afraid not. I'm strictly the chauffeur today – I've got to drive him to another session.'

'Shame. Well, come and see us soon.'

'Yes, I will,' she lied. 'All right, darling, we're going now.'

She ran Peter to earth in his dressing room, and met his agent, John Goldsmith, coming out of the door as she went in.

'Hello, Julia. We've got some good news for you,' he said.

'No, I'll let him tell you. I've got to dash now. See you on Tuesday!'

'Yes, all right,' she called after his receding back. She put Nathan down gratefully and followed him into the dressing room, saying, 'What was all that about?'

'There's my boy! Oof! What do you feed this child on – concrete? He gets heavier by the minute.'

'Particularly when you're carrying him,' Julia agreed. 'Hello darling,' she prompted.

'Hello darling,' Peter said obediently, kissing her. 'Had a good morning?'

'Pretty good,' she said, sitting on the edge of a table and watching Peter and Nathan with quiet pleasure. 'I got a good bit done. I've nearly finished Lady Peacock now. Boy did a remarkable painting too, didn't you, Boy? He says it's an ashtray, but I rather think he means asteroid.'

'Does he?' Peter said, startled. 'Do you? What did you paint today, Boy?'

'Ashtray.' At least, that's what it sounded like.

'Where would he get that from? I mean, how would he know what an asteroid is?' Peter asked her.

'From us, talking. Don't you remember, I asked you what an asteroid was – when I was listening to *Journey into Space*?'

'Would he pick it up from that?' Peter asked, doubtful, yet willing to be convinced that his son was as intelligent as that supposed.

'Oh yes – no, Boy, don't eat that! Peter, he's got your rosin, darling, take it away from him. Yes, I think he did, because when I asked him about his ashtray, he said it flew in the air. He is very quick on the uptake, you know.'

'Of course,' Peter smirked. '*My* son would be.' He gently

removed the rosin from Boy's fingers, grimacing at the stickiness, and steered him back towards his mother. She looked pretty today, he thought. That casual style of dress suited her, and with her hair in two bunches behind her ears she looked hardly old enough to have such a large, stout son. Though, actually, Boy wasn't fat. He was large-boned and tall for his age, but really quite thin for a child. Nothing to worry about in that, however. Better a thin child than a fat child, and he was so full of bounce no one could doubt of his being healthy.

He loved to see Julia with the child, for she had such an easy way with him, a comfortably casual motherhood that Joyce had never managed. Her words about her painting conjured up for him the image of her, as he had seen her a few days ago on his return home, kneeling on the floor with Boy between her knees, holding a piece of paper steady for him while he dabbed multicoloured paints with gay abandon over the surface with his fingers. Julia had been wearing her 'smock' as she called it – it was an old shirt of Peter's – and had paint on her face, presumably from a wilder dab than usual on Boy's part, or maybe from pushing back her hair which was tumbling forward. Both she and the child had been laughing, and he had wondered why Joyce had never romped with her children like that. Julia never worried about dirt and scratches, and hardly at all about housework. She thought having fun was more important than the house being spotless or Boy appearing in white socks and starched knickers.

'What was John sounding so thrilling and mysterious about?' Julia was asking him now. 'He said you had good news. What is it?'

'Oh, that,' Peter said, and failed utterly to look casual.

Julia grinned, reading him accurately. 'It's something big, isn't it? Oh *tell* me, please.'

'You know about the festival in Bath?'

'The music festival? Yes.'

'And you know who was doing the three big concerts?'

'Oistrakh, wasn't it? But—'

'Well, he's had to pull out, and they've asked me to do it instead.'

'*Peter!*'

He nodded, fielding Boy who was heading for his open violin case again, without taking his eyes off Julia.

She stared at him with astonishment and pleasure, and then, disconcertingly, began to laugh. 'You standing in for Oistrakh!'

'I don't see why that's funny,' he said indignantly.

'Oh no, I'm not laughing at you. I'm thrilled to bits about it. It's just that I've never – I never shall get used to the idea of your being famous. To me you are always so very much the man I live with, my Peter.'

'Probably a good thing. Save me from getting big-headed. Listen, we'd better get a move on if we're to get to Holborn in time. Did you have lunch before you came out?'

'Boy did, I didn't. Why?'

'Well, if you'd like to hang around until I've finished, we could go out and have an early bite together.'

'In celebration?'

'Of course.'

'Somewhere swanky?'

'As swanky as possible, bearing in mind it'll have to be somewhere that won't mind Boy.'

'Any really good restaurant won't mind him,' she said with dignity.

'The Cafe Royal?' Peter suggested with a wicked grin.

'Don't tempt me,' she said, and then exclaimed, 'Oh Lord! Boy's eating something.'

'Is he? Oh dear, yes. Come here, son. What have you got in your mouth? Give it to Daddy. Spit it out, Boy.'

His son stood his ground, his face now immobile, and gave him an owly look that was pure Julia. Coaxing had no effect on him – opposition merely made him freeze and his ability to hold out in this defensive position outclassed any hedgehog. In the end Peter was forced to the indignity of prizing Nathan's jaws apart, and the contraband comestible turned out to be a small piece of the Elgar violin concerto torn off the corner of Peter's part.

'That just proves he's musical,' Julia laughed. 'What's the saying about eating, drinking and breathing music?'

'It only proves he's his mother's son,' Peter said, gathering his possessions together. 'As I remember, you told me you used to eat paper too – blotting paper mainly.'

'The things you remember,' Julia marvelled.

Julia had assumed that she and Boy would be going with Peter to Bath, as they accompanied him almost everywhere else. It was a shock to her, therefore, when, a few days before, he looked up from the accumulation of mail he was dealing with and said, 'Oh, by the way – it completely slipped my mind to mention it, but I said Rowland could stop here overnight on Saturday. You won't mind putting him up and cooking him breakfast, will you?'

Julia was standing at her easel by the window, varnishing the finished portrait of Lady Peacock, which she was going to deliver and (she hoped fervently) be paid for at the end of the week, and she was so deep in her thoughts about this and about the implied promise of a further commission from Sir William Peacock if he liked Madam's picture, that she was slow to look up and comprehend what he had said.

'On Saturday?' she repeated, and Peter, seeing her vagueness, hurried on to press home his advantage.

'Yes, just for the night, I think. He has to catch a plane on Sunday morning, and he doesn't think he could make it up in time from Suffolk. You don't mind, do you darling? You like Rowland, and he'll be company for you.' Julia opened her mouth to speak, and he hurried on, 'He's written me a note here, and he says he thinks he's got another commission for you – neighbour of ours back home. Mother of a girl I used to go out with, as a matter of fact—'

'Yes, but Peter,' Julia interrupted, 'I shall be with you in Bath on Saturday. You mean this Saturday?' She considered his expression for a moment, and then said, 'I thought we would be coming with you as usual.'

'Well, I . . .' Peter looked embarrassed. 'I hadn't thought of it. I was rather thinking of doing it on my own, you know – just this once. I thought I'd like to – well, I felt I'd want to be alone.' Strange how a few past tenses have a muting effect on something outrageous. 'It's such a big occasion—'

'Yes, of course it is,' Julia said. 'That's why I thought you'd like us to be there.'

'I'll be so busy,' he said evasively. 'I wouldn't have time to take you round. You'd be bored stuck in a hotel by yourself all the time.'

'Since when did I ever get bored?' Julia asked with justice. 'And I'd like to see Bath – the architecture – the places I've read about in Jane Austen. I could do some sketching. And then, to see you doing your first big public performance . . .'

There was a lot more she could have said, and had she presented him with the simple vanity of wanting to be seen as the wife of the solo artist, it might have moved him; but after looking at him for another moment she said, more puzzled than offended, 'You don't want me to go. Why?'

'Darling,' he began, but she shook her head.

'No, I'm not cross. But do tell me. I just want to know.'

'Well,' he said hesitantly, and then, as if determined to get it over with, said quickly, 'I had thought of going to see the boys on my way back.'

'Oh.'

He always said 'the boys', never 'Joyce', but for her the one always implied the other. She did not see why this plan should stop her coming to Bath for the festival, for she could come straight back by train and he could then go on in the car to Shaftesbury; but a moment's reflection made it plain that Peter must be able to work this out quite as well as she could. If he didn't want her to come to Bath, he didn't want her. She would not do herself the disservice of arguing with him.

She drew herself up slightly and said pleasantly, 'No, of course I don't mind Rowland coming here. He can have the folding bed in the corner of the sitting room. If you'll just clear your things off the table there before you go, I'll get it made up for him. I wouldn't want to move them in case they're in some special order.'

'The order of chaos, that's all,' Peter said. 'But I'll do it anyway.' He wondered whether to say anything more about Bath or Shaftesbury, and decided against it. She would never quarrel with him, or argue with him except as an intellectual exercise (how different from Joyce!), and it certainly made some things easier for him, such as now. But this particular kind of pride troubled him sometimes, made him feel the strength and stature of her separateness from him, when he wanted to feel always only her closeness and dependency.

They spoke no more about it during the evening; in fact they didn't converse at all. Peter, having finished his letters, read a chapter of the book he had been trying on and off to finish for months. He sat in the big wing chair by the fire while Julia sat on the floor in front of him and sketched his joints, neck, and ears in preparation for the (possible) portrait of Sir William. At ten she went in to look at Nathan and then made some Bournvita and brought it in so they could drink it together by the last of the fire.

As she sat or sprawled on the floor, disjointed as a toy, Peter studied her anew, wondering what it was that made her, for him, so different from anyone else. Whenever he had started a new affair, there had been at first a tremendous excitement for him, and the object of his interest had always stimulated him to an almost painful degree for the first few meetings. But there it had always stopped. The excitement had waned, and after it the pleasure, and at the first smell of boredom he had ended things. A familiar, invariable pattern.

But not with Julia. She excited him always, as if every time were the first. The sight of her right now; her bare brown legs stretched across the carpet; her narrow body twisting round so that she could look at him over her shoulder; her face, her exquisite, so very human, extraordinary face! It was as familiar to him as his own, and familiar in the same way, as something so absolutely and utterly his own that he could not conceive of being without it. Had he looked in a mirror and seen her face reflected instead of his he probably would not have noticed for a few seconds. The sight of her right now was exciting him so that he could feel himself begin to tremble.

He put down his cup, holding out his hand to her, and she stood up obediently and took his hand, and he led her into the bedroom, forcing himself to take the time to pull the curtains, switch on the bedside light and close the door before he went back to her. She stood still and let him undress her, watching him steadily from her dark eyes. It was like being watched

208

from the undergrowth by something strange and dangerous. She was utterly familiar to him, but with every movement, every time he touched her, she was also strange to him, more strange than another person could be, as strange as something from another world, an unthought-of species.

Then when she was naked, he had to stand still while she undressed him, and then at last he could draw her to him, lay the whole length of his burning body against hers, go into her, make love to her. He could never get close enough to her; it was like being thirsty and knowing nothing would ever quite quench it. Sometimes when they were making love he would put his face against hers and just breathe into her nostrils, the way horses do; to breathe her breath was some way of getting closer to her. Now as he neared climax the wild thought crossed his mind that he should eat her, or be eaten by her; that would be the final consummation.

But now her hands were on his face, putting him back a little from her, and he could see her little white face, taut with the agony of loving, her eyes now opening, now closing as her body arched under him. He was helpless, no more in control of his movements, gabbling something, he didn't know what, and she said, 'Peter, oh Peter', and he felt it coming, the inevitability of it, like a fugue returning to its home key. She was bringing him home, her movements were bringing them both home, coming home together.

He lay collapsed against her, his face in her neck, and she folded her arms across his back to keep him warm. After a while she said, into his ear, 'Do you know how gypsies marry?'

'No,' he said. 'Tell me.'

'There's a part of the ceremony where the bride and groom both urinate into a bucket, and the elder then picks up the bucket and pours the contents on to the earth, and he says, "As these waters are mixed, and can never be divided, so are these two people one, and can never be put asunder".'

He said nothing, and after a while longer, her breathing told him she was asleep. He slid off her, and she turned, murmuring, in her sleep and put herself into his arms to be held, like a child. She often seemed to know what he was thinking. He kissed her

209

brow and put a strand of hair away from it, and held her as he would have held Boy to send him to sleep.

He loved her, she was everything to him, and that was why he needed to get away for a little while, to rest. He didn't think she felt this – there was a kind of robustness about her emotions. He thought of Byron's poem:

> *For the sword outwears the sheath,*
> *And the soul wears out the breast,*
> *And the heart must pause to breathe,*
> *And love itself take rest.*

Not for Julia. But for him – he could not sustain this pitch of emotion all the time without suffering some depletion. It used up the stuff of him, and he had only so much to give. Greek warriors used to deny themselves the pleasures of Aphrodite Pandemos before battle: great feats of arms precluded other great feats of arms, so to speak. He had his first really important solo coming up – he had to prove himself the equivalent of Oistrakh, and he meant to prove himself superior. And that meant . . .

Exhausted with love he fell asleep, and woke an hour later to remember they had left all the lights burning and the fire untended.

Julia took the painting round to Campden Hill Square, received a cheque and, just as gratifying, her client's cries of pleasure, and came away with some photographs to study and an appointment to go back in a week or two and take some sketches of Sir William for his portrait. Because she had Nathan with her, she went back via Holland Park, enjoying a walk under the trees, and caught a 49 home from High Street Kensington. She and Nathan both loved riding on the top of a bus – even more than riding in taxis.

Peter was in when she got home, already packing up his things for the weekend.

'Oh, let me do that,' she said, seeing his dress shirts hastily bundled in. 'You take my boy into the kitchen and make some tea, and I'll pack your case for you.'

210

'All right,' Peter said, happy with the swap. 'Don't forget my cummerbund, and ties – and shaving tackle.'

'As if I would. Don't panic, darling, I've packed for you hundreds of times.'

'So you have,' he said cheerfully, kissing her.

'D'you know what I thought of coming home,' Julia called out a while later. 'I thought I'd telephone Sylvia at work tomorrow and ask her to come over for the weekend. We could have a cosy time together, and she'd love to meet Rowland.' Peter didn't answer her, and she turned her head over her shoulder and called 'Darling?'

'Yes,' he called back from the kitchen.

'Did you hear what I said?'

'Yes.' Long pause. 'Good idea, why not. She'd be grateful I expect.' Another long pause. 'Hey, did you know this child is going *bald*?'

'What, that patch at the back of his head? Yes, I noticed that. I think it's where he rubs his head on the back rails of his crib. It's really too small for him.'

'More than time he had a proper bed.' The next time Peter spoke it was from right behind her, and she glanced up to see him standing in the doorway, holding Boy in his arms, and Boy eating a finger of bread and butter with his favourite Marmite on it. 'Our son's growing up, eh Julia? Buying the first bed must be some sort of an occasion, like cutting the first tooth, don't you think?' He smiled at her tenderly, and Boy's face too lit up in one of his adoring, adorable smiles as, in a gesture of uncontrollable love, he offered her the chewed end of his Marmite finger, showing his teeth like a row of tiny seed pearls.

Peter left straight after breakfast, and, having installed Boy at the kitchen sink with a large pot of water and the plastic Bournvita mug to play with, she rang up Sylvia's office.

'Could I speak to Miss Jacobs, please?'

'Is that Mrs Kane?' The girl on the switchboard knew Julia's voice tolerably well by now. 'I'm afraid she isn't in today.'

'Not in? Is she off sick?'

'Oh no, nothing like that. She's gone away for the weekend,

and she's taken one day of her holiday now so as to make it a long weekend. She'll be back on Tuesday.'

'Oh. I see. She didn't tell me she was going away,' Julia said.

'Didn't she? Well, I think it was a bit of a last-minute thing actually. She got an invitation from someone and arranged it all in a hurry.'

'Did she say where she was going?'

'I didn't hear. All she said to me was something about she was going to stay with a friend of her brother's, or the brother of a friend, or something like that.'

'She hasn't got a brother, so it must have been—'

'Vice versa – yes. Oh well, she's got nice weather for it.'

'Yes, she has. Perhaps you'd just say I called, when she comes back?'

'Okey-doke. You going away?'

'Not on my income,' Julia laughed.

'Shame. Get that famous husband of yours to take you somewhere.'

'Fat chance. Well, thanks anyway. Cheerio.'

'Bye.'

She put the phone down and went back to Nathan, who had got an empty milk bottle from the draining board and was now with great concentration pouring water into it from the mug.

Later that afternoon Rowland telephoned. 'Look, on Saturday I'm coming down around six-ish, and I want to take you out to dinner – okay?'

'Well, it would be lovely, but—'

'Oh no, no buts. Listen to me, I've arranged a very nice girl I know to babysit with Nathan for the evening, and I'm going to take you out and wine and dine you. All is arranged – all you have to do is to be dressed in your best, ready to leave, by half past six. You see, I've even booked an early table so that you won't have to be back too late. How's that?'

'That's very kind of you, Rowland, but—'

'What's there to "but" about? Will you do me the honour of dining with me, Mrs Kane?

Julia laughed and yielded. 'I shall be delighted, Mr Kane. How funny that sounds, to call you Mr Kane.'

'Not half as funny as for me calling you Mrs Kane. I'll see you tomorrow. Don't have your hair in bunches. None of this bohemian lark for me.'

'I'll do my best to look prosperous,' Julia promised.

Rowland had changed very little since the first time she met him. He was a little more stunningly handsome. His looks had matured with him, and he now looked pretty much like Peter as Julia first remembered him, except that Peter of course had never been so handsome.

'Hello, little sister,' he greeted her at the door. 'No kiss? I'm allowed to kiss my sister, you know.' He was a good three inches taller than Peter and Julia badly misjudged the turning up of her face, so that Rowland had to stoop awkwardly to make contact.

'Come on up,' she said. 'You're early. What time does your friend get here?'

'I told her half past six. She's usually punctual. A very reliable girl. That's why I like her.'

'Girlfriend?'

'That depends what you mean by girlfriend.'

'I often wonder how you managed to escape marrying all this time.'

'I'm too beautiful,' Rowland said, turning an innocent blue gaze on her that she recognised first from Peter and secondly from Nathan. 'No one wants to marry me.'

'What can you mean?'

'Well, every girl I go out with thinks I must have a dozen others on a string, and that makes her jealous, and *that* makes her hate me. So we quarrel, and then she says "I knew you were like that" and stalks off. Self-fulfilling prophecy. It happens all the time. No one understands me.'

'It's easy to see whose brother you are,' Julia said. 'You have a line of patter that's unmistakable.'

Having re-introduced Nathan to his uncle, Julia left them playing together in the sitting room while she went to bathe and change. She took great care with her appearance, finding that she was really looking forward to the evening. She was rather shocked with herself, but all the same she couldn't help feeling that it would be nice to have a night out without Nathan, just this once. She bathed, powdered herself with expensive talc – a Christmas present from Sylvia – and put on her underwear. There is something very luxurious about the feeling of putting on a new pair of nylons. In her slip, she sat down at the dressing table and rubbed cream into her face and, as an afterthought, her neck, and then considered herself in the mirror. She ought to do something to her face, to make it look special, but for the life of her she didn't know what. She had sometimes experimented with makeup, but it simply made her look tarty. She thought it likely to be true that there were some people for whom makeup really did nothing. She certainly looked better without than with it, but sometimes she regretted it.

At least she had a lovely dress – a very plain, sumptuous-looking thing of white knitted silk jersey. A white dress always looks special, and she loved to wear this because it felt so nice. She had just learnt to wear black with white: black patent-leather shoes and handbag, and she finished it off with a black-and-white silk scarf round her neck. Her hair was long again, and she arranged it in a large soft coil on the back of her head and disposed the short wisps at the front into Empire-style curls as best she could. A dab of scent, a quick backwards-on squint to see that her seams were straight, and then she was ready.

'Still too early,' she said as she went back into the sitting room, to find, to her relief, that Rowland had Nathan on his knee and was reading to him – she had feared they might be playing some riotous game that would make him so excited she wouldn't get him to bed. 'Do you want to wash or anything? I'll put Boy to bed.'

'Yes, all right,' Rowland said, delivering up his charge. 'I'll finish that story another time, old chap.'

'Will you come and say goodnight?' Nathan asked him, and, rather flattered, he agreed. Julia picked the child up and took him away, sleepy and smiling, to clean his teeth and tuck him up in bed, where he did not look like being able to stay awake long enough to get the benefit of the promise. Julia kissed him and left him, feeling odd because she would be giving up responsibility for him for an evening.

She felt it did her good. The evening was so pleasant, and it was as stimulating to converse with a fresh mind as it was flattering to have such a very handsome and attentive partner. The meal itself was not such a novelty to her, for she and Peter ate out fairly often, but it was certainly something new to be eating out as a (temporarily) single person. She found her companion amusing, enough like Peter to start out with her affection, enough unlike him to intrigue her and to keep them talking.

They drank wine with the meal and had a liqueur after it, and Rowland got just a little, very nicely drunk. Julia thought she had too, but it was the effect of the atmosphere and the occasion, not the alcohol. With his elbows among the coffee cups, Rowland lowered his voice and talked nonsense to her, the kind of pleasant nonsense which, had she ever been courted in the ordinary way, she would have remembered from early dates. She listened with more attention than it warranted, amused and flattered, but once they were outside the restaurant, going home, and she discovered that she was not drunk after all, she wanted no more of it. She no longer responded, and Rowland remained quiet in the taxi.

When they reached the mews they discovered that the babysitter's husband had already arrived in his car to drive her home, and they refused Julia's offers of coffee and drinks and went straight away. Julia gave her coat to Rowland to put away, and went in to see Nathan, and remained a long time looking down at him in the hope that Rowland would either sober himself up or fall asleep before she had to go back out and join him. She straightened the covers over her small child and his assorted bedfellows – a golly, a teddy bear, and an amorphous knitted toy called (more with faith than with conviction) Lambie – and indulged herself in a little motherly thinking about him. It wasn't a thing she often did, for she didn't often feel like his mother, usually more like his favoured companion. Then at last various noises in the rest of the house drew her away.

Rowland had installed himself on the sofa, and had poured out two drinks, one of which he held out to Julia as she came in.

'Come and sit down, and be comfortable,' he said. She took the drink from his hand and went to sit in the chair, away from him, but he caught her wrist and stopped her. 'No, not there – on the floor. Sit on the floor. He told me that's where you always sit.'

'He told you?'

'Peter told me. Sit down. He often used to talk about you to me. Well, not often. Sometimes.'

Julia sat as directed, lifting her skirt out from underneath her carefully to keep it clean, and said, more for something to say than because she wanted to know, 'What did he tell you about me?'

'Just about how you were. I knew then, even before you came down – that time, remember?'

She took it to be a rhetorical question and said nothing, but he insisted.

'Remember, when you came and visited us that time with Peter and Michael?'

'Yes, I remember.'

'I knew before I even saw you how it was between you and Peter. And d'you know what? I was glad. Not for you. For him.' He stopped for so long that Julia thought he had fallen asleep. His eyes were closed, and she risked a look at him, for she had been avoiding his eyes up till now. He looked, even though drunk, divinely beautiful and not at all the way a drunken person ought to look. But then, Peter never showed drink either. He opened his eyes again.

'You're too good for him. I knew that even then. I told you so, didn't I? And you said you knew all about how bad he was. I thought that was just bravado, but you did, I think.' He frowned. 'It was always like that. He's a bastard, but people love him, people will do anything for him. He's my brother, and I love him, but he's a bastard. Oh boy, is he a bastard.' He fixed Julia with a penetrating blue gaze. 'He'll destroy you, you know. Well, not destroy, maybe, but he'll be rotten to you. He'll . . .' He stopped himself with an obvious effort.

Julia felt it was time to interrupt. 'Perhaps you don't know what he's like now,' she said gently. 'He's changed, you know.'

Rowland shook his head. 'He hasn't changed. I know him. He loves you, Julia, he loves you as he's never loved anyone. He never did love anyone before. He married Joyce because he thought he ought to have a wife, but he never loved her. But he'll hurt you. Even now – even at this very moment . . .' He stopped again, and then stumbled on. 'When I saw you for the first time, I thought you were too good for him. I wished it was me. I would have – I wanted you instead. But it was always him. Listen! You must trust him.'

'I do trust him,' Julia said, bewildered.

'You must. A man as dishonest as him must have an honest wife. Honest enough for two. That's why Joyce was no good. She was as dishonest as him. She knew how to get what she wanted. She married him because she wanted a house of her own, and she's got it, without even having to have him. But you, you're wide open, and he'll do you. But he'll never let anyone else do you, and that's why you must believe in him. Even when you find out about him, don't believe it.'

He looked so troubled and anxious that she did not take offence at his strange ramblings, believing they were meant kindly, but she felt he ought to be shut up, and she got up as far as her haunches and laid a hand on his knee and said, 'Rowland, I think you should go to bed now. I'm grateful for your advice, but you mustn't worry about me and Peter.'

'Julia,' he grabbed her hand and held it, even against her reluctance, and looked straight at her, and said in a steady voice, 'I'm a little drunk, but not as much as you think.' He paused for thought, and then gave a little shrug and said, 'Thank you for being with me, for a very pleasant evening.'

'Thank you for taking me out. I really enjoyed it,' she said, getting to her feet. He stood up too. 'The bed over there is made up. It's quite comfortable. And if you need an extra blanket, there's one on the chair.'

'Thank you.'

'Goodnight, then.'

He stood aside for her to pass him, and as she did he said very quietly, 'I love you, Julia.' She walked on without pausing, as if she hadn't heard him, but when she reached the haven of her bedroom and closed the door behind her, her face was scarlet.

It was a long time before she got to sleep. Naked under the sheets she lay on her back and felt the blood whispering about her body, intensely aware of herself, and listening for any sound from the rest of the house. He was only just a few feet away from her, divided from her by a wall, and she was as conscious of him as if he had been lying beside her. She half expected, was half afraid that the door might open, that he might come in and slide into bed beside her. She thought of his body, of what he must look like without his clothes, of whether he would look like Peter, and, afraid of her thoughts, pushed them jumpily away.

Of his weird warnings she thought nothing at all. No outside influence could affect her feelings for or her thinking about Peter – they existed only between the two of them, independent of all other circumstances. What she did think, over and over again, was that Rowland desired her. Another man had wanted her, had said he loved her. She listened to her own breathing, and felt the sheet touch her body, and was aware of herself almost as Peter was aware of her.

The door handle didn't turn, and after a while she dozed, and then slept, and dreamt of Peter for only about the third time in her life, until she was woken at six by Nathan rattling the bars of his crib, his usual signal that he had exhausted his early morning pursuits and wanted to get up.

Rowland was up before she could call him, coming into the kitchen fully dressed as she was pouring boiling water into the teapot, and he smiled at her without embarrassment and said, 'Good morning. Did you sleep well?'

'I don't remember,' she said. 'I was asleep. Tea?'

'Oh, yes please. Hello, Boy. You're up early.' He crossed the room to talk to his nephew, and Julia might have thought that he had forgotten their late conversation except that he hadn't been that drunk; and because after a moment he came back and stood beside her, and laid his hand gently over the back of hers. She looked up, and he met her eyes and smiled at her, a warm, undemanding smile, as if they had been lovers the night before and had nothing now to prove and no barriers to surmount.

She felt that whenever they met again in the future it would be like that, that they would share this particular kind of intimacy which they had never done anything, so to speak, to deserve.

Eleven

May 1961

O nce when searching for something in the understair cupboard back home, Julia had stood up too quickly and hit her head a stunning crack on the underside of the stairs. There had been no pain, only a sense of violent shock and harm together with a grasping nausea.

She felt like that now. All the weeks of gnawing anxiety and nameless brooding fears had been resolved. They knew the worst, and it was the worst. She looked at Peter, a thousand miles away across the room. She wished she could touch him, so that she would not feel so alone. *This can't be happening. This can't happen to us!*

Peter saw Julia look towards him. Her eyes seemed enormous and black, like holes cut out of her face, and her head was up. He knew that posture, the lift of her head when she was threatened, and for a moment he forgot his own pain in wanting to help her, and wished their seats were closer together so that he could touch her or hold her hand. But any respite could only be brief.

In a moment he spoke again. He felt he was expected to ask something, but his mind was as dry as his mouth. 'Could it have been anything to do with – I mean, when he was born, it was a very difficult birth, and—'

The doctor shook his head. 'No, not at all. It's a very mysterious thing. We know very little about it, and one of the things we don't know is why it attacks some people and not others. We all, all of us, have a propensity towards cancer, but why cancerous cells develop in some people and lie dormant in others we just can't tell. It seems to be completely random.'

'Like lightning,' Julia said, and the doctor looked briefly, encouragingly at her. He hoped she would speak, for in his experience shock was better coped with if it could be talked out straight away.

After a moment she said, 'But he's so young. Only four years old. I didn't think you could get cancer so young.'

The doctor shook his head again. 'This particular form of cancer, I'm afraid, is no respecter of age. Over half the people who have any of the forms of leukaemia are under twenty-one.'

Peter had trouble finding his voice, as if it was hiding from him deliberately, but now there was something he had to ask, though he didn't want to be told. 'What are the chances of curing him, doctor?'

The pause which followed, though it lasted only a second, seemed to draw his life out on a thin thread. The doctor laid his two hands on the desk in a curious gesture that seemed to ask to be forgiven and said, 'At present there is no known cure for this form of the disease. We have ways of slowing it down, of impeding its progress, but we can't cure it.'

The nausea had passed, and shock was now making Julia feel light and hollow, like an empty seed case – which, her mind told her with a bitter twist, was exactly what she was. Everything seemed to be happening a long way off, and curiously slowly. When she spoke, she hardly knew she was doing it. 'Then he will die?'

To Peter, Julia's voice was without emotion one way or the other, merely asking a question. How could she be so calm?

The doctor, though his face was full of concern, responded in the same way, matter-of-factly.

'Yes. Unless there is some breakthrough in the research field in the next few months and, frankly, you understand that while such a thing is possible, it would be irresponsible of me to allow you to pin too much hope on the possibility.'

'You think it unlikely.'

'Very unlikely. I'm sorry.'

Peter became aware of a pain in his hand, and looking down he saw that his fist had balled up, and his fingernails were digging into his palm. He uncurled his fingers slowly and saw the red crescent marks he had left. He wanted to whimper, but another part of him was in control of him, though still not,

221

apparently, of his voice, for it came out as a croak and he had to clear his throat and start again. 'How – how long will it take? How long do we have?'

'If the present rate of development does not alter, I should say three or four months. There is a tendency, however, for the progress of the disease to accelerate as the patient's resistance weakens, and this is particularly true in the case of a child. Children have fewer physical resources. In that case, I should say probably three months.'

'Does he suffer?' Julia asked abruptly.

'Not at the moment,' the doctor told her. Neither of them looked at Peter, as if they knew he could not bear it. 'Later on he will probably experience a certain degree of pain, but we can give him drugs at that stage to control it. He will begin to feel more and more tired, and to reject his food as he has done, and it may be necessary then to feed him intravenously. But at present you can just carry on as usual, in between regular visits to me here.'

Julia nodded. She seemed calm and controlled after that one desperate look of appeal she had thrown at him, and Peter wondered if perhaps she had known for some time what was going on. But if she had, she would have told him, wouldn't she? She wouldn't keep such a thing to herself.

'Is there anything else you would like to ask me? Don't hesitate to ask, if there's anything at all you want to know, however trivial.'

Peter shook his head, and Julia said, 'No, nothing, thank you.'

'Well then, would you like to make an appointment for, let's see, next Tuesday morning? And if there's anything that occurs to you in the meantime, don't be afraid to call me up.' He scribbled a prescription and handed it to Julia saying, 'Have this made up at the pharmacy before you leave, and give him one after each meal. And Sister will give you the diet sheet I mentioned.'

'Thank you, doctor,' she said. 'I'll see you on Tuesday then.'

'Goodbye. Goodbye, sir.'

He ushered them out, and they passed through the passage

and into the waiting hall where about twenty people were scattered amongst the rows of iron chairs, and perhaps a dozen children ran up and down, their footsteps and shrill voices echoing hollowly from the high ceiling. There was no sign of Nathan, but as they hesitated the department sister came towards them, smiling cheerfully.

'Nurse took him to the playroom. He'll be back in a minute. Have you to make an appointment?'

Again Julia was ready with speech. 'Yes, for Tuesday. And you have to give me a diet sheet.'

'Oh yes, that's right. Would you like to come to the desk, then?'

'Yes, of course.' She turned to Peter. 'Darling, why don't you take this to the pharmacy – down that corridor, there. I'll meet you back here.'

He took the prescription obediently and followed her directions, and handed the paper to the prescriptions clerk, who poured some red pills from a large jar into his palm and then counted them into a small bottle, wrote a label for it, and handed it back. Peter was glad that it did not involve speaking. He put the bottle in his pocket and retraced his steps, and as he reached Julia's side he saw his son, hand in hand with a pretty young nurse, coming towards them from the other side of the hall. His hand reached blindly for hers and it was there at once, holding on to him as though she were drowning. He did not dare look at her, but he knew her heart was breaking. He drew a breath that was almost like a sob.

And Julia said, quietly, for him only, 'We must act normally in front of him.'

'Yes,' he said. We must smile, he thought, or we'll frighten him. His mouth muscles didn't seem to be responding. Smile, damn you!

His son caught sight of him and broke into a run, pulling the nurse with him.

'Daddy,' Nathan called, and several people looked round and smiled as Nathan broke free from the nurse and ran to his father to be swept up into his arms. Peter hugged him, and at the touch of his son's small, compact body everything welled up in him in a scalding surge of grief. He buried his face in the child's neck and smelled the sweetness of his skin and his clean hair. *Oh God, don't take him! Don't take my boy!*

Julia watched them, in agony. As if she were inside Peter's skin she felt and knew everything he felt and thought. Across Nathan's shoulder she met her husband's eyes and the contact seemed to burn her. Oh Peter! We must be normal for him. But how can we? I can't bear this. I'm not strong enough. I can't do it.

The hug had lasted only an instant, and now Peter put the child back a little to look at him, and smiled – waveringly, but it was a smile.

'What's this – tears?' he asked, touching Nathan's cheek. 'You weren't crying, were you, Boy? Big men don't cry.'

'It's all right, Mr Kane,' the nurse said as she reached them. 'He wasn't hurt. He just didn't want to leave. There's a rocking horse in there, you see.'

Julia smiled then, and if it was a travesty only Peter would know that. 'Oh, that's typical of my boy,' she said. 'However did you get him away from it?'

'I said his Daddy was waiting for him. He really is a Daddy's boy, isn't he?'

'He certainly is,' Julia said. 'Unfortunately Mr Kane has to be away from home a lot, so he always makes a fuss when Daddy comes home.'

'He looks ever so much like you,' the nurse said conversationally.

'Do you think so?' Julia had never thought of Boy as taking after her.

'Oh yes – he's the spitten image of you. Have you any others?'

'No, just the one.' Peter heard the catch in her voice, and reached out his hand to draw her away. 'Why do you ask?'

'Oh, I just wondered. Ah, here's Sister with your cards, by the look of it. Well, cheerio, bye-bye, Nathan. See you next week. Bye-bye.'

Nathan, holding hard on to Peter's thumb, was overcome with shyness and buried his face in Peter's shoulder and wouldn't come out until they had passed through the door and out into the courtyard. Peter wanted very badly to hold Julia's hand, and he asked Boy if he wanted to walk, but Nathan merely shook his head and began to suck his little finger, a habit he had had since babyhood. Out of the corner of his eye he saw Julia open her mouth automatically to reprove the child, but he forestalled her, saying, 'Let him, just this once. At least it's better than a thumb.'

'I'm glad you've spoken,' Julia said. 'I was beginning to be afraid you would never speak to me again.'

'I'm sorry,' he said. They walked on a little way in silence – the car was parked at some distance down the road – and then he said, 'It's the shock, I suppose. I just can't believe it. I can't take it in.'

'Do you think I can? Don't try,' she said. 'We'll know it soon enough. Peter, I don't want to go home yet. Can't we go somewhere? To the zoo or something. I want to do something, so I don't have to think.'

'Darling, I can't,' he said gently. 'I have to go back to town. I've got a session.'

'Can't you give it a miss, just this once?' she cried.

'God, I wish I could, but I can't. You know what it's like. Everyone's booked and it's the last day we've got the studio. We have to finish today. I'll drop you off somewhere. I'm sorry, darling—'

'It's all right,' she said, dully. 'I know you have to work. Nathan, get down and walk now, Daddy's carried you far enough.' Nathan immediately released his hold on Peter's neck, as obedient to his mother as she had always been to Peter, and Peter lowered him to the pavement and took his hand instead. 'You can drop us off at Baker Street,' Julia went on. 'We'll get the bus up to the zoo from there.'

'All right.' They reached the car, and got in in silence, and Peter drove off, turning left into the main road. 'There's a circus on up here, look. Shall we go one evening? Would you like that, Boy?'

Julia interrupted him. 'Peter, come straight home after the session. Please.'

'Of course I will,' he said.

'Come straight home,' she said again, as if he had argued

225

about it. She sounded nervous. She didn't want to be alone with it, he thought. He understood that. Neither did he.

They drove past the place where the circus tent was pitched, and Nathan knelt up on the back seat to stare at it. 'Look, Daddy, look. There's a fair.'

'Are you kneeling on my violin case?' Peter said automatically.

'No, Daddy. Can we go to the fair?'

'Yes. It's a circus, though.'

'When can we go? Tomorrow?'

'We'll see,' Peter said, again automatically, and then recollected himself. 'Yes, yes I expect so. Tomorrow.' And at that, Julia began to laugh. She managed to stop herself almost immediately but while it lasted it was a horrible sound, a bubbling-up of something dark and uncontrollable.

'How's the kid?' Martin Newman asked at the session. It was a scratch orchestra and Peter had made sure he had been booked for it. One of the pleasures of being a soloist was being able to confer benefit on one's friends. Peter had told Martin the day before that he had to go up to the hospital to see the consultant. He remembered how when he had said it, he had thought his time was being wasted, that it would be something Julia could very well deal with on her own. Oh God, what an idiot he had been! And blind, blind.

Martin was an old friend. Peter told him.

'Oh God, no. That's terrible. Oh, Peter, I'm so sorry.' He stopped, and Peter felt rather sorry for him – after all, what can one say? 'He looks such a healthy kid. When did you notice there was anything wrong?'

'I didn't notice. But Julia's been worried for weeks. He's been off his food, and he started getting indigestion, and being sick, and she thought he might have some sort of blockage, or intestinal trouble. We never thought of this.'

'I've never heard of it,' Martin said frankly.

'We hadn't either,' Peter said. He shook his head. 'I can't really take it in. He's just the same, just as bright, always on the go, interested in everything. He doesn't even look ill. I can't believe it. I just can't believe it.'

226

'How's Julia taking it?'

'She's very calm, but I think she's frightened.'

'Frightened?'

'Frightened of him, of being left alone with him. I feel guilty about it, but I'm glad I had to work today. Is that awful of me?'

Martin was saved from having to answer this by the orchestral attendant calling him. Almost at the same instant the conductor called across, 'We're ready for you now, Peter. Could you . . . ?'

It was a world into which he could retreat, pulling the door closed behind him. Putting the bow to the strings was the first movement in a ritual that made him something else, changed him alchemically from dross to gold, from human and ordinary to spirit and extraordinary. It was to him the addict's morphia. He played, and he was safe in the convolutions of music that nothing could change or harm, the music that was the same always. He walked about inside the composer's brain and was washed through with the composer's emotions, a flood of grief and anguish and passion that, being unconnected with him, did no damage and left no hurt in passing.

The knowledge of them was there, in the background, but he did not think of them while he played. His wife and child: tiny tesserae in a great magic pavement whose picture changed every instant, and yet was always recognisable as a whole. His grief, their grief, was only a part of a universal paradigm, and as such was bearable, even beautiful.

As soon as the red light went off the orchestra applauded as one man, and the studio staff joined in, and even the conductor leaned over and said something pleased and polite before he went back to the sound room to consult with the producer. Peter knew that he had been good: there was something like an after-image in his mind of his sound, the music he had made. He had been *good*. The players sat relaxing, their instruments ready, talking quietly amongst themselves, ready at a word to play again, or to dash off to the pub, as the command should indicate.

Peter too stood waiting, avoiding all eyes, and was almost disappointed when the conductor came back out and put his thumb up and said, 'Excellent. Excellent. That'll be it, then, boys. Thank you all very much.' He extended his hand to Peter, who took it numbly. 'Congratulations,' he said, and strode away again. His time was worth a hundred pounds a minute, Peter thought.

He might very well have remained standing there, had not Martin seen his predicament and touched his arm and said, 'Can I give you a lift anywhere?' He knew Peter had a car, but it was a way of attracting his attention.

'I want a drink,' Peter said abruptly. 'Come with me, Martin.'

Martin thought of Julia, but his hesitation was only momentary. He expected to 'chum' Peter for just one drink, and then see him off for home; but his good intentions were doomed, for as they were finishing their first drink, a crowd of men from the orchestra came in, and Peter greeted them with cries of delight and bought a round. From there it developed into a kind of party, and if Martin noticed the desperate quality of Peter's wit, it was obvious that none of the others did. It was after nine before he could manage to prise his companion loose from the bar and get him outside, and by then Peter was certainly not fit to drive.

'Let's go somewhere else,' Peter said when they were outside on the pavement. He looked slightly ruffled and bleared, but otherwise, to an inexperienced eye, he appeared sober.

Martin was not deceived. 'Not a chance,' he said. 'I'm going to drive you home.'

'Not yet, not yet. Let's go somewhere else first,' Peter insisted. It was like a superstition: the act of returning home would make the nightmare he had dreamed come true.

Martin looked at him kindly. 'Peter, old man, you've got to face it sometime. I'm sorry to have to say this, but, look, she's on her own too. The longer you put it off, the worse it will be. Come on, now. I'll drive you home in your car, and come back for mine. Where are your keys?'

Defeated, Peter drew them out from his pocket and handed them over. Martin was right of course, but who wanted to be right all the time? He wanted very badly to be wrong just now, to go out and not come home all night, and end up in some girl's bed he'd never seen before and would never see again. He didn't want to face the truth. He wanted to abdicate, just for one night, just this one time, just for one last riotous, drunken, debauched evening.

Instead, he was being driven home, with the windows wound down so that the cold air sobered him frighteningly quickly. Martin drove into the mews and made a guess as to where Peter normally parked. He set the brake, pulled the key out of the ignition and handed it to Peter. 'Here. Lock the car and put the key in your pocket. If I were you I shouldn't tell her I drove you home.'

They got out. Peter held out his hand, quite steadily, and shook Martin's, and said, 'Thanks, old boy. You're a great pal. Too bloody great.'

'Okay. I'll be seeing you.' Martin turned to walk away, and then turned back and said thoughtfully, 'Counter-irritant. The only thing that stops you feeling a pain is another one. You could try hers.'

Julia was in the kitchen, sitting at the table with her hands resting before her as if she was waiting for a waiter to bring her meal. He recognised the gesture as the same the doctor had made just before he told them that Boy was going to die, and he wondered what terrible thing Julia was going to say. But she said only, 'He's in bed and asleep. I said you'd say goodnight when you came in, but if he's asleep, don't wake him.'

He stood still in the doorway, waiting for her to reprove him, but she said nothing, only looked at him wearily.

'Aren't you going to say I'm late?' he said. She shook her head. He thought that she knew everything that had happened this evening; she knew he had been drunk, knew what he had intended, knew about his struggle, and by what a narrow skin-of-the-teeth chance he had come out on the right side of it. 'You know everything, don't you,' he said, and it sounded drunkenly accusing, and he was surprised, because he hadn't really meant it that way.

Her voice was tired. 'Peter, don't make me fight your battles for you. I haven't the wit always to judge by intentions.'

'I'm drunk, Julia,' he said.

She stood up and came round the table to him. 'No, I'm

229

afraid you're not,' she said, as if he had asked rather than told her. She stood very straight, and because he was sagging a little, she seemed tall to him. Tall and strong, like a tree. Only he knew that she was in agony, and that this was her way of coping. He fumbled for her hand, and finding it, closed his round it blindly, as if he really was drunk. They turned and walked together to the child's room, and went in to look at him.

'He is asleep,' Julia said. The child was asleep on his back, his two fists palm up on the pillow on either side of his face, his head turned towards Golly and Teddy and Lambie. His face looked slightly moist and flushed, the way a sleeping child should, the way Michael and James always had. There is something special about one's own sons when they are sleeping.

'All sons,' he said aloud. 'I never had a daughter.' Boy had pulled the covers about as usual, and had exposed his feet to the night air. Julia stooped automatically to pull the covers straight and tuck them in. Boy stirred, flung an arm out across his toys and said 'Train', and was still again, and as Julia straightened up, Peter's control began to break.

'I can't bear it,' he whispered. 'Oh Julia! Oh God, don't let it happen!'

She put her arm round him and hustled him out of the room and into their own bedroom, and sitting down with him on the bed she took him in her arms. 'Oh God, don't let him die. My little boy . . .' The crack widened, and with his head on her shoulder and her arms round him, bit by bit he gave in, drew a convulsive breath, and began to cry.

Julia did not speak nor move. If she had tried to speak, her own tears would have broken free, and she was afraid of them, afraid of what she would let loose. She must be the rock while this lasted. They had so little time – she dare not waste it. She felt so tired, and yet she wondered if she would ever sleep again. She sat quite motionless, her head resting on his, her eyes dry and staring at nothing, holding him while he wept.

The progress of the disease was bewilderingly swift – two months is so short a time. Peter was luckier than Julia: he had

230

his work, though he turned down a lot of engagements and did nothing far enough afield to necessitate staying away from home, even for a night. Julia spent all her time with the boy and seemed so calm you could almost have believed she was resigned to losing him. It was as though she had determined to make the most of the time she had, taking him to see everything she had ever promised him, playing with him, reading to him, talking with him, his constant companion, drawing everything she could out of the little scrap of time that was left.

Peter worried about her, for she would not let him in on her suffering. She never cried, never even wavered from her calm, reposeful behaviour, and he was afraid that she would break badly, all at once, if she didn't break a little, now and then. She saw no one but him and the child and the doctors and, feeling that she needed company while he was out working, Peter asked Sylvia and Rowland and Martin to call round when they could. Rowland, who was staying with friends in London for a holiday before the serious work on the farm started, was there a lot, and she seemed to derive some comfort from him that she could not get either from her husband or sister. Peter understood, or thought he did – that he himself was too much a part of it, that he and she were two raw surfaces that had better not rub together – but though he tried not to feel hurt, he still did.

There was a short respite after the first breaking of the news, when Boy seemed well, and enjoyed all the treats that were coming his way, all the outings and the fun and the special things to eat, and Daddy being home so often, and all going out together. Then the little symptoms of being easily tired, and fretful in the afternoons, and being unable to eat, seemed to snowball. Overnight he seemed to change, and Peter could only watch helplessly as his son's grip on life slipped, and loosened.

Julia too began to show the strain. He came home one evening to find her walking up and down with the sobbing child in her arms, looking worn out and frightened.

'Give him to me,' he told her. 'Come Boy, come to Daddy. There, that's right. Don't cry any more. Shall I read you a story? Put the kettle on, Julia, and make some tea, while I put Boy to bed. There's a good girl.'

231

She obeyed him, and it tore at his heart to see how heavily she walked, her proud uprightness broken. It took a long time to settle Nathan. He had to sit by the bed, Nathan holding his finger, and tell him the long and intricate story of the Wild Swans – from memory, for Nathan would have no reading – before he at last dropped off to sleep from sheer exhaustion. Peter covered him up and tiptoed out to join Julia in the kitchen, leaving the door open. They never closed it now.

'He's gone off all right,' Peter said, trying to sound cheerful for her sake. She had made tea but had forgotten to pour it out, and he did the honours while he talked to her. She walked about the kitchen restlessly, touching things, listening to him, but he could see that for the first time in weeks she was really *there*, the barrier she had put up between her and the rest of the world was down and she was communicating again.

'Oh Peter, I can't bear it,' she broke in after a while, cutting across his rambling account of his day. 'He's suffering. His poor bones ache, and he's sick all the time.'

'Didn't you give him the pills?'

'Oh yes,' she made an impatient gesture. 'It kills the pain. But he still suffers. He knows he's ill. He does!' she protested to Peter's grunt of surprise. 'He worries about it – have you ever seen a little child worrying? He said to me today, "What's wrong with me, Mummy?". He knows he's ill, you see. He heard that woman at the corner shop complaining about her back – you know the way she does – and when we came away he asked me if that was what he had, lumbago.'

'Drink your tea,' he told her, and she picked up the cup obediently, and looked at it, and then put it down again without knowing what she had done. She walked round the table again, and then stopped in front of him with a kind of desperate appeal.

'They don't let animals go on like this – it's so cruel. If I could, if I had the means, I would kill him.'

'You wouldn't. Don't talk like that,' he said. 'I don't want him to die. He's my son.' She turned wearily away from him and put her hands over her face. Peter reached out to her tentatively and put his hands on her shoulders. He had been afraid to touch her recently, she had seemed so distant.

Now she felt brittle. She didn't shake off his hands, and he thought that in a moment he could have held her, and knew at the same time how much he ached to hold her; but before anything more could pass between them Boy cried out from the bedroom, and she jerked into movement at once.

'Let me go,' he said, but she still went, with no sign that she had heard him. He followed her into the nursery, where Nathan was lying in his cot, watching the door and crying – not sobbing as earlier, but crying softly and weakly, as if to cry cost him as much effort as to bear himself in silence. Julia stood beside the cot looking down at him, making no move to touch him and then turned to Peter in a kind of desperate appeal. He put her gently aside and picked the child up. Nathan was light, too light – he had always been a sturdy, stocky little boy – and his head seemed too big for him, like that of a fledgling bird. Peter held the child against him and began to walk up and down the room, talking soothingly, saying anything that came into his head, and it seemed to work, for Boy stopped whimpering; the heavy head leaned down on his shoulder, and the finger slid into the corner of the mouth for comfort.

Julia, who had watched motionless, her arms wrapped about her as if she was cold, reached out a hand automatically and said, 'Don't let him suck his finger, Peter. He'll grow up with a deformity . . .' and then he caught her eye and saw the same thought occur to her. He did not really need both arms to support Nathan, light as he was now. He reached out and put his other arm round Julia's shoulder, drew her to him, and she came slowly, and leaned her head against his chest, and in a minute Boy's other hand reached out and fastened in his mother's hair.

Later, when they had got Boy to sleep at last, Peter mixed them both a nightcap and then took Julia to the bedroom. It was not late enough to sleep yet; it was still light outside. They lay down on the top of the bed, just for ease of getting close. She was almost as bony as the boy, he discovered as he pulled her against him and held her. She spoke after a while, her voice quite clear, but distant, like something heard over a radio.

'I didn't mean it. Of course I wouldn't kill him. That's the worst of it. Even though he's suffering I can't let him go. I want every second I can screw out of life, however much it hurts. I want to hold on to him until they tear me away. It's so selfish of me.'

'It's natural,' Peter corrected. It was easy to be big and brave when she was lying in his arms asking him for comfort. Any weakness in her showed up as strength in him. 'Do you think I'm any different?'

'I don't know,' she said. 'I don't know how you feel. He isn't your only child, after all.'

'Darling, don't,' he chided her gently.

'You're out so much, away from it – I don't know what you are going through.'

'Julia, don't. Don't take it out on me. You know—'

She drew a breath. 'Yes, I know,' she apologised. And then she went on harshly, 'Oh Peter, I try to accept it, but I can't. Such a little life, so little of everything and all to be gone in a few weeks. I can't believe it. I can't understand it. All the things we were going to do together, and we'll never do them. We'll never see what he grows up like. How can it happen?'

'Darling, darling.' He held her tighter, and she clung this time.

'The worst of it is, I want so desperately to enjoy every moment we have left with him, but I can't. The thought of what's coming stops me. I can't get it out of my mind enough to be happy with him *now*. I'm wasting having him, for thinking of losing him.'

'I know. I do know. It's just the same for me.'

She was silent for a while, and Peter caressed her hair, glad that she was communicating at last. This was the only comfort they could offer each other, the knowledge that they both felt the same pain.

'I love you so,' she said. She had wanted for so long to take comfort from him, but had not been able, afraid to let go of the iron control which was all that kept her upright. But just now, in his arms, it seemed to be all right to be weak. 'I love you, Peter.'

'I love you too. So very much.'

It was growing dark outside. 'When he was born,' she said after a while, 'I felt that we had done something to the world –

made it different in some way, changed it irrevocably, so that we could never go back to what we were, any of us. And now it's being rubbed out, as if it never happened.'

'It's not like that,' Peter said. 'Not as if it never happened—'

'What will we do without him, Peter? How will we be?'

He held her hard, desperately wanting to comfort her but knowing of nothing he could do or say. He wanted to make love to her, so that he could be sure of making contact with her, but he knew that she didn't want him to. She would not have refused him, and that somehow made it impossible even to ask. He could only be glad of the contact they had made. She fell asleep in his arms, and he lay still for a long time, unwilling to move for fear of waking her, until when at last she sighed in her sleep and turned over, releasing his arm, he found it was quite dead, and he went through silent agonies as the blood returned to it.

They didn't know it then, but that was the beginning of the last phase. The next morning the boy was obviously worse, and after two days of seeing him too weak to do anything but lie in his bed or his mother's arms, they gave in, and took him in to hospital, knowing deep down that they would never bring him home again.

Ward rules were that he could only have one toy with him in his bed, and having said goodbye in tears to Golly and Teddy he settled down on his pillows to enjoy what comfort the favoured Lambie could furnish. The visiting rules were very strict – parents were held to be an upsetting influence on hospitalised children – and they were sent away almost at once, and told they could come back at three for visitors' hour.

On intravenous feeding his condition improved, and on the second day Julia and Peter found him able to sit up in bed, his arm splinted to keep it still, ready to tell them all about the nurses and the puddings he had enjoyed. The improvement lasted for a couple of days, and he talked of being out of hospital in time to go to school in September, something that had been looming large in his mind since it had been suggested back in March.

On Thursday the third of August, Julia went in to the morning visiting session alone while Peter was at a rehearsal, and found Boy very much worse. He was lying down again, and apparently having difficulty in breathing. He could not speak to her, but lay back on his pillows, clutching her hand and staring at her with enormous eyes. Even while she was there it got worse. He was waxy-faced and gasping, and the nurse grew alarmed. The houseman was sent for and came to administer a drug by injection which eased Nathan's breathing. By the time visiting hour ended he was asleep, but Julia refused to leave him. When the doctors arrived for their round she insisted that they let her wait outside until they had finished and then come back to his bedside.

When Peter arrived in the afternoon Boy was awake again; flushed and feverish, and with glands hugely swollen, he was nevertheless apparently in no pain. He smiled a little when Peter appeared, and listened with signs of pleasure while Peter talked to him, holding his hand tightly. After a while he began to drift off to sleep, and his grip on Peter's hand slackened.

'Are you going to sleep, Boy?' Peter asked, tentatively drawing his hand away. Boy's grip tightened convulsively, but relaxed again almost at once, as sleep drew him inexorably.

'Tired, Daddy,' he murmured.

On the morning of Friday the fourth of August, he was weaker, unable to talk. Julia sat with him all day, but at last was persuaded by Peter to go home and sleep for a while, while he continued the vigil.

'I'll telephone you if anything happens, and you can be here by taxi in ten minutes,' he said. 'You need to rest, darling. Go home and get something to eat and then lie down on the bed, and I guarantee you'll drop off to sleep.'

She agreed reluctantly and went – that was about four o'clock. Not long after she had left, Boy took a turn for the worse, and at half past six, on the doctor's advice, Peter called her to the hospital to say goodbye.

By the time Julia reached the hospital, Nathan was in a coma; and at about three o'clock on the morning of August the fifth he died, without regaining consciousness.

*   *   *

They went abroad almost at once. Peter's agent, who had been refusing offers that all his professional training screamed at him to accept, made a timely suggestion that Peter should do a five-week American tour which had been put his way. Peter thought it would be the best thing for them both to get right away, and accepted.

The tour was packed full both with work and incident. Peter received tremendous ovations at every performance, and Julia, who had begun to collect his press notices a while back in a spirit of irony, was by the end of the tour almost in awe of her husband for the attention he was attracting. The States loved him, and it seemed likely that they could make a return visit every year for the rest of their lives if they felt like it.

Apart from the concerts, there were press receptions, sight-seeing tours, and parties, parties, parties. Everyone who was anyone in the world of the arts, and any society hostess who thought anything of her own reputation, wanted to have been hostess to Peter Kane. He was everyone's darling, and Julia came in for quite a share of the limelight too. She had gone over there with only one evening frock of any sort in her luggage, but while she was there she had to buy so many new things, particularly evening and cocktail dresses, that she had to buy a new suitcase as well, to bring them back in.

There was little time to think, no time to brood. Every night she went to bed either tired enough or drunk enough, or a little of both, to ensure sleeping. Peter had other things to exhaust him. Julia found it was possible to fill her mind with her husband's concerns, his performances, his receptions, his future successes which looked like being assured; and here in a strange land amongst a strange people there was nothing to remind her of the great emptiness waiting for them at home.

From Hollywood they travelled back by aeroplane, a novel experience for Julia, and arrived in England on a cloudy October day, late in the afternoon. From the terminus at Victoria to Gloucester Road was a journey of a few minutes by taxi, and they did it in silence, uncommunicating, untouching. It seemed to Peter to be an age since they had talked together of anything but the small daily concerns of eating and drinking, dressing and travelling; and an even

237

longer age since they had touched in more than a perfunctory, accidental way.

He took secret glances at her face as the taxi whirled them through the pre-rush-hour traffic, and it told him nothing – it was as sealed to him as her mind had been for weeks past. He believed that women must feel the loss of a child differently from a man. His own sorrow and pain was not less, and would never go away; but he could shut it off in a separate compartment of his mind, and live in his work, his career, for much of the time, where the grief could not debilitate him. But he thought it must be different for a mother, that the love was somehow much more fundamental, and the loss a wrenching away of what was virtually a part of one's own body and therefore self. He would have liked to talk to her about that, but had been afraid to do it while they were away and on tour. Now they were home, perhaps he could find a way to make her open up to him. They had been everything to each other before Boy. Surely they could be again?

He paid the taxi off in the mews, and as they turned towards the flat together Peter wished he had had the foresight to cable someone to be there to receive them, to have the place warm and lit up. Instead they made their way up the stairs in darkness, and the house had the cold, musty smell of a place long unlived-in.

They dumped their cases in the passageway and went into the kitchen.

'There's no milk, of course,' Julia said, 'but we could have some black coffee.'

'The shop down the road is probably open,' Peter suggested. 'I could nip down there and get a few things. We'll want something for breakfast too, won't we?'

'No,' she said.

'It wouldn't take me a minute,' he went on, feeling that she needed the comfort of hot tea and perhaps a meal, but she shook her head irritably, and he thought perhaps she was afraid to be left alone, and didn't press it.

'It doesn't matter,' she said. 'I'll just take my coat off, and then I'll make some coffee.'

'All right. I'll put the water on,' Peter said. She went out

238

of the kitchen and he heard her footsteps along the passage towards the bedroom; heard them pause, and when they didn't go on, he knew what had halted her.

She was at the open door of the nursery, staring at the empty bed. It had been stripped, of course, and the mattress wrapped up, but Nathan's cot-toys had been dropped there carelessly. The sight of them, abandoned, lost, their eyes staring in bewildered appeal, wrenched her heart with dreadful, ridiculous pain. *How can you feel such pity for inanimate objects? Stop it! Stop it!*

She forced herself to go in, picked up the golliwog, seeing her own hands moving as though at a great distance, not attached to her. *It's just a toy*, she told herself. And the other part of her mind cried, *His toy. He's gone, he's gone. You'll never, never see him again.*

Peter came to the door behind her and saw her pulling the golliwog about in her hands as if she meant to pull it apart, her mouth working as though she were trying to speak. 'Darling,' he said. He walked in behind her, reached out to touch her shoulder, and she threw the toy violently away from her, and, trying to evade him, ran blindly into the door jamb.

Her forehead made a surprisingly loud crack against the wood, and Peter exclaimed in sympathetic pain and reached out for her again. Recoiling from the door, she saw the movement of his hand. 'No,' she cried, and turning violently from him crashed into the wall. She seemed to bounce off it, hit the wall opposite, and began to scream, not loudly, but a thin, faint scream of desperation.

From wall to wall she stumbled, hitting them full on as blindly as a bird hitting a window-pane, crying, 'No, no, no' in a desperate grief which horrified, almost sickened Peter. He wondered if she was deliberately hurting herself: he remembered Martin Newman's words, counter-irritant. But he couldn't bear this. He grabbed her, but in trying not to hurt her misjudged her strength and lost hold of her again. It was some moments before he could catch and subdue her, by which time her face was bruised and her lip cut and bloody. She struggled wildly when he caught her. In a shaking voice he spoke to her, until after a few moments she made a sound like a hoarse sob, and then broke into tears.

'My love, my darling,' he heard himself saying. 'It's over.'

Would to God that it were! He slipped an arm under her knees and round her shoulders and picked her up and carried her into their bedroom. He loosened her clothes, bathed her face with cold water, and then held her hand, dumb with misery, until she should have cried herself quiet. He brought her aspirin, covered her up, and saw her at last settle to sleep.

She woke again in the middle of the night, crying – not violently, as before, but a quiet, lonely crying that was far harder to bear than her earlier frenzy had been. He had thought that nothing could be worse than that horror, but as he held her to him and listened to the desolate weeping that went on and on as if there could never be an end to it, he felt that his heart was breaking.

Twelve

October 1962

The hard times were over. Now everything was coming his way – praise, fame, money, the double sweets of success and sureness of his own achievement. They moved to a new place, a house in Pelham Crescent, and furnished it from scratch, taking with them from the old flat only the leather chesterfield and the black and white Adam print. Peter had outgrown the latter, and would have left it behind with the rest of the stuff, but Julia was attached to it, and insisted on taking it with her. She hung it in their bedroom in the new house, so that Peter should not be ashamed in front of their guests. In the drawing room of the new house, in pride of place, hung the large portrait in oil of Rowland that Julia had finished a few weeks ago. Peter was very proud of it, and Julia was happy with it too.

'It's the next best thing to the picture of you that I can see in my mind's eye but can't get on to canvas,' she said. She had never been able to make a portrait of Peter that satisfied her. 'I'm too close to you,' she said. 'I see you too much in detail to be able to get the overview.'

Peter's success had followed on from the American tour just as expected. He was on his way to being world-famous, and was not only very highly thought of by musicians and the musical public, but had also crossed that mysterious barrier into the esteem of the Ordinary Man in the Street, to become one of the few names, like Menuhin and Beecham, which are instantly familiar to everyone, however unmusical.

Julia accompanied him everywhere, to every concert, on every tour, to every party and reception. They entertained at home a lot too, and their parties, through the eagerness of everyone who was there to *be* there, were invariably successful.

241

How much of Julia's own personal success she owed to Peter she could not judge. The emptiness of the hours when Peter was rehearsing or recording, or otherwise engaged in an activity she could not share, had driven her to her easel again with renewed vigour. Peter's new contacts had produced commissions for her. Interest in anything to do with him had probably gone a long way towards ensuring her pictures would be hung, and securing her a solo exhibition. He frequently had to assure her that interest in her would hardly have been sustained unless her work had been good.

In any event, everyone loves a portrait, particularly their own, and if she received neither praise nor attention from the more avant-garde sections of the world of fine art, she was unlikely to notice it in the steady stream of praise and attention from the rest of the society around her. Magazine articles appeared about both of them, individually and as a couple, and when they attended public functions they were often photographed for the papers: 'Peter and Julia Kane arriving at the opening night of *Idomeneo.*' 'The talented Kanes were guests at the Grosvenor House charity dinner on Saturday.' At their parties the world of art mingled with the world of music, with the world of fashion looking on; and in the centre of it all Julia, gowned to swooning point, played at being the hostess.

It was all play – even Peter, with vested interest in not believing it, knew that. She had the knack of getting on with anyone, as had Peter himself, but unlike Peter she cared nothing for this kind of entertainment and this kind of friendship. Probably she was the better hostess for being uninvolved, but Peter knew she was not happy, and although she displayed not the slightest sign of it to anyone else, he knew it all the same and felt, again and again through that year, that somehow he had failed her. They had never had that talk – he had funked re-opening the wound, even while aware with the back of his mind that it would not be a case of *re*-opening, since it had never healed. But there was so much else to do, and his career was so demanding, and as long as everything functioned properly, the temptation to leave well alone and trust to time-the-great-healer was overwhelming. Yet from time to time he could not avoid the feeling that they were drifting apart; along with a faint irritation that she would not make more effort to be happy, for his sake.

Perhaps the time he chose to bring the subject up was not the most propitious. He was just home from an editing conference at the recording studios and had had only enough time to bathe and change for their party that evening. He came downstairs into the drawing room to get Julia to put in his cufflinks for him, and found her arranging dark-red and gold chrysanthemums in a vase in the alcove.

'Here, fix these for me, will you, darling?' he said. She turned languidly and held out her hand in an automatic gesture that spoke of depression.

'What's the matter?' he asked her in concern.

'Nothing,' she said. 'What makes you think something is the matter?' She raised to him a face so calm and composed it was almost a blank, and then looked down at her hands again as she put his links in with unhurried movements. He thought for a moment, painfully, how very beautiful she was. She was wearing an evening dress of emerald green velvet, close-bodiced and loose-skirted, exquisite in its simplicity, with no other ornaments but her gold locket on a chain round her neck, and her thin, cheap wedding ring – she never would let him buy her a better one. Her hair was arranged in a high soft crown designed to show up the fairest parts of it where the sun had bleached it silver; her skin was creamy against the darkness of the dress, and her eyes were dark in the pallor of her face.

He ached for her; and loving her, and being aware that their relationship was weakening with each day that passed in mutual reserve, he determined suddenly to find her out.

'Julia, why are you so unhappy? Please tell me, I want to know.'

She finished fixing the cufflinks, settled the cuffs and said, without looking up, 'Why should you think I'm unhappy?'

'I don't think you are, I know you are. You are my wife, I know everything about you.'

'Nonsense,' she said unemphatically.

'Well, if I don't know about you, it is because you won't let me know. You don't talk to me any more. We hardly communicate at all. When you listen to music, it's always the noisiest stuff you play – Shostakovich, Berlioz, Prokofiev.'

'And what does that prove?' she asked, actually looking up for a moment in her surprise.

'Oh come on! When you are happy you play chamber music and church music and quartets: you can't be miserable and enjoy that kind of music.'

She turned away, reaching for a cigarette from the mantelpiece and lighting it. 'You are absurd,' she said, trying to laugh. 'Such trifles on which to base a theory.'

'It's no theory.'

'I agree.'

'Don't use sophistry on me, my girl! It's not a theory, it's a fact. And you never used to smoke,' he added.

She turned to face him, leaning against the fireplace wall in an attitude of negligence, but her eyes did not quite meet his. 'You are being carried away by the desire to make an impression,' she said. 'As the sharp-eyed sleuth you might do better if you were ever in my company for long enough to observe anything.'

'What do you mean by that?'

'Just what I say. You are hardly ever at home – except for parties like this one.'

'Where am I then?'

'Anywhere but here. You think you know me, Peter, but you don't know yourself. You are the one avoiding contact. You're always out working, visiting people, giving interviews, at receptions.'

'So it's my success you don't like,' he said. 'You were happy enough when I was a struggling rank-and-filer, but you don't like it now I'm a successful soloist? Are you sure it isn't just plain, simple jealousy?'

That made her look at him all right, and her eyes flashed for a moment. He would have been happy if she had joined battle – at least when they were quarrelling they would have been communicating – but either she knew he did not believe that was the case, or else she thought that if he did believe it, it was not worthy of rational opposition. At any rate she did not trouble herself to argue. She merely sighed a little and pushed herself off the wall, crossing the room in search of an ashtray, into which she crushed the whole, just-lit cigarette with uncharacteristic wastefulness.

'Julia, why won't you talk to me?' Peter tried again.

'I do talk to you, of course I do,' she said in a voice whose reasonableness made him want to throw things.

'I know you are still grieving for Boy,' he said – boldly, because she never mentioned the child, to him or anyone else. It was hard enough for him to speak of Nathan, and to speak of him to her was even harder. He made an effort. 'Don't you think I miss him too? For God's sake, he was my son as well as yours.'

He saw she didn't like that. She turned sharply for the door, saying, 'You'd better put your shoes on. Your guests will be here in a minute.'

She had never so abruptly refused to converse with him – usually she was more devious in avoiding issues. As often as he could during the evening, he observed her closely. She was always to be found in conversation with somebody, or with several somebodies, often smiling, sometimes laughing. Where she was, the crowd seemed always a little more dense, the talk a little more earnest. He watched the expressions of her face, the turn of her head, the movements of her hands, the posture of her body, and he saw that she was nervous, jumpy, depressed. She started violently when the telephone rang, moved too abruptly towards the door when it opened to admit a newcomer, smoked too rapidly, hardly ever more than halfway down a cigarette. (When had she started smoking anyway?) Had she been ten years younger he would have likened her behaviour to a teenager waiting for the person on whom she had a crush to arrive.

That, however, was one solution he never even considered. She had been his for so long – since before she even knew she would one day be anybody's – that he could not think of her in the context of anyone but himself.

At one point in the evening Julia was standing in front of the fireplace with a group of people who were admiring Rowland's portrait, and comparing it with the original. Peter stood opposite Julia, smiling sardonically, but hardly ever taking his eyes from her. Julia looked up at the painting, and then at Rowland, and Peter saw her face redden, and the smile she had been wearing drop away, leaving her expression naked – bleak.

It had not occurred to him before, but he wondered now whether Rowland might know more about Julia's state of mind than he did. He knew that they had a strong friendship, and had he been less sure of Julia he might even have been jealous and suspected that it was more than friendship. Even as it was, it took him some time to work up enough determination to ask his brother the potentially humiliating question. Cornering Rowland alone later in the evening he said, 'Do you know what's wrong with Julia?'

'What's wrong her?' Rowland said, with a fair imitation of Peter's intimidating eyebrow. 'In the circumstances, that seems an odd question to ask.'

'I was wondering if it wasn't something else, apart from that,' Peter said patiently. 'I wondered if she'd said anything to you.'

'Why would she?'

Why indeed. Peter struggled a little with this one. 'Oh, I don't know. Perhaps it might be easier to talk to someone who wasn't involved.'

'You could try asking her.'

'Oddly enough, I had thought of that.'

'And?'

'She denied that there was anything wrong.'

'Then perhaps she doesn't want you to know.'

'That's what worries me.'

Rowland looked away a moment. 'She hasn't confided in me. But I can see that she might find it difficult to confide in you.'

'What do you mean by that?'

'Ah, the defensive reaction,' Rowland said. 'You have changed, you know. When you two lived in that little flat, you muddled along happily together, two mice building a nest. Now all this –' He waved his hand round to encompass the room and the glittering guests. 'The fame, the money, the notice – it is different. You're not equal any more.'

246

Peter felt a depression coming over him. 'Then it is jealousy. Jealousy of my success.' It was comfortable to say, but he didn't believe it. There was something wordless inside him that did not consume that and feel satisfied.

Rowland did not answer the implied question. Instead, after a pause, he said, 'Maybe she wants another baby.'

That surprised Peter, and then seemed too simple. 'But then why wouldn't she tell me so?'

'You think it would be that easy?' Rowland said, sounding surprised in his turn.

'We are husband and wife.'

Rowland sought for words. 'Maybe she's afraid to ask you, in case you have another and it gets the same thing. Or maybe she's afraid that you don't want another, so she daren't ask.'

Peter opened his mouth and then shut it again. He and Julia had never talked about having another child, and the omission now for the first time struck him as remarkable. Had she concluded from the absence of discussion that he didn't want another? Did she perhaps think he blamed her for the boy dying, or believe he blamed himself? For that matter, what *did* he feel about it, beyond the monolithic loss? It was a closed door he did not want to open, and his work was not only the refuge from it but a satisfactory reason not to have to. Why wasn't it the same for her? He felt an obscure irritation that she should go on suffering so much that he was forced to notice it.

As he and his brother watched, Julia slipped away from the group she was talking to and out of the door. It was a perfectly normal action, but in the wake of their conversation and Peter's thoughts, it looked significant.

'I expect she's gone to see about the snacks,' Peter suggested.

'Yes,' said Rowland neutrally.

'I think perhaps I'll go and help.'

It took him a while to get out of the room, for people wanted to talk to him, and he couldn't make too obvious an exit after his wife, or it would appear they were having a row. He worked his way gently round the sides of the room and at last managed to slip out behind someone's back. Julia was not in the kitchen, where the help hired for the evening were arranging the food on ashets. He tracked her down eventually in their bedroom, and she turned sharply as he came in. He closed the door behind him and leaned against it, and Julia stared at him as if bayed.

They regarded each other for a few moments as their unspoken thoughts filled the atmosphere around them like smoke. Then at last Peter said, 'Rowland thinks that perhaps you want another baby.'

'Did he volunteer that thought, or did you ask him?'

Peter felt faintly embarrassed. 'I know you and he are close. Do you?'

'Would it trouble you if I did?'

'I don't know. I think it would trouble me if you didn't – positively didn't, I mean.'

'Maybe that's part of it, but part as a symptom is part, rather than the whole disease.'

'Then what is the whole disease?'

'That you don't know what is wrong, is what's wrong.'

'You're talking in riddles.'

'No, not really. You listen in riddles. No, that's not true. You listen in clichés. You don't ask questions to get at the truth, but to hear the answer you want. Even now, you aren't really here with me.'

He stirred impatiently. 'This really isn't the time for a deep discussion, with a houseful of guests.'

'Then why are you trying to have one? Because you know you won't get one,' she answered her own question.

'Look, I am making the effort—'

'They're your guests.'

He stared, trying to penetrate the barrier, but her face was closed to him. 'I was right then, it is jealousy.'

She made a tired gesture. 'Don't bring that up again. It isn't true, not in the least.'

'Then what is *wrong*?' he asked, exasperated.

'I don't know if I could explain it to you. I don't really want to try. I'd sooner you worked it out for yourself. If you can't, then there's no more to be said.'

'For God's sake!' He hated this 'there's something wrong

and you have to guess what it is' that women went in for. But this was Julia, his love. He curbed his irritation and tried to smile. 'Don't I even get any clues?'

She thought for a moment, and then said, 'I'll tell you one thing, Peter. Anything that doesn't grow is dying. Change is growth, and even if you don't like the direction of the change, you shouldn't resist it. You should welcome it. Do you know why you married me in the first place?'

It sounded like an abrupt change of subject, and he was taken aback for a moment and couldn't find the answer. 'Do you want me to tell you, or are you going to tell me?'

'I can't know. I can only use my imagination – but wasn't it because I was unpredictable, and you'd got used to Joyce?' She turned away from him, saying, 'Don't try to answer that, just think about it, when you've time – in bed, or in the car, when you're alone – and tell me what answers you come up with.'

'And do you think that will help?' he asked, thoroughly puzzled. She began to walk towards the door, and he stood aside automatically and opened it for her.

'I can't possibly say; but the thinking about it can't be anything but salutary.'

'Oh God,' he groaned quietly, and followed her back to the drawing room.

He did think about it, a little, once or twice, and it seemed to him to be like one of those impenetrably deep conversations that his mother had used to have with the Monsignor when he was a child, about Catholicism, when nothing seemed to mean anything solid or real, when what he saw as simple, they found obscure and difficult. To him as a child, the concept of God had been so easy to assimilate – such a thing of clear and happy certitude – that he had been baffled as to what his mother found to puzzle and argue over with the sesquipedalian priest. When he had grown up a little more, he had rejected the organised religion, 'seen through it' in his own choice of words; but still there had not seemed anything four-dimensional about it – indeed, it was the same simplicity which had once convinced him, which now seemed to him to disprove it all.

Julia, it seemed, saw something wrong – something difficult

– in their relationship, where to him it all seemed quite plain. Things had, surely, been more complex before, when they were not married, when there were all the complications of Joyce and the boys, and then shortness of money, and uncertainty about his career; but she had not been troubled then.

Since he could not think on her level, not knowing what or where it was, he tried to think of a straightforward answer to her distress; and, failing to find one, gave it up. Overtly they went on as always together, but there was a feeling of distance, of separation – it was like following someone who was always just out of sight, just one corner or one set of swing doors away. But Julia's trouble was no longer discernable, and gradually he forgot about it.

Failure sat on her chest like indigestion; not precisely painful, but uncomfortable, sharpening sometimes, then fading again as something else caught her attention.

She didn't know, she didn't know, how to reach him, how to make whole again what was broken. How could she tell him what was wrong if she didn't know the words for it? And how could she expect him to do anything about it if she didn't tell him what was wrong? Her few attempts were abortive, succeeded only in irritating him and shaming her, and she sought relief in silence.

She remembered with painful poignancy their joyful closeness, when they had understood each other without words, when their thoughts had kept pace through silences; when they had been on the same side. It was not only Boy's death, nor Peter's career, but what the combination of the two had done to them. He had gone to fame and success as though they were a place, and on a fundamental level he had not taken her with him. She had, she thought, become his wife, the background shape that took care of his house and decorated his arm at functions; the person who could be trusted to take phone messages and remember his dry-cleaning. He had gone somewhere she could not follow him – into international stardom – while she had gone another way, into loss, where he did not want to tread. The part of their life they had always shared had become, because of Nathan's death, too painful.

They rubbed against each other like two raw surfaces, and it was easier for him – she saw it and did not blame him – to avoid the contact than to go through the protracted discomfort of healing. She longed for him, needed him to grieve with, and found herself when with him too numb and dumb and – yes – too cowardly to break through the civilised crust into the chaos beneath.

She began to withdraw a little from his society – to stay at home sometimes instead of going everywhere with him, pleading the pressure of work – and in avoiding him there seemed some kind of solution, for when they did meet again there was such a spontaneous upsurge of pleasure that their old relationship seemed renewed.

She even toyed with the idea of admitting the Simple Solution – Sylvia had plenty of them to offer: 'You're seeing too much of each other. Everyone needs a break now and then. Most married couples spend less time together in ten years than you have in the past two. It's good to get away from each other now and again.'

It was comforting to think of human beings working on universal rules like that, like popular family cars coming off a conveyor belt, so that whatever went wrong, you could simply fix it by consulting the manual and having the right screwdriver or wrench to hand. It was comforting to think of a relationship as a sort of trigonometrical problem, where a startlingly wrong answer came right if you remembered to subtract the cosine correction instead of adding it – or vice versa, whichever it was. So for days on end she would be tolerably happy, accepting the Sylvia view, until she became dissatisfied with the basic premise – that her and Peter's relationship was something that, like toffee or a popular song, you could get tired of. Then her own too-slick words would come back to chase her round and round her brain: 'What doesn't grow, is dying.'

Sylvia was around a lot more often these days. She noticed it vaguely, and was happy enough that it should be so, for she felt that Sylvia, living in a flat now with two other 'bachelor girls' in Bayswater, was sometimes in need of a little peace and quiet and stability, not to mention a square meal. Julia thought Sylvia might have a fancy for Rowland, who dropped by when he was in London, often at the same time as Sylvia. Rowland seemed interested in Sylvia, and often gave her a lift home. If he and Sylvia were there when Peter arrived home, he seemed at pains to take Sylvia away at once. Julia's explanation of that to herself was that Peter's arrival meant Rowland was not worried about leaving her alone and gave him the chance to make time with Sylvia. It crossed Julia's mind that they might eventually marry. It would be a nice tidy thing to do, to square everything up. Sylvia wanted only the opportunity to be a very good wife to someone. She had all the right womanly qualities, and great physical attractiveness into the bargain, which most men seemed to value highly.

Gradually they settled into the new routine, and habit confirmed the contrivances and made them custom. Julia only went to concerts in London now, and then only on special occasions, where it was virtually obligatory for a star to display a wife. The rest of the time she worked at her painting, kept house, arranged parties and soirées, visited galleries and exhibitions. She took up riding again and went twice a week to a stables in Richmond. She took a greater interest in clothes, and started to do a little dressmaking herself.

Her time got used up, and she felt content, and Peter, no longer having to worry about her, was happy too, slipping back into the old pattern he had known with Joyce, of a wife who was a separate entity, functioning within a known sphere. If his sexual desire for her was more frantic than before when they were together, he put it down to the fact that they had fewer opportunities for satisfying it, for she, too, clung to him as if each time might be the last.

Julia was completely unprepared for what happened. She came home one day in April, in the early afternoon, from inspecting some new work in a Bond Street gallery. It had puzzled her and depressed her, for she couldn't see where it was leading, and, moreover, someone whose opinion she was used to respecting had seen in the pictures a whole lot of things that Julia had not. She had taken them to be fairly simple ideas expressed in the modern idiom, which tended to be involved; he had told her quite categorically that they were in fact highly complex ideas, working on something like eight different levels at once, and for the life of her, she couldn't see it. Either she was distressingly lacking in insight, or someone was conning someone. She hardly knew which alternative was worse.

So she did not stay for the drinks reception, but made her excuses and left before the press arrived. She was glad to get home. Here in Pelham Crescent, at least, one could be sure of what was good and what was not. Taste was not a two-edged knife, and 'good taste' was not a term of disparagement. The house stood quiet, white and sun-bathed, like four o'clock in a fairy story. The quietness affected her too, and she let herself in silently to the lavender-scented hall. She took off her hat and laid it with her handbag on the hall table; inspected the afternoon mail without interest; ran a hand wearily through her hair, and then went upstairs, up the thick, royal-blue carpeted stairs with the ornate, white-painted banisters; hesitated on the landing, and then went on up to the next floor, to her studio.

She turned in the doorway and stopped abruptly. Peter was there, facing three-quarters away from her, kissing Sylvia. His left arm was round her and his right hand was on her left breast; both Sylvia's arms were round his neck, and they both had their eyes shut. It was an odd picture, framed by the doorway, and seemed to persist in her mind like the impression of a bright window lingering on the retina. Sylvia's hair was ruffled; she was naked to the waist. Peter's shirt was undone and pulled out from his trousers. The velvet-covered, cushion-filled 'posing' couch was behind Sylvia, ready to receive them, and even at such a moment Julia appreciated that he had not wanted to use the marital bed. It was his form of loyalty.

But she could hear their breathing, and remembered in minute detail what it was like to be kissed by him like that, with his hand cupping her breast and his arm strong in the small of her back so that he could bend her under him a little. That it was Sylvia and not her he was doing it to hit her with a violence of shock that was, unexpectedly, nauseating. For an instant she really thought she might be sick.

As she looked, bemused, the significance burned into her mind, etching itself in deeper and deeper pain for all the few seconds during which they remained unaware of her presence.

Then Sylvia's eyes fluttered, the lids parted a little, and bolted open. She made an indistinguishable noise through his mouth that sounded rather like a squeal. Julia knew in that instant that she could not bear a confrontation, that it would hurt her to a degree from which she might not be able to recover. This was not just a kiss – he had done everything to her, everything, and she saw them in her mind in a lightning-flash revelation of revolting clarity. Her husband had defiled her. She turned and fled, just as she saw Peter's eye open and roll round to see what Sylvia was looking at without pausing for an instant in his kissing.

As she ran down the stairs, her mind was racing, but not, marvellously, panicking. It was desperately important to get away; it was desperately important that he should not speak to her, and she knew that if she stayed in the house he would come to her and try to explain, perhaps try to justify, perhaps lie. She was in terror that he would lie to her. She didn't want to hear it, any of it. She understood perfectly what had happened, she had comprehended everything in that Kodak snap framed in the doorway, and if he spoke to her it would not be to tell her what she knew.

So she had to get out of the house. On the landing below she paused, looking towards the bedroom while she calculated whether she had enough time to pack anything and instantly rejected the idea. Nightdress, dressing gown, change of under-wear, spongebag – these were the 'essentials' she would pack if she were to pack, and she could just as easily buy any of those in any shop she passed. No, no packing. She ran on down.

Money was the real essential. She picked up her handbag, knowing that she had around twenty pounds in it, dashed into the drawing room for her cheque book which was lying inside the open bureau, and heard the sounds of pursuit from above her.

'Julia! *Julia!*' Peter's voice. Of course not Sylvia's – Sylvia would no more want to walk into a row than Julia had, all those years ago in the Kanes' hallway in Spenser Road. She ran back into the hall and had her hand on the front door latch when Peter reached the turning of the stairs and called her again.

'Julia!' His voice, so near and unmuffled made her stop and turn, and she saw him, one foot on the landing, one foot two steps down, one hand on the bannisters, leaning forward to see her under the slope of the flight above. His face was a little flushed, his hair a little ruffled, his eyes bright blue. He was angry, not anxious, she thought: in his own mind he still had not done anything terminal. She loved him so searingly, despite everything, that she knew in that instant she must make it impossible for herself to come back, or she might just crawl home like a dog to the comfort of his hand. She scrabbled in her handbag for her front door keys and flung them down the hall to the foot of the stairs. And then she opened the door and stepped out, shutting it firmly behind her.

She ran the ten yards to the corner, but once she had turned into Pelham Place she walked, for she was out of sight to him then from the front door, and she knew he would not pursue her down the road – especially not with his shirt loose and open. It was too undignified, and he was an international star now, with a reputation to lose. And of course he would not believe she was going for good anyway. He would think she was running out blindly to cry and would be back in the evening to be explained to. She walked briskly towards the station, her step strangely light, her mind oddly painless. That was shock, of course. She walked as a headless chicken does, not knowing it is dead. She went not knowing in the least where she was going, except that it was away.

Thirteen

1963

In November her father died. Julia heard about it from Sylvia, in a letter sent to her at Martin Newman's address, where she had been staying since her return from Ireland. The letter avoided any mention of Peter or the trouble, so Julia wasn't able to guess whether Sylvia was with him or under his protection or what. The letter was addressed from Milton Street where Sylvia was staying for a week or so to help her mother over the shock.

'It was a heart attack,' the letter said. 'He went into his study to work as usual after lunch, and when Mother went in to tell him dinner was ready, he was lying forward over his desk. He must have died almost immediately after lunch, so the doctor said, and apparently it was instantaneous. That is a comfort, at least. Mother is taking it very well. She hasn't said anything, but I think she would like it if you were to come to the funeral. It is to be on Tuesday.'

Julia finished the letter, and then leaning forward dropped it on to the fire – not from any dramatic urge but because she liked to watch paper burn. She thought a little about her father, but she felt nothing. She had still had a little residual affection left for him; but her mind was so numb with the shock of losing Peter that the blow fell on an already-amputated limb. She did not reply to the letter, nor attend the funeral. Her parents had rejected her, thrust her unceremoniously out of the nest so long ago that her life had become quite detached from theirs. They were strangers, and one did not attend the funeral of strangers.

There was a curious aftermath, however. Firstly there came from a firm of solicitors a letter concerning her father's will. His share of the copyrights of his books had been left to her mother for her lifetime, and to Julia thereafter. The term of copyright was fifty years after the death of the author, so given that her mother was now sixty-three, it was likely that Julia would inherit before the term ended – if the copyright was worth anything by then. The solicitors did not quite put it in those terms, but they said they would be grateful if Julia would keep them informed of any change of address in future.

Julia was surprised and oddly touched that her father had remembered her in his will – though it was possible that he had simply forgotten to change it after her disgrace. But there was another consequence of his death which was even more surprising. A week later she received another letter, again forwarded from Milton Street; in consequence of which she found herself one day having tea at Fortnum's with her aunt Ethel.

'Oh, call me Etty, love. I never liked that silly name – though it was all the rage when I was a girl, and believe me or believe me not it was thought quite pretty – and I can't think of any reason you should have to call me "aunt", given that you haven't clapped eyes on me since you were knee high to a grasshopper. You don't remember me at all, do you?'

There was a slight wistfulness to the question, but honesty compelled Julia to say, 'No, I'm afraid I don't – though I think I have heard Mother talk about you.'

'It'd be a wonder if she did,' Etty snorted, 'given we had a falling-out, as they say; but it was none of my doing that it wasn't made up, so I hope you believe me. My, this is a posh place, isn't it? Do you think that snooty waitress is deliberately ignoring us? I'd have picked somewhere cosier, dear, but it had to be somewhere we both knew, and I haven't been to London since VE Day, so I was afraid everything would've changed. Only I was sure Fortnum's must still be there. It was that or the Ritz and I thought the Ritz'd be even posher.'

Julia regarded her unknown aunt with deep interest. She was prosperous, peroxided, and dressed in pink, which was not only surprising for someone her age, but surprising for December when everyone else was in dark suits and furs. She had thick makeup on, too, which did not so much make her look younger as made it impossible to calculate her age, since it looked quite unnatural – a mask, like kabuki. She had on a small hat with a net, and earrings that looked as though they might be real diamonds; and when she loosened the scarf around her neck she let loose a gust of heavy but expensive perfume. Yet she looked around the Fountain Room with the open curiosity and frank enjoyment of a child. Julia liked her instantly and hugely, so much that she regretted her own proper dark suit and hoped her aunt would not find it a reproach, or notice that she stood out like a buttercup on a bowling green.

The waitress came to them, looking as though her feet hurt. She had a red nose and watery eyes.

'Now then, dear,' Etty said to her firmly, 'we'll have a pot of tea and some scones and – what about a nice poached egg on toast?' she asked Julia.

'Oh, no thank you. Nothing to eat.'

'Why not? It's my treat, and I'm good for it. You don't look as though you eat half enough. I know, a nice Welsh rabbit. Do you the world of good. Two Welsh rabbits, dear,' she said firmly, turning back to the waitress to prevent argument. 'And put a poached egg on top as well. Have you got a cold? Yes, I thought so. Well don't you go sneezing on us, or there'll be no tip for you. My Desmond takes a cold at the drop of a hat and I don't want to be carrying your germs back to him.'

The waitress went away with a lift of her eyes as though now she'd heard everything. Etty turned her attention back to Julia. 'Well, now, love, let me have a look at you. My, you do look like your father, God rest his soul. I bet that was a comfort to him.'

'Do you think so?' Julia said.

'What, do I think you look like him, or do I think you were a comfort? You weren't at the funeral, I notice, though Sylvia said you were invited.'

'I wasn't exactly invited. Sylvia told me when it was to be—'

'And you wondered if your mother knew she was telling you, is that it?' Julia did not want to go into her situation with Sylvia, and nodded. Etty primmed her lips. 'Phyllis is a fool. I'm her sister and I love her, God help me, but I know a fool when I see one. A fool and a snob, and look where it's got her. Desperate

258

to be respectable, marrying out of her class, looking down on me and Desmond, but there she is in that miserable little hole, while we've got a brand new bungalow in Surrey, *and* a car. I admit money isn't everything, and there's no denying your dad was a good few cuts above us, but what's he left her?' She cocked her head at Julia. 'In case you're wondering, I told her I was going to see you today – *and* I told her I was going to tell you everything, so you needn't worry. None of this is behind her back, though it'd serve her right if it was.'

Julia felt she was being flattened. Etty seemed so large and ebullient and unstoppable, like a mountain torrent. Julia could trace a resemblance in her face to her mother, but her mother's guarded, tight-lipped expression was missing, and in its place a pink, slightly crumpled mobility registered a succession of feelings, all endearingly on display. Aunt Ethel also smoked, and her slightly husky voice spoke of a lifelong habit. Her mother thought it 'common' for women to smoke.

'What do you mean, tell me everything?' Julia asked, grasping at the most significant phrase in the outpouring.

Etty gave her a significant, sideways look, knowing as a parrot. 'About her and Bernard – your dad – and you and Sylvia and all the rest of it. She never told you anything about all that, did she?'

'She never told me anything about anything,' Julia said. 'Neither of them did.' She found a wonderful relief in admitting it. One naturally defended one's parents, and she had never spoken disparagingly of them to anyone – consequently, had never allowed herself to criticise them. But the further she moved from her childhood, the more faults she saw in the way her parents had brought her up. The stiffness, silence, isolation – the utter lack of communication – they were relics from another age: modern parents talked to their offspring. And the way they had cast her off, which she had accepted as her just deserts, now seemed to her wrong and unwarranted. Shouldn't they have stood by her, however much they disapproved?

'I know. And I know how they let you down when you got in your bit of trouble, and I know why you wouldn't go to your own dad's funeral, so I wanted to explain it all to you. I mean, for one thing, you've got the right to know, and for another

259

– well, it might make you understand Phyl a bit better and maybe take pity on her.' She regarded Julia's face a moment and added, 'Yes, I know what you're thinking – why should you? But it's for children to understand grown-ups, you know, love, not vice versa, because grown-ups can't change once they get set in the mould.'

The waitress came with a tray and began laying things out, and Etty desisted from speaking until the woman had left again. Then she said, 'Tuck in, and I'll tell you a story. Once upon a time there were two sisters.'

'And their names were Ethel and Phyllis,' Julia supplied with a smile.

'Sharp, aren't you? Well, these two girls weren't posh, but they weren't poor. Their dad owned his own shop, a seed merchant's, and back in those days where we lived was quite a country sort of area, not really part of London at all, so the shop did quite nicely. Apart from the farmers, nearly everybody kept a few hens or rabbits or pigeons, and there was dog meal and biscuit as well, and cage-bird seed and so on. But things started to change during the war—'

'The first world war?'

'Of course, love. The Great War we called it – of course, we never dreamt there'd be another. Anyway, the shop started to go downhill a bit, and after the war things just got worse. There were big new companies, chains, selling seed and fodder, and they undercut the little man, with their discounts and packaged stuff. So we found ourselves getting poorer, and the prospects for me and Phyl weren't too rosy. For girls like us, there was only marriage, or staying home with mum and dad. Well, Phyl was pretty, and I was smart, so we hoped for the best. But there wasn't much choice back then, in a country place, what with all the boys who never came back from the war, and I wasn't for marrying just anyone. I wanted a man with something about him, and a bit of cash to spend. So I took a correspondence course and learned to type and then I upped sticks and went to London. Got myself a job, and then a better one, and – well, this is not my story, so to cut it short, I ended up at a small engineering firm in Ladbroke Grove and married the boss, and I've never looked back. You couldn't want a better husband than my Desmond, and though we've never had any kiddies we've been very happy. But the upshot,' she said with an air of dragging herself back to the nub of the matter, 'is that I wasn't there to keep an eye on Phyllis, and she went and got herself into trouble.'

'What sort of trouble?' Julia asked.

Etty gave her an arch look. 'Oh, the usual sort, dear. Does that surprise you?'

'You mean . . . ?'

'Got herself in the club with some local boy, one of the ones who *did* come back – but nobody special, he wasn't, for all that Phyl was so pretty, *and* thought so well of herself. He was just a farm labourer before he went away, from all I could gather.'

'My *mother*?' Her mother, who was always so proper, who disapproved of so many things, who had been so unforgiving of Julia's sin, had been a sinner herself?

'Yes, dear. Hard to believe, the way she is now. A prig and a prude and oh-so-proper. But I suppose she might say that she knows only too well where bad behaviour leads.'

Julia felt bewildered. 'So – what happened?'

'Oh, the boy scarpered as quick as you like. Mum and Dad were shocked and furious too, but they did right by her, and looked after her until she had the baby.'

A light came on in Julia's memory. 'Was that the other sister – Lydia – the one who died?'

'Yes, dear, only she didn't die, of course. Given away, she was, to a rich couple who hadn't got any kiddies of their own. It's a shame it wasn't a few years later, after I'd married Desmond, or we might have adopted her ourselves, but I hadn't even met him then, so there was nothing I could do. So anyway—'

'So she's still alive?' Julia interrupted. 'My sister Lydia is still alive?'

'Well, I suppose so,' said Etty. 'I've never heard of her since, for of course it was all kept a deadly secret where she went and who they were and everything. Don't even know what her name would be now. But she's probably alive. She'd be – what – in her forties now.'

Julia was so enchanted by the idea of her sister's being alive she hardly heard the last part. She had fantasised all her childhood about the kind older sister who would understand her and be a confidante and protectress. And now it seemed there really was such a person – somewhere. If only she knew where!

Etty was continuing. 'Anyway, dear, that's not important. The thing was, of course, that your mother had spoiled her chances. She was damaged goods now, and no one would take her, so she had to get a job. A barmaid, that's what she became. Yes, it's true! Pulling pints in a bar, under the eyes of every Tom, Dick and Harry – that's what she came down to. Well, she didn't want to stick around at home where everybody knew her, so she moved to Oxford and got a job in a pub there. I think she thought she might meet some nice gullible young undergrad that she could con into marrying her, but it didn't work out that way. Years passed and she got older and though she was still handsome there was no use looking at undergrads any more. And then when she was in her thirties she met David Underwood.'

'Uncle David!'

Etty gave her a wry look. 'Yes, Uncle David. Well, he was a handsome rogue, that's what he was. Had money, too – inherited. Never been married, but never denied himself the pleasure of ladies' company, if you understand me.'

'I remember him just a little bit,' Julia said. 'At least, I don't really remember what he looked like, but I remember that I liked him, even though I was in awe of him.'

'Yes, dear, females always liked him, even little girls. I was quite smitten myself, though I was accounted for, of course, by the time I met him.'

'When I was very little he sometimes used to lift me up until my head bumped the ceiling,' Julia said. No one else ever did anything like that. In fact, once they had moved to Milton Street, she didn't remember anyone ever touching her at all, except from necessity. Her mother never tucked her in or kissed her goodnight. As to her father kissing her – it was impossible even to imagine.

'Oh, he was a charmer all right, was David Underwood,

and he took a fancy to your ma, and she – well, I don't know whether she was in love with him or if she just hoped he'd marry her. But he wasn't the marrying sort. Lifelong bachelor, like a lot of these university men. Anyway, it was through him of course that she met Bernard – your father. Now he was another lifelong bachelor – he was already in his forties when she met him – but he was a different proposition from David. Very unworldly, your father. Nose so deep in his books he hardly knew what century it was outside, never mind what day of the week.'

She paused to refill the teacups, and said, 'My, this is turning out to be a longer story than I expected. How are you standing it, love?'

'It's fascinating,' Julia said. 'I knew nothing about my parents' past. I didn't even know my grandfather was a seed merchant.'

'She never talked to you about any of it?'

'She never talked to me at all.'

'Didn't even show you the wedding photos?'

Julia shook her head. 'I didn't know there were any. We weren't really a photograph family. We didn't own a camera, and there weren't any framed photos on display, the way you see in some people's houses. We had a school photograph done once a year but I don't know what Mother did with them. They were never shown.'

'I expect she has them tucked away in a box somewhere,' Etty said wisely. 'She can't be so unnatural a mother she throws away her own childrens' pictures.' She took a long draught of tea and said, 'Now, where did I get up to?'

'Meeting my father, I think.'

'Oh, right you are. Well, now I have to guess a bit, because Phyl wasn't exactly confiding in me, but I think David and her both decided separately that Bernard was a good prospect for her. She was desperate to be respectable and get married, and I suspect David wanted her safely tied up so she couldn't bother him – but he didn't mind the idea of having her somewhere handy, if you get me. Am I shocking you, dear?' Julia shook her head. 'That's not my intention, so I hope you believe me. But you see, I can't see how it could have been done without

263

David's help, because, as I say, your father never looked up from his books for two minutes together. But look up he did, and fell in love with your mother.'

'Did he?' Julia was astonished and, she found, delighted by the idea. She had always hoped, though increasingly hopelessly, that her parents had not always been as she knew them. It seemed too dismal. It was impossible to imagine her parents in love, but, oh, she was glad to learn they had been, once.

'Well, she was still handsome, and she knew how to charm when she wanted to. Whether she was in love with him I can't say, but she wanted to marry him all right, and he was too old-fashioned and respectable to do anything without marriage, so the long and the short was that they got hitched.'

'Was it a lovely wedding?' Julia asked. 'You were there?'

'Oh yes, I was matron of honour. Well, I wouldn't call it *lovely*, exactly, but it was nice. Registry office do, of course, but your mother looked very nice indeed, in a beautiful lilac crêpe dress and matching hat. Beautiful tucks in the bodice, fitted sleeves – a bit like the outfit Mrs Simpson got married in, if you know what I mean, only not with such a long skirt. Then it was back to David's house for a bit of a do. Lots of champagne, and all sorts of smart people, friends of David's, I suppose, because they weren't the sort you'd meet in a pub, if you understand me. Then your mum and dad went off on honeymoon, and when they came back, well, now –' her expression changed from pleased reminiscence to pursed disapproval – 'that was when the tricky bit came in, and the reason I always suspected there was a what-you-call-it between them, you know, collusion.'

'Between Mother and Uncle David?'

'Yes – because, you see, your father had lived in bachelor lodgings up to then, so he hadn't got a house to take your mum back to. So David said, why don't I take a house big enough for all of us to live in. We work together and it makes sense for us to be on hand when queries come up, rather than have to arrange to meet. He had money, you see, dear, and your father didn't, only his royalties and lecture fees. Well, Bernard was as happy as could be with the arrangement, so David took that big house by the park and they all settled in like one big happy family.'

The tone of the last part was sardonic, and Julia looked at her aunt doubtfully. 'You mean – you think there was something going on between Mother and Uncle David?'

'I can't put my hand on the Bible and swear there was, because of course she wouldn't tell me a thing like that and the last thing she wanted to do was to risk her nice respectable marriage. All I can say is when Desmond and me visited sometimes there was an atmosphere. There were little looks and little hints I picked up—'

'But – but I thought Uncle David *liked* my father. They were colleagues for years and years!'

'I'm sure he did like him, dear,' Etty said comfortingly, 'but you know, with rakes like him, nothing counts for anything when they're on the prowl. David was a real charmer, and he was clever, but he was the sort who thinks himself too clever, do you know what I mean? He'd have been convinced he could have a romp with his partner's wife right under his nose, and get away with it. He'd have believed he'd never be found out.'

Julia looked at her with dull shock. 'But he did get found out?'

Etty said, 'I promised myself I'd tell you, because I thought you ought to know, given the way everybody's been so down on you – not that I approve of messing with married men, and divorce is a terrible thing, but we're all human, only some people don't like to remember that. But Desmond said I should let sleeping dogs lie, and now I see how upset you are, I wish I'd listened to him.'

Julia shook herself. 'No – really – I'm glad you told me.'

'I know it's a surprise to you, dear, but you mustn't judge people too harshly,' Etty said.

'I'm the last person to make judgements. You know about my wicked past, obviously.'

'You were young,' Etty said, 'and if I know anything about Phyl and Bernard, you were innocent. And I bet the man was a real charmer, like David.'

'Yes,' Julia said dully. 'A real charmer.'

Etty leaned across the table and patted her hand. 'There, I've

265

upset you, and that wasn't what I wanted. I'm really sorry love. I won't say any more. You forget everything I've said. It was all my fancy, I dare say.'

'No, no, you must finish. I want to know the rest. I *need* to know, to understand. Don't you hate it when you don't understand things?'

Etty nodded slowly, and then said, 'Well, if you're sure – there's not much more to tell, anyway. First Sylvia came along and then you did, and everything in the garden seemed lovely until the war. Well, at least your dad was too old to be called up, that was one blessing. But then that bomb fell on the house and changed everything.' She hesitated, and then squared her shoulders to the task. 'You know that your father wasn't at home when the air raid started?'

'He and Mother had gone out somewhere together.'

'No, dear. That's what they said afterwards, to save face. But it wasn't quite that way. He'd been giving a lecture in London and he was on his way home when it started. He had to take cover in the public shelter, and when the all-clear sounded he carried on home, and found the house a ruin. The housekeeper, Mrs Hooper, had taken you children down to the shelter in the garden, and she was in hysterics that David was still in the house somewhere. He never would go in a shelter, not for anything, so she hadn't even asked him, but just grabbed you girls and went down herself.'

'And my mother?' Julia asked, though she thought she had guessed.

'Mrs Hooper thought she was out, like your father. She did *go* out, apparently, after your father left, but she must have come back and slipped in without Mrs Hooper knowing. Anyway when the rescue team dug in the rubble, they found her with David. The bed had gone straight down through the floor with them in it. He was on top of her, and that's what had saved her. I suppose he threw himself over her when it happened, or maybe . . .' She coughed and thought better of that sentence. 'Well, at all events, he'd taken all the rubble and stuff on his back, and his body had protected her. He was dead but there was hardly a scratch on her.' She paused a moment, and then went on musingly, 'It was a funny old thing, the blitz. You

266

never knew who would survive and who wouldn't. You could have two people standing side by side and one'd be killed and the other perfectly all right. And you'd have people step out of ruins you'd think a mouse couldn't survive in. You just never knew. Anyway, that was how your mother was found. David was dead as a nail, and the house was his, of course. Your mum and dad were left practically without a stick, just what they could salvage from the ruins.'

There was a silence while Julia reassembled her thoughts. Then she said, 'So you think the affair had been going on all along?'

'I can't say that,' Etty said briskly. 'It's only what I suspect. But all those lectures and talks and things your father did, that helped his income so much and bought Phyl the nice clothes she liked – it was David arranged them all. He knew people, he liked people – your father was too much of a recluse. No, David got him all those engagements.'

'So he could be alone with my mother.'

'Maybe. I can't say more than maybe. But after he was killed, the lectures pretty well dried up.'

So that explained the difference between 'before' and 'after', Julia thought. With the house destroyed and David dead, her parents had moved into the small rented house and lived in the 'reduced circumstances' of depending on his royalties. No more lecture tours because no David to arrange them. And no more love or trust or conversation or laughter, only the sterile business of restoring respectability, keeping the past secret, and bringing up the two girls not to make their mother's mistakes. No wonder her mother had always been so keen on their becoming secretaries, like the respectable and lucky Etty. No wonder they had been so savage with Julia when her sin was exposed. No wonder . . .

She became aware of her aunt's eyes fixed on her. 'You're upset, I can see it,' Etty said. 'Do you think I shouldn't have told you?'

'No,' Julia said, and then again, more firmly, 'No. I'm glad you did. It explains so much. But why did you and Mother fall out? Was it because of – of her being found the way she was?'

'Oh no,' Etty said, sounding quite surprised. 'I would never judge another human being for making the best of what they'd

267

got. I thought your mother was a fool to risk everything, but maybe she had to. Maybe it was the price she had to pay for the "everything" in the first place. I was shocked like everyone else when it happened, but I was more thankful she and you girls had got out alive. But I said things to her afterwards, things I shouldn't have said. It was in the shock of the moment, really, and I apologised afterwards many a time, but she had a resentful temper, your mother, and she never really forgave me. We offered them help you know, Desmond and me, but they wouldn't take it – or your mum wouldn't, anyway. I don't know if she ever even told your dad. Offered them a home with us to begin with, and cash to tide them over, but they wouldn't take it. Well, they were lucky to get that house in Milton Street – of course, bombed out and with two little kiddies they were priority, but even so. But it all seemed to have taken it out of your dad, and to my mind he never really tried afterwards, just shut himself up and went on with his books, and your mum – you know how she became. I'd have liked to help – at least have you girls to stay sometimes, give you a bit of a treat now and then, but no. She wouldn't have it. Since you left home, I've written to her a few times and she's eased up a bit with me. At any rate, she invited me to your dad's funeral, which is quite an advance. Now I've got the "in" I shall stick by her, you needn't worry.'

'But what was it you said that was so unforgivable?'

Etty hesitated, but then said, 'In for a penny, I suppose.' She patted her lips carefully with her napkin and said slowly, not quite meeting Julia's eyes, 'I wondered why it was that Sylvia looks so different from you. Anyone can see *you* look like Bernard, but Sylvia—'

'Sylvia looks like Mother,' Julia said, shocked. 'You don't think— ?'

Etty coughed slightly. 'Doesn't matter what I think. But I think your father wondered sometimes. Before the bomb, I used to catch him looking at her, and looking from her to your mother and then to David. He was unworldly, but he wasn't a complete fool. It's just that sometimes it's better to shut your eyes and not rock the boat.'

'Have you told Sylvia this?'

'No, of course not. What do you take me for? Anyway, Sylvia's never been thrown out to fend for herself like you.'

'You saw her at the funeral. How did she look?' Julia asked bleakly.

'Very well. Smart and pretty. Upset, of course; and she talked a lot about you, and wished you'd come.' Etty eyed her consideringly. 'Is there some quarrel between you and her? It wasn't just because your parents sent you away that you didn't go?'

Julia didn't answer directly. 'I was a fool, too, like my mother – only I didn't have her excuse. She did what she did to survive. I did it for love.'

'Well, I don't say there wasn't love in it for your mother as well. David Underwood was a handsome man, and a charmer. Was yours like that?'

'He's not handsome, not in the usual way.'

'But you love him?'

'I'll never love anyone else.'

'Oh, you can't say that! Things change, people get over things. You learn in a long life that you can't ever say never.'

'I've learned in a short life that you can't trust anyone,' Julia said, and her aunt tutted.

'No, dear, no. That's not the attitude. I don't know what happened between you and your man, or between you and Sylvia, but time heals all things. And Sylvia's your sister – you can't get away from that. I mean, she'll always be your sister, no matter what. And when you get to my age, you'll know that flesh and blood is what counts most.'

Julia only shook her head, bewildered by all the new information. It would take days, if not weeks, to sort it all out, and discover what she felt about it all. It explained so much that had latterly come to puzzle her. She understood now her mother's desperate struggle to achieve respectability at all costs, what she had undertaken for it, and sacrificed for it, and her sullen fury at the daughter who put it all in jeopardy through a frailness she didn't understand. Julia believed that – believed her mother had never been in love and therefore did not comprehend what had driven Julia to do something which could bring her no apparent gain. Looked at in that light, Julia had behaved like a madwoman, first committing adultery, then being involved in a divorce, and now – oh, now! Throwing it all away for nothing, was how she supposed her mother would see it, leaving Peter when he was rich and famous and therefore the perfect husband. She was glad now she had not gone to the funeral. Her mother might have been goaded into telling what she thought of her. It was evident that Aunt Etty did not know what had happened between her and Sylvia, so she suspected Sylvia had wisely kept quiet about it with their mother. Julia didn't blame her for that. In Sylvia's position she would have done the same. She, Julia, had simply been too young when her own crunch came – too young and too innocent – to dissemble, to make herself a position to defend. She would handle it better now – though of course it was impossible that such a thing could happen now. She had been the victim of timing, that was all.

To understand all is to forgive all, so they said. But no, she could not forgive, not her parents nor Sylvia – not yet. Still, she understood, and that was a beginning. But all this revelation did not help her in the least to know what to do about anything, or what her life in the future would hold. She felt as utterly at sea and without guidance as in those days just after the discovery by Joyce of her wickedness, and her own discovery of Sylvia's.

Fourteen

D uring those first months after leaving Peter she had behaved rather like a victim of shell shock. As when Joyce had confronted her, as when Boy had died, her first instinct had been to run and hide, and she had obeyed it. It was hard to run in any direction that did not remind her of happier journeys with Peter, and at last an almost random movement had directed her to Ireland. She had gone over the long way, by train and boat, spending a long, weary, bitterly cold night travelling. The entrails of the boat had been at the same time stifling and cold. There had been no seats, and the passengers were pressed together in a slowly milling throng like cattle, their droning, slurred voices sounding en masse rather like cattle too. There had been nothing to do but drink, and Julia, in common with almost everyone else, had drunk all night long, falling in at last from sheer propinquity with a family of father, mother, three boys, two girls, small baby, pushchair, and a young Olympus of luggage. They talked to her kindly and unintelligibly, shared their sandwiches with her, and let her take turns with them sitting on the largest of the suitcases.

Julia, dazed though she was with drink and tiredness and shock, recognised their kindness, and the awareness of it and the inability to express the awareness added to the sense of nightmare with which she recalled that extraordinary journey afterwards. On arrival in Ireland she hired a car and drove south and west, and spent her whole time that way, simply driving from place to place, through endless narrow lanes, past endless wet, empty, green fields. Each night she found a town, booked into a hotel, and spent the evening drinking in the saloon bar watched by the local

271

old people, faintly hostile, like cats, in the presence of a stranger.

The soft wet air seemed to seep into her brain and her bones so that she slowed down, and could not think or remember. Inside her somewhere was the hideous wound, bleeding internally, a pain just waiting to be wakened by an incautious movement; but for the time being she was completely anaesthetised. Her driving grew slower and even less purposeful, and if she came across anything remotely resembling a view, she was likely to stop the car and sit and stare at it for anything up to an hour before moving on. The instinct to run and hide was satisfied: she really was somewhere else.

It was instinctive, too, on her return, to go to Martin. He had been in on the story from the beginning; he was Peter's best friend, and had always been kind to her, but more especially he had a way of remaining calm and impersonal which Julia thought would be important to her in her present state. She was not mistaken in her trust. He took her in unquestioningly, gave her the freedom of his flat, and was ready with his advice and help as soon as she asked for it.

She behaved, and felt, as if she would never move again; but after the shock of her father's death, and when she had had time to assimilate all the new information revealed by her aunt, she felt at last that the time had come for her to move out, and to set about recreating her own life.

'You don't have to go,' Martin said first of all, mildly, never wishing to interfere. When, however, she persisted, he said more strongly, 'I wish you would stay. I like to have you here, and I don't think you should be on your own yet awhile.'

'Thanks,' she said, really grateful. 'But I have to make a start sometime. So far all I've done is prove what I can't do. I've failed at everything. When I've succeeded at something, then I'll be fit for company again. I have to try to get on my feet.'

'What will you do?' he asked.

She could only make a practical answer. 'Get a job. Get a place to live. Do what everyone else does. Somehow or

272

other I got spared those things the first time round – now I've got to catch up.'

Martin shook his head. 'I can't see it somehow. Oh, don't mistake me – I know you're capable of it: but that's for ordinary people. I've always felt there was some kind of special fate reserved for you.'

'If there was, don't you think I've already had it?' she asked, her mouth curving in a bitter smile.

'Cross the gypsy's palm with silver. I see letters, a fair man, and journeys across water. Beware of the dog. Do not alight from moving train.'

Julia laughed. 'You almost make me want to stay. If it wasn't for . . .' She stopped.

'If it wasn't for what?'

But she wouldn't tell him. She had thought that if it wasn't for the fact that he was primarily Peter's friend, and that her association with him on a long-term basis would effectively end that old friendship, she would love to stay. But it was better that she should try going it alone – she had been right in that.

The practical parts of the matter were easy enough. She got herself a small flat in a two-storey house in Clapham Common, ready furnished, for a rent which was small enough for her not to worry about what she anticipated would be the greater difficulty of getting a job. But times had changed since she had disappeared into marriage, and she emerged into an easier, more relaxed world. The 'sixties had arrived. Austerity was over, business was expanding, new companies were popping up, and jobs seemed suddenly as plentiful as blackberries. Advertising in particular was a growing industry. She studied the cards in the windows of the new proliferation of employment agencies, and was sent for an interview with an advertising agency whose offices were in a tall, narrow, sooty building in Chancery Lane. The offices inside were as little inviting as outside, being old, ill-lit, dusty and inconvenient; but the studio, which was at the top of the building, occupying the whole floor, somehow attracted her.

It was as dusty, and far more untidy than the rest of the

273

offices put together, with overflowing waste-paper bins, an indescribably dirty floor, and no uncluttered surface to be seen; but the light was good, the walls were decorated with posters and pen-and-ink sketches, the clutter was mainly composed of such agreeable elements as coloured cartridge paper, sketching blocks and poster paints. Above all, the four faces – three male and one female – which lifted to examine her when she was brought in to look round, seemed friendly, intelligent and interesting.

She accepted the job, went back to the agency to report and receive instuctions on how to acquire an employment card, and went back to her flat in Clapham wondering how she was going to get through the days until she started work. There was nothing to do at home – she had to get used to calling it that. Once she had bought one or two items of food and made her bed, there was nothing more to be done in the matter of housework. She foresaw the time when she would be glad of the excuse to go down to the launderette, just to pass the time.

She knew no one in the area, and didn't know the area itself either, or what it had to offer. South of the river was terra incognita to her, which was pretty well why she had chosen it. Even the tube line – the Northern – was new. Apart from Waterloo (for the Festival Hall) and Borough (for Henry Wood Hall) its stations had no associations for her.

All her books had been left behind with Peter – likewise her painting gear, though even if she had had it with her she would not have wanted to do any painting for herself. That belonged to another life, a life in which there was Peter and their marriage and children. Her loss welled up inside her, and she leaned against the window and cried – not for Nathan, but for Peter. The loss of the baby was a completed and absolute thing, with nothing to be done about it, but the loss of Peter was a present and ongoing suffering. He had been her life for more than ten years, and being parted from him was like being torn in half. It was many weeks before she could get through a whole evening without tears.

Her job, however, from the very first day turned out well. The studio team welcomed her so openly and pleasantly that she hardly felt like a newcomer. It reminded her a little of being back at college. The five of them arrived each morning with varying degrees of unpunctuality and spent the first half-hour of the day making tea, trying to get the heaters to work or the windows to open, depending on the season, reading the papers, complaining about the state of the studio (the cleaner was erratic) and gossiping. They talked voraciously and with catholic inclusion all day long, and to Julia the conversation was one of the best parts of the job.

At lunch time they would take turns to go down to the sandwich bar run by an elderly Italian couple on the corner of Cursitor Street and fetch up the orders for everyone. They would spend the rest of the lunch hour playing darts on their own board which was concealed behind a poster in the corner. On Fridays they got paid, and they would go down to The Old Leather Bottle and have their sandwiches with beer. They bickered amicably, criticised each other's work, borrowed each other's erasers, pens and brushes, denied borrowing each other's rulers, swapped newspapers, and were half-resented, half-envied by the rest of the staff, who viewed them as a privileged clique, a Bohemian elite of the newly swinging age.

They all had their eccentricities. Christina, for instance, was forever eating, and her waste-paper basket overflowed before anyone else's and spread a tide of orange peel and chocolate wrappers along with the usual paper, cardboard and pencil shavings. Malcolm, who was rather fey and wore a cardigan, covered every available surface with potted plants – geraniums, spider-plants, tradescantia. Gordon was a fresh-air fiend, and Bob could only work to music, either on the radio, or his own whistled versions. Julia fitted very neatly into the group and was soon famous for her good humour, her willingness to make the tea even when it wasn't her turn, and her cartoon portraits of members of the staff.

She liked her job, and loved the company she had at work, perhaps the more so because of the miserable contrast her home life provided. She kept the two rigidly separate, and nothing of her past life or present misery intruded into her office personality. She had reverted to her maiden name, so

275

there was no reason for anyone to connect her with the famous Peter Kane, and if any of them knew there was a connection, they certainly never mentioned it. The divorce was mentioned in the papers, but either money or interest kept the reporting to a minimum. In the musical periodicals it received better coverage, with a photograph, but even so it was not general knowledge.

Time passed. Julia continued to like her job, and was successful at it. She created an advertising figure called Freddy Fox for Fox and Fuller, the biscuit manufacturers, which was a sudden hit and became a minor cult, earning her a substantial bonus and more of the top account work. An art exhibition was announced that roused her interest enough to tempt her out to it one weekend, and as she left she was handed a leaflet announcing the opening of a new gallery. A fine day decided her to book a ride at a hacking stables in Wimbledon. She found a local pub that was pleasant to drink in now and then.

Piece by piece, she was rebuilding.

1965

'Hello! Come in, come in. My dear, it's been an age since I saw you.'

'Am I late?'

'You're not the last.'

'Tactful man!'

'Let me take your coat.'

Julia turned her back and slid out of her coat as Giles took hold of the collar, and then turned again to receive her due admiration.

'You look ravishing!' he said with every appearance of sincerity. She didn't really mind one way or the other, because she knew she looked good – black velvet made a marvellous effect against her pale skin and fair hair – but it was nice to have it said anyway. 'I must say divorce seems to agree with you. I must see if I can't persuade Louie to give it a try.'

Julia could even take that now without flinching. 'Many people here?' she asked calmly, preceding him towards the open door of the lounge, where she paused to look round with a feeling of satisfaction.

Life was very good just then. She knew she was looking at her best, and the recent large increase in her salary allowed her to spend enough on clothes for it to appear that she spent much more. Christina had left work to get married, and in her place had come two young boys straight from school, so Julia was no longer the newcomer. She never made the tea now, and the arrival of two people junior to her had seemed to necessitate the pay rise, which had gratified her.

With work going well, she had at last begun to appreciate the potentialities of her freedom. She had no one to please but herself, and nothing to spend her wages on but what she chose. She had had a holiday in Edinburgh for the Festival – a fortnight into which she crammed three and sometimes four performances a day, seeing everything from the Usher Hall to the Traverse Theatre. She was planning to go to Greece on next year's holiday. She went out almost every night of the week, and had acquired one or two admirers who took her to the theatre and to dinner seemingly for the sheer pleasure of her company, for they never offered to do more than kiss her on the cheek on parting. From a process of contagion, she had built up a new circle of acquaintances who provided a steady stream of invitations, one of which she was fulfilling tonight.

The room she was surveying was handsomely furnished and pinkly lit with concealed lighting, and was filled with people who were all attractively dressed and who all had an appearance of affluence and happiness. No group conversed without laughter, or at least smiles. Some standing, some sitting, some holding glasses, some with cigarettes, some talking, some listening, they all seemed happy and polite and ready to be pleased with whatever happened. She knew that there was no one here who was more than superficially acquainted with anyone else in the room, that more than likely they never would be, that certainly they did not want to be. Everything was light and frothy and undemanding and pleasant, and she was happy that it should be that way. Anything more intense might be an attack on her

277

new-found freedom, and Peter was not so deep beneath her surface that he could not be joggled into life by any kind of rough weather.

Julia's eye was caught by her hostess – Louie – and in obedience to a flap of the long freckled fingers she went across to pay her respects.

'So glad you could make it,' Louie said with affectionate fervour, hooking Julia into the group with a skinny arm. She was in her forties, painfully thin, with loose thick skin like a chicken's, plentifully dusted with freckles. Her hair had been sandy in youth, but had since gone grey, though she had had it died pink for so long that no one remembered it any other way, and the eccentricity went unnoticed. It was cut very short by one of the new 'trendy' West End hairdressers, and she was wearing a leather catsuit like Emma Peel's: only a woman of enormous charisma could have got away with it at her age.

Louie had been married very young to an aspiring poet who was a student at the University of Edinburgh – her home town. When he had expressed his pique at being unrecognised by a rather spectacular suicide actually on college premises, Louie had devoted herself and her inherited money to getting his poems published posthumously.

Nothing in life could have become his work so well as the leaving of it to his wife. She found a publisher, the poems made a splash, she dug up and polished some more and published those too, and now had the satisfaction of knowing him to be read by the modern literature class in the university that had ignored him to death. Her success had confirmed her as a Literary Lion, and she had pursued the career ever since, with a removal to London and two more husbands to help her along.

Julia had fallen in with her at the Festival, and had been oddly attracted to her. Louie was loud and blunt, with a hoarse, cigarette voice and a debased Morningside accent. She smoked perpetually with an eight-inch ebony holder which she waved to emphasise points in her arguments. She drank whisky like a soldier and lionised shamelessly and inclusively, regardless of the branch of the arts in question. She had recognised Julia at a matinee at the Playhouse and fastened on to her. Julia had been a painter, and had been married to a musician – that was more than enough.

Julia was amused by it all, but she recognised all the same Louie's genuinely kind heart and real interest in the arts – together with a comforting indifference to the shame of divorce – and she allowed herself to be adopted and encouraged. She had even, since meeting Louie and her present husband, Giles, actually done a little painting for herself. It had cost her an effort at first, and she had found it both difficult and painful, but it had also given her a release that she had been unable to find elsewhere.

'We haven't seen you in an age,' Louie was saying. 'Tell us what you've been doing.' Since that question, with Louie, always signified painting, writing, sculpting or other work in the field of the arts, Julia shook her head.

'Nothing, nothing at all. I haven't as much as picked up a pencil.'

'You write?' asked a dark-haired young man with the lantern face and hollow chest of a footballer.

'No, no, Julia paints. This is Roger Harrap, who is writing a novel about Sicily, Julia, and his young lady, and you know Bella and John, and this is George Crichton, an old friend of mine from back home.' Louie conducted the round of introduction with her cigarette holder. It was the last-named who held Julia's attention, and as she held out her hand to him she found herself subjected to a scrutiny no less thorough than her own of him.

What, Julia wondered, as she looked at him with a sensation of delightful shock, what is so familiar about him? Why does he remind me of Peter? The man had, like Peter, very blue eyes and reddish-dark hair, but she didn't think it was that alone – the combination was not so very uncommon. He would be a year or two older than Peter, and an inch or so shorter. His face was broad and firmly fleshed, the sort of face that was confirmed in its own lines so that you knew it would not change noticeably for the next fifteen or twenty years; a face of maturity and authority, the face, perhaps, of a teacher or a father. Whatever he was, he was a man on whom responsibility sat as recognisably as a uniform, and yet it did not irk him: he was happy in the responsibility, and liked the people who brought their problems to him. One more thing she could know – he was not only a happy, but a good man.

None of this was like Peter, she thought. Peter was not a man to seek out or be comfortable in responsibility. He had never known or wanted authority, being a man first and foremost for himself, an individual who would love one or two other individuals and barely know the rest of the world existed. He was essentially self-centred. He was many exciting and lovely things, but he was not Good, in the absolute sense that she read goodness in this man's face.

'How do you do,' said Crichton. His accent was very slight, his handshake warm and dry. Though a small man, he was powerfully built – she could see the breadth of his shoulders and the muscles of his upper arms, and though his suit was in fact perfectly well cut, he gave the impression that he might burst the jacket if he flexed his muscles.

'How do you do,' Julia replied, and added impulsively, 'I am very pleased to meet you.'

He smiled at her, and Julia was rather shocked with herself as she felt a pang of unmistakable physical attraction. It was the first time since she had left Peter that it had happened. Perhaps that was what was familiar about him, she thought: that he exuded sexuality rather as Peter did, so that she registered awareness of him all over her body. Louie was talking again, and she was forced to turn her attention away from the man, but she continued to be minutely aware of him standing beside her – a sensation like the heat of the sun on her bare skin.

'Roger is the person to tell you about Greece, Julia.'

'What did you want to know?' Roger asked, and exchanged a sidelong glance with his girlfriend, which Julia interpreted as, 'Here we go again'.

'I was thinking of going there for a holiday next year,' Julia said mildly. 'Do you know Greece well?'

'I lived there before the war,' he said.

Julia was surprised. 'I wouldn't have thought you'd have been anywhere before the war,' she said.

He frowned suspiciously. 'What do you mean by that?'

'She means you look too young,' Louie said abruptly. 'For heaven's sake stop being so touchy and tell her about Greece. Do you recommend it for a holiday?'

'That depends what she wants to go there for,' Roger said. His hostility was just apparent.

'There are some awfully good hotels,' said the girlfriend sweetly.

Julia, unsure of her ground, was not ready with her next remark, and Crichton stepped into the breach by saying with a voice of friendly interest, 'I expect you'd be wanting to know about the landscapes? I was in Greece a few years back, and though I can't claim to know anything about painting, I can say that the scenery was magnificent, and the colours really extraordinary.'

'Apparently the light is something very special in the Greek Islands,' Bella joined in. She ran a print shop in the Charing Cross Road and she and Julia had met once before at one of Louie's parties. 'You paint landscapes, do you?'

'I have done on occasion,' Julia said, 'but it isn't my speciality.'

'What is your speciality?' Crichton asked as if he really wanted to know.

'Like you, George, she's a physiognomist,' Louie answered for her, drawling out the word comically.

'Oh yes, I remember now, I have heard something about you and portraits,' Bella nodded. 'Well, you should get plenty of material in Greece – all those gnarled peasants and fishermen and bandits and whatnot.'

Julia raised her eyebrows. 'It isn't really like that, is it?'

'Bella gets all her ideas from Barbara Cartland,' John said, looking at his wife over the top of his spectacles. 'Greece is all car parks and guided tours now, isn't it, Roger? And the bandits all very clean and picturesque posing for photographs at half a quid a time.'

Roger, finding his authority on Greece a subject of jest, disdained to answer, but Bella didn't wait to find that out.

'Oh, yes, like those fishermen in Cornwall! Do you remember, Louie, John took a picture of them, one either side of me, and the boat in the background, artfully draped with a fishing net?'

The conversation turned esoteric from there on, and after listening for a few minutes, Julia glanced at Crichton, and finding he was looking at her, decided to satisfy her curiosity about him.

'What did you do in Greece?' she asked him. 'Did you paint?'

'Oh no. I'm afraid I don't know anything about art. But you paint portraits? That must be interesting.'

Julia was annoyed with herself for having asked two questions at once, and tried to answer dismissively, so she could get back to the first question. 'I used to.'

'Why did you stop?'

'Well, I didn't really stop painting, but I stopped doing it professionally. Lack of time mainly.'

'What do you mean, professionally? Did you use to go round to people's houses and have them sit for you, like Gainsborough and Reynolds and so on?'

'Well, yes, though I was never in that league, of course. People would ask me to do a portrait of them, and I'd have a few sittings with them and do the rest from memory or from photographs.'

'Photographs?' He sounded surprised, and she fathomed his thought.

'Oh yes,' she smiled. 'The modern techniques can be very useful – and necessary in some cases, when the subject isn't available for more than one or two sittings.'

'But surely that's—'

'Cheating?'

'No, I was going to say isn't it for the sitter to fit in with the artist's time? I would have thought that the artist was the important one.'

'Perhaps in the case of a great artist that would be true – there are one or two like that – but I'm just an ordinary old hack, and in my case it's a matter of he who pays the piper.' She stopped, feeling herself being carried away. 'Or I should say, it *was* the case. As I said, I don't do it professionally any more.'

282

'I should have thought,' he said slowly, 'that it wasn't the sort of thing you could just stop. Isn't it a case of once an artist, always an artist? If it's in your blood – not just painting, but anything like that, like being a musician . . .'

For a second Julia thought that he knew who she was, and that this was a pointed reference, but his face was so innocent of guile she dismissed the thought as soon as it occurred. He must have seen an expression of reserve cross her face, though, for he stopped and said again, 'Perhaps I am talking nonsense. I'm sorry.'

'No, no, not at all. I think you're right in a way, in that you never stop seeing with the single eye, or hearing with the single ear. If thine whole body is an eye . . .'

'Pardon me?'

'It's a quotation. Something like that. But what I mean is, I look at everything in a particular way because I was a painter, and I don't think I would ever stop doing that just because I'm not using the material I gather any more. But I don't know that that has anything to do with being an artist.' Unlike Crichton she used the word in its proper sense. 'I always looked at things that way, before I ever took up painting, and I suppose I always will, even if I never pick up a brush ever again.'

'Perhaps you became a painter *because* you looked at things that way,' he suggested.

'Which came first, the chicken or the egg? I hadn't thought of that.' She considered, applying the principle to Peter to see if it worked, but came to no definite conclusion.

As if he had followed her process he said, 'Perhaps the two can't be separated, the one being part of the other.'

Julia felt she hadn't talked so much to anyone for ages, and thinking thus made her suddenly aware of him as a stranger. Her ease evaporated, to be replaced, not by unease, but by the sense of heightened awareness she had had at first. To fill the space, she asked a question. 'Do you have children?'

'I don't even have a wife,' he said. He didn't seem surprised by the question, but she felt she had to explain it anyway.

'I wondered. You seemed to me to be like a man with children.'

'I have a great many children of that sort,' he said, smiling as if he understood her.

'Oh, are you a teacher?'

'No, not exactly. I'm an officer in the army.'

'Oh.'

'What do you mean, oh?'

'I meant, oh, that explains everything.'

'Does it indeed? Such as?'

She picked out one thing from the many. 'The way you stand.' As she said it, she found the similarity to Peter that had bothered her: George Crichton was a small man, and like Peter he stood very erect, with his chest out and his shoulders back – like a soldier, of course. Perhaps Peter had been taught his posture by his father? 'How did you come to join the army?'

'I didn't have much choice at the time. I left school just before the war, and there were no jobs around at that time in Scotland. It was the army or nothing, and I preferred the army. I signed up, and that was that.'

'So you came up from the ranks – is that the expression? I didn't know it happened outside story books.'

'It doesn't so much now, but in the war promotions of that sort weren't uncommon. In an emergency, being a soldier is what counts for most. I got my stripes almost at once, there being a shortage of NCOs, as always—'

'Why as always?'

'Because it's the NCOs who are in the front line, so they always get killed first.' He smiled at her surprise, and said, 'Who did you think leads the men into battle? Not the captain – the sergeant.'

'I didn't know,' Julia said humbly. 'So, how did you manage to stay alive and become an officer?'

'Just luck I suppose. It was ironic, really. We'd entered an area that was much more heavily defended than we expected. I suppose you might say we were ambushed. We crawled and crawled under what they call "withering fire", and among all the casualties, one by one our officers were killed. I was the senior sergeant surviving, so I took over until they should send us another officer. It never occurred to me that they'd simply make me up.'

284

'It must have been hellish.'

'Oh, it was bad enough.' His eyes were reflective, and Julia stood close, feeling the cold he saw, unaware of the people round her. 'We lost a lot of good men that day. I was just lucky.'

'I'm sure you earned the promotion.'

'I never wanted to be an officer – too rarefied for me – but I don't regret it. On the whole, I've never regretted it, nor that I joined the army in the first place. It isn't a job, it's a life.'

'And you enjoy it?'

'It's different, of course.' He answered more than she had asked. 'It's mainly an administrative job now, but there's still some soldiering goes on, and I do quite a bit of instruction.'

'Instruction of what?' She had been right, then, about his being a teacher.

'Gunnery. Tanks. We're a cavalry regiment.'

'Oh.'

He cocked his head a little and looked at her. 'A different sort of "oh" that time? I'm talking too much, boring you.'

'No, not at all,' she protested, but he was not swayed.

'And I am,' he affirmed. It was the first real piece of dialect she had heard from him. 'We'll talk about you now.'

'That sounds funny,' she said. 'As if we're to talk by rule.'

'Might be a good idea where some people are concerned,' he smiled, rolling his eyes at the rest of the room.

She laughed softly. 'Don't you like this sort of thing?'

'No. Do you?'

She did not match him in frankness. 'Why did you come, then?'

'Claims of old friendship. Mrs Barnes's brother was with me in the war.' Julia had to think for a minute before she identified Mrs Barnes.

'You must be the only person in the world who calls Louie that. Apart, of course, from the Inland Revenue.'

He made no comment upon this, and she thought perhaps she had offended him in some way. Perhaps he thought she was laughing at him? She did not want him to move away from her, and casting about for a neutral subject, said seriously, 'Aren't those flowers simply lovely? I do think Louie has a marvellous way with them.'

Crichton turned his head to look at the tall white vase in the corner with its striking arrangement of bronze chrysanthemums and white daisies, and then turned back to her again. He had such a direct way of looking at her that she felt warmed merely by being the object of his attention, whether he spoke or smiled or not.

'Do you like flowers?' he asked abruptly.

'Yes, I do. I love them, all of them. Except, perhaps, tulips. They always seem so artificial.'

'I should like to send you flowers,' he said. There seemed nothing she could say to this, but she had the idea that she was blushing. 'It's an odd thing, but now I come to think of it, I've never sent anyone flowers. Except for my mother, of course, on Mother's Day, but they were given, not sent.'

'Well, that shows you're a nice person,' she said lightly against the shyness.

'Why?'

'Nice men are always nice to their mothers.'

When he really smiled, his upper lip curled so far it showed the edge of his gums – a funny smile, an endearing smile, oddly boyish for the strength of his face. They talked on – except when interrupted by other members of the party – for the whole evening, discussing her job, his childhood in Scotland, their tastes in music and books, likes and dislikes and ambitions – or rather, his ambitions, for at that time she could not be said to have any.

'To command the battalion,' he said. 'That's my dream, and it will happen. Not too long now, and it will happen.'

'What would you be then?'

'Sorry?'

'What rank, I mean – major or colonel or – or – general . . .'

He smiled again at her military ignorance, but it was a gentle smile, not a superior one. 'Colonel. I'm a major now. Then after that if you keep going up, it would be brigade rank, and you'd have to go to headquarters. Even more of a

286

desk job. I don't want to go that far. I wouldn't like to leave my men – no, full colonel's good enough for me.'

'I suppose it would be rather like being promoted to headmistress when you really loved teaching,' Julia mused.

He gave this careful thought and then said, 'Yes, I expect it would.'

'And do you have any other ambitions?' she asked.

His pellucid gaze seemed to examine the contents of her head, without dissatisfaction. 'Oh yes,' he said. 'There's another thing that I'd like very much. Will I get you something to drink? Your glass is empty.'

Sunday mornings were hard for her, bringing back as they always did memories of Sunday mornings as they used to happen in the mews flat years ago (it seemed more years than it was). Then she had woken slowly, knowing she had the time, to the knowledge of perfect content. To lie half-dozing, with Peter beside her; slowly, luxuriously to roll over and be engulfed by his sleepy arms; to make love and then doze again with her head on his shoulder; to bathe and breakfast together and share the Sunday papers in perfect companionableness: these things had been the ingredients of the best day of the week for her. Even now to lie in the half-waking state and remember brought back a little of the pleasure; but it evaporated as soon as she woke properly and knew that it was all over.

She tried to build up new traditions round her Sunday mornings that would make them something to look forward to. She had the *Sunday Times* delivered instead of the *Observer* which Peter used to take; she always had half a grapefruit and a boiled egg for breakfast and took it back to bed on a tray, instead of egg and bacon in the kitchen; but for all her effort, the anticipation was never very sweet. She never really wanted to get out of bed.

This morning was no exception. She propped her head up on her arms and looked round the room, noting the dust on the polished surfaces shown up by the bands of sickly winter sunlight coming in through gaps in the curtains. Her clothes of the night before were lying over a chair, the black velvet dress smoothed out carefully, the underwear dropped anyhow. Her eyes moved to the corner of the dressing table and the heap of pins she had taken out of her hair when she let it down. She picked up a handful of hair and pulled it before her eyes to examine it. The ends were splitting, but that was not unexpected given the length it had reached. It was very fair still, almost white in the longest parts. It was a sort of comfort to think that no one would ever notice when she went grey.

Will you still love me when I'm a white-haired old lady, she had asked Peter once, and he had said how would I ever know you'd gone white? That was before the mews flat, that was in the bedsitter. She closed her eyes and felt the tears burning behind them. There were sounds outside the window, of cars and sparrows, London noises, muted by Sunday, but noises all the same of people being alive. They seemed utterly remote from her, as if she were a ghost. She remembered the way she had felt coming out from the hospital when she had first been told she was pregnant. She had stood still on the street and heard the traffic noises from a great distance, and had felt her separateness from it. She had felt then that she would never be lonely again, that she was immune from loneliness in the secret place she shared with her new child. It was like that now, too, though without the pleasure. Nothing could touch her. Perhaps she would never speak to another soul, ever again.

The telephone rang. Unlike a film heroine, who reaches out a languid hand to the white telephone by the bedside, Julia had to get up and pad through to the sitting room to answer hers. She took her time, and would not have minded if it had stopped ringing before she got there, but whoever it was was persistent.

'Hello?' she said without much hope.

'Hello, Julia. Were you asleep, my pet?'

'Oh, Louie. No, I wasn't asleep.'

'Well you should have been. Getting up early's for old birds like me. You get your beauty sleep.'

'If I had been asleep, the telephone would have woken me,' Julia pointed out reasonably.

'Och, no, dear, if you'd been asleep I would ha' rung off. I wouldn't disturb you for worlds!'

Julia laughed unwillingly. 'How's the washing-up going?'

'Oh my dear, I always say the only thing to do after giving a party is to move house! People drop things in the *oddest* places. But I suppose I should welcome it as a sign of success – if they'd had time to go and find an ashtray, it would probably mean they were bored. I'm *so* glad you've given up, by the way.'

'Given up what?' Julia said, thinking she meant painting.

'Smoking, of course. It never looked right on you, you know.'

'I think that's why I started – defiance. How on earth did you know I'd stopped?'

'I saw you. Or rather, I didn't see you. You didn't light one all evening.'

'I don't know how you could notice a little thing like that in all that crowd.'

'I had special reasons for watching you,' Louie said happily. 'How do you like him?'

'Who?'

'Don't be coy – the major, of course! He is an absolute pet lamb, and he and Eck were like brothers in the war. He was with Eck when he was killed, you know.'

'Yes, he mentioned that.'

'I had a fancy that you'd like him. And you scored quite a hit there, dearie.'

'Now, Louie—'

'Don't "now Louie" me! I'm neither blind nor deaf.'

'You certainly aren't dumb.'

'Now now. Don't be rude. I just wanted to know how much you liked him. Because, you see, I don't want him hurt. He is one of the *goodest* people I ever knew, and I adore him, and you mustn't break his heart.'

Julia had heard Louie's effusions before, and took them with a handful of salt, but she thought it odd that Louie should pick out one of the things she had noticed – his goodness.

'What do you mean, the goodest?'

289

'*I* don't know. He just is. Anyway, he's going to ask you to go out with him.'

'How do you know he's going to ask me out?' Julia asked, amused.

'Because he asked me for your address.'

'Did you give it to him?'

'No.'

'Why?'

'The chivalric ordeal, I suppose. He has to prove he's worthy. A little effort will be good for him. Listen, sweetheart, if he does contact you, you will be nice to him, won't you?'

'Why wouldn't I? But I'd like to know if you think I'll be good for him, or he'll be good for me.'

'Him for you, of course. I hardly know the man.'

'Oh, you're impossible!'

'Let me know all about it. Goodbye just now.'

'I might. Bye.'

She was just lifting her spoon to rap her egg when the doorbell rang, and her first horrified thought was that it was the major himself. She thrust that idea away, wrapped her dressing gown round her, and went to answer it.

'Miss Jacobs? Sign here, please.' A youth in some kind of uniform put a long flat box into her arms and at the same time held out a piece of paper to her and indicated a gap in the list of signatures that he wanted her to fill.

'What on earth is it?' she asked, taking the stump of pencil he offered her and leaning the paper on the passage wall to sign it.

'Special delivery,' he said in a bored voice. The reaction was universal.

'On a Sunday?'

'That's why it's special.' It sounded like a joke, but he seemed eager to be off so she concluded it wasn't, scribbled her name and handed back the paper and pencil. He took them and was gone without another word.

Julia shrugged and took the box into the kitchen. She laid it on the table, undid the white raffia string that was round the box, rolled it neatly into a coil, and lifted the lid. Roses. She stared. Red roses, those very dark red ones that look almost black. At this time of year they must be hothouse grown or flown in from somewhere. Wildly extravagant, either way. She counted: eighteen of them. Beautiful, beautiful. She lifted them to her face, but of course they had no scent, only the faint, damp green smell of a florist's shop. But she liked that smell anyway. She put them down, touched a velvet petal, and then thought to look for the card. It had fallen on the floor, a small white square, the most chaste of calling cards with an address and telephone number in one corner and in the centre in unfussy print, 'George Crichton'.

She held the card like a talisman, tight in her hand, and then lifted a single red-black rose to smell it again, and the tears she had defeated before broke through. She sat down at the table and wept while her breakfast egg cooled, forgotten, on the tray.

He telephoned at lunchtime. After the exchange of identities there was a silence, which he broke by saying, 'Are you all right?'

'Yes – yes. I made a fool of myself this morning over your flowers. They were so lovely and so unexpected that I cried.'

There was another pause, and he said, 'I think I should feel flattered by that. I hoped that they would have an effect on you, but – you *are* all right?'

'Yes. Why do you ask?'

'I don't know. I hardly know what I expected you to say.'

Julia didn't know herself. She was handicapped by the fact that she did not know what to call him, and she wondered if he was troubled by the same idea. She said, 'I can't thank you adequately for sending them. It was so kind.'

'I enjoyed your company so much last night. I can't remember when I enjoyed an evening more. I phoned to thank you, and to ask you if you would have dinner with me tonight.'

She was impressed by his courage in coming right out with it. 'I'd love to,' she said without hesitation, glad that he had said tonight, and not given her more time – time in which

291

to forget what the evening with him had been like, time to get cold feet and find an excuse.

'Shall I pick you up? Would seven be too early?' He sounded eager, like a young man, and she smiled.

'That would be lovely, not a bit too early.'

'Good, good. That's fine. Well, I'll see you at seven, then.'

'Yes. Thank you, again. Goodbye.'

He rang off, and as soon as she put the receiver down she realised that she had not told him, nor had he asked, her address. But then, of course, in some mysterious way, unless Louie was havering and she really had told him, he knew it, didn't he? He had sent the roses – and he knew her phone number too. A pleasant mystery with which to occupy her blank moments during the day, over lunch, in the bath, while she waited for it to be time to dress for the major.

Fifteen

J ulia stood at the window staring out at the sky. The sun was setting. Out there, under those grimy roofs, millions of people were working and eating, drinking and sleeping, playing cards, reading books, watching television, copulating, suffering from hideous diseases, dying; and each perfectly, unshakably sure that the world revolved round him, each the centre of a conscious universe. And out there somewhere, possibly quite near, quite accessible, was Peter. He might even be thinking about her – it was the right time of day for it.

She was suffering for him something almost physical in the way of loss. She seemed to herself somehow diminished; when she looked in the mirror she appeared to be smaller, as if she had been wearing a pair of magnifying spectacles, and had now taken them off. Everything she did seemed slightly less big, less important. She had thought that the loss of him would ease with time, but it had not. It became increasingly difficult to persuade herself that there was any point in doing any one thing rather than any other.

I *want* you, Peter, she thought irritably. Why should I have to suffer so; why can't you be here; why do you have to make *me* pay for your weaknesses? Why indeed, she answered herself. She turned her head, and looked into the room, which seemed darker since she had been staring at the western sky. There, in the corner. Well? The plastic side of the telephone gave off a slight gleam in answer to the last light coming in at the window. Well? What about it? It would be easy enough to find him, you know. A couple of telephone calls – you know the numbers to ring. You know within three guesses where he is at this very moment. He's probably lonely for you, almost as much as you are for him. Why on earth suffer? Cui bono?

293

She stared at the telephone as if she could make it ring by looking. Out of her longing she conjured up the smell of him and the sound of his voice, but unlike those lucky people in films, whose memory always recreated every detail of a past happy moment and lost love, she could bring forth no visions, and her eyes were hungry too. The sight was so important, as important as the touch. She wanted to see him, just to see him; she would settle for that. The eyes have it: the eyes dominate everything; God, how terrible to be blind, to know that never again would you *see* what you loved – and even in that permanent dark how could you ever stop yourself *trying* to see?

She walked over to the table, picked up the receiver, lifted it up to her face. The sound of the dialling tone brought her up short. No, she couldn't, not possibly. If he were to phone her, she could have found the words, but she couldn't call him, and he didn't know where she was. Well, he could have found out, of course, but if he had not done it in all this time, why would he now? He had never pleaded with her, never tried to change her mind, accepting her right of self-determination in a way that few people ever did with someone they loved. It was a compliment, she supposed, of sorts, that he had never tried to get her back. Of sorts. A feeling of hopelessness weighted her hand, and she put back the receiver and wandered away to the kitchen, deflated, and made herself a cup of tea.

As she carried the cup back into the now dark room, the telephone gave a preliminary chirp and began to ring. She started violently, and the cup chattered in its saucer. Peter! Her thoughts had reached him across London; he had heard her! Terrified now that it would stop ringing before she got to it she put the cup down on the floor and ran across the room, grabbing at it in the half-dark, dropping and catching it again, getting it to her ear at last, and all she could manage to say was a feeble, 'Hello?'

'Hello? Is that Julia? Hello?'

Not Peter. Oh, not Peter. She couldn't speak for disappointment.

'Hello? Hello?' with the insistence of a parrot.

'Yes, this is Julia.'

'I thought I must have the wrong number when you didn't speak. Oh dear, you sound terribly fed up. I hope I didn't disturb you?'

'No, it's all right, George. I was just thinking about having something to eat.'

'You haven't eaten yet, then? I was just phoning you to ask you to have dinner with me. I'm glad I caught you in time. Would you like to? Anywhere you like. I'm at your command.'

Julia wanted company, but it was Peter's company she wanted. The idea of being with anyone who *wasn't* him was momentarily sickening. She opened her mouth to refuse, and then visualised her evening if she did. Alone. Depressed. How could she bear now even to turn on the light? She would have to say yes. Then she thought about the effort of dressing, going out, ordering food in a restaurant, making pleasant conversation, entertaining him by way of payment, and she blenched.

For a long, horrible moment she teetered to and fro like a neurotic, and then, picking the answer out of a hat, 'I'd like to have dinner with you, George, but I can't face going out. Why don't you come round here?'

There was a silence as he digested the invitation. He had always been careful not to intrude on her privacy, and doubly careful not to trap her into inviting him to her house, and she knew it, and was thankful. This, of course, was not the way to invite him in for the first time, but she hoped – fervently – that he would understand. At least she knew he would never take advantage of her. He was a thorough gentleman.

'If you're sure that's what you'd like, of course I'll come round,' George said at last, carefully. Bless him, so carefully!

'Yes, I'd like that,' she said, and to ease the tension, dressed up the invitation lightly. 'Bring a bottle of something, and we'll listen to some soupy old records and get nicely tipsy together.'

'I'll be there in fifteen minutes,' he said, and she smiled, though he couldn't see it of course, grateful that he understood how she felt. He had gently relieved her of the necessity to make decisions; her hand holding the receiver began to tremble and she felt tears gathering behind her eyes.

'Yes,' she said, and he said goodbye and put the receiver down.

Julia was still standing there when the doorbell rang a quarter of an hour later. The noise made her jump, and she hastened through the dark room to answer the door, forgetting the cup of tea she had left on the floor, knocking it over in her progress. It was the last straw. By the time she had got to the door her resistance had given out, and the first sight he got of her coincided with the first tears welling out of her eyes.

Wonderfully, he had the sense not to ask her what was wrong. He put an arm round her shoulders and escorted her to the sitting room, and when he put the light on and saw the spilt tea he further had the sense to realise what was wrong, and he propelled her, still sobbing and still manoeuvrable, into the kitchen where he left her crying at the table while he cleared up the mess. Then he put the kettle on and while it was boiling he sat in the chair beside her and gently took hold of her hand. He didn't stroke it or fidget with it, just held it quietly and uninsistently while she finished her cry.

At last the tears stopped, and belatedly he seemed taken with a sort of shyness, detached his hand, and, placing his clean white handkerchief before her, got up and turned away to make the tea, giving her the privacy of his back. Julia blew her nose on one half of the exquisitely laundered cotton, wiped her eyes on the other, brushed her hair back with her fingers, and then merely sat hiccoughing gently and watching him while he capably made the tea, cut and toasted bread, and then buttered and jammed it.

'Now,' he said as he put plate and cup before her; his first words since he arrived, 'all you have to do is eat it.'

'Thank you, George,' she said – rather quaverily, to her disgust. She was aware now that red-eyed and red-nosed she was not looking at her best. But he smiled at her with the same warmth and admiration as always.

'That's all right, think nothing of it,' he said.

He sat down, opposite her this time, and she was conscious of a great sense of comfort which simply seemed to radiate from him. His presence alone made her feel less like an abandoned starveling, and she could not think of anyone else who would have had that effect on her. In her present state, to have anyone else witness her tears would have been intolerable. In the eight months or so since she had met him, he had come that close to her; but it must be a function of him, not of time passing, for there were others she had known much longer and would not have turned to for comfort.

His choice of hot toast and jam revealed a depth of psychological understanding that surprised her – it was quite impossible to eat it and still feel tearful, for the taste and the crunch were so essentially cheerful, and the concentration necessary to avoid spilling melting jam and butter everywhere pushed out all other thoughts. By the time she had finished she felt immensely better, and only her puffy eyes were not back to normal.

She licked her fingers and eyed him cautiously. He glanced up and smiled his angelic, good-humoured smile and said, 'Better?'

'Much,' she said. 'What makes you such a good nurse?' He raised an eyebrow. 'How do you know what will please me?'

'I love you,' he said, 'so of course I know.'

Just like that. A stillness fell over her. It reminded her perilously of what Peter had said once – 'I married you – I know everything about you' – and yet the echo of the words raised no anguished spectres; perhaps because it was the one true thing to say to someone you loved. Knowledge, love – almost synonymous; or at least, love could not exist without knowledge, and perfect knowledge was not likely to exist without love.

She didn't need to be surprised: she had known for a long time that he loved her. He wasn't the sort of man who needed to conceal the fact – he didn't seem to feel weaker for loving, but stronger. Yet his saying it seemed remarkable. Men in general – she generalised from what other women said – were reluctant actually to say the words, whatever their behaviour might have implied. But George was an old-fashioned sort of man, and a brave one. He would not shirk the consequences of his words, nor ever say more than he meant. When he said love, he meant the whole thing; but the confession mutated between his lips and her ears into some kind of a preliminary, as if there was something horribly final, something like an ultimatum, to follow. She said nothing, only looked at him apprehensively.

'I do love you,' he said again, as if she had denied it. 'I've never loved anyone before. I've had affairs, I won't pretend I haven't. A soldier's life, you know – it seems to be part of the job,' he added deprecatingly. 'But I've never been in love before I met you. I know I've only known you for a few months, but the moment I saw you – that does sound corny, but it's literally true – the first time I ever clapped eyes on you, I loved you. That's why – I must admit it – why I rather mercilessly thrust myself on you. I hope you won't hold that against me. I really had to, you know.'

'Yes,' Julia said. She could not look away from him. The clear, candid look he gave her, the shining of his face, made her feel strangely muddled and ashamed, as if she had in some way cheated him or hurt him. She felt smeared and bedraggled; a dull, sooty flame to his clear shining.

'You're the sort of person that men love easily; I expect you know that.' Oh, echoes of Peter again, Peter loving her, helpless to resist it, oh God, oh God, how can I bear it? So many years, and it never seems to grow less. 'I don't believe anyone once in love with you could ever stop. I know I couldn't.'

'Why?' she said – croaked, almost. '*Why* do you?'

'Love you? Because you're different. All the other women I've met are – I don't know how to say it – conventional, I suppose. It's as if they have it all written out, like a play, from the beginning. You say something and they say something, and they know it all beforehand, every word and action. If you stepped out of the script they wouldn't know how to handle it. But you – I've seen you do it: you listen to the words, think about them, and say what you think. One can talk to you, really talk, and know you are there. You, not some automatic response out of the training manual.' He smiled a little, but his slightly anxious eyebrows showed how serious the point was for him. 'You are a real *person*. I feel I've come close to you in this short time, and the thing I'm most afraid of in the world is losing that. I'd never find it again with anyone else.'

She said, 'Yes,' not from any meaning or response inside her but just to stop him, to acknowledge his words so that he should not flounder on alone in the tangle of his sentences.

He reached out and took her hands across the little space between them, and she gave hers to him readily – at this point in their acquaintance it was not such a huge step – still looking into his face, reading the love and the absence of guile, of shadow or concealment or desire to hurt. This man was to be trusted, said her mind to her. 'I want you to marry me, more than anything in the world.'

He stopped, but she was not sure, from the phrasing of the last words, whether he had asked her the question or not. Even had she known that, she would not have known how to answer. Her mind and her heart were blank, and she was silent.

He went on, 'I know you have been married before,' How the hell did he know that? Louie, she supposed. 'I'm guessing that he hurt you badly, and it may be hard for you to trust anyone again. You won't want to hurry your decision, and I wouldn't want you to either. This is too important to me to hurry it. I don't expect you to answer me now; but I wanted to tell you. Will you think about it?'

She nodded, helpless as a white mouse before a python. Go on then, her mind urged him, bathe me in your digestive juices, break me down into pulp, dissolve me, assimilate me; take me or don't take me, but don't make me make a decision!

But he only smiled and held her hands quietly, with that blessed unfussiness, that soldierly stillness which was one of the particular things about him; and she knew that she was unfair, that that was not the kind of yes he wanted. He deserved better than that. Wearily she hauled herself back up inside her skin, reached out for the control panel, looked out through her eyes. 'Yes, I will think about it, George. I won't keep you waiting long.'

'No hurry. I'll wait. There's all the time in the world.'

They spent the evening listening to music and drinking vermouth, talking a little and almost normally. Julia got a little drunk, enough not to be able to tell if George was sober or not, enough to relax with him and feel happy.

His scruples would not let him see her the following evening, so that she should not feel dragooned into making a decision.

At least, that was how she interpreted it to begin with; but when at around nine o'clock she found herself at a loss for amusement, and thinking about him, and wishing he were there to entertain her, she remembered his astuteness over the toast and jam, and wondered if there were not another reason. Absence making the heart grow fonder? It was not, she retorted sharply, as if she were totally dependent on one man for her leisure and pleasure. She argued with herself, but in her mind's eye she saw his face shining its innocence, and knew that she could never have got so far even as accusing him of such duplicity.

That made her laugh – round one to him! With a weapon as intangible as that, up against her convoluted argument, probably all the other rounds too. But there was no denying that she did want his presence and his company; and if that was not love, not traditionally enough to marry on, she knew that, once married to him, she would give herself to the marriage unstintingly. It was an upside down kind of way of looking at the thing perhaps, but of all things she hated uncertainty and would prefer to force herself into a situation than to remain in any kind of limbo.

What was her life, after all? What was she for, as she was? Even without the loneliness, aloneness seemed to her without purpose. She needed to have demands made on her; she needed a human yardstick against which to measure herself and her world; she needed, not to euphemise, to be wanted, personally and sexually. And for the matter of that, she thought she would probably be happier with him than without him.

That only left his side of it to be settled. She telephoned him.

'Will you come round and see me?'

'When?' he asked equably, as if there were nothing more in the balance that a friendly call, a drink, a chat. She could still get out of it, if she wanted.

But she had bitten the bullet. 'Now,' she said.

'I said I wouldn't tonight,' he reminded her gently.

'Yes, I know. But I believe that was for my sake, not because you didn't want to come. And if it was for my sake, then let me choose. I want to talk to you.'

He chuckled softly, a sound that raised the flesh between her shoulders. 'I'll be there very soon,' he said, and rang off.

He was dressed casually, for a change, in a sweater of a dusty shade of blue, grey slacks, and, soldier-like, a white shirt open at the neck. In the parting of the top button Julia could see where the reddish, inveterate tan of his face and neck ended and a man's tender whiteness began below it; and her skin tingled with the shock of desiring him – a man, a stranger. She wanted him, and it was the beginning of something that now could not be stopped.

'Well?' he said pleasantly. She cleared her throat, but could think of no possible words that would do. 'Let's sit down, shall we?' he said helpfully. They sat down on the sofa, edgewise on so that they were facing, a polite distance apart. She would have known how to begin with Peter – but then Peter would probably have known what she wanted to say anyway. Perhaps George knew, but if so he wasn't going to help her. George: that was a good way to start.

'George,' she said, and the rest fell into place, 'do you really want to marry me?' He nodded. 'You're sure?'

'Quite sure,' he said.

'You know that I've been married before.'

'Yes.'

'How?'

'There are things about you to suggest it. It's easy enough to tell.'

She nodded. A brief silence, and then he asked, 'Were you divorced?'

'Yes. Should I tell you about him?'

He considered, and then said carefully, 'If you mean, am I curious about him, then no, I'm not particularly. But if you want to tell me about him, then do. I want you to have no restraints when you talk to me. You don't have to say anything, but any time there is something you want to say about him, go ahead and say it. Only . . .' He paused and regarded her as if afraid he might give offence, 'Only, if you don't mind, I'd rather you didn't tell me his name. Just in case I ever meet him.'

Why, she wondered – because he would be upset, or because

he might punch him on the nose? She didn't ask, however. She only said, 'I don't think it's very likely you'll ever meet him.' There was another silence, and then she said, 'You haven't asked me for my decision yet, though you must have known that was why I asked you to come here tonight. But,' she went on without giving him a chance to assent or deny, 'you wouldn't ask me, because that would be pressurising me.'

'How well you know me,' he said, smiling.

'Do I?' she said, and paused. 'I want to be honest with you,' she resumed.

'That sounds ominous.'

'I don't know that it is. I don't think I want to tell you about him, only to be fair with you. I think perhaps . . .' She paused again. This was painful, more painful than she could have expected. She dragged the words out of their hiding place. 'Perhaps there is something that you give to one person, that you only have once, that you never have again to give to anyone else?' She hadn't meant it to come out as a question, but it did.

And he nodded, calm and sure – oh blessedly understanding man. 'Yes,' he said. 'I think so. You are my one person.'

The words hit her, pierced her and sank melting into her flesh. He loved her that much? She held out her hand to him, and he took it and held it on his knee. Quietness seeped out of him, lapping round her. She stared, held by him, but lost, lost within his very certitude. She did not know him, he was quite wrong, quite wrong. She knew nothing of him, of how he thought or felt, and even when she had been with him long enough to be able to predict his words and actions, she still would not know why. Peter she had known like the inside of her own mind, but George was like a Martian to her, so utterly alien that she would never more than catch a glimpse of his thought processes.

And yet – what were most people to each other? He understood that she had not that one thing to give again, but he wanted her all the same. Or did he think she might prove herself wrong at last and find another well of it somewhere in her? At all events, she discovered now that there was no decision to be made. His lapping quiet was the calm flood that would bear her away, and bearing her up would never let her sink or drown.

All hesitation left her. 'Let's have a drink,' she said, and got up to fetch them while George remained quite still, only his eyes moving, watching her move. She stood before him, holding out his glass, and said, 'We must drink a toast.'

'What to?' he asked, standing obediently and lifting his glass into the operative position.

'To our marriage,' she said, and drank.

He drained his glass, and in the same movement they put down their glasses on the table, and then put their arms around each other. She trembled at the first contact, but his hands moved gently over her, soothing her, and he said softly into her ear, 'I love you. Don't be afraid. I will make you happy. I love you.'

She was a Martian to him, too, and though, because he was good with animals, he would often make the right guess about her, there would be many times when he would be wrong – like now. She was not afraid: she desired him, and was rather shocked at the sensation, but he had misunderstood, and she could not tell him, even though she knew he desired her too. She knew she could not tell him, though she did not know why, and that was how it would be for the rest of their lives. The rest of their lives.

'I will marry you, George,' she said, as though she had not already given him the answer.

Sixteen

E xperience governs anticipation. Julia had been married to Peter, and therefore when she accepted George's proposal she did not even consider the events which normally follow an engagement of that nature, and was quite unprepared for them. The first thing that happened was that George arrived the following evening to take her out to dinner in celebration, and presented her with a ring box printed with the name and address of a Hatton Garden jeweller. She opened the box and looked with an incomprehension bordering on inanity at a gold ring set with the biggest diamond she had seen in real life; an Elizabeth Taylor kind of ring, gorgeous in its opulent simplicity.

She looked at the ring, and then up at George, and could not think of anything to say that was adequate to the moment. It was so terribly like something in a film that she could not associate it with herself or with him. She had not expected an engagement ring – to tell the truth she had not considered their agreement to marry in the light of an engagement – and if she had, she would never have imagined anything like this. It was in the realms of mink coats and £500-dresses from Dior, it came from a fairy-tale world displayed in films from Hollywood and breathed of in magazines like Vogue and Harpers, a world to be visited in occasional self-indulgent daydreams but not really believed in.

George's expression had altered minutely with a creeping in of anxiety. Since Julia didn't seem to be on the verge of speaking, he said, 'I do hope you like it. I judged that you would prefer to have something plain, but if you would like a cluster, or a coloured stone perhaps, you must say so. After all, it is for you, and you are the one who will wear it for the rest of your life.'

'No, no, you were right – I do prefer plain things, and one stone is always better than many.' She stopped, feeling inadequate again.

'But what's wrong? You don't seem pleased,' George asked her.

She forced herself to look at him, though she could feel her cheeks burning. 'I am pleased, truly – it is the most beautiful thing. It's just that it doesn't seem real. I hadn't expected – I didn't expect you to buy me a ring, and this . . . !' She looked at the brilliant, light-filled thing again and drew breath. 'I've never *seen* anything like it, let alone thought of owning one. It must have cost the earth! I shall hardly dare to wear it.'

Now he was smiling, sure of himself again. 'I've been saving for years, not with anything particular in mind, but just saving because I hadn't anything particular to spend my money on. I'm glad to be able to spend it now on something so worthwhile,' he said. 'But you haven't tried it on. If it doesn't fit we can have it altered – the chap I bought it from will do it for me. He's a friend of mine – I met him in Germany after the war – so we can trust him. Send it to him to have it cleaned, by the way, when the time comes. Don't trust anyone else.'

While he was talking Julia had taken the ring out of its box and was turning it in her fingers to catch the light, gazing in wonder at the blue fire in its depths. She did not want to try it on because she was sure it would not fit, and that would be such an anticlimax. But when at last, under his silent urging, she did slip it on, although it was a little tight it could be worked over her joints, and once on it fitted snugly.

'That was lucky, wasn't it? I hoped it would fit because I wanted to see it on you. How do you like it?'

'It's beautiful, George,' Julia said, and again it felt like a scene in a film; nothing like this had ever happened to her before.

'As long as you're happy, that's all that matters,' George said, drawing her hand to him to kiss it. A mere form of words? Usually, but in George's case it was true. He would do anything – anything, that is, that he did not consider immoral – to make her happy, and that was all that did matter.

The Ring (she always thought of it with a capital letter, like Mr Tolkien's) was only the beginning: Julia was soon

305

to find out what most girls discover much earlier in life, that getting married is not just a case of two people pleasing themselves. Firstly there was the ceremony itself, and George was very surprised but relieved to discover that Julia had no preconceptions or even preferences as to how it should be carried out, for he had set his heart on a regimental marriage, but would not have even mentioned it had Julia wanted something else.

As it was, she agreed in a bemused kind of way to everything he suggested, and after the first few minutes her imagination failed altogether, and she was never able to form any picture at all of what it would be like.

'I wish we could get married in the regimental chapel,' George said. 'You'd love it – it's beautiful, and steeped in tradition, with all the old standards from famous battles, some of them so old they're practically dust now. And the windows – memorial windows – are beautiful. I'll take you to see it. You'd like the chaplain too – he's a great old boy. Not a bit stuffy. Marvellous sense of humour, and a voice like an organ. I wonder, if I had a word with him, whether he would agree to marry us.'

'But George, I've been divorced.'

'I know, but divorcees can be remarried in church. It's up to the individual priest to decide whether he'll do it, and I think the padre would do that for much for me, if I explained the circumstances. He's very open-minded, and you weren't the guilty party, after all. Would you like me to talk to him?'

'By all means.' Julia nodded, watching his face, wanting to please him in any way she could over this affair that seemed exclusively his.

'Well, wherever we have the ceremony, we must have a slap-up reception afterwards,' he went on. 'We'll invite every-one we know, a proper sit-down meal and dancing afterwards, and the officers' mess chef can make the cake. He'll take it as a compliment to be asked, you know, and he is first-rate. And then, after the reception, we'll go away to – where would you like to go?'

'Go?' she asked, bemused.

'For the honeymoon? Where would you like to spend the honeymoon?'

'Honeymoon?' She sounded vague, and though she smiled she saw a slight hurt in his eyes as if he thought she was taking the matter too lightly.

'Isn't there anywhere you've always wanted to visit? Surely there must be.'

Seeing it was important to him, she roused herself from the dream and thought a moment. It was no use her choosing Paris or the South of France: it would have to be somewhere improbable; somewhere obscure enough for him to believe it would be the fulfilment of a lifetime's dream for her. Mexico? Japan? Zanzibar? Zanzibar sounded exotic, but if he asked her why, would she be able to be convincing, given that she knew nothing about it?

'The Camargue,' she said suddenly, remembering a film she had once seen of a misty marsh peopled only with aery white horses and exotic, scarlet flamingos. 'I would love to go to the Camargue.' And as she said it, it became real, and she was able to invest the words with enough enthusiasm for him.

'Then you shall,' he said, his face alight with pleasure again at giving her her desire. One day, she thought, perhaps he will take from me; but for now I must consent to his giving, always giving.

She was taken to meet the chaplain, who, as promised, turned out to be an amusing, liberal and shrewd man. He obviously thought highly of George, and having talked seriously to Julia about her divorce and her intentions, pronounced himself willing to marry them in the chapel.

'We all lead irregular lives in one way or another,' he said. 'I think it's more important for the Church to tidy things up than to bear grudges.'

That settled, the date was set; but only when it came to drawing up the guest list did George discover that Julia had no one she wanted to invite.

'But you must have!' he exclaimed. A wedding without guests on both sides seemed hardly legitimate to him. 'You must have some family? Parents, brothers and sisters? Uncles, aunts, cousins?'

Julia shook her head. 'My father is dead, and my mother turned me out years ago. I haven't seen her since, and have no intention of seeing her.'

'Not even for your wedding?'

'She wouldn't come.'

'Oh surely, to her own daughter's wedding . . . ?'

'I was married before, remember, and she didn't come to that. And she disapproves of divorce.'

'Invite her anyway,' he suggested. 'You may be surprised.'

'No,' she said firmly. 'I don't want her there. I have nothing to do with her any more.'

'You mean,' George said slowly, 'that you haven't one single living relative to ask to your wedding?'

She shook her head again. She avoided mention of Sylvia. She did not want to talk about Sylvia with him, now or ever.

He said, brightening, 'But you have friends.'

'Not friends, really. Just acquaintances, not people I feel close to. It doesn't matter, George, I don't mind not having anyone. I've always been a solitary kind of person.' Not true, not really, but Peter and I shared everything, and when I left him I left it all behind. The friends I had belonged to my life with him, and they don't translate.

'What about Louie and Giles, and Bella and John, and all that crowd? Louie introduced us, after all. We must have her and Giles. Think how hurt they'd be to be left out.'

She thought it an odd criterion, to invite people to this most important and intimate ceremony on the grounds that they would be upset by *not* being invited; but she realised that in the matter of weddings she had no experience and was clearly going against tradition. No one had been at her wedding to Peter, so that had become her yardstick; but George had different expectations, and this, after all, was his first and only. It must be as he wanted. She was being ungracious and spoiling it for him, and she must not do that. She brightened her expression.

'Yes, of course, silly of me. Of course we must have Louie.' George was still looking perplexed and unhappy, and she hastened to comfort him. 'I wasn't thinking clearly. Of course we'll invite all our friends. We'll have all that crowd.' She hit on something else that might make amends. 'I'll tell you what!'

'What?' he said suspiciously, thinking she was going to make another sacrifice and further denude his expectations.

She laughed at his expression. 'No, no, you'll like this. And so shall I. The regiment can be my family. We'll invite them all, and they can fill up the bride's side. And some of your fellow officers must have children, I'm sure, who would like to be bridesmaids.'

He took the bait, or so she thought.

'But of course – they'd be only too delighted. And the CO can give you away. He can stand in for your father.'

Ever afterwards, Julia was unable to decide if he had been joking or not, but in the event it turned out like that, joke or not. All the arrangements about the ceremony and the reception were made with the regiment in close and private consultation with George. After that first discussion he took over the organisation and she encouraged him to think that she would sooner have him arrange the whole thing as a surprise for her, like a surprise birthday party. She spent the two months of the engagement sometimes in a state of somnambulism, and sometimes feeling as though she were being bounced in a blanket, breathless and confused.

She was taken to meet George's brother officers at dinner in the mess, where she was toasted ceremonially. She went to fittings for her wedding outfit, a silk suit in a shade of ivory and a hat with an eye veil – compromise between her divorced state and George's marital virginity. She chose blue georgette for the bridesmaids' dresses and eventually also met the bridesmaids, aged ten, eight and seven, all daughters of friends of George.

The Chief Catering Officer was supervising the banquet and the cake, or rather The Cake, as it promised to be. The civilian guests were to be lodged in nearby hotels (except those who lived within easy reach) and brought to the chapel in hired cars. Elderly aunts and seldom-seen cousins of George's were coming down from Scotland to attend. Army guests were to wear their Blues. Photographers were hired.

Presents arrived at Julia's flat from people she had never heard of, and she made lists of the gifts and the donors so that she could eventually write and thank them all. She left her job and had a farewell drink at the pub with Bob and Malcolm at lunchtime on her last day. They were very curious about the whole thing and she wondered if she should have asked them to the wedding, but it seemed rather late in the day now. Besides, she had enjoyed working with them but could not have laid her hand on her heart and said she regarded them as friends.

There was an announcement in the newspapers of the forthcoming wedding, and it caused Julia a sharp pang – the first touch of realism about the whole affair – as she realised that Peter would see it, or would hear about it from somebody who saw it, one of their former common friends. She knew how he would feel, knew the exact mixture of anger and hurt and loss that he would feel at the news. For days after the announcement appeared she went round in a dither of anxiety in case he should phone or write, or even call round to remonstrate with her, or merely to be sarcastic and hurt her. But the days passed and he did not contact her – of course he did not! – and as she relapsed into her dream-state again she realised that she had rather hoped he would. Painful as it would have been, she had wanted that badly to see him again! She felt guilty about it, chastised herself inwardly, determined to put him entirely out of her mind from then on.

It was like, she thought as the day approached, a society wedding, it was all so elaborately, so carefully arranged. They even had a rehearsal, with her and George and the groomsman and the bridesmaids, Louie as the maid of honour, and Colonel Truscott who was to give her away – a tall and handsome man with beautiful and anachronistic mutton-chop whiskers, who reminded her of Peter's father. She began to feel that she was acting a part in a school play – a very minor part which required very little rehearsing, in an unusually lavish production that needed a great deal of rehearsing – for there was exactly that air of concentration, suppressed excitement, and organised confusion about it all.

George was loving it, and she begrudged him none of it, and even managed to put up a lively performance of being there during all the anticipation. It amazed her that getting married could call for such organisation, and it amazed her even more, with only Peter for comparison, how much thought George was putting into it. He approached all the thorny subjects

310

gravely and thoughtfully and with so much genuine care for her well-being that she hid her surprise that such things should need to be discussed and took her first real steps towards his life and away from Peter's.

The first of these discussions took place in her flat where, with various documents and notebooks spread out on the table, he went into the subject of money with her. He explained to her how much he earned and when and how it was paid, and what regular bills had to be met from it, and how much he thought they could afford to spend on food and clothes and so on. It was obvious that she was not expected to work – how her mother would have approved!

Julia said, 'I have some savings, and the interest on them.'

'That's your money,' George had told her firmly. 'You keep that and do whatever you like with it – it's your own private money.'

And she had accepted that that was another thing she was not to give him. He told her carefully about his expectations and the pension he would receive when he retired, and showed her his various savings accounts and investment accounts. He showed her also the draft of the new will he was having made, and explained what widow's benefit she would receive if he died.

'I've taken out some life insurance too,' he said. 'If anything did happen to me, you wouldn't want, I've made sure of that.'

'I see you have,' she said. 'You've thought of everything, I believe.' She was to be dependent upon him for everything, even for her independence – it was another step, a longer one this time.

He had been so self-assured over the financial side of their marriage, that Julia found it refreshing that he should be shy over what to her was equally basic. This conversation took place in Richmond Park where they had gone for a Sunday afternoon drive to get away from the sight of the wedding presents that were silting up Julia's small sitting room.

George pulled over and stopped the car in a convenient spot, and then turned to Julia and said, 'I'd like to talk to you, dear.'

He often called her dear now, never darling, and in those

311

modern days when the coinage of love-words was so far debased, the small, unfashionable word seemed to her an expression of particular tenderness.

'I like it when you call me dear,' she said on an impulse, and he reached over and touched her cheek.

'You are dear to me. You do know that, don't you?'

'Yes, I do,' she said comfortably. 'What did you want to talk to me about?'

His eyes slid away from hers momentarily in uncharacteristic indirectness and she realised from the distinctly bushy look about him that he was shy. That was what warned her what he was about to say.

'I wanted to talk to you about birth control,' he said firmly, taking a firm grip of the subject's collar. 'Having been married, you'll know about the various methods, and I would like the decision to be yours as to which method we use.'

There is something, Julia thought, very indecent about such frankness, except when you read it in government pamphlets. She didn't really know what to say, being unable to imagine using anything at all, and George plunged on into the uncomfortable silence.

'If you would prefer to take the precautions yourself, or if you wanted to try taking this new pill thing, then I shall be quite content with the arrangement, but if you would rather I saw to that side of things—'

'What?' she asked, startled.

At last a gleam of amusement crept into his expression. 'My dear, you must know about the various devices—'

'What, those horrible rubbers? How dreadful!' Her look of genuine horror tickled George and he began to laugh, despite himself. She went on quickly, 'Oh George, I should hate anything like that. Don't you want to have children?'

'I should love to have children, but I wouldn't like you to be perpetually pregnant, like a Catholic.'

'That's all right,' she said promptly. 'When we've had enough, we'll just avoid the dangerous times.'

'It isn't a safe method,' he warned her gently.

She made an impatient movement. 'I don't *want* everything to be safe,' she exclaimed, and then thought about

312

that, and changed the emphasis. 'I don't want *every*thing to be safe.'

She smiled at him, and he ached suddenly with wanting her, but could do no more than take her into his arms and hug her. He thought briefly of his past love affairs and sexual encounters, and then of Julia, and wondered what he had done to be so blessed.

'How can I deserve you?' he asked aloud. 'You're so pure.'

Pressed against his chest, Julia had no chance to answer this, which was probably a good thing, for she had time to consider, to get over the first reaction to the word, and wonder what exactly he meant by it. Pure, impure? Perhaps like sin it was a matter of intent rather than deed. What was it Peter had said? That the love between them was like chastity: she had understood that only wordlessly at the time, like so many of the things he taught her, and the thoughts he had put into her head matured like endowments at various moments of her life. Perhaps George, like her, understood these things without having the words for them; perhaps that was what he meant by purity. She wished passionately at that moment that she knew him. She thought of his clear firm face which was so utterly opaque to her and wished she understood what went on behind it, what he thought and wanted and believed in. It all seemed so terribly hard.

Perhaps it just needed to be worked at. Perhaps after long years of study she would one day find herself proficient, fluent in Martian. She saw herself as one of those dedicated naturalists who safari into the wild lands and live for ten years with a colony of lemurs until they know everything there is to know about them, and even speak lemur language and are looked upon by the lemurs as one of the tribe.

Would George ever look upon her as one of him? He kissed her head and she worked it free so that she could look up into his face, and she wondered – strange thought – if he even knew she wasn't.

The night before the wedding Julia spent at the hotel where the majority of the wedding guests were staying. Some of them had arrived a couple of days beforehand, and when she arrived at the hotel there were already two reunions and a party going on, all of which she quietly avoided, though it surprised and pleased her to discover that the wedding was being looked upon as the social event of the year by the section of society which had been invited to it. It was strangely flattering, even though she knew most of the anticipation was for George's sake rather than hers. He had, she had discovered, a wide circle of what she would have called acquaintances, but who, in the gruff, undemonstrative way of men, qualified as real friends. She actually heard one man say to his companion at the bar, 'I wouldn't miss old Crichton's send-off for the world. It's going to be the biggest beano since VE day, you mark my words!'

Is it indeed, she thought, passing on her anonymous way upstairs. Well, I'm glad I got my invitation early.

Her room had a private bathroom, though in all other respects it fell far below the standards of luxury George would have liked to secure for her for that night, but she had been firm.

'I'd feel uneasy in anything grand, George.'

Her suitcase was there, already packed for the honeymoon, and a second smaller case for her overnight needs. Her wedding outfit was hanging in the wardrobe. A barber who was a friend of George's was coming over to the hotel to do her hair for her the next day – he was apparently equally good with women's hair.

Julia had a bath and rubbed scented cream into every part of her she could reach, and then surveyed herself in the full-length mirror in the bathroom – a luxury she was not accustomed to in her own flat where such surveys were done inch by inch in a hand-mirror. The bottom half of her, she decided, was better than the top – fine legs and haunches, and a good back – screwing her head over her shoulder to see – but her chest and shoulders were too thin, and her ribs stuck out like a dairy cow's. I need to put on some weight, she thought. Skinny women always look older.

Not much like a bride, she decided, and then looked at her face. She hadn't done so for some days, and it was a shock. White and exhausted, with blue-shadowed eyes, the face stared back at her with a kind of numb expression, and through tears she saw tears gather in the eyes. She shut them and the tears squeezed out past her lashes. There was only one thing in her mind, the impermissible thought, and she tried to dismiss it with the worry that she would look like hell at George's wedding tomorrow, but for the time being she couldn't worry, she could only grieve. It was as if Peter were dying, for after tonight he would be gone from her irrevocably, she would never be able to see him again, she would be lost, exiled. Her misery spilled over, and she sat on the floor beside the bath and cried into her hands for Peter, and for Boy and the life that had been taken from her.

Eventually she stopped crying, sniffed a little, blew her nose, and then said aloud and with determination, 'Well, I shall never do that again.'

She got up, put on a dressing gown, and went into the bedroom. She had brought a book to read – a P.G. Wodehouse had been her choice as being the right sort of mood-setter – and she suddenly decided on self-indulgence as a cure for the blues. She rang room service and asked them to bring her up a roast beef sandwich, a glass of milk, and a double brandy. When it arrived she set the tray on the bedside table, turned out the main light and turned on the bedside lamp, and then got into bed.

She ate her sandwich, and poured the brandy into the milk and sipped it, and read her book until she felt drowsy, and then she slipped down under the covers and turned off the lamp. I'm not getting up to clean my teeth, so there, she thought, and in a very short time she was asleep.

At a quarter past one – or rather at thirteen-fifteen as she would now have to learn to call it – Julia, not looking at all numb or exhausted but wearing the kind of smile a bride should wear, walked out of the front entrance of the hotel, escorted by Colonel Truscott, and climbed into the beribboned Rolls-Royce which was to take them to the barracks.

The colonel made no conversation during the short drive, beyond, 'It's a lovely day for you – not a cloud in the sky.'

'Yes, I'm glad.'

It was lovely. Indian summer, she thought – one of those almost heraldic blue-and-gold affairs, with the sweetness of dying leaves beginning in the air, and the clearness of autumn washing the sky. Limpid, frank blue sky, reminding her of George's eyes.

'If I might take advantage of my position *in loco parentis*, you look very beautiful, my dear. Radiant, in fact.'

'Thank you,' she said. 'So do you. Your uniform is gorgeous.' And he laughed.

Her bridesmaids (whose names she had never managed yet to apportion correctly) were waiting at the door of the chapel, and the oldest and tallest, who had been appointed chief bridesmaid, stepped forward as Julia climbed out to hand her the bouquet – yellow and white roses. She had not wanted to carry flowers but George had wanted it, so she had stipulated that it must be small. Louie was standing behind them in a suit of old-gold gros-grain. She had abandoned the pink of her locks for the occasion and dyed them a bronze shade to go with the suit, so she looked like a chrysanthemum: a beaming, freckled chrysanthemum with indisputable tears in her eyes.

Julia smiled at her, and as she did so there was a rapid gunfire of clicks from the posse of photographers waiting there. She was surprised, almost taken aback, but Louie hurried over to speak to her and persuade her to stand in various postures for five minutes while more pictures were taken. Then the colonel indicated that the time had come, the little girls, well-schooled and breathlessly determined to get it right, scuttled into position behind her, each clutching her posy of yellow rosebuds so tightly that the poor things were already wilting, and Julia laid her hand on the crook of the military sleeve and walked in at the open door of the chapel.

The sunlight fell across the dark chapel in four brilliant bars so that the aisle she walked up was a zebra crossing of alternate light and shade. At the end of the aisle stood two figures in identical, immaculate Blues, a tall slim one, Bryce, the groomsman, and a shorter, stockier one, whose back she could already pick out from any company, Crichton, the groom. On both sides of the aisle were the dark masses of the guests, mostly in uniform, and here and there a splash of pastel colour and a gaudy hat marking out a female. A ripple of pale faces turned to watch her as she passed.

She felt, irreverently, like the Queen Mary being docked, for the colonel guided her up to her berth in front of the altar as if she would not have made it alone, and the little girls bobbed behind her like tugs under her massive freeboard. It was the civilians, she realised, who were turning to look – the army guests were maintaining proper military discipline. Even George did not peep until she was deposited at his side and he could look at her without moving his head.

I should be feeling something, she thought in a panic; love or reverence or excitement, or at least a sense of *occasion*, but I only feel as if I'm not here at all. The flowers, all white or yellow, were massed everywhere and the air was heavy with their scent. It doesn't smell like a church, she thought. Oh I'm so hungry – I hope I don't rumble. She glanced up sideways under her lashes at George, and saw a little rough patch on his cheek where he had shaved over-zealously. He should have had his barber friend do it this morning before sending him over to me. The sunlight was just touching the side of his head, and she saw with microscopic clarity the tiny almost transparent hairs over his cheekbone, the slight droop of his eyelid at the outer edge, the way the laughter-lines ran out three ways from his eye corner. The sun laid a sheen of gold over his foxy hair so that it shone almost auburn. Auburn hair and blue eyes, like a film star. I wonder what his children will look like, she thought, and then looked at his mouth, and felt a shiver of desire run down her, like cold water.

She had not been listening, but picked up her cue all the same, coming to at the point when the congregation was asked if they knew of any reason etc. The words, familiar as the words of the death sentence to every true Englishman, rolled sonorously on, and with a suddenly dry mouth Julia saw the padre looking straight into her eye and asking her to repeat after him. Me, I, I have to speak, aloud, in front of all these people. Stage fright. She wasn't sure how her voice worked any more.

'I, Julia Maitland Jacobs.'

'I, Julia Maitland Jacobs.' Her voice did it on its own, and it sounded surprising, small and very female, in this large and very masculine chapel. George looked at her now, and he looked surprised too, as if he had just woken up and realised that the dream was not a dream, but here and now.

'Take thee, George Alexander Crichton.'

'Take thee, George Alexander Crichton.' She hadn't heard him say his bit! How shameful! She hoped she had looked in the right place and not displayed her absence to him. To be her lawful wedded husband. Husband. This man. This one, my husband. She couldn't make it real in her head. The whole thing was an elaborate dream, and sooner or later she would discover – but this one's mine, and I am his, and only death can part us now. Unless we change our minds. She made, without realising it, an instinctive, escaping movement of her head, and George, who was good with animals, knew it for what it was, knew both that small struggle and the quietness that followed it, having seen it in trapped birds. A weight settled on him, and though he never referred to it, or even really thought about it consciously, it stayed with him always, that foreknowledge of defeat.

They went with the chaplain into the vestry to sign the register while the chapel choir sang an anthem which Julia would have loved to stay and listen to. Bryce and Colonel Truscott were the witnesses, and they both claimed the right to kiss Julia, and did so, one on each cheek.

Then she turned to George and said, 'And now *I* can kiss *you*,' which made them all laugh for some reason. She looked very happy, and George looked exultant, as if at any moment he might jump on to a table and yodel with the glory of it all. From the quiet, distant dream she passed into a noisy colourful dream in which she moved and laughed effortlessly, and smiled as though she had been born like that; and appropriately the hiatus between the two had been that moment at the altar when she had looked at George and desired him and been afraid.

They paraded down the aisle again, and out of the main door, and there was an archway of swords for them to walk under and more photographers, and yet more photographers, lining the way as they walked from the chapel to the mess hall, doing a kind of a leapfrog always to keep in front of them. Julia's hand was held firmly between George's elbow and his side and he slowed his soldier's pace to something more suitable to Julia's step. She had not looked at him yet, but she knew he was smiling much as she was. At the door he took pity on the photographers and turned with her on his arm to face outwards for a snapping moment, and then they went in.

The tables were laid all the way up the hall, covered with white cloths and a glitter of glass and silver, with a cross-table at the top, banked with flowers for the important people, Julia thought, before realising that she was one of the important people at this 'do'. She and George stood just inside the door and welcomed the guests in, as they formed a kind of slow-shuffling queue outside apparently for the privilege of shaking George's hand and kissing Julia's cheek. She knew very few of the faces, but they all knew George, of course – and liked him, as was apparent from their affectionate remarks and smiles. He stood erect and proud, shaking hands and saying just the right thing to everyone, and she wished she had his social sense. But she smiled the right sort of smile, it seemed, and all the men said gallantly that George was a lucky fellow.

At last they seemed to be all inside, and she and George could walk up the hall amid a hurricane of clapping, cheering, and stamping to take their places at the middle of the top table. Best seats in the house, she thought to herself. Mention my name . . .

She was glad she had been hungry, for course followed course in seemingly endless succession, and there was wine and champagne in such plenty that she was quite soon drunk – although that is a word that one never applies to a bride on her wedding day. Radiant is usually the adjective for her state of alcoholic euphoria.

There were speeches, with cheerful heckling, reminding her of a political rally. George had to stand up and answer them, but they might have been speaking Swahili for all she understood of what was said. She heard her name spoken, and saw George, still standing up, looking down at her with a tender smile, and she smiled back rather blearily.

'Are you all right, dear?' he asked her when he sat down again.

She gave him the full frontal effect of her radiance and said, 'Tis naught but the blushful Hippocrene.'

'You're drunk, you gorgeous little maenad,' Peter said.

'And tonight is the Dionysia,' she replied, *but Peter told her what the women did at the Dionysia, and she took it back hastily.*

Meanwhile, in the real world, George looked across her to his groomsman and said in the same exultant tone, 'My wife's drunk!' That was apparently very funny too, and all those who overheard it laughed.

It was, as predicted, the best beano since Mafeking. After the meal the chairs and tables were cleared away like lightning by the mess stewards and there was dancing.

'The band is very good,' Julia said as she revolved in his arms, alone on the floor for the first bars of the first dance. George said they had better be, or they'd hear all about it next day from the colonel. Julia laughed into his eyes and said, 'I think there must be absolutely everything you could ever want in one regiment. Any kind of expert you need, you'll find one amongst your friends in the army, be it a barber, or a band—'

'Or a carpenter or a taxidermist.'

'Or a walrus,' she added confusedly.

George laughed. 'You've just discovered something about army life.'

'I've just discovered something about you,' she countered. 'I wonder how often you're going to produce "a chap I know" to perform some service for me – or you – and think he's doing it because you're both soldiers.'

'Well, that's what it's like in the army,' he said, nervously.

'You're a simpleton,' she said sweetly. 'They do it because they love you.'

He shook his head at that, but she could see that the idea pleased him.

The celebration continued. A phenomenal amount of drink seemed to be consumed, and a wonderful good humour prevailed. Everyone wanted to dance with Julia, and she only ever

320

got half of any dance with George before he was 'excused' and she found herself in the arms of a dashing soldier who seemed bent on showing her that he was the most magnificent hero and dancer in the world while at the same time telling her earnestly, as if she doubted it, that the Major was the greatest hero, soldier, and friend in the world and the best oppo a chap ever had. Had the love that was flowing about that hall had the same intoxicating effect as the alcohol they would all have been incapable by the time Julia and George had to leave.

'How long will that go on, now we've left?' Julia asked him when they had been waved by the revellers out of sight and had settled back in the car that was taking them to the airport.

'All night, in one form or another,' George said with satisfaction. 'They're a good lot, aren't they?'

Julia laughed, and he asked her what was funny. 'Remember I said, "Let the regiment marry me?" I feel as if I've married the regiment!'

'I suppose you have in a way,' George smiled, and then reached out for her hand. 'But most of all, you've married me.'

'Yes,' she said, and lifted his hand to her cheek.

'I love you, Julia.'

'And I, in common with everyone at that wedding today, love you.'

'Do you really?' He sounded anxious.

She laughed and moved closer to him and draped his arm round her shoulder. 'Of course I do.'

He was trembling and his arm tightened round her convulsively and he kissed her fiercely as he had never done before. 'Tonight,' he whispered into her mouth.

'At last,' she whispered back.

Seventeen

While it turned out that being George's woman was pretty much like being Peter's woman – all men being brothers under the skin to a surprising degree – Julia soon found that being George's wife was nothing like being Peter's wife, so her experience stood her in no stead at all.

George got his battalion very soon after his marriage, soon enough for Julia to do all her adjusting in one go. For a few weeks they lived in Julia's flat, and then his promotion came through and they moved to Scotland, and she discovered that a colonel's wife was a very public figure indeed. She had married the regiment with a vengeance, and it took a close interest in everything she said, did, or wore. Julia was not long in observing that the colonel's wife, like Caesar's, had to be above reproach.

The only trouble between her and George in the early months of their marriage, in fact, came about because of her initial refusal to understand that she was no longer a private person. Eccentricities were not lovable, and it took her a little while to realise that she could not behave with the same freedom. One quarrel with George arose quite early on because she visited a pub alone one day when he was on duty, and another because at a party she had talked and laughed too freely with a group of men. The quarrels left Julia tearful and bewildered, feeling that she had been punished for something she hadn't done, but George was patient with her, and gradually she learnt the rules as she learnt the language. It would have been stupid to rebel, since she had chosen her fate herself, and there was a satisfaction in dedicating herself to the job and knowing herself to be growing skilful at it.

At Christmas, her first Christmas as Mrs Crichton, she had

a letter from Martin wishing her well on her marriage and enclosing a Christmas card from Sylvia which she had sent care of him. 'I don't know whether you will have heard,' Martin said in his letter, 'that Sylvia and Peter are to marry in the New Year. I don't think it has been a planned thing – they seem to have been on and off ever since you left, and I don't think anyone expected this. I hope it won't upset you too much.'

It was a vain hope. She had not seen or spoken to Sylvia since she had caught her with Peter in the studio, and thought she had managed to wipe the whole business from her mind. For Sylvia, having taken that step, not to go on and secure marriage to Peter would have been foolish and – more to the point – most unlike Sylvia, who was her mother's daughter in valuing respectability, if in nothing else. Julia could never imagine Sylvia as Peter's mistress: abandoned love-making and Sylvia did not seem to go together in any credible way. Equally, she could never have imagined Peter choosing to marry Sylvia – why should he, indeed, when he had already enjoyed her without committing himself to the shackles of marriage? Yet it had happened, and it struck her to the heart with a bitter sense of betrayal.

She told herself it was only Peter doing what Peter did – had he not, after all, betrayed Joyce to marry her? How was it different? But she had always believed it *was* different between her and him, and that difference was the only justification for her sin or his. And for him to marry Sylvia was worse than for him simply to sleep with her now and then. It diminished *her* marriage to him, to know he would do it – apparently – with anyone.

Oh, but that was not fair to Sylvia. She was a good-looking woman, and knew how to behave; she dressed well, and would be an excellent wife to Peter of the sort who is primarily for being seen on his arm at receptions and for acting as his hostess in order to advance his career. Peter would know how to value that; he need not be in love with her, and he was a man, in any case, who did not function well as a bachelor.

Was it worse, or better, to think of him marrying Sylvia without love? She ground out the arguments inside her mind through sleepless night after sleepless night. And did Sylvia love him? She must do, surely? Surely it could not only be cold ambition of their mother's sort? Would that be worse, or better? Sylvia, helpless victim to Peter's charm (Julia knew all about *that*), driven to betray her sister by her heart and her hormones, or Sylvia, opportunist, shrugging over the split milk and thinking there was no sense in everyone's losing out? In her stew of misery, Julia decided at last that she did not want anyone to be a villain. She would sooner they were in love after all. Let there be some gleam of sunlight somewhere. Let them be happy with each other. She was out of it now. She had no right to let it hurt her.

But, oh, Peter, Peter! She could forgive – that was a cerebral exercise – but she could not forget: that was visceral, and beyond any exercise of self-will. Her marriage to George had brought her happiness, but also unhappiness, more than she could have expected. She had thought he would slip into the spaces Peter had left, fill them, fill her out, use her up. She hadn't reckoned on his reminding her so constantly of Peter, of being so like him, superior to him in so many ways and yet falling short in those unthinking, wordless aspects that were nothing to do with merit but simply to do with her need of one particular person. Sometimes when they made love, and her eyes were closed, she would involuntarily see Peter behind her eyes instead of her husband, and that made her feel not only miserable but guilty. Then she would hold him tightly and say, 'I love you, I do love you,' and the tears would squeeze out from under her eyelids.

She did love George, it was true. She admired him and respected him, liked him and desired him. Their physical relationship was marvellous – in a purely technical sense, he was a better lover than Peter had ever been, more sensitive and more thoughtful of her. Inasmuch as she could be happy with anyone who wasn't Peter, she was happy with him. But that did not stop her being lonely. In a paradoxical sort of way she was lonelier than she had been when she was living alone – she was lonely for her loneliness, for that isolation which had protected her to some extent. George gave her companionship, but sometimes the deficiency in that companionship was harder to bear than its absence would have been. Sometimes when they were at home at night, sitting either side of the fire reading like the picture of domestic content, she would glance at him covertly, at his firm, fine profile, his strong neck, his blunt, sure hands, and she would feel the huge distance between them, feel the silence between them of all the communications she could never make; and then she would almost hate him: something that frightened her.

She used to pray sometimes, mocking herself, with a parody of a prayer she had learnt at school: 'Teach me, good Lord, to love him as he deserves – to take and not to count the cost, to keep silent and not to heed the wounds . . .'

But, inevitably, she settled in. She grew used to him, adapted herself to his way of life, his needs and requirements. The fierce struggle she had sometimes felt died away, and her love of him increased in proportion. Just as it would have been stupid to fight against the social rules she had inherited, so it would have been stupid to suffer for the lack of something she could not have, and as soon as she stopped wanting that intimate communion with her husband, she discovered a great fund of contentment in the communion they did have.

She was helped by her physical removal from the scenes she had shared with Peter. Here everything was the army, and the outside world barely penetrated. Her concerns were the colonel's; her friends were other officers and officers' wives. She found that it was very easy for her to become a kind of figurehead to the young soldiers, and the more she concerned herself with the regiment the more it seemed to please George. Faint echoes sometimes reached her from her old world – occasionally a letter from Martin or a card from Rowland, sometimes a mention of Peter on the arts page of a newspaper – but it all seemed so distant when compared with the immediate realities of an upcoming regimental cocktail party, or of young Hamilton's inexplicably going AWOL, that it meant nothing to her.

Julia was not concerned by the fact that she did not become pregnant straight away. In fact, she never thought about it, but even had she thought about it she would not have been surprised, for she had been Peter's mistress for some years before she conceived Nathan, and she had assumed that that was the way it was. George, however, was eager for a child, and her public more or less expected it, and so bit by bit she began to be aware of the subject. She began to be aware of her periods and to expect, month by month, as each finished that it would be the last. She came gradually to understand that George was, in the vernacular, 'trying for a baby' – an expression that made her think of hoopla – and that they were not succeeeding.

She would always have been willing, if asked, to have an examination, but it never occurred to her that it might be necessary. George, however, felt that his bombing was sufficiently on target to have been met with some success, and eventually his worry communicated itself to her. About eighteen months after their wedding George finally took his courage into his hands and spoke to her about it, and suggested, very hesitantly, that they should both have tests.

'Of course, darling, if you're really worried,' she said.

His relief was evident. 'You don't mind, then?'

'Of course not,' she said, surprised in her turn. 'Why should I?'

'I thought it might hurt your pride.'

'Don't be silly,' she said. She might have said more, but her brain was working quickly, and she had got to the stage of thinking if it isn't me (and presumably it isn't since I have had a child – something she had never told George, for Nathan was too painful a subject even now for her to broach, especially as it would have meant talking about Peter, which she could not and would not do with him) then it must be George, and pride works both ways.

'I think it would be best if we made an appointment to see a specialist in Edinburgh. But we'd better think up an excuse for going – take a couple of days' holiday perhaps, go and see a show or two. I don't want this discussed all round the barracks.'

'Not any more than it is already, you mean,' she said, unperturbed. 'You know the whole town is holding its breath for me to present you with an heir.'

'It can hold its breath, as long as it holds its tongue,' George said succinctly. 'So we'll go to Edinburgh, then?'

'All right, George, just as you like. But I'm sure there's nothing to worry about.'

'I hope not,' he said. 'Maybe I'm being silly. It hasn't been that long, after all. But we're neither of us in the first flush of youth and I'd prefer to know sooner than later if there is anything wrong.'

In the event, the tests and examinations could find nothing obviously wrong with either of them. They were both apparently normal, and the specialist told each of them separately and then the both together that conception was a mysterious thing and depended on so many tiny factors being just right that it was a wonder to him sometimes that anyone ever managed it.

'But millions do, every year, so don't worry. You're both healthy, and there's no reason I can tell why you shouldn't have a fine big family. Try to forget about it, that's my advice. In my experience, the more you worry about it the more you interfere with that delicate balance. Get the whole business right out of your minds and you'll be expecting a wee one in no time.'

When they left the hospital, Julia glanced up at George's grave face, and reached out for his hand. 'Don't worry,' she said. 'As he said, we must just keep trying.' He looked down at her, unsmiling but with love, and she went on, 'We will have a child. I know it. I feel it in my bones.'

'Prophetic bones, now,' he said, smiling.

'It's true. We will, we will. Believe it.'

'I believe you,' he said, pressing her hand, and drawing it up into the crook of his arm. 'I've a vested interest, but still I believe you. We will have a child. I can't let you down.'

'Don't think of it that way! Why should it be you letting me down and not the other way about? Besides, I didn't marry you for children. I married you because I love you, and if we never have any children that wouldn't change – but we will.'

It would have been more true, though less tactful, to say that she didn't care about having children; but she didn't care mainly because she didn't believe they couldn't. As time passed and she didn't conceive, her wish for a child developed in proportion with George's fear that it would never happen. But, as was often the way with her, the more she cared, the less she spoke about it, and it was at once the thing they never discussed and the thing that drew them together.

April, 1969

'Are you sure you don't mind?' Julia asked again.

George smiled with his infinite patience. '*I'm* sure I don't mind – the question seems to be, are *you* sure I don't mind.'

'Sorry. Am I being a bore?'

'Of course not, dear. The trouble is you don't go out often enough – it's too much of a novelty to you.'

Standing in the hall of their semi-detached house, commanding officers for the use of, wearing a cardigan over his kilt, he looked shorter and stockier than ever – broad, bull-necked, but somehow vulnerable. Why did cardigans make men look vulnerable? He had his hands clasped behind his back, a real soldier's pose – they learnt it when they were stopped from putting their hands in their pockets. She even caught herself doing it sometimes. She had not gone out without him for months, and she was beginning to wish she wasn't going at all, for the house was snug and comfortable, there was a fire and a good book, and her own dear husband, amiable and companionable. He had duties to attend to that meant he could not go, and would have to go up to the barracks for a while later on; but she could have spent a quiet evening by the fire, reading, and listened to the concert on the radio, and then, when he returned, they could have had a nightcap together and gone early to bed.

She hesitated, painting the joys of a domestic evening brighter because she knew, really, that she couldn't change her mind now. It would irritate George, for he hated indecision; and besides, she had to go.

'What time will you be back? What time is your train?' he asked.

She had the details pat enough to satisfy even him. 'There's a train at twenty-two oh-six, which I might get if the concert's over early. But in any case, the last train isn't until twenty-three twenty-two, which gets in at oh-oh twenty-six, so I've plenty of time.'

He nodded approvingly. 'And what time will the concert end?'

'I don't know, but the usual thing is for it to end between nine thirty and ten.'

'Oh, you'll be all right then.'

'Oh yes. It's only five minutes from the station.'

'Good. Well, if you can telephone me from Waterloo and say which train you're getting, I'll have someone come down and meet you, save you the walk up the hill in the dark.'

'There's no need, darling.'

'And there is,' he said firmly. 'You're the colonel's wife.'

'Aye, and I am,' she said, gently mocking.

When it was time for her to go he said, 'Have a lovely time, darling, won't you,' and stepping forward to kiss her: 'You look really beautiful. It's worth you going just to see you dressed up.'

She felt a tremor of pleasure as she always did when he said something like that to her. 'If you have the chance to listen to it on the wireless, you may hear me cough,' she said.

'I'll try and catch a bit of it,' he said. 'Go on, now, or you'll be late. Have a good time.' He kissed her and pushed her out of the door, and she turned at the gate to wave, knowing just how he would look in the doorway of that ridiculous house with its bits of stained glass, like the nineteen-thirties' mock Tudor houses that line the arterial roads. Then she set a brisk pace for the station, allowing the excitement inside her to escape just a little from the iron control she had set over it.

After all, she argued with herself, there's nothing to be guilty about. I'm only going to *see* him, that's all. Just sit in an audience with a couple of thousand other people and watch him play – there's nothing wrong with that. And it's been such ages since I went to a concert, live. Not since that once, at the Usher Hall, and that was – what? – two years ago? Must be. Now they had moved down to Aldershot, she thought happily, and were so handy for London, she could go to concerts more often. Very deep in her mind, too deep for her to be immediately aware of it, was the thought that if she went to other concerts at which Peter was not playing, it would dilute the wrongness of going to one at which he was.

As she reached the station approach she saw a couple of squaddies up ahead of her, going in the same direction, and she slowed her pace, not wanting to walk with them; but fate was against her. One turned his head and saw her, and they both waited politely for her to catch up. Oh well, she thought resignedly, I suppose I should be pleased they like me enough to want to talk to me.

They were in mufti, but unmistakably squaddies by their short hair – that alone gave it away in these days of flourishing mops – by their short sideburns, nicotine-stained fingers, and more especially by their dress. Why it was she didn't know, but the soldier off duty always wore a beautiful clean shirt with the top button open and no tie, slacks, an expensive jacket – suede or leather was fashionable at the moment – and a watch like a young chronometer that looked as though it must weigh the wrist down 'somethink cruel'. She found it amusing that these boys who were so eager to get out of uniform in their off-parade time should dress themselves with such unmistakable conformity.

'Evening, M's Crichton,' one mumbled shyly as she reached them.

She fell in beside them and smiled pleasantly. 'Hello, Harris.'

''Lo, ma'am.'

'Hello, Buchanan.'

They were excruciatingly embarrassed, and she chatted pleasantly to set them at ease. They seemed to her impossibly young to be soldiers at all – they looked no more than about fourteen, and Buchanan particularly had soft rosy cheeks that seemed never yet to have known the kiss of steel. She knew that they must be seventeen, but knowing is not believing.

'How's your mother, Harris? Is she better?'

'Yessm. I'm going home now to see her, but she's out of bed and Dad says she'll be back at work next week.

'Oh, that's good. You've got a forty-eight, have you?' She glanced across to apply it to both of them, and they nodded. 'And what are you doing with yours, Buchanan?'

'I'm going to Weymouth to see my girl.' Well, thank heaven for that. Harris's home was in Exeter, so she wouldn't have to travel up to London with either of them. They were good boys, but she wanted her thoughts to herself at the moment. They fought each other briefly to open the door for her into the booking hall, eager to please her, both because she was very popular with all George's men, and because she belonged to the colonel whom they adored. He was almost a god to them, and to the boy-soldiers, as George called the cadets, he was a legend.

'Well, this is where I leave you,' she said when they reached the platform. She had to cross the bridge for the up line. 'I'm going to London for the evening. To a concert,' she added, knowing they would be wondering why she was going out alone without the colonel, but would be unable to ask her. 'I hope you enjoy your leave. Goodnight, boys.'

'Thank you, ma'am. Goodnight, ma'am,' they said, and she headed for the other platform as quickly as she could, almost in a panic to be alone.

She travelled first class, one of the blessings of being a colonel's wife, and she had the compartment to herself. She settled herself into the corner seat by the window, happy because she loved train journeys, and because at the end of this one was the prospect of seeing Peter again.

Just to see him: she hadn't known how much she wanted to see him. The four years, almost, in Scotland had passed like a dream, though until she had come back south it had seemed real enough, and her former life had been the dream. Yet she had never forgotten him, never would. He was the first love of her heart, and though she was happily married, settled down as the saying is, with a man who was twice the person Peter would ever be, yet still there was a part of her that longed, wistfully, to see him again. Perhaps if she could see him just this once, the wistfulness would go away and leave her free to live George's life with him without shadow.

She wanted to believe it, and most of the time she did believe it, but sometimes a restlessness would come over her, and she knew that something in the past, though dead, would not lie down.

She toyed with the idea – just to pass the time on the journey – of what would happen if she actually met Peter face to face. It would be different, of course. A meeting between Peter and Mrs Crichton, a mature and socially stable woman of thirty-two, would be on a completely different footing from a meeting with Julia, the schoolgirl mistress, or even Julia the ex-wife. He would be grave, dignified, treat her with a little deference, listen to her with polite attention as his equal, or even his superior – or would he? A vivid memory of his face and his cynical, all-up-one-side smile gave her doubts. Peter would always be Peter, self-assured, arrogant, king of his own kingdom.

She arrived at Waterloo half an hour before the concert was due to start, so she went to the hall and bought herself a drink at the downstairs bar. She had always loved the Festival Hall, and to be back there after so long was like a homecoming. She revelled in the sights, the sounds, the smells that were all so familiar to her, and felt the excitement building up inside her, clammy hands and queasy stomach, in anticipation of the music. Finishing her drink she went to wash her hands and check on her appearance, and then made her way to her seat.

She was in the middle of the front row of the stalls – not a popular seat from the music-lover's point of view, and perhaps not a tactful seat, since it would mean she was sitting virtually right in front of the soloist, but of course he would not be looking for her to be there, and she did not think the soloist ever really saw the audience, except as a mass. To recognise one individual would require a change of focus; and in any case, she must have changed so much, he wouldn't recognise her if he did see her. From her point of view it was a marvellous seat, for she would get her wish of seeing him, and seeing him really close to, and she would be able to hear and observe his playing and determine if and how he had changed in the years in-between.

She settled herself and looked around, watching the hall fill slowly, and was pleased to note that it was going to be a sell-out: you could always tell, for the lower boxes were taken. There were a lot of evening dresses and furs, and a lot of glittering from the boxes, which was a compliment to Peter, and she was pleased about that. In the choir stalls, the cheap seats behind the orchestra where she had used to sit, which Peter always called 'steerage', was the usual combination of students, school parties, and young female orchestra-fans.

She heard a few stray notes of tuning-up from behind the curtains that led to the dressing rooms, and visualised the scene back there – the strings and woodwind beginning to queue up near the entrance, the people with guests making their excuses and ushering them out, the attendant wandering about looking dazed with a piece of paper in his hand (orchestral attendants were permanently harrassed), and in the bar a few diehards, a couple of trumpets and some basses, finishing off their drinks and putting in their orders for the interval: 'Put us up a JC, Gwen, there's a love!'

Now the musicians were coming out, carrying their instruments, looking deceptively smart in their black tailcoats. Close-up, she knew, many of the tails would not bear inspection, abused, as they were, like overalls. She remembered unironed shirts and grubby 'white' ties; grey stains under the arms of maculate coats, threadbare patches, frayed cuffs, shiny spots; she had seen these uniforms rolled into a ball on the back seats of cars and thrown off on to the floor with a sigh of relief. But from a distance they certainly looked good, and a tailcoat, like a kilt, does something for every man.

Like reliving a dream, she watched the orchestra assemble, tune up, and then wait, poised and ready for the conductor, each player an individual, an artist, but becoming just one part of a larger instrument in the hands of the man with the white stick. He arrived, bowed, was applauded; the house lights went down, and a silvery silence settled and prevailed until the first notes of the music took its place.

It was Kodaly's *Hary Janos Suite*, with that peculiar opening that musicians call 'the sneeze'. Julia was at once absorbed by the familiar music, oblivious to everything while it was playing, but at the end of it, while the conductor was bowing, someone on the platform caught her eye, smiled and nodded. She frowned to recollect, and then remembered him – Jim Overton, a cellist who had played in the same orchestra with Peter – and smiled back. He mouthed something at her which she couldn't understand. Laboriously he tried again, and again, while she shrugged and looked apologetic. Laboriously he tried again, and again, while she shrugged and looked apologetic. Then he pointed to the curtains, and she realised he was saying 'Peter'. She smiled and nodded, and then, thinking perhaps he was asking if she wanted Peter told of her presence, she shook her head, and then shrugged. The applause had stopped and people were standing up for the interval now. Overton smiled pleasantly and got up to file off the platform.

Still, just in case Peter should be hanging around the curtains, though she couldn't in the least imagine his doing such a thing, she went out of the auditorium and climbed up to the level where there was a balcony overlooking the river, and stayed there admiring the view until the gong sounded for the second half. A perfect 'A', the gong was. She remembered being told by a flautist, when she first visited the hall, that the musicians who played there most had petitioned to have the gong tuned to a concert 'A' to protect their delicate musical sensibilities, and she had believed it at the time.

She returned to her seat. There was only the one piece in the second half: the Brahms violin concert. It was a mark of Peter's fame that he was now considered a big enough draw to have the post-interval section all to himself. The orchestra filed on and settled down, and a hush ensued which to Julia seemed to be unnaturally protracted. Her tension built up and her eyes fixed on the left-hand curtains burned from their unblinking stare, until the curtain was flicked aside, and her heart gave a convulsive bang in her chest as the familiar black-and-white figure came out and ran lightly and jauntily up the steps to the platform, followed more sedately by the conductor.

Hungry for every movement, every gesture, she watched him thread his way between the desks of first violins, with a smile and nod here and there to players he knew. His fiddle was tucked under his arm, and over his wrist, like a waiter, he carried the white cloth he used to protect the shoulder of his coat.

At the front of the platform he paused and bowed, smiling slightly; three bows, one left, one right and one centre. Then he turned sideways on, spread his white cloth over his shoulder, and nodded to the first oboe, who gave him an 'A'. He tuned, quickly and without parade, nodded to the conductor, and lifted his bow to the strings.

Through the few bars of the introduction, despite her hammering heart and childishly clammy palms, Julia took in every detail of his appearance, feeding on him against the famine that was to come. He was wearing his hair a little longer, a little fuller than before – partly no doubt because the fashion had changed, but also, she suspected, to compensate for the increasing expanse of forehead he was displaying. She knew his vanities, and they were not complex.

Otherwise, he had changed very little. She had not expected that he would. His playing was more assured, and more brilliant in a way she could not exactly define, but his stance during rests was the old cocky stance, and he looked around the auditorium in the same self-assured way, which she had used to liken to a stallion looking over his mares.

In her pleasure at looking at him she had forgotten how close she was to him, and that she was not, after all, invisible. In the pause between the first and second movements he saw her. His eye, travelling idly along the front row stopped on her with a jerk. She saw his hairline shift back as he stared at her, shocked; and then a slow, lopsided smile curled his mouth, and one eyebrow went up quizzically. Too long had intervened for her to be sure what that smile and eyebrow meant, and she could only return enough of a smile to acknowledge them.

But he had seen her! He knew she was there, and whatever her conscious wishes about him, while she listened the rest of the hall melted away and she was alone with him while he played for her, for her only, as before. Her eyes never left him, and he spoke to her with a surer tongue than his own, one that could never be misunderstood, while she listened with more than just ears – she was the instrument on which he played and there was no distance between them. She wanted it to go on for ever, and fought against knowing the music was ending. When it was over, and the last shining notes were done, under cover of the applause she drew a long shuddering breath.

It was over, and now he was a public man again, bowing to his audience, shaking hands with the conductor and the leader, doing all the things which were not his gestures because they were stereotyped; no longer Peter but The Soloist, a distant figure, unreal, a cardboard cut-out. Nothing more passed between them, not even a glance, and then he was gone, the lights came up, and the concert was over.

Julia joined the slowly-shuffling queue heading for the exit and felt hollowed out, as if she had done some strenuous physical exercise. She was tired, ready for sleep, deflated; she wanted to go home, to get into her warm bed and snuggle down beside her man, curl up against his hard, hot back and sleep. Outside on the street she glanced at her watch. Because it had been a short programme, it was too early for the train. She hesitated, watching one or two musicians issue from the side door and hurry towards the station. What about a drink? Might as well, just for fifteen minutes or so. But not the station bar – too cold and inhospitable.

She turned away from the station and walked along the dark road that led past the artist's car park. Down there, there was a little pub called the Rose, a nice little pub that was never too crowded. She would have one drink there and then go back for the train. She firmly suppressed any tendency to remember that it was the pub to which Peter had always taken her in the early days, preferred by him at the time because few of the orchestra used it.

She pushed open the bar door cautiously and went in. Beyond the screen, in the public bar, the locals were watching television, but this bar, the saloon, was absolutely empty. Ashamed of the thought she had so resolutely not thought, Julia walked across to the bar, took her seat on a high stool, and when the barman came up to her, cheerfully ordered a gin. So much for that. She would have this one, and then get off home. George would be waiting for her, glad to have her safely home, and she was happy to be going back to him. She was cured, she thought, of all that silliness: *of course* he was not here waiting for her, and she was glad he was not. That part of her life was all over, and now she had seen him once, his ghost was laid, and she could go home in peace to her new life.

She lifted her glass to drain it, and then the door of the

bar was pushed open, and she knew by the rising of the hair on the back of her neck, without even turning round, that it was him.

She turned her head slowly. Peter was standing half in and half out of the pub, holding the door back with one hand, like the demon king making his entrance in a pantomime, smiling his satyr's smile.

'Well, well, well,' he said. 'Look who's here.'

'Well, well, well,' she parodied, 'if it isn't Father Christmas.' Her voice sounded to her surprisingly self-assured. Part of her wanted to get up and run, but the other part kept her sitting still, very still, on her stool. It was a good high stool, and that, oddly enough, comforted her, as if it gave him less advantage over her not to be looking down at her.

He turned back and ushered a man and a girl into the bar, and said to them loudly and cheerfully, 'I say, do you mind if I kiss this woman? I haven't seen her in years!'

They smiled indulgently at him – good old Peter! – and he pranced across the bar and took her by the shoulders and kissed her mouth. The ceremony performed he drew back, still holding her shoulders, and looked into her face as if to see what she was like, and she got the feeling that he had kissed her out of a sort of desperate courage, because if he hadn't kissed her then, right away, he would have turned on his heel and run.

'Won't you introduce us?' the girl asked, laughing.

'Certainly I will.' He turned to Julia first. 'This is Mike, who's a professor at the College, and this is Sue, a pupil of mine, who will be brilliant one day.' Then he turned to the others, and she saw that he had cleverly made it unnecessary to mention Julia's surname, for of course he did not know what name she was using. 'And this is Julia, a very old friend of mine.'

'How do you do,' Mike said.

The girl held out her hand and said, 'Were you at the concert?'

'Slept all through it, didn't you?' Peter jumped in before she could answer. 'The old standard repertoire holds no excitement for you. Heard it all a thousand times.'

'Well, and haven't you?' Julia countered.

Sue looked from Julia to Peter rather sourly, alerted by something in the quality of the exchange; and the look she gave Peter alerted Julia in the same way. She knew at once that he had had this girl, perhaps was still sleeping with her, and it seemed the girl knew him well enough to know the same about Julia.

Julia, however, could look at Sue without any jealousy, for she would not in any circumstances have liked to be her. Whatever Sue now had with Peter, Julia had had the best part of him, and the way he had called her his old friend had warmed her through. A kind of peace enveloped her, and she sat very still and very high on her stool and was aware of the other girl's hostility only with pity, and from a great distance.

'Do you play?' Mike asked her politely, just as, at Louie's parties, writers had asked her if she wrote, and painters if she painted.

'Oh no, I'm afraid not – to my regret.'

'Julia paints,' Peter said hurriedly – he really was nervous, she thought, afraid that someone might say the wrong thing about her or to her. Now he wanted to remove the shame of her not being musical before Sue could get hold of it.

'Really? Would I know you? What's your name?' Mike asked.

'Jacobs was the name I painted under,' Julia said, putting Peter temporarily out of his agony. 'I don't paint any more, though.'

'I've never heard of you, I'm afraid,' Sue said blandly.

Julia smiled. 'Don't be afraid. I've never heard of you either.' It was pleasantly meant, and in any other company would have been accepted pleasantly, but Sue took it amiss and bristled.

Peter broke in hastily with, 'Let's have a drink, shall we? What would you like, Sue? Mike, what are you drinking?'

'Oh, a pint of special for me, Peter, thanks.'

'I'll have a vodka and lime,' said Sue.

'What's that you're drinking?' Peter asked Julia. 'Gin and polly? Right, that's a pint, a vodka and lime, two gins, and one tonic, please.' The barman nodded and moved away, and

338

Peter leaned an elbow on the bar and said to Julia, 'I take it you came up especially for the concert?'

'You take it right. I don't come here just to drink, you know.'

'What did you think of it?' Mike asked her.

She hesitated, wondering whether he was simply being polite, or if he wanted a discussion, and while she paused Sue jumped in with a different emphasis: 'What did you think of Peter?'

It was clumsy, it was wrong, just the wrong tone of possessive smugness to expose the fact of the sexual relationship between them, which was something she would want known and Peter would want kept secret. Julia winced privately knowing that Sue was cooking her own goose. She did not look at Peter, but she knew what his expression would be. She said gently, 'I thought he was very good.'

Sue blushed a little, and defiantly attacked again. 'How did you come to know him? He says you were an old friend?'

Now Julia did glance at Peter, and seeing him blench was amused. 'Oh, I'm a very old friend,' she said heavily, and let him get as far as opening his mouth before she took pity on him. 'In fact, he's my brother-in-law.'

'Oh, really?' Mike said.

'Yes, he married my sister.' It was mean, really; but sneaking a look at Peter, she saw that he had never thought of it like that before. He didn't quite know what to say.

'They haven't met Sylvia,' was what he did eventually say.

'Does she never come to concerts?'

'Oh, she has her own occupations. It can get to be a bore for a soloist's wife.'

That was cruel, and a tit for tat for her earlier scored point. Now they were even.

The drinks arrived, and Peter engaged Mike in conversation of a technical sort in an attempt to avoid any further difficulties. Julia finished her drink and was thinking about her train, for though she would have loved a conversation with Peter, she didn't like the company of the other two. She put her glass down, preparatory to making her excuses.

339

Sensitive to the movement Peter turned to her, breaking off in the middle of a sentence, and said, low and quickly, 'Don't go.'

There was a short silence, as the whole truth dawned severally on the four of them, and then Mike, who had been well brought-up, summoned his social sense to say, 'I have to be going, actually, Peter. Got to get an early night tonight. Can I give you a lift, Sue?'

Sue opened her mouth to refuse, looked from Mike to Peter, from Peter to Julia, and then, as Mike nudged her none too subtly, closed her mouth in fury. There wasn't a thing she could do, and she picked up her handbag and stalked to the door. Mike covered up as best he could with polite leave-takings, and then at last Peter and Julia had the bar to themselves.

'Let's have another drink,' he said. She nodded slightly, and he called the barman and ordered the drinks, and then hitched himself on to the stool next to her.

'Sorry about that,' he said. 'I didn't want to bring them along, but I couldn't seem to lose them on the way down.'

'You don't mean to tell me you knew I'd be here?' Julia said, surprised.

'Of course I did. Where else would you be? Not the Pill Box or the Hole in the Wall. Anyway, this was always where we came.'

'But how did you know I'd be waiting for you? I might have gone straight home.'

He shook his head. 'I never thought of that.' He glanced towards the door and she saw the direction of his eyes.

'That poor girl,' she said. They exchanged a long look that equally expressed and forbade several subjects, and it was a while before they could hit on one which it was possible to discuss.

Eventually he said, 'When did you decide to come tonight?'

'Last week. I saw it advertised.'

'But you've never come before.' It was half a question. 'Why all of a sudden, after so long?'

'Well, we've only just come back to England,' she said.

'Oh, you were abroad? I never thought of that,' he said, ignoring the 'we' that had slipped out.

'Not quite abroad,' she smiled. 'Scotland.'

'What part?' He seized on that eagerly, for here was a subject they could discuss. Julia told him of her experiences, avoiding any mention of George or marriage. The atmosphere between them was of pleasant companionship, only a little unnatural because of the gaps that had to be left. They finished their drinks, and a silence fell.

'I have to go,' she said, glancing at her watch.

'I'll give you a lift,' he said.

'I'm only going to the station,' she said. They picked up their belongings and walked out on to the street, and Julia could not help feeling how familiar an action it was to leave this pub with him.

'My car's just up here,' he said.

She responded more or less instinctively to the request in his voice and followed him to where his car was parked by the kerb, but there she stopped and said again, 'I'm only going to Waterloo.'

'For a train?'

The foolishness of the question told her he was not quite so much in command of himself as he appeared.

'Of course for a train. What did you think?'

'Where to?'

'Aldershot.'

His brows shot up. 'What the devil are you going to Aldershot for?' he said explosively, as if it were the end of the world.

'I live there,' she said.

'In *Aldershot*?' He stared, disbelievingly. 'Why, in God's name?'

'That's where the army is.'

'Oh yes. I'd forgotten.' His voice was flat, expressionless. 'Well, get in.'

She hesitated, not sure of where they'd got to. 'Where do you live?' she temporised.

'I have a flat in Kensington,' he said. He seemed to see a question in her expression and went on, 'She's not there. She's in High Wycombe.'

'High Wycombe?'

341

'I have a house in High Wycombe,' he said.

He sounded rather shamed, and she quite didn't know why, except that it seemed as impossible a place for him as Aldershot was for her. She said again, in his own tone of astonishment, '*High Wycombe*?'

Then they caught each other's eye, and the tension exploded into laughter. They laughed until tears ran down Julia's cheeks, and Peter had to hold on to the roof of the car, breathlessly.

When eventually they recovered themselves they got into the car, and Peter turned to her and said simply, 'Where to?'

She looked at her watch. There was still time for the train. She looked up, saw Peter's mouth tremble, and hesitated.

'Oh Julia,' he said, and reaching out a hand drew her head to him, not to kiss her, but to put his cheek against hers. 'Where have you been?'

'Away,' she said.

Eighteen

December, 1969

The servant put down the coffee pot in front of Julia and went out. She lifted the pot, holding back the sleeve of her dressing gown with the other hand, and as she reached across the table to fill George's cup he said, 'Peter Kane – isn't he the violinist?'

The hand wavered a little, and the perfect column of liquid was broken by the edge of the cup so that a few drops splashed over into the saucer. George observed from under his eyelashes, but did not look up from the letter he was reading.

'That's right,' Julia said, her voice unconcerned. She filled her own cup and opened the *Sunday Post* to the cartoon page. After those years in Scotland, breakfast wasn't the same for her without the *Sunday Post*, and they had it on order from the local newsagent along with the *Sunday Telegraph*, which George preferred.

'Do you know him?' George asked.

'Why do you ask?'

'Well, I'm sure I don't, and he's invited us to a party on the fourth of December, so it must be for your sake. It's at his place in London – Wynnstay Gardens, wherever that is.'

She looked up now, meeting his eyes without embarrassment. 'It's in Kensington – a block of private flats. Enormous, very swanky. He must be well-off to live there.'

'You know the place, then?'

'One of Louie's crowd lived there, years ago. It's just off Kensington High Street – off Allen Street.'

'Oh yes. I know where you mean.' He regarded her for a moment and then reverted to his former question which she had avoided. 'You know him, then?'

Now she knew why he wanted to know it wasn't so bad. She sipped her coffee and then said in as off-hand a way as possible, 'Yes, I know him. He married my sister, actually.'

'Your *sister*?' George screwed up his face in astonished amusement. 'You never told me you had a sister. In fact, I distinctly remember when we married you said you had no relatives at all.'

'Well, we don't talk. I haven't seen her in years,' Julia said, buttering toast with unusual care. 'We had a' – she remembered Aunt Etty's term – 'a falling out and parted on bad terms, and I haven't seen or heard from her since. That was before I even met you, so you see as far as I was concerned I *hadn't* any relatives.'

'You really are the oddest person,' George said. 'Your family seems to me to be lacking in some very basic instincts. Your parents threw you off in your extreme youth, and now after all these years I find out for the first time that you actually have a sister, who's also thrown you off.'

'Oh well, people are funny sometimes,' she said dismissingly. She didn't want to get on to troublesome ground with him this early in the morning. She glanced at the letter in his hand and longed to read it, though she could not trust herself to ask him for it in any kind of a normal voice. Instead she said, 'How odd of him to invite us. You'd think if he was asserting a family connection he would have got her to write.'

'He doesn't mention her at all,' George said, glancing down, but not offering the letter to her. 'He just asks for the pleasure of the company of Colonel Crichton and his wife at a – however you pronounce it. Anyway, at an evening party.'

'Not soirée? He doesn't say soirée?' Julia exclaimed. 'Oh really! How shockingly pretentious!' And she began to laugh.

George carried on regardless. 'Nuisance is, he doesn't say what we should wear. People who use those sorts of words ought at least to have the decency to say "dress" at the bottom.'

That stopped her. She stared at him. 'You don't mean you're going?'

'Certainly. Why not?'

'Well, as you say, you don't know him.' She was floundering.

'You do, though. Don't you want to go?'

'But – well, I shouldn't have thought that sort of thing would appeal to you at all.'

'How do you know what sort of thing it will be?'

'Well, it's obvious, isn't it? I mean, he's a famous violinist, and his friends will be the terribly smart, fashionable sort of people who hang around the fringes of the artistic world.' She thought of a comparison, and added persuasively, 'Like Louie's parties, only worse. All false and glittery. People calling each other "darling" and posing for imaginery cameras.'

'Oh, that's how you see it, is it?' He nodded intelligently. 'Well, I don't agree as it happens. He's obviously a very brilliant man, and from what I've read about him he comes across as intelligent too. He's bound to collect like-minded people round him. I think it would be an excellent opportunity to meet some interesting new people. Besides –' he smiled at Julia – 'you must be sick and tired of nothing but army talk all day long. It will be a chance for you to get back amongst your own sort of people.'

'But George, I love army people and army talk. I am amongst my own sort of people already, however could you think I'm not?'

She protested in vain. He was determined to do her good.

'My dear, you don't need to comfort me. I quite understand, really I do. You are very good at mixing with my set, but I know you get restless sometimes for a bit of intellectual conversation. I think it's very kind of this fellow to ask us. Reading between the lines, now I know the score, I wouldn't mind betting he's trying a spot of reconciliation between sisters, which is praiseworthy. You should never spurn an olive branch, dear. I shall write and accept for both of us.'

She shook her head, but said nothing, for she had learnt long ago the folly of arguing with George when he had decided on something. What upset her most was that he should suspect her of only pretending to be happy amongst 'his set' as he put it. She was genuinely happy in her situation, and hated to have him think otherwise.

345

As to why Peter had sent the invitation, she didn't need to wonder. She knew perfectly well that this party had only been arranged as an excuse to invite them. There was nothing praiseworthy about it – reconciling her and Sylvia was the last thing on his mind. It was a monumental tease, that was what it was. There was a strain of the prep-school bully in Peter which meant that he liked to torment people – only people he loved, it was true, but all the same it was reprehensible; and in the present instance she was very much afraid of the consequences. George was adept at playing the bluff, kindly colonel, but he was sharp and observant when it came to people. But to try to persuade him out of going now would be to court suspicion, and all she could do was to hope for the best, while fearing the worst.

Peter himself opened the door to them with an alacrity that suggested that he had been opening the door all evening.

'Oh, it's you. Good, come in, come in. I'm glad you could make it. Julia,' he put a hand on her shoulder and gave her a 'society' kiss on the cheek, but she felt the hand tremble, and when he stepped back she looked up into his face and saw the feverish brightness of his eyes that spoke either of much excitement or much whisky

'Hello, Peter,' she said as warmly as was compatible with her embarassment. The introduction she had dreaded was now imminent. 'This is my husband – darling, Peter Kane. Peter – George Crichton.'

'How do you do? I know you by repute, of course,' George said holding out his hand cordially, ready to like anyone until they proved themselves otherwise.

Peter took the hand and shook it, looking slightly down at George from his two inches vantage, and said, 'Ah, yes, Colonel Crichton – I've been doing my homework on you. DSO and bar wasn't it? That was a pretty piece of work.'

Julia mistook his tone of voice for mockery, longed to smack him, and prayed that George would not notice it; but George said the right sort of modest things and didn't seem at all put out. He didn't expect evil of people, and so he rarely got it, and in fact in this case he was right and Julia was wrong. One thing Peter did know how to value was a military reputation, having been brought up to it.

'You have a lovely flat here,' Julia said nervously. Peter looked at her with a softened expression.

'Do you like it? I hoped you would. I'd like you to have a good look round and tell me what you think of it.' He glanced at George and said in an explanatory sort of voice, 'I value Julia's opinion, you see.' She knew he only meant to make her uncomfortable, but George thought Julia the most remarkable person in the world and so could not see anything unusual in someone's consulting her opinion. 'Let me take your coats, and get you a drink,' he went on. 'You know where the bathroom is and everything, don't you?' It was said as casually as may be to trap her, but she was on her guard against his tricks and said nothing, though she gave him a sharp look.

George merely shook his head, smiling politely, and said, 'No.'

'No, of course you don't. What was I thinking? Well, it's down the passage, last door on the right. And everyone's in the drawing room – that door there. What can I get you to drink?'

They ordered their drinks from him and then drifted into the drawing room. Julia already knew the room, of course, but was still ready to pause in the doorway and admire it. It reminded her a little of the old houses in Scotland, for it had the same kind of very high ceilings and long windows. The walls were distempered plain white, as had been the walls of every place she and Peter had lived in together. The fireplace was enormous and beautiful, marble and brass, and a real fire burned in it. On the mantelpiece, between a pair of silver candlesticks was a cowrie shell they had brought back from Portsmouth in the summer after Boy was born. Apart from the old leather chesterfield, which occupied the far wall, it was the only thing that had lasted through from the old days, and she was painfully touched that Peter, the least sentimental of men, should have kept the worthless ornament.

The first time she had come here – that night after the concert – she had been on the verge of mentioning it, but she could not just yet bring herself to speak of Boy, not even to him. But she had looked, and turned to him, and he had known what she was thinking, and it was enough.

Peter paused in the doorway with their drinks and looked across the room at them with a mixture of love and bitterness. There she was, elegant and lovely – in his opinion there was not another woman in the room to touch her – and there beside her was a man he knew from the first glance he was not going to be able to hate as he wanted to, needed to. In the past few months he had come to realise how much of his life had been wasted. He had been content enough in the intervening years, absorbed in his music and the furtherance of his career; but now he had met Julia again, and it came to him that he was in exactly the same position as he had been sixteen years ago – he had gained nothing, nothing.

He was married to a woman he neither loved nor respected and frantically wanting another woman, but with this grotesque difference – that before, Joyce had been his wife, and Julia the other woman. Now he was married to Sylvia; but Julia was his wife – always his wife, he could not think of her as anything else – and there was so much to keep them apart.

Since their first meeting, back in the spring, he had seen her again several times, but by no means as often as he wanted, or had pressed for. She was very, very cautious, had spaced the visits, and changed the venue around – like Julia in *1984* he thought. Despite the infrequency of their meetings, he had found to his surprise that sex was no longer the main thing he wanted from her – oh, they always made love, and always at his instigation, but that was more to make sure of her, a kind of reminder of ownership. He felt that in some way it gave him power over her, to possess her, a power which he was no longer sure of in other spheres. He had to fight off the feeling that she was going to leave him again, back out of his life completely.

That was one of the reasons he had invited her and Crichton here tonight. At the back of his mind, hardly acknowledged, was a thought of forcing a reckoning; at the front was a simple desire to find out the cut of a man who could call forth such unreasonable fidelity from Julia – who was *his*, damnit, *his*, and always would be!

He carried the drinks over, and George said pleasantly, 'Are we not to have the pleasure of meeting your wife the night?'

Julia blenched inwardly at the very thought, and Peter smiled, lifting one corner of his mouth in that cynical way of his, saying, 'I'm afraid not. She's at our house in Buckinghamshire. She couldn't be here.'

'That's a pity. I'm sure Julia would have loved to see her again. That is right, they're sisters?' George asked him hesitantly, clearly puzzled by the relationship.

Peter looked at Julia in surprise. It had not occured to him to wonder how she had explained him – and the invitation – away to her husband. 'That's right,' he said.

'And could you not have had a wee word with her, to patch up this silly quarrel?' George asked gently. 'To be frank, that's what I thought the invitation was for – an olive branch, d'ye see?'

Peter shook his head. 'When women fight, I keep out of the way. Now, if you'll excuse me, I have to circulate a little. Please make yourselves absolutely at home, and if there's anything you want that you don't see, don't hesitate to ask me. Let me just introduce you to Paul and Miriam.' And he scraped them off on the couple nearest at hand and made his escape before Crichton could pursue the question of why, in that case, had they been invited.

It really was a very good party, viewed dispassionately. There was plenty to eat and drink, of good quality and in good variety. The two rooms being used were large and beautiful, and well-heated without being stuffy. The people he had invited were a good mixture, and some of them were really fascinating to talk to, while all of them were easy and unaffected. Julia and George were soon separated, drawn apart by differing streams of conversation, and as in a battle you can move as much as a hundred yards while seeming to fight on the same spot, they moved around in the course of their conversations so that after a while she lost sight of him altogether.

Some time later music started up in the other room, and as she stood temporarily alone Peter came over to her with a full glass to replace her almost-empty one, and stepped into her small vacuum.

'Enjoying it?'

'Was I supposed to?'

'What kind of a question is that? Why do you think I asked you?'

'Well, why did you?'

'Why do you always answer a question with a question?' he said, exasperated.

'Why do you?' He glared for a moment, and then burst out laughing. 'All right,' she went on, 'but tell the truth, now, and save a sailor. Didn't you invite me here tonight for the sheer joy of tormenting me?'

'Why should I want to torment you?'

'I don't know, but you do like it, don't you?' You always did, she added inwardly, and he saw the tiredness in her face, and was sorry.

'I asked you because any party without you would be a failure.'

'You always sound so convincing when you're saying things like that,' she said. 'It's so tempting to believe you.'

'Then do,' he urged, his face guileless. 'Why all the fencing? I thought we were friends again.'

'Ah, yes, when I'm alone with you. And when I'm away from you. But when I'm here between you, with my husband on one side and my lover on the other—'

'I'm your husband,' he interrupted. 'I don't believe in divorce.'

'That's a dangerous road to pursue. You had to divorce Joyce to marry me in the first place, don't forget.'

'I don't want to remember that. Anyway, I was never really married to Joyce. You're my wife, never mind the law.'

'A very convenient philosophy,' she said drily.

'You don't believe me,' he said, injured.

'As it happens, I do,' she said. 'I believe you believe every word of it.'

'I love you,' he said. The words knifed her, as always.

'I believe that as well,' she said, a little more shakily. He turned so that with his back he cut off the rest of the party, and put a hand on the wall behind her shoulder and leaned on it, closing her in.

'I want to kiss you,' he said.

He looked down into her lovely, living face, every feature of which was so familiar to him that he could have found her blindfold, by touch alone – familiar and dear, the thing he loved more than anything else in the world. He had taken her lightly, all those years ago, back in the beginning; but she had stuck to him like cobweb. He had done that thing and given no thought to the consequences – had never even begun to suppose there could be any consequences to something he had slipped into so easily. Here on the further side of it, it was hard to believe he had been so – what? – irresponsible? But it was not that he had shirked or shunned responsibility; rather that it had seemed like something to which no responsibility could attach. He supposed it had been a kind of madness. Common sense had been suspended. He saw that now, from this vantage point of maturity, but he was still far from understanding it.

He understood only that he loved her in some fundamental way. This was the love that was mixed up with every other love he experienced – music, sunlight, health. He did not say, because of you, nothing else matters, but, because of you, everything matters much more. But he didn't know how to tell her, he had never been able to tell her, except by playing to her. All words were so mixed up with other associations and other meanings that they could never express even the shadow of what he wanted to say.

As for Julia, this close to him she found herself growing weaker, wanting more. She felt the difficulties building up in her life, snowballing, and she wanted, weakly, for life to sweep her away, careless of the consequences, as it had when they were younger, when in her ignorance and innocence and the freshness of first love she had felt no sense of responsibility for Joyce's children upstairs, and for Joyce herself in hospital.

She hated the loss of her freedom, she hated George's dependence on her. She had always believed that of any couple, one always loved more than the other, and having been the loving and insufficiently loved partner, she had thought it was the worst thing to bear. Now she knew better. She had left Peter, but she could never leave George, simply because she did not love him enough. Oh, far, far better to be the deceived than the deceiver.

She had left Peter on a point of principle, and had lived to betray those same principles herself. Well, it was not an unusual situation – many people said one thing and did another; but in her case she cared desperately.

'Ah, there you are!'

Peter jumped back from her in alarm, but Julia gave no guilty start as George appeared beside her. It amused her to see Peter, the debonair, caught on the hop.

'Hello, darling. Having a nice time?'

'Isn't it strange that the only person you can never speak to at a party is the person you came with?' George said.

'That's why parties are parties,' Peter said with an effort. 'You can talk to your wife any time.'

'I must say you've got an interesting crowd here. Julia was afraid I'd be bored – I think she felt I'd be out of place amongst all these arty types.' He smiled to show her he was only joking. 'But I've had some very interesting conversations.'

'Did you meet Brigadier Barrow?' Peter asked.

'Oh yes, we had a wee chin together.'

'I'm glad. He was a friend of my father's. They were in the King's Own together – cavalrymen, like you. I believe your regiment had something to do with the King's Own during the Remargen campaign?'

Julia liked to hear them talking about such a safe mutual subject as the army, and saw that Peter went up in George's esteem simply through knowing a little about the army and the war. What odd creatures men were, affected by the most unexpected trivia, she thought.

Peter wandered off again, and George said, 'They're dancing in the next room. Would you like to dance?'

'Yes, I think so – for a little while. Then let's go home. It's been a nice party, but I want to get home and into bed with you.'

George's brilliant smile warmed parts of her, and his arm round her as they walked to the next room was comfortingly solid and real. She had no wish to think wrong thoughts any more. She wanted an end to all complications, but there was

352

one thing on her mind that she knew was going to give her more trouble than anything else in her whole life.

When George went to find their coats, Julia went to find Peter to say goodbye.

'Can't you stay a little longer?' he asked her. She had found him in the kitchen and as the other person present went out, leaving them alone, he pushed the door closed and said, 'I don't like to think of you going home with him.'

'That has nothing to do with anything,' she said shortly. 'As you should knowing, taking Sylvia into account.'

'One doesn't take Sylvia into account,' he said easily. 'Now if you hadn't gone and got married—'

'There would still be Sylvia,' she persisted.

'You don't really mind about her, do you?' he asked. 'It was for your sake really that I married her.'

'It takes a mind like mine to understand a statement as crooked as that.'

'But you do?'

'Understand?'

'Yes.'

'In a way.'

'Thank God. There has to be somebody in the world who knows what I'm talking about. Don't go.'

'I have to.'

'You don't have to. You don't ever have to go away again.' He was serious now, and she was silent, trying to outwill him, fighting for foothold on a slippery slope. She could hear his breathing in the quietness of the kitchen, and in the background a tap dripping with a clink like coins being dropped. 'Julia,' he said, putting his arms out to take hold of her, and she felt herself snapping like static.

'Peter, don't. How can I face him if you do this?'

'You've managed other times.'

'Oh . . .' Why did he refuse to see what was obvious? The frustration of not being able to get through to him made her blurt out the news that she had intended to save until they were really alone.

'Peter, I'm pregnant.'

He seemed to freeze. 'What?' He had no voice but a whisper.

'I'm pregnant,' she said, more gently this time. She watched pleasure begin to win through over shock, only to be dispersed again by doubt.

'Is it – is it me?'

'Yes. Yes, it's yours.'

'How do you know?'

'I know.' She waved away all that with the flat of her hand. She would not, could not, tell him about George's growing anxiety that there was something wrong with him. She had never told George that she had had a child, but he was too chivalrous in any case to think the fault might be hers. He was older than her, and he had wondered whether his age was telling against him. In four years of marriage to George and regular congress with him, she had not conceived; she had met Peter again, and almost at once found herself with child. In her own mind she was sure, but it was not capable of proof or explanation, and that made it harder for Peter.

'Are you really sure?' he urged.

'Yes. Believe me.'

It was painful to see the dawning joy on his face. He looked down, as if he was shy, and murmured, 'Thank God. Thank God.' He put his hands over his face for a moment, and then looked at her, beginning to exult. 'Julia! We have a child.' He was smiling now, and he put his arms round her shoulders. 'I'll have a son! Oh Julia . . .' He put a hand against her belly as he had done the first time she had conceived, and looked at her questioningly as if he were not sure if she understood.

'I'm glad it's yours,' she said. 'I'm so glad to have a child of yours. I never wanted to have children from any-one else.'

'You will never bear any man's son but mine,' he said fiercely, and the thought of George came to them both at the same time. 'Does he know?' Peter asked.

'Not yet.' She began to draw back, remembering that George would be looking for her. 'Peter, I must go.'

'What?' He looked surprised.

'Yes, I must.'

354

'You're not going back with him, after what you've just told me? You can't!'

'I can't throw everything to the winds, just like that. I can't leave him, just like that.'

'Why not?'

'Because I can't. Peter, be reasonable. George is my – oh, I'm married to him, for God's sake. He loves me.'

'So do I.'

'But you're different, you're different.'

'So it seems.' He was cold with anger now, and she knew that he didn't see it, that he never would. For him it seemed obvious that she should not go back to George, nor he to Sylvia; but he had never had any sense of responsibility towards other people. He was for him, and for her. His child was in her belly and that was the only reality.

'I must go back with him tonight,' she said, her voice dull.

He dropped his hands to his sides and said, 'All right. If you must, you must.' She stared at him for a moment, and then began to turn away, but he caught her back. He took her face between his hands and kissed it, and his tenderness, as always, was harder for her to bear than either his anger or his passion. Tears started in her eyes.

He saw them, and said gently, 'Don't sleep with him tonight. Not tonight.'

'I won't,' she said.

It was a lie, and they both knew it. Peter changed tack. 'When will you tell him?'

'Soon. When the opportunity arises . . .'

'Tonight.'

'Not tonight,' she said irritably. 'Soon . . .'

'Soon,' he said firmly. He moved back from her as the door opened. George came in, holding their coats.

'Oh, there you are. I wondered where you'd got to,' he said. He stood quite still, like a soldier, just inside the door, looking from one to the other of them.

'Yes,' Julia said. Her voice sounded weary even to her.

'We were just saying goodbye,' Peter said and she winced inwardly at the cynicism in his tone that surely could not escape George's notice.

355

But he only smiled, holding out her coat, and said cheerfully, 'Well, time to go, I'm afraid. We've rather a long journey back, and I think Julia's tired.' He helped her on with her coat, giving her shoulder a loving squeeze as he settled her collar, and she prayed silently, Oh God, oh God. She looked from one to the other, from George, short and solid, handsome and ruddy and smiling, to Peter, elegant, dark, self-assured, always cynically amused, and felt herself being torn in half.

She wanted to give in. It would be so easy to give in, to stay with Peter – it would even be reasonable. The possibility beckoned her like sleep. But it was not a possibility. She looked at George, who loved her more than she could ever deserve, and she knew she would never tell him that the miracle had not happened.

Nineteen

1975

The men had taken everything now and loaded it on to the van – everything except this one last suitcase into which Julia was packing a few odds and ends. When that was done, it would really be all over, the end of a life and of ten years of marriage. The end of everything.

She pressed down the clothes in the case and looked around. Just the things on the dressing table to go in: the pair of photographs, one of Catherine at three years old, sitting in an armchair with her legs stuck straight out before her, her hands twisting in the skirt of her dress with self-consciousness; and one of George in uniform, a rather classy studio portrait he had had done in Germany, not looking much like him because it was too posed and stiff.

George had framed them himself, carefully measuring and mitring the four sides, cutting out the rebate by hand, making the back card and cutting and glueing the supporting leg; only the glass had been bought cut to size. It was a neat job. George had always loved to make things, and was so painstaking that anything he undertook would end up as a professional-looking job.

She put them into the case, face-downwards, pushing down the hollow feeling in her chest which she knew only too well from the past weeks, and packed in the little boxes in which she kept pins and brooches. She had a passion for boxes, and George had indulged it – all of these were presents from him: a little black and gold Chinese lacquer box from Hong Kong; a porcelain snuff box from one of the many antique shops of Perth; a pokerwork box from Portobello Road; a dear little miniature pirate's treasure chest carved out of wood and embellished with minute brass bands and nails; and her favourite, an ivory box shaped like a rose, which had been his last Christmas present to her. She did not put this away at once, but held it cupped in her hands as if it were an egg she was warming, while she looked around the bedroom.

It had been their home since Cathy was born: George had been posted down to Lulworth shortly before her birth. It was also the house they had lived in for longest in their married life. He had not always been here, for he had had to go where they sent him, but once she had the baby he had thought it better for her to be settled. If there had been a long separation, she would have moved with him, but he had never had to be away for more than a few weeks at a time. His last absence, six weeks on exercise in Germany, would have been their longest separation. His last absence, she thought, and it would never be over.

It had happened on the last morning of the exercise, in the darkest hours just before sunrise. The tank in which he was riding had come off a bridge and been disabled, and he had left the crew and started back towards camp on foot. The crew, in the inquiry, said that he had given them no reason, had simply told them to stay put and had gone walking back down the track they had made.

The driver of the other tank had never seen him. It was pitch dark and of course they were not using lights, it being a night exercise. Julia had never been expressly told, but she understood there was not much left by which to identify him when they finally found him.

A few deaths were expected on an exercise of that size, but the grief and horror that swept through the ranks was enormous. They had brought him home and buried him with military honours, and the funeral had been beautiful and moving; so moving that during the playing of the pibroch at the graveside many of the men had sobbed. They had lost in him something more than simply a leader: he had been the heart of the battalion. Julia had known and felt this, and her own grief operated on two levels; for the loss of the colonel; and for the loss of her man. George, the loving, the loyal, her gentle husband, was dead; the fine, hard body she slept beside was torn to shreds, and he would never touch her again.

358

She had his last letter still – it was lying on the dresser now, the last thing left to pack. She knew the shape of its fold and the texture of its paper by heart now. He had written it on the evening before his death, when they had come into camp to rest up for a day. It thanked her for her letters, spoke a little about the exercise, touched on the political situation that was causing the army's commanders anxiety; but mostly it had spoken of her and Cathy. It was, after all, a soldier's letter, written while lying on his bed in one of the periods of inaction between bouts of strenuous exertion; and so he had written, as soldiers do, of his wife and child.

'When the war ended,' it said, 'I thought that I had had my finest hour, but I know now that I had hardly begun. All I did then was nothing compared with my greatest achievements, you and Cathy.' Then he had gone on to talk of the death of one of his young squaddies – the ink had run here where Julia's tears had dropped on to the page. The last paragraph she knew by heart:

> Remember, if you want me, just close your eyes, and I will be there, as you are with me, you and Cathy, always, wherever I go. You are beside me in the dark now, though I can't see you, and when I finish this letter I shall kiss you goodnight and hold you to my heart while I sleep. Goodnight, my darling, God bless you.

She was crying again now, and had to blink to clear her sight, because her hands were not free. She stared down blankly at them, having forgotten what it was she held, and saw the little box, rose-shaped and warm as an egg in her hands. She put it into the case, dropped the letter on top, and then stood for a moment, her head down and her hands hanging useless by her sides. She felt defeated.

'Excuse me, ma'am – are you ready?'

She jerked her head up and saw the driver looking in at the door apologetically. 'Yes – yes, I'm ready.'

She still did not move, and after a moment's hesitation

he came forward and closed the case and carried it out of the room.

She followed him automatically, and said, 'Where's Cathy?'

'The little girl, ma'am? She's downstairs – been helping us. Kept us laughing – she's a card, isn't she!'

The card appeared at the foot of the stairs at the sound of descent and looked up at her mother. She was extremely dirty and untidy – from 'helping' no doubt – and although she was looking cheerful enough now, her face was streaked where she had been crying earlier on.

'Come on, Mummy, hurry up – we're all ready,' she called impatiently.

'All right, I'm coming,' Julia answered. 'My stars, what a mess you're in. What have you been doing?'

'Getting Angus out,' Cathy said. 'He got packed into the van by mistake, and I was the only one small enough to get in where he was.' Angus was her doll – a rag doll, in fact, that George had brought home from Holland when Cathy was about two. She had rejected it at first, thinking it, for some reason, beneath her to play with a girlish thing like a doll, but George had had the idea of making it a boy-doll, and by cropping the yellow hair and giving it a kilt made from a piece of tartan lining out of a mackintosh instead of a skirt, Cathy had been induced to accept it as something rather novel and exciting. The doll had been christened Angus Rory Ian McIntosh (the last because of his tartan, of course) and he had since achieved the status of Linus's blanket.

'Couldn't you have left him there, darling?' Julia said, automatically tucking Cathy's blouse back into her skirt. 'It's only until we get to London, after all.'

'Oh no, he wanted to look out of the window. He'd 'a been *miserable* shut up in there,' Cathy said firmly.

'Your cardigan's buttoned up all wrong too – here . . .'

'No, I'll do it – I can do it.'

Julia let go at once, recognising a touchy area. Since her father died, Cathy had been a little difficult to handle, sometimes reverting to babyhood and asserting inability to button a button or tie a shoelace, and sometimes refusing to have the least thing done for her. Julia did not insist either way on these occasions, feeling that Cathy would find her own level again once the waters calmed. It was not worth quarrelling over a button.

Cathy, breathing hard with concentration, started buttoning again. As clear as a recording, George's voice sounded in Julia's head: 'Start from the bottom, that's right, and just work up, one by one.' She saw him again sitting on Cathy's bed while the latter took her first lesson in dressing herself. The lesson had held good. She saw Cathy had started at the bottom of her own accord, and was getting it right.

The child looked up suddenly with a flash of blue like a Siamese cat, and said, 'Have you been crying again?'

'Yes,' Julia admitted.

'Well, you mustn't, you know. It'll be all right.' It was George all over again, the mock severity – did Cathy know she was imitating him, or was it unconscious?

Julia took hold of a bunch of dark curls – Cathy had darker hair than either George or Peter, with no glint of red in it – and said, 'I'll try not to. What happened to your hair ribbon?'

'It got lost,' Cathy said, concentrating on her last button. 'Done it!'

'Got lost how?'

'I don't know. It just comes off. Come on, they're starting – where's Angus?'

Cathy heard the engine from outside, and grabbing up the doll ran out to the van. Julia followed, taking a last look back and pulling the door closed after her. At the gate she paused again to look back, but Cathy was calling again, impatiently, so she obeyed and climbed up into the cab beside her, glad, at least, that Cathy seemed to have no regrets in leaving the place that had been her home for five years, for the whole of her life so far.

Catherine's birth had been quite another affair from Nathan's. She had arrived like clockwork, dead on time, after the briefest possible labour, so that Julia had practically felt let down at having keyed herself up for nothing. She had been disappointing to look at – a small, wizened baby, like an old apple. She had not opened her eyes or yelled or

361

exuded any personality at all. Her crumpled face screwed up with determination, she had slept for the first two days of her life, resisting all attempts to wake her up, even for food.

'Don't worry, dear, she'll fill out once she starts feeding,' the nurse had said when Julia, quite truthfully, had said the baby was like a wrinkled old woman. 'I often think being born takes it out of these small babies more.'

And George, hanging over the cot with proud adoration, had said, 'It's the little wrinkled apples that are the sweetest – everyone knows that.'

So they had taken her back to the new house in Lulworth, and Catherine had proceeded to justify her father's faith by proving to be the sweetest-natured child anyone had ever come across. Even as a baby she exuded sweetness: she never cried, even when her feed arrived late; she learnt to smile almost before anything else, and once having mastered the action she had used it on every possible occasion.

As soon as she could sit up, she used her hands to pull herself upright. She rejected crawling almost as soon as she learnt it as being too slow, and clinging to her father's finger she had stumped forward with determination, smiling sunnily at her own achievement. She loved everything that moved, quite indiscriminately, and often frightened her mother by her fearless approaching of unpleasant-looking dogs, but despite her catholic taste she very early in life exhibited a preference for her father's company.

As Julia said of her, 'She'll make a great business woman – she invests where she's sure of the highest return.'

George, of course, adored her, but proved to be a very sensible father, and unless showering her with love could be called spoiling her, she was not spoilt. He loved most of all to teach her things, and it was he who gave all the lessons that normally fall to the mother's part, like teaching her to dress herself, for instance. He took her out to show her off whenever he had the chance, and Colonel Crichton out walking with his daughter was a more frequent sight than Colonel Crichton out walking with his wife.

He, of course, had never allowed her to be ugly, and

362

again to prove him right, she grew into a pretty baby, and a beautiful child.

George, sitting her on his knee to brush out her black hair, would sometimes say, 'Do you think she looks like me? I think she's more like you, really.'

But Julia would only ever say, 'I think she looks like herself.'

In fact it was the truth; but then little children have everyone's face – it's only as they grow older that their features settle into a pattern, and favour one side or the other, or more often both.

Julia saw likenesses to Peter from the time Catherine was about four, but then of course she was looking for them. It did seem, though, that she was growing more like him, especially in the shape of her nose and mouth, and sometimes when she was doing something teasing her face would take on an expression of suppressed glee that was so like Peter it would start gooseflesh down Julia's back. It seemed to her frightening that Cathy's features should imitate someone she had never known, as if her flesh, her very cells, had a memory of him that could not be wiped out.

Julia wondered if George would have noticed one day, and recognised another face in that of his daughter; and if he had, what effect would it have had on him? Her life had not been all happiness, but it was right that she should suffer a little to protect them both. Peter had never seen the baby, and that had been a grief to her, for she knew how much he had wanted the child. She hoped he had not continued to suffer after she had gone away.

It had been a terrible decision to have to make, when there was only the possibility of one of them being happy, but once having made it, she had to stick to it, whether it was right or wrong, and that in its way had been a comfort to her, knowing she could not go back on it. And she thought, looking back, that she had been right. She could not have known that George would die – and if she had, would it have made any difference? She did what she thought was right in the end. The years had been good, very good, and though that only served to make her present grief the worse, she would not have them different.

*　　*　　*

Before the move, the most surprising thing to come out of George's death had been a visit from Sylvia. It had begun with a phone call, one afternoon about a week after the funeral.

'Hello – is that Julia?'

'Yes. Who's that?'

'It's me. Sylvia.' Julia was so surprised that she could not immediately think of anything to say, and a silence fell which Sylvia broke anxiously. 'Hello? Are you still there?'

'Yes – yes. I didn't recognise your voice.'

'I didn't yours either.' Sylvia gave a nervous laugh.

'How are you?'

'Oh, I'm all right. How are you?'

'Bearing up.'

A short silence. 'Oh, Julia, it's terrible. I don't know what to say.'

'Don't say anything, then. There's nothing to say. Where are you calling from?'

'Well, actually,' hesitantly, 'I'm at the station.'

'Oh yes? Where are you off to?' Julia asked, not understanding.

'I'm not off to anywhere. I'm here. I'm at the station.'

'What – you mean *my* station?'

'Yes – what's it called – Wool. I wanted to come and see you.'

'Well, why didn't you tell me? Why didn't you ring me before, you ass? I would have come and met you,' Julia said.

Sylvia made a sound that could have been a sigh of relief. 'I thought about ringing, but then I wasn't sure if you'd want to see me, so I thought I'd just come and present you with a fait accompli, as it were. And then when I got here I lost my nerve. So I phoned you. I hope you don't—'

'Oh Sylvia, of course I want to see you.'

'Do you?' Sylvia said with a lift of hope in her voice. 'I know we haven't – I mean, there's so much that's happened between us, but – well – blood is thicker than water, isn't it?'

Shades of Aunt Etty. 'I'd better come and pick you up,' Julia said.

'I can get a bus – there's one outside now.'

'You, on a bus? Anyway, you don't know where I live. You wouldn't find your way from the bus stop. No, I'd better pick you up. Stay there, I'll be down in ten minutes.'

'All right. I'll wait by the phone box.'

Julia put the phone down. 'Cathy!' she yelled.

'I'm in here,' she called back, and followed it up as she always did by answering the call in person, coming out of the sitting room with a comic in her hand. 'I was just going to start my practice,' she said defensively.

'Never mind just now, darling, you can do it later. We have to go down to the station to pick somebody up.'

'Oh, who?' Cathy asked, brightening. She loved company.

'Your Aunt Sylvia. She's come to visit us.'

Catherine considered. 'Have I seen that one before?'

'No, she's never been here.'

'Is she a real aunt?' Cathy was mildly interested, for all her other 'aunts and uncles' were merely friends of her parents.

Julia smiled. 'Yes, this one's a real, flesh and blood, dyed in the wool aunt. But I daresay you won't know the difference. She's my sister.'

Catherine appeared to consider this a point in her favour for she nodded approvingly. 'Good,' she said.

'Run and put your coat on, then, darling, and I'll go and turn the car round.'

'Can Angus come? He likes going in the car.'

'Yes, if you want.' Angus had been much in evidence since her father died, but Julia decided it was better, at least, than thumb-sucking or nail-biting, or even worse things that might have come out of the state of shock.

Julia recognised the solitary figure by the phone booth as she pulled the car into the station car park. She and Cathy got out and walked across, and for a moment the sisters looked at each other in silence, before Julia made the first move and put her arms out, and they embraced.

'My, you smell expensive,' Julia said. 'What is it?'

'Balenciaga – Le Dix,' Sylvia answered absently. She was staring at Julia. 'You've changed,' she said abruptly. 'I would hardly have recognised you.'

'It's been a long time,' Julia reminded her. 'What is it – eleven years? Twelve years?'

'Twelve,' Sylvia said, showing that she had been counting.

'I would have known you, though. Still the same Sylvia – except –' she looked her up and down admiringly – 'a much wealthier Sylvia by the looks. You're very smart and elegant. You make me feel quite shabby.'

Sylvia made a throwaway gesture in her shyness, and looked down at Cathy, who was holding her mother's hand, so awed by the vision that she quite forgot to smile.

'This is my daughter Catherine,' Julia gave the child a little prompting push.

'Hello, dear,' Sylvia said, stooping a little and holding out her arms. 'I'm your Aunty Sylvia. Will you give me a kiss?'

Cathy was not used to people who talked like that, and she started at her aunt, and then at her mother with a look that said quite plainly, *must I*? Julia gave her a look in return and another gentle shove which said just as plainly *yes – it won't kill you*, and Cathy reluctantly reached up and kissed the powdered and scented cheek that was offered.

'Let's get home – we can talk in comfort then. It's too cold to stand about,' Julia said when this ceremony had been performed, and they got back into the car.

Julia had been speaking the truth when she said Sylvia had not changed. Her youthful slimness had become thinness, but the flat and fleshless look was certainly very fashionable at that time, and the lack of lumps and bumps made immaculate tailoring the easier. Sylvia was very, very smart, and very attractive. Her suit was of grey flannel and looked handmade, fitting her as if she had grown it. With it she wore a dark-blue-and-white striped silk blouse, with a very attractive gold brooch at the neck. Her shoes, gloves and handbag were all of soft dark-brown leather, and she had with her a crocodile-skin overnight bag with her initials on it in gold, S.M.K. – Sylvia Maitland Kane. So Sylvia still stuck to the 'Maitland' with which they'd both been endowed at their registration – Maitland was the maiden name of their father's mother.

Her makeup was faultless, her perfume expensive, and her

366

dark hair was styled to a perfection of soft waves that can only be achieved in a hairdresser's salon, and showed no thread of grey. Finally, her gold wedding ring, gold wrist-watch, and gold stud earrings were all as solid as that very solid gold brooch. She looked what she was – the expensively-kept wife of a successful man.

Looking beyond the straightforward appearance, Julia decided that her sister was neither contented nor particularly happy. Sylvia had always wanted what she had now, marriage to an important person, a large house, plenty of money, beautiful clothes, but presumably it had not answered, for though Sylvia looked less than her years, her thinness, her restless hands, and the bottle of pills Julia saw in her handbag when she opened it to get out a handkerchief, told their own tale.

Back in the house Julia put the kettle on and made tea, cut some sandwiches, and got out a cake, and carried a tray through into the sitting room.

'Oh, goodness, I hope this isn't for my sake,' Sylvia said. 'I don't want to put you to any trouble.'

'No trouble. We always have tea by the fire about this time, don't we Cathy?'

'I haven't done my practice yet,' Cathy answered obliquely.

'I know, darling. Have your tea first, and then you can do it. Is the fire on in the other room? Well, run and put it on now, and then the room will be warm for you to start.'

Cathy ran out to obey her, and Julia explained to Sylvia, 'She feels the cold in her hands, and of course she can't play with cold hands.'

'What does she play?' Sylvia asked.

'Piano and violin at the moment. She'll decide for herself what instrument she wants to take up as first choice later on.'

'Is she good?'

'I think so.'

Cathy came back, and Julia poured out. 'Hand Aunt Sylvia a sandwich, darling. Did you have a good journey down?'

'Not bad, except that I made the mistake of trying to get to the buffet for a cup of tea. It was packed with soldiers, all drinking like fish, and they are so coarse when they get together.'

'They do get a bit rowdy, I suppose,' Julia said mildly. 'But they don't mean any harm – they're all good boys, really. I always see them on their best behaviour, of course – they wouldn't misbehave in front of their CO's wife.'

Sylvia bit her lip. 'I'm sorry – I forgot.'

'Don't be sorry. I have to talk about him – I can't expect people to be tactful for the rest of my life.'

'Are you going to stay on here?' Sylvia asked to change the subject.

'I don't think so. George left me well provided for, but I think I'd like to go back to work, at least part-time. While Cathy's at school, you see, I would have nothing to do at home.'

'What will you do, then?'

'Move back to London, I suppose. There's more choice there.'

'And what about you, Cathy? Would you like to live in London?'

'I don't know,' Cathy said. She was being surprisingly shy with Sylvia. 'I think so.'

'You could come and visit me at my house – that's in the country, but near to London.'

'Do you have a dog?' Catherine asked, brightening momentarily.

'No. But we have a cat.'

'That's no substitute, I'm afraid,' Julia laughed. 'Cathy's mad to have a dog. Never mind, darling, it will happen one day. Remember how you always wanted a dog, Sylvia?'

'Oh yes, and I brought home that awful stray one day, and mother went nearly mad and sprayed everything with Jeyes fluid in case it brought some disease in with it.'

Julia laughed, and then was silent. 'Have you seen her recently?' she asked after a moment.

'Oh, yes. I still go there every now and then – I suppose about once a month. She's still quite active.'

'She's still at Milton Street?'

'Yes, she manages all right, and she prefers to be independent. Father's royalties are still coming in, and Peter tops it up, so she's comfortable.'

The first mention of his name between them was got over that easily – but the idea astonished Julia. Peter pay her mother a pension! Her mother accept it! It was extraordinary, to say the least. Now his name was out, she thought it best to talk about him. She glanced at Catherine, but she was staring at the fire, not attending to grown-up talk that was incomprehensible to her.

'How is Peter?' Julia said, looking at Sylvia steadily.

Sylvia looked back at her doubtfully. Peter was what she had come here to talk about, but she had often wondered how she could ever introduce this particular topic to her sister. Their lives had been so strangely tangled, and she had never known how Julia felt about his marrying her. Catching them in flagrante had been enough to make Julia abandon her marriage and her family, but would Sylvia's marrying him have made her sin worse or be just part of the same sin? But in the common parlance, she had stolen her sister's husband (though it did not feel like that from her point of view) and Julia had so resolutely maintained silence since then that Sylvia had hardly thought she would receive her, let alone be so affable. She had certainly never thought the topic of Peter would be so easily arrived at.

Julia had been wondering from the beginning, from the moment of the phone call, whether Peter had told Sylvia that he had had an affair with Julia after his marriage to her. She would not put it past Peter to do it out of sheer love of mischief, but from the way the conversation had developed so far, it appeared that he must have kept the secret. Discreet for once – or was there some other reason for his reticence?

So, into the breach: 'How is Peter?' she asked.

'Professionally, or personally?' Sylvia said.

'Either. Both. Professionally, I know he's still at the top of the tree. Does he feel he's playing well?'

'Oh, his work's all right. He's taken to conducting, now, you know. This new idea of the soloist conducting the orchestra – well, of course, it isn't a new idea, but it hasn't been the fashion for about a century, so it seems new.'

'Yes, I heard that Zukerman had done it,' Julia said.

Cathy was listening again now, for music she regarded as her special subject.

369

'That's how it started, anyway, but now he's also conducting without playing – ordinary conducting, you know.'

'Well, I'm glad he's getting on successfully,' Julia said blandly. She was trying to conceal from herself the great pleasure she felt in mentioning his name again. She had never, since the very early days when Sylvia had been her confidante, had the relief of being able to talk about him to anyone, and the last years had been more of a strain on her than she had known. She could not, even now, of course, talk to Sylvia about him in the way that she would had their situations been different, but even just to hear of him was good.

In the silence that followed, Cathy decided that nothing more was going to be said about music, and gulping the last of her tea she stood up, saying, 'I'm going to go and practise now, Mummy.'

'All right, darling. Are your hands clean?'

'Yes.'

'Scales and arpeggios first, don't forget. At least a quarter of an hour.'

'A'right.'

Cathy darted off, and Sylvia looked after her and said, 'What a pretty child,' but she wasn't really thinking about it. After a minute, the soothing background sound of ascending and descending scales came from the next room and in the security of the sound Sylvia turned back to Julia and began the subject again. 'He's in New York, you know.'

'Working?' Julia helped her on.

'Oh, yes, he's doing some concerts. Solos, and some guest conducting with the New York Phil. He – he doesn't know I'm here, of course.'

Julia suppressed a smile. Sylvia was taking a long way round to the point, but she had guessed now that this visit was not primarily to comfort Julia in her loss, but to air Sylvia's own troubles. How typical that was, she thought; but you had to work with the grain of people. There was no use in trying to change them – as Aunt Etty had said. The guilt between them was probably about evenly apportioned by now, and they were sisters. Should they not stand by each other?

She helped Sylvia on again. 'How is he in himself? How is he with you?'

'Oh, Julia, that's just the trouble.' It came out now, in a rush. 'I don't know how he is. He seems moody and unhappy, but I can never get near enough to him to find out what the trouble is. He won't let me get near him. Was he like that with you?'

In some ways it was an unforgiveable thing to ask, of course, but that was Sylvia all over. Her clumsiness was pathetic rather than offensive. Julia said patiently, 'Well, of course, it was all rather different in those days.'

'I suppose it was.' Sylvia did not even know she had been clumsy. 'He was probably at home a lot more, for one thing. Sometimes, you know, I don't see him for a week, even when he's not abroad. The worst thing is, he never gives me any warning. Sometimes he goes up to town, saying he'll be a couple of hours, and then he just doesn't come back. So I wait up for him, and keep dinner waiting, and then he'll phone at some unearthly hour and say he's staying in town, and not to expect him back.'

'Does he stay in a hotel?'

'Oh, no, we still have the flat.' Sylvia's pride in that was just evident. 'He stays there. I know that, because I've phoned him there sometimes – not often though. He'd be furious if he thought I was checking up on him.'

Julia realised she had read more into the hotel question than Julia had meant. She smiled inwardly and asked, 'And are you?'

'Am I what?'

'Checking up on him?'

'Oh – no, not really. Well, in a way, I suppose I am, a bit, but it isn't that that I'm worried about. Actually, though you may think this is silly, I'd be happier if he *was* being unfaithful to me. At least I'd know where I stand. If I knew he was, I mean – because of course he may actually *be* being, only I don't know about it.'

'Do you think he is?'

'I don't know. I've nothing to go on, I mean, I haven't any evidence or anything to make me think so. But of course he's a very attractive man, talented and rich and famous, and it would be natural enough, I suppose, if he did have someone. But it's all the uncertainty, that's what I hate. If he had a woman and I knew about it, I'd know where I was with him. I could put up with it, or do something about it.'

She paused and looked at Julia, hoping for some comment, but Julia was not going to be drawn, and merely looked encouraging. She already knew much more than Sylvia could tell her. She was beginning to get a picture, a sad picture, of what her sister's life was like with her husband.

'I never know where I am with him,' Sylvia went on. 'I can't tell if he's serious or joking, making fun of me, and if I ask him, he just slides away from it and says something vague. He can be absolutely maddening like that – it's like trying to argue with an eel. He *won't* argue, that's what I hate most! He's so much better with words than me that he can always get out of everything, and just baffle me with his . . .' She waved a hand helplessly.

'Persiflage,' Julia supplied neutrally.

'And then, he never lets me in on any of his plans – I never know what's coming up. It isn't so bad when I expect him home and he doesn't come, but when it's the other way round – sometimes I see him off, say, for a week, and then in the middle of it he'll turn up, without warning, and expect me to be ready for him. Then if I'm out when he gets back, or I haven't got a meal ready for him or something, he creates hell, and if I complain he hasn't given me any notice, he says I don't want him at home, and he'll go somewhere else if that's my attitude, and that sort of thing.'

Poor Sylvia, Julia thought, genuinely sad for her. Sylvia was so earnest, so serious that she could never see that Peter was playing a kind of elaborate parlour game with her. If she could have laughed at herself, Peter would have been won over on to her side, but she took his teasing seriously, and that was playing into his hands. It was an enormous practical joke he was playing on her, and he would never take her unhappiness seriously while she did it for him.

It was the old conflict, the same that had been between him and Joyce. Sylvia wanted an orderly life, with regular meals and organised hours, while Peter wanted to live according to his own whim. Joyce had fared better because Peter then was younger with his wings still untried, but even so the first full stretch of them had broken the marriage apart. Now that he was older, richer, and famous to boot, there was nothing that could control Peter. He lived by impulse, directed by a perverse sort of humour, and he had discovered that the best way to stop Sylvia annoying him was to keep her in a state of continuous confusion.

Of course, it was great cruelty to Sylvia, and from a man who, having married her for insufficient reasons, had the more duty to behave properly by her. But Peter, of course, would not see it that way. He had not seen any call of duty in Julia's relationship with George; his mind just didn't work that way. But it was no use expecting innocent, conventional Sylvia to understand.

The worst thing of all, the thing that really made Julia sad, was the realisation that Sylvia loved him in spite of it all. It was something that perhaps she should have expected, knowing Peter's power, but she was too little used to thinking of him in relationship to other people, and Sylvia, of course, in the very beginning, had despised Peter and thought Julia mad to waste so much time on him. When had the change occurred? Or had that early contempt merely been a cover-up, perhaps subconscious, for another emotion? Well, whatever had taken place, Sylvia loved him now, and Julia's heart was heavy knowing it.

The scales stopped, there was a pause while music was found and set up, and then Catherine began playing her set piece. It was a Chopin berceuse. Julia, having heard it from the first slow, tentative try-out, was not aware how it must sound to someone hearing it for the first time, and was not expecting Sylvia's comment.

'Is that still Cathy playing?' she asked.

'Yes. Who did you think it was?'

'I thought maybe it was a record. She's very good, isn't she? I mean, *really* good!'

'Oh, yes,' Julia said, bringing her thoughts back with an effort. 'She has real talent. We hope she may make music her career one day.' Sylvia's stare told her that she had slipped up, and at once she recalled the 'we' that had slipped past her wariness. Tears stung in an instant reaction. She had forgotten for quite ten minutes, and the agony of returning thoughts was the worse for the respite.

Sylvia reached across and took her hand and squeezed it. 'Oh Julia, I'm so sorry! Here am I going on about my problems, and quite forgetting that you – oh my dear.'

Now Sylvia was crying, and that was a major disaster, considering the three layers of mascara, not to mention eyeliner. Julia controlled herself hastily and dropped to her knees in front of her sister. 'Here, Sylvia, don't cry, for heaven's sake. Here, take this,' and she thrust a handkerchief at her. 'Listen, don't cry. I don't want Cathy to come in and find you like this. And think of your mascara. You'll look like a zebra. Take a deep breath – now blow!' She held the handkerchief over her nose and pinched it, and by cajoling and joking managed to stop the tears and get instead a watery sort of laugh.

Cathy had heard something and stopped playing, and the next moment she would be coming in. Julia called out over Sylvia's shoulder, 'Why have you stopped?'

'I've finished. What are you doing?'

'Never mind. Aunty Sylvia wants to hear you play *Für Elise*.'

'All right.'

The music started again, and Sylvia dabbed her face cautiously and stopped hiccoughing.

'Oh Julia,' she said. 'You're so brave. I don't know how you do it.'

'Oh, I know,' Julia said drily. 'When the next war starts, they'll call me up first thing. Listen, I've got two medals,' and she revived an old joke, pointing first to one shoulder and then the other. 'I got this one for bravery, and I'm scared to tell you what I got this one for.'

Sylvia was laughing now. 'Oh don't!'

'You're like spring weather,' Julia said. 'Tears one minute and laughter the next. Here, you'd better have a look in the mirror – that'll sober you up. I don't know why you wear all that stuff on your face. You're a really pretty girl, you know.'

'Girl!' Sylvia exclaimed. She took the mirror and inspected and dabbed again, and said, 'I don't know why I do either. I just feel naked without it.'

'Better?'

'Yes. You're marvellous.' She had forgotten what Julia could be like, had forgotten the stalwart independence and courage she had often displayed when they were children, standing her ground, not swayed by fashion or popularity or teasing by other girls. Julia would always be what she would be, no matter if others laughed at her, or disapproved. 'I don't know how you can stay so cheerful,' Sylvia said.

'Oh hush,' Julia said, squeezing Sylvia's hand and pushing it back at her.

'I do love you, you know.'

'She's stopped playing – here she comes. Now for heaven's sake pretend you were listening,' Julia muttered.

'I was listening,' Sylvia said, turning to see Cathy come back in. 'That was lovely, darling, you play really well.'

Cathy was not to be put off by compliments. She looked from her mother to her aunt, and then said to the latter, 'Have you been crying?'

Julia saved her from answering. 'No, she's been laughing, actually. Haven't you ever heard of someone laughing till they cry?'

Cathy looked at her suspiciously, until she saw the suppressed smile, and then she smiled and ran to her mother and flung her arms round her neck. 'You're being silly,' she exclaimed. In her language that was a compliment.

Julia kissed her forehead and pushed a strand of hair back from her face. Cathy looked so much like Peter in that moment that it made her catch her breath. 'Where's your hair ribbon?' she asked. It was all she could think of to say.

'I took it off. What shall I play now? Did you hear the berceuse?'

'Yes, I did. I think you've got it now. Play me that one I like – the one I call the walking music.'

'Oh, I know, you mean the *Ballade Opus 38.*'

'That's the one. Play me that.'

'I can't do the middle bit yet.'

'I know, but play me the beginning.'

'All right.' She was away again in a whirl of energy, and in a few moments the piano started again.

'She's a lovely child,' Sylvia said, and this time she meant it.

Julia was lying awake in the dark. It was past two o'clock, but she couldn't sleep. The bed was too big for her, even though she filled half of it with spare pillows to try to give the effect of occupation. She dreaded going to bed, for she could hardly ever sleep, only lay awake thinking and thinking about George; and if she did fall asleep, she had terrible dreams about him, bright vivid dreams in which his loved face contorted and threatened her, grew enormous and overwhelmed her until it filled her and choked her like flannel in her lungs.

She wished she had suggested to Sylvia that they shared the bed, but she hadn't been sure how Sylvia would take to that suggestion. It would have been a comfort to hear someone else's breathing in the dark. It was so silent here, except when there was a high wind. It would be better in London, where there is never silence. Silence let in things from the dark that she wanted kept out. Many, many nights she had lain in this bed, stretched out on her back like this, but with the big hulk of George next to her, breathing softly, busy in sleep. She would reach out hand and foot and lean them lightly against him, and thus kept anchored to sanity and the world through his warm life, she had listened to the silence outside and let it come in, slowly, gently, to carry her away. But as fear of a dog makes a dog savage, so now her terror made the silence a cruel thing. The first night she had screamed aloud, and Cathy had come running in, sobbing, terrified. So now she fought it off, and lay tensely awake, waiting for it to get light. She kept her curtains drawn back so that she would be able to see the first streak of approaching day as soon as it was apparent.

When the phone rang she was almost glad. She put the light on and looked at the clock, and thought it must be a wrong number. At least, though, it could not be bad news. With Cathy tucked up safely in the next room there was nothing to fear from phone calls in the middle of the night, or telegrams by day. There was no one else she cared for.

She went downstairs to the hall and picked up the receiver, and heard the hollow, tinny sound of a long distance call. Definitely a wrong number, then.

'Hello?'

'Hello, are you Bindon Abbey 78? I have a call for you from New York, hold the line please.'

There was a long pause, filled only with the hollow clanging and hissing and crackling, and then at last a male voice emerged from the din saying,

'Hello! Hello! Who's there?'

'This is Mrs Crichton. Who's that?'

'Julia. For God's sake, you've been a hell of a time. What a terrible line this is! Hello? Are you still there?'

Though no one else ever said her name quite like that, it took her a moment to believe she was hearing aright. Perhaps she was dreaming this? – but her bare feet on the hall lino were convincingly cold.

'Yes, I'm still here. I can't think why. What on earth do you mean by calling me at this unearthly hour?'

'What are you talking about, you dummy? It isn't an unearthly hour – it's only half past nine.'

'Where you are, perhaps. All right, have it your own way. Why are you calling me at this perfectly reasonable hour?'

'Why shouldn't I call you? You don't sound very welcoming, considering it took me nearly an hour to get through. Where in hell is Bindon Abbey?'

'How did you get my number?'

'Hah! My *wife* gave it to me. I suppose she told you I didn't know she was there?'

'Sort of.'

'I thought so. Prompted, no doubt, by the knowledge that I would call her at home, she arranged with the GPO to transfer incoming calls to your number.'

Julia laughed. That, again, was just like Sylvia.

'How drunk are you, Peter?' she asked.

'Very, very drunk indeed,' he said solemnly. There was a short burst of interference, and he said again, 'Are you there?'

'Yes, I'm here.'

'I wish you weren't. I wish you were here. You should see

377

this, my Julia. I'm at a party given in my honour by what we innocent bystanders call a business tycoon. Typhoon would be a better description. I have been devoured by the hungriest lioniser I have ever come across. You'll be glad to know I have been completely flattened. She's pure Aldous Huxley – the Lilian Aldwinkle of the space age.'

'Well, for the sake of international amity, don't be rude to her,' Julia laughed.

'I already have been. But it's no fun, Julia – she likes it. I'm in the mood to do something outrageous. I might precipitate the third world war.'

'So why are you phoning me? Or did you want to speak to Sylvia?'

'God, no. Not Sylvia. I wanted to know if she's been behaving herself?' He sounded suddenly sober. She knew these moods of his, when his drunkenness was self-induced, and nothing to do with his intake of alcohol.

'She's been pouring her heart out to me,' Julia said.

'Oh God. I'm sorry, Julia. You shouldn't have to put up with that sort of thing.'

'It's all right, really She didn't say anything you might not be the better for hearing.'

'That isn't the point. You shouldn't have to put up with it.'

'It's the least of my worries at the moment.'

'Julia, I can't say all I mean over the telephone, especially with this line, but I'm truly, truly sorry – it shouldn't have happened to you. He was a fine man, and I know you loved him.'

Even the bad line did not disguise Peter's real sympathy, and Julia's eyes burned again with tears that seemed to be always so near the surface these days. There was a brief silence, and then he said, 'Does she look like me?'

For one astonished moment she thought he was talking about Sylvia, before she understood. She used the old evasion. 'She looks like herself. Who's paying for this call?'

'Mine host, Saint Brigid be praised! Not that I couldn't afford it, of course, but it might have been Sylvia who answered.'

'You can be the cruellest person, Peter.'

'Listen! I want to see you when I get back. I have to see

378

you. Say yes, that's all, because I have to go. Someone else wants the phone.'

'I don't know. I don't want—' she said in anguish, and he cut across her.

'I have to go. Look, I won't ask you now, but I'll be back on the fifteenth. Around midnight I expect. Give me a ring at the flat on the sixteenth.'

'I don't know,' she said again.

But he shouted at her, 'Promise!'

'All right,' she said miserably. She ached for the want of touching him, but though her body knew its master's voice, her mind was still wounded by any thought of infidelity.

'Good girl,' he said, and she could not mistake the joy in his voice now. 'I'll wait in all day. Don't let me down. The sixteenth.'

He was gone. The tangled web was there to hand, ready for her to begin weaving again.

Twenty

April, 1979

'**M**ummy! Are you home?'

'In here, dear,' Julia called back from the living room of their flat. They usually called it the studio, for it had been built as a studio, and had a north-facing floor to ceiling window which made it the very devil to heat in winter. The rest of the flat consisted of a bedroom which they shared, and a kitchen. The bathroom was on the floor below, and they shared that with one other tenant, a very quiet, decent old man who had lived in the house all his life.

Nine-year-old Catherine came running down the passage and into the room, and then stopped at the sight of a visitor, a tall, thin man with elegantly-waved grey hair, dressed in a very fashionable suit of mulberry-coloured velvet.

'Uncle Martin!' she exclaimed with pleasure, and ran forward to hug him.

He laughed and returned the embrace, and said to Julia, 'I see I haven't outworn my welcome, then.'

'You wouldn't do that if you came here twice as often.'

Martin Newman had remained a great friend to her, and had helped her out of many difficult spots. It was his friendship that had got her over the difficult adjustment period after George's death when she had come back to London. 'Uncle Martin's got a surprise for you, Cathy.'

'Oh, what is it? Is it something to wear?'

Julia laughed at that. 'You see her opinion of you, Martin. To her you're a fop and a dandy.'

'No, it isn't something to wear, missy,' he said, tugging a plait. 'It's much nicer than that.'

'Oh what? What? Please tell me!'

'It's nicer than chocolate cake, too,' Martin said, rolling his

380

eyes and licking his lips.

'Don't tease her,' Julia said.

'All right. It's a concert. Tonight, Albert Hall, Esterhazy playing the Brahms Violin concerto. How's that?'

'Oh, Uncle Martin! How absolutely *divine!*'

Martin burst out laughing. 'Where on earth does she get these words from? Divine indeed!'

'School, I suppose, I don't think I ever say that,' Julia said. 'Cathy, you'd better run and have your bath now, darling, before tea, because there might not be time afterwards.'

'All right,' she said, giving Martin a kiss on the cheek and jumping up.

'Oh, and what homework have you got?'

'I did it on the bus coming home,' she said cheerfully. 'See you in a while,' and she ran out.

'She's a beautiful child,' Martin said. 'It's no wonder you keep on painting her.' And he looked around the studio at the various portraits Julia had done of her, going back five years.

'I never get tired of looking at her,' Julia said. 'She's—'

'She looks like Peter,' Martin said bluntly.

Julia looked at him pleadingly. 'Martin!'

'Yes, I know. I wouldn't give it away.' Martin stood up abruptly and walked over to the window, and looked down at the traffic that raced past along Talgarth Road, heading for the M4 and freedom – a bottle-neck in reverse. He spoke again without turning round. 'I can't pretend to understand it, but I'll respect your decision. But you still love him, don't you?'

She didn't answer, and he turned his head and saw her watching him, gripping the arms of her chair.

'What *is* it about him, Julia?'

'I don't know. God, I wish I did, then perhaps I could dig it out and end it. Have you come to plead for him?'

'No. No, I've been Peter's friend for a long, long time, but I wouldn't plead for him in this case.' He turned his head away again and said, 'For the past twenty-five years I've watched him hurting the only woman I've ever loved. I wouldn't plead for him.'

'Martin, no!'

He left the window and walked back to stand in front of her, and smiled comfortingly as she stared up at him anxiously.

'Oh yes,' he said. 'You know it's true, Julia. I always loved you.'

'I wish you hadn't told me,' she said miserably. 'Really, I didn't know. I mean, we've always been friends . . .'

'Don't let it upset you,' he said kindly. 'It doesn't upset me, not any more. When you left Peter I thought I had a chance. I thought once you'd got your divorce and got over the shook, I could step in – but I was too slow. Someone else beat me to it.' He was making fun of himself now to lighten her anxiety.

'I was always very fond of you, Martin – I still am,' she began.

He held his hand up and flapped it gently. 'Hush, infant. You don't need to make any explanations. I knew even then that it was Peter – first, last, and always, as far as you were concerned. I'm quite happy, believe me. I like my bachelor life now, and I'm happy to be your friend and your daughter's favourite uncle.'

She smiled uncertainly at him, and he walked away again and picked up a canvas and studied it so that she could recover herself.

Eventually she asked, 'Why did you tell me, Martin? After all this time?'

'So that you'd know whose side I'm on, in the event of any dispute. When you asked me if I was pleading for him, it hurt me to think you might suspect I was a spy from the opposite camp. I would like to see you reunited with Peter, certainly I would, but not for his sake – only because I think you'd be happier with him. But if you don't think it would be right for the child, I respect your decision.' He grinned suddenly. 'That doesn't mean I agree with it. I think you're a bloody fool. But then I'm not Cathy's mother.'

'You're the next best thing,' she said.

'A dubious sort of compliment.'

'I mean it in the nicest way,' she said, standing up. She came across to where he stood, holding the painting in one hand, and took his arm in her two hands. 'There have been two people in my life who have loved me a lot more than I deserve,' she said.

He kissed her forehead. 'That's your opinion,' he said. 'Tell me about this one – who is it?'

'Oh, that was a rather unfortunate mistake,' she said laughing. 'I was commissioned to do the portrait of the new principal of a college, and while I was working on it, they changed their minds and elected somebody else. They wrote and told me, but the letter got stuck in a bunch I couldn't be bothered to deal with, and it wasn't until after I'd finished the picture I got round to opening them.'

'So you were left holding the baby?'

'Yes, unfortunately. Oh, it isn't so bad – I can use the canvas again, and I still got the commission for the replacement picture – it's only my time that was wasted. But I was sorry – I thought it was rather good.'

'I can't tell if it's a likeness, of course,' Martin said, looking at it. 'All I can see is your style – most of your pictures look the same to me.'

'A dubious compliment. I love your honesty.'

'I can't help it. Take it as a mark of my respect for you as a person. I couldn't flatter you if I tried.'

'Well, anyway, most faces are the same, aren't they? I mean, two eyes, a nose, a mouth . . .' She drew it in the air.

'You sound like Humpty Dumpty,' Martin said. 'How's the job working out?'

Julia was back at the advertising agency. 'Oh, excellently. I feel rather a fraud, taking money for so little work. It's like a rest camp there. I potter in, do a bit of drawing, drink some tea, and then potter home again in time for lunch and a whole afternoon doing what I like. Really, I'm indecently well-off.'

'Don't complain. You worked hard enough for it in the past.'

'I'm not complaining. It means I can put George's money aside for Cathy. In about five or six years time she's going to want to buy a first-class instrument, and the money's going to be there for her.'

'You think she's got real talent?'

'I know she has.'

'A mother's bias?'

'You know better than that.'

'I know it's hard to be objective where you love.'

'True. Well, I can't ask your opinion. It seems odd that you've never heard her play.'

'I just never seem to have been around at the right time. Never mind, you can fix it up for me – a special concert in honour of my birthday next week.'

'Your birthday? I didn't know.'

'Yes, I'll be fifty-five, God help me. Ten more years and I can draw m' pension.'

Julia snorted irreverently. 'That'll be the day, when a musician can retire. Anyway, I'd better get some tea ready. Do you want a bath or anything? Because if you do, you'd better haul that child out. She's just getting to the age where a bathroom holds an awful fascination.' Martin laughed. 'Kids are funny, you know. When they're little, you can't get them out of the bath. Then comes five years or so when you can't get them *in*. And after that you have to grab a bath when you can.'

'Only girls, not boys.'

'I've never brought up a boy,' she said.

There was an awkward pause. 'I'll manage with just a shave,' he said. 'I've got my tackle in the car, with my tails.'

It was very odd to be walking in at the artists' entrance again at the side of a man in tails carrying a violin case – a mixture of the familiar and the unfamiliar. Catherine was unnaturally quiet, but glancing down at her Julia saw it was only because she was too thrilled to speak. She had been to concerts before, but never in the company of one of the musicians, and never going in at the 'stage door'. Julia smiled in sympathy – she had felt very much the same the first time she had done it, though she had been a lot older, and a lot less innocent.

'I must go and warm up,' Martin said when they reached the auditorium door. 'Here's the tickets. Come down to the bar in the interval – you know where it is, don't you? I want to hear Cathy's criticism of the soloist – unless she's too starry-eyed to have a criticism.'

384

'Of course I won't be,' Cathy said indignantly, and then she saw she was being teased, and she gave her closed-mouth smile that was pure Peter.

They took their seats – very good seats, too, front stalls, halfway back on the violin side – and Julia was glad to be occupied with answering Cathy's endless questions, for it was all so painfully familiar to her. The effect never wore off, however often it was repeated.

The orchestra filed on, and Catherine was silent for a few minutes while she looked for Martin. As soon as she spotted him she tugged Julia's arm and hissed loudly, 'There he is, there he is! Look, Mummy!'

One or two people looked round with indulgent smiles, and Julia loosened the fingers from her arm and said gently, 'Yes, darling, I can see him. Yes, I know he's waving.'

'He's saying something, Mummy. What's he trying to say?'

'I don't know.' Martin was making some kind of dumb show, but she couldn't make it out. Probably something to amuse Cathy. Julia shrugged to show she didn't understand, and he redoubled his efforts; but the leader came on, and his chance was gone.

The overture was *Coriolan*, to which Catherine listened with calm interest: it was a piece she knew very well. When it finished, she turned to her mother with shining eyes of anticipation for the concerto that was to come, smiling so hard her jaws must have ached. Julia smiled and nodded sympathetically. There was some kind of delay backstage, and after the spare players had filed off and the replacements sat down, an attendant came out and walked to the front microphone to make an announcement.

'Ladies and gentlemen, we very much regret to announce that Mr Stefan Esterhazy has been taken ill and will not be able to play tonight. We are very pleased to say, however, that Mr Peter Kane has kindly agreed to fill the breach, and we are very grateful to him for agreeing to honour us at such very short notice.'

I'm imagining this, Julia thought. There was applause, but to her everything seemed to have gone very quiet, as if the auditorium was holding its breath, and she felt as if every eye was slowly turning towards her. That must be what Martin had been trying to say, then. But he must have known beforehand, surely? Unless Esterhazy had gone sick literally at the last moment and Peter was going to play without a rehearsal, he must have rehearsed with them this morning. But that would mean that Martin had played a deliberate trick – a plot to get Cathy and Peter together – and he had sworn he was on her side, not Peter's. Her pulse was returning to normal, the applause for the announcement had stopped along with the roaring in her ears, the normal sounds of shuffling and coughing were fading in. No, Martin would not do such a thing – would he?

She saw Cathy looking at her with a puzzled expression. My eyes must be standing out of my head, she thought, and she smiled at her daughter reassuringly.

'He's very famous,' Cathy whispered. 'I don't think I've heard him before, though, have I? Will he be as good as Esterhazy?' Cathy asked.

'Better,' Julia said.

The door to the platform opened, and Peter walked out, brisk, jaunty, his fiddle under his arm and his cloth over it, like a waiter, and Julia's nails dug into her palms. She hadn't seen him for four years, since she had wrenched herself away again, for Cathy's sake, and for Sylvia's. The applause was good for him – he had never failed in popularity, and there was extra for him now on account of his sporting acceptance of a last-minute date, saving the evening for the audience.

The conductor took his place, the applause stopped and the audience settled down, and while the stillness expanded to fill the hall, Peter tuned his fiddle, nodded to the conductor, and stood poised. Then the haunting opening notes of the Brahms concerto eased on to the air, building to the first tutti climax of shrilling violins, while Julia could only stare at him, still full of the shock and astonishment of his sudden appearance, and a twisting knife of pleasure, and the anticipation of his playing.

His hand came up, he settled his weight, and he was into it, sweetly, like an Olympic diver cutting into the water without a splash. Now she was away, carried down the years to the time when they had been together and she had sat watching him play almost every day. Around her, everything familiar – the rustle of silk dresses, the muted coughs, the smell of her own perfume, the warmth and muted lights of the hall, and the slightly blurred black and white mass of the orchestra; and most familiar of all, and most blurred of all from being stared at so intently, Peter – playing to her, for the sake of her single ear: her man, the father of her children.

And now, beside her, a new element: Catherine, her child, his child, knowing nothing of him; taut as a drum skin stretched by his music, already hero-worshipping him, but as a stranger. She shook her head to clear it.

In the pause between movements, Peter turned and borrowed the leader's rosin, and exchanged a few words with him, and they smiled. They were old acquaintances, of course. Julia watched every gesture and expression greedily, hungry for knowledge of him. He rosined his bow, and looked around the auditorium with his old, insolent look, and she stiffened, afraid of catching his eye – as if he could have seen her in that throng.

Then the music started again. It poured from him faultlessly, as easily as song pours from a bird's throat. With music Julia had always prided herself on being an impartial judge of performance; now she was held still and scarcely breathing, unaware of anything but the silvery threads of notes that were woven round her like a net to capture her and draw her to him. All consciousness was focussed on the pinpoint that was Peter, and from him the notes rose high and perfect, beautiful almost past comprehension, so that it hurt to listen. Tears seeped from her eyes, but she was not aware of them, nor of her hands clasped or her body bent forward under this love; only aware dimly of praying, *let it never end*.

After the last notes, there was a second of silence before the applause broke crashing into it like a sea wave. Julia was shaken back into herself and joined in the applause, smiling wildly. Catherine, too, was grinning, as were other members of the audience – it was a common emotion. Cathy's eyes were shining, and she clapped until her palms burned. Peter went off, returned for his ovation, went off again. The clapping died away, apart from one diehard in the cheap seats who solo'd a moment in the hope of another bow; and then stopped, and the excitement subsided into a happy bubble of murmured conversation.

Julia didn't want to hear people talking about the performance – it was a thing she had always hated – particularly if the performance had been good – finding that it dispelled the magic too brutally. As soon as the applause stopped, she jumped up and, pushing Cathy before her, headed for the exit. They still got stuck behind some slow-moving people, and by the time they passed through the door, Martin was already standing there in the curved corridor waiting for them.

He lifted his hands at her reproachful look, and said, 'I didn't know, Julia. I swear I didn't know. Esterhazy collapsed about an hour before the concert – appendicitis apparently, poor devil. A few of us thought he didn't look well this morning, but apparently though he was in pain he was determined to do the concert and not let us down. So then they had to phone round frantically to see if there was anyone available with the Brahms in their repertoire. It had to be a name, someone in London, and someone who was willing to do it without rehearsal. Peter just happened to be at home and free when they phoned and of course the Brahms has always been his piece. I didn't know anything until I got backstage. I can tell you, it had us all on our toes, not knowing each other's speeds and markings.'

'That must be why it was such an electric performance,' Julia said. 'The impromptu nature of it all.'

He thought she was being sarcastic. 'I didn't know. I swear to you.'

'Did you tell him I was here?'

'I didn't need to. He was waiting when I came off, and he just looked at me and said, "Is she with you?" I pretended I didn't know what he was talking about and dodged off, but he knew all the same. God knows how.'

'He saw me in the audience I suppose,' Julia said. Once they had been able to do that, to pick each other out in any crowd, but that was long ago. Cathy was looking from one to the other of them, feeling an atmosphere but not being able

388

to make any sense out of the conversation. Julia touched her dark head and made herself smile reassuringly. Catherine was the important one. She must be protected.

'What will you do?' Martin asked.

'We'd better go, I think. It can't be helped. I believe you, Martin, about not knowing.'

He looked grateful, and said, 'Must you go?'

'I think it would be better.'

'Mummy, we're not going home?' Catherine was beginning to catch on.

'I'm sorry darling, but yes.'

'Oh Mummy, why?' she wailed. 'Can't we stay for the second half?'

'No, I'm afraid not. I'm sorry, but it's just one of those things.' She spoke firmly, and the child closed her mouth again, knowing when it was useless to argue.

'Look,' Martin said, 'you'd better hang around for just a little while. He's bound to be going straight off now, and we don't want you bumping into each other at the exit.'

'True.'

'Come down to the bar and have one with me, and then when the coast is clear I'll see you out.'

'All right.'

They made their way down the stairs to the artists' level and trotted along the seemingly endless curved corridors. They turned a bend and arrived outside a bar, and there, looking as if he had simply been waiting for them, was Peter.

They stopped still in front of him, three of them, but he only looked at her, holding her eyes, his mouth lifted at one corner with the half-mocking smile. The fans, or perhaps music students, who had been gathered round him stared at her resentfully for the obvious loss of his attention. In the background John Goldsmith was talking to what could have been reporters or at least arts critics; his blurred white face turned towards her, frowning, but she could not spare more than the corner of her attention for him.

'You must have willed this very hard,' she said eventually.

'You couldn't escape me for ever,' he said.

'I could, without bad luck.'

389

'Luck has nothing to do with it,' he said. 'Don't you know I always had the power to bring you back—'

'"With a twitch upon the thread",' she finished for him. She sounded dazed. Martin was standing to one side, but between them, as if ready to keep them apart if it came to a fight.

Catherine was staring hard and wide-eyed at The Man, the soloist, the star, her hero, whom her mother inexplicably but wonderfully seemed to know. Then his eyes were turned on her, and she looked down and blushed.

'Cathy,' he said. She looked up again, surprised out of shyness by the fact that he knew her name. He smiled at her, a warm, affectionate smile, and she smiled back instinctively. Even Julia was shocked at how alike they were when they smiled.

Peter turned to Julia again. 'You were wrong,' he said. 'She does look like her father.'

Twenty-One

Peter had a little sporty two-seater car, and Julia went with him while Catherine, half-disappointed, half-relieved – for it takes practice to breath the same air as a god – got into Martin's car. Julia could see her, just ahead of them, chattering eagerly to Martin and now and then turning round to wave, and stare doubtfully at the illustrious stranger who turned out to be an old friend of her mother's. Martin, too, kept looking back – Julia could see the tilt of his head as he looked in his rear-view mirror at them – and she could make a guess at what he was thinking. She wondered how he was fielding the child's questions.

'I'm going to lose them for a bit,' Peter said suddenly. 'It won't hurt them to wait outside for ten minutes.'

'Cathy has her own key,' Julia said absently, and Peter glanced sideways at her and grinned.

'Oh, you abandoned woman!'

She looked confused. 'I didn't mean—'

'I know what you meant.'

He slowed and allowed a couple of cars to overtake him and settle in between him and Martin's Rover. Then traffic lights conveniently allowed Martin through and stopped him. The former disappeared into the distance and when the lights changed Peter stuck his arm out and made a turn into the park. Julia, who had only just stopped trembling, started again, vibrating with some kind of excitement – or apprehension, maybe? Peter drove them a little further into the park and then turned into a lay-by and stopped the engine.

'This is where you turn to me and say, "You look lovely by moonlight",' she said flippantly, to cover up her emotion.

'Moonlight can be awfully deceptive,' he countered, ducking

his head to look up out of the front windscreen. 'Fortunately we have sodium light instead, which of course never lies.' He edged round in his seat to face her. 'I just want to have a proper look at you.'

One of the things she didn't want was to have a proper look at him, but she could hardly avoid it now, and it was just as disturbing as she had feared. Peter at fifty-four was very different from Peter at twenty-eight, but she had seen long ago what he would become, and it was no surprise to her that he had got there. His hair, having receded to the top of his head, had kindly stopped there, giving him the benefit of a very high forehead which was pleasing rather than otherwise. He wore his hair brushed straight back to emphasise it – a leonine effect. His hair had begun to go grey all over, and the silver hairs mixed with the dark rather attractively, but his sideburns were still foxy, and sparked with ginger, and for some reason she found that infinitely touching.

But the great blue eyes under their heavy lids were still the same, though the lids were softly wrinkled now; the odd-shaped nose, and the almost lipless, always smiling mouth were uniquely him and unchanged. The same man looked out from within Peter's older flesh as had first looked over the top of his newspaper at a small, solemn schoolgirl with plaits.

'You're getting fat,' Julia said, determined not to yield.

'I'm not fat, just well-nourished.'

'And bald. And your hair's too long at the back. There's nothing worse than a balding man who won't submit to it gracefully.'

'You should see Rowland,' Peter said, unmoved. 'He's gone thin on top and wears the bald patch carefully thatched. He looks a sketch, but there's no telling him. But you – ah, you haven't changed at all.'

'Tosh,' she said. 'Of course I have.'

But he merely nodded. 'I always said I would never see you go grey. Your hair is silver here –' he touched the top of her head very gently – 'but it always was in the summer. It just looks like sun-bleaching. You haven't changed, my love.'

My love, he thought. She had grown older, grown less

392

beautiful in the expected ways of a woman grown older, but in fact she was remarkably like herself, say, twenty years ago. Still the same beautiful, living face, more thoroughly alive, he thought, than anyone else around her, and the thinness of her face served only to emphasise that the features were the same. All his senses ached for her, for what was rightfully his.

'Well,' he said.

'Well what?'

'I want to know if you still love me as much as before – despite my being fat and bald.'

'No.' His eyebrows shot up. She sighed. 'More, much more. If you were completely circular and as smooth as a hard-boiled egg, I would still love you more and always more and more.'

'You mad fool,' he grinned faintly. 'You don't mind admitting it, then?'

She did, but she said, 'It can't hurt me now. How's Sylvia?'

It was not the non-sequitur that it appeared, and he knew it.

'Much the same,' he said abruptly. 'I don't want to talk about Sylvia.'

'Poor Sylvia.'

'I never could understand why you married George.'

It was slightly petulant, but she took it at its face value, and said musingly, 'You know, shameful though it is to admit, he reminded me of you. I left you in a fit of determination, but ever afterwards I kept looking for you in other people.'

'Yes,' he said slowly. 'I think that's why I married Sylvia.'

'Uh-huh.' She denied that firmly. 'You married her to spite me. You always did like to spite people.'

'You don't sound very much as if you love me,' he said, aggrieved.

'Oh, I do,' she said sadly. 'Much too much.'

He would never know, she thought, of the sadness that had fallen on her when she walked out of the house, never to leave her. Even when she was married to George, the loneliness had still been there, the difficulty of finding a reason for going on; but her need to be loved then had been stronger than her instinct to love. That – the loneliness she had concealed from George – and her betrayal of him, had been the guilt she had

393

carried ever since, and if Peter had suffered, as she believed he had since Cathy was born, it was only a just expiation.

Something in her had died when George died, some centre of resistance, and since then she had not wanted to struggle – there had only been Cathy, and everything she had done since then had been for her, as it should be. But now she was with Peter again it was like the easing of some long-ignored discomfort. Just to be near him, to see him and talk with him was so good, so easy. Loving him seemed to come from outside of life, as though it were a continuing stream that simply ran through this incarnation from somewhere long before to somewhere long after, something incapable of explanation, something that just *was*. She had never understood it, but without him she had been less than a person, she had been only what existed, purposelessly, because it did not die.

'Julia, it's been hard for me, too,' he said at last, painfully. He had never wanted to admit any kind of need for her, and long uncertainty of her reaction to any possible plea made it harder for him. But, oh, he wanted her. She was his, he had made her, taken her as a child and formed her in his image, as if she were the seed of his body, and his existence was the justification of hers. He could not explain it to her. His wanting to be in her, a part of her, was like a thirst he could not quench, because no human act could bring them close enough.

He put his hands out, and she took them and put them to her face, but the physical contact was such a small part of it, was nothing, and his eyes strained into hers, searching for the assurance that she understood. Dark eyes, warm and expressive: but what he saw there was only what he wanted to see, there could be no assurance. He closed his eyes in anguish, and pulled her head to him and held it against his chest.

'I've done some bad things in my life, but it was never because I didn't love you. That has never changed. I wish you could understand,' he said.

She nudged harder against him, as a dog will, and said, 'I understand. There's nothing about you I don't know.'

They drew apart, and he started the engine at once and put it in gear, though it was a moment before his sight cleared so that he could drive off. He searched for a subject on which to begin, and finally said, in a polite sort of voice, 'Did you know your mother died?'

'No, I didn't,' Julia said. She searched inside herself for reaction, but there was none. She had not seen her mother in over twenty years, and had been too detached from her for too long to feel anything about her death. 'When was that?'

'About six months ago. Sylvia was very cut up about it – she seemed to have been very fond of her after all.' He sounded faintly surprised.

'They were always closer than the rest of us. Mother approved of Sylvia. She was like her, I suppose that was why.'

'The solicitors asked us for your address. They wanted to contact you about your father's royalties. But of course, we didn't know where you were. Otherwise I would have made Sylvia ask you to the funeral.'

'Made her?'

'She was glad we hadn't got your address. She didn't want you to be there.'

'I suppose not.'

'It was hard for her.' He was a little surprised to find himself defending his wife. Julia noted it but said nothing, keeping her expression neutral. 'She felt guilty, even though it was all my doing rather than hers. And she was – not jealous, exactly but – oh, you were a hard act to follow, I suppose.'

Still neutrally, Julia said, 'It doesn't matter. I didn't care about my mother.' And after a moment she added, 'What surprised me was your attitude to her.'

'To your mother?'

'Yes. Sylvia told me you paid her an annuity.'

He looked faintly embarrassed. 'Oh, that. Well, in a way, I admired her. So completely wrong-headed, but sticking by her judgement through thick and thin. We used to have fearful rows, you know. She never would admit she was wrong to have turned you out, and I really admired the old dame. You are a bit like her in that way – no, don't snort! You have her courage, that same bull-headed courage.' He mused for a moment. 'Do you know what she said, the first time I met her after – the first time with Sylvia, I mean. She said, "You seem to have a taste for my daughters." That was all.'

'I'd have thought she'd have been livid.'

'No. She was cold and haughty at first but I think she got quite fond of me in the end, in a rough, undemonstrative way.'

'It would have to be that.' She remembered her father. She remembered her unkissed childhood, and it was like opening a cellar door and feeling the black cold air come through.

'I was male company for her, and she was not a woman to have female friends.' He smiled suddenly. 'I used to take her to the Albert Hall sometimes.'

'She wasn't interested in music.'

'Not for music, for the boxing.'

'*Boxing?*'

'Yes, she liked it. She watched it on television sometimes. That and the wildlife programmes and the news were the only things she ever watched.'

Julia had nothing to say to that. There had been no televison in her childhood. She could not have guessed what her mother's viewing tastes would be. But then, she had never known much about her mother at all.

'What did she die of?' Julia asked.

'Old age, I suppose. They put bronchitis on the death certificate but the doctor said she was just worn out. There was no lingering. She was only ill for about a week. She was very spry, right to the end, hopping about the house in those dreadful overall dresses she used to wear – you know. She used to make me macaroni cheese. She was so funny about that: I hate macaroni cheese, but when she was staying with us she used to volunteer to cook supper from time to time – to pay her way, I suppose – and she'd make it, and I'd say "No thanks," and she'd say, "But you like macaroni cheese," and I'd say, "I can't stand it – I told you last time." But she never got it through her head. Every time the same. In the end I almost started to believe I must like it after all.' And he chuckled again.

Julia had nothing to say on the subject. It all seemed too strange. Instead she asked, 'How are the boys?'

'Oh, very well. Michael's in Hong Kong at the moment – he's a captain now. He came to see us last time he was on leave, at Christmas.'

'Is he married?'

396

'No. I think he takes after Rowland – a confirmed bachelor. He makes a joke of it – he always says he's going to stay a bachelor like his uncle.'

'And what about James?'

'Oh, Jamie is married – I expect you knew that. He has two children now, both boys.'

'You, a grandfather!'

He made a face. 'I don't feel like one. I don't see much of them. Jamie was always more of a mother's boy. He goes to see Joyce most weekends, or has her over to his place. He never really forgave me for leaving her, and then I compounded it by leaving you, too. He thinks I'm unreliable.'

'Thinks?' She raised an eyebrow at him, and he shrugged.

'I don't think he likes the idea of Sylvia, either. Michael, of course, treats it as a huge joke.' He looked at Julia, a sudden flash of blue. 'You'd like Michael – he's our sort.'

'I don't suppose he remembers me,' Julia said wistfully. She liked to think of them being her children, for the simple fact that she couldn't bear the idea of anyone else having babies by him.

'No, I don't suppose he does,' Peter said vaguely, not having heard the hopeful note of her question. His mind had rattled on ahead of hers. 'I want Cathy.'

'No.' It was jerked out of her by surprise, and she saw his expression tighten. 'She doesn't know about you. As far as she's concerned, George was her father, and that's the way it's going to stay. She's going to have a normal life.'

'Normal! What's normal about it? It isn't normal to have no father.'

'It's normal enough to be an orphan. You know what I mean – don't be deliberately obtuse.'

She turned her head away, anxiously, and stared out of the window. He reached across and fumbled for her hand, and finding it, drew it back with his to the gear lever and drove like that.

'Julia,' he said, 'listen to me. When George died, I thought you would come back to me. We could have been happy together, and brought her up as our child. All right, I'm not going to argue about that – you did what you thought

397

was right, and we both suffered for it. Oh yes, I did suffer – more than you can imagine. But anyway,' and he gave her hand a shake to ensure her attention. 'But anyway, it can be all right now. Now I've found you – I looked for you, you know, but that bastard Martin would never tell me where you were.'

'Martin's a good friend,' Julia said.

'To you he is.'

'To both of us. Don't abuse him.'

'All right. But now I've found you again, it can all be all right, can't it?'

He didn't mean the note of pleading to creep in, but he could feel her resistance hardening as he spoke. She tried to withdraw her hand but he closed his grip and unconsciously drove faster.

'No. Definitely not.'

'But why? It makes no sense.'

'Because you're already married.'

'Sylvia doesn't matter –'

'Oh? I think she does. She's your wife, whatever your reasons for marrying her. And besides, can you imagine what it would do to Cathy to be told the father she loves and reveres wasn't her father at all? That her mother betrayed him, that she was no better than a whore?'

'I could hit you when you say things like that,' he said angrily.

'It's true.'

'It isn't, and you know it. We were married and we should never have been *un*-married. There should never have been anyone in your life but me. That isn't being a . . .' He didn't even like to say the word. 'What you said.'

'Whichever way you look at it, Peter, what I did – what we did – wasn't right.'

'Oh damn your wrong and right! To hell with it! All there is, Julia, is three people who ought to be happy together, being miserable away from each other.'

'Cathy's not miserable.'

'Cathy's my daughter.'

'I disagree,' Julia said very quietly. There was a pause.

'What did you say?'

'Don't threaten me,' she said in the same low voice.

'Are you trying to tell me, after all this time—'

'Oh, don't be a fool,' she said irritably. 'You can see Peter Kane written all over her face, as you've already commented. But that isn't the point. Being a father is not just a matter of fact – being a father is an action, a continuous action. George cared for her, brought her up, educated her. They loved each other, and as far as anything that matters is concerned, he is her father.'

'Except,' he said viciously, 'that he needed someone else to get her for him.'

She turned her head away, and this time withdrew her hand without opposition.

In a moment he said, 'I'm sorry.'

'Forget it.'

They drove in silence for some minutes, and then he said, 'If she finds out, she'll hate you for keeping it a secret from her all these years.'

'I'll take that chance,' she said stonily.

'At least let me see her. Just that.'

She looked round at him, studied his face for a moment, and then said flatly, 'No. I don't trust you. You'd tell her.'

'Of course I wouldn't. But if she should guess, I wouldn't deny it.' She continued to look at him steadily and at last he grinned. 'All right, I would tell her. Too bloody right I would!' The tension eased between them. He glanced down at her as he drove on faster, and he seemed suddenly gleeful, full of energy. 'I'm going to fight you for her.'

'Peter, no!'

'All the way. Like old times, Julia, you and me, tooth and nail, locked together in mortal combat—'

'Except that it's a child's life at stake,' she said bitterly.

'Oh no,' he said, wounded. 'I would never hurt her. I might very likely kill you, but I would never hurt her.'

'Then leave her alone.'

'Julia, think about it. Think what I could give her. Not just money and position, not just stability and a proper home – though that's important. Two parents, security. Children want that. But in Cathy's case, there's something much, much more important I can offer. You know what that is.'

'Music,' she said, almost inaudibly.

'There's so much I can teach her. Martin said you think she has real talent. Think what it would mean to her to have me teach her. And if she *is* good, when she's ready, I can launch her into the music world better than anyone else on earth. You know that's true. I have the influence and the contacts. Peter Kane's protégée would get breaks other youngsters can only dream about. And Peter Kane's daughter . . . ! Would you deny her that? To be a soloist – the dream of her life?'

'Why can't you help her without—'

'Oh, you know it wouldn't work,' he said impatiently. 'The tutor-pupil relationship is intensely intimate in music. I couldn't work with her closely day after day while pretending to be nothing to her. And I wouldn't want to, either. My being her father will be a matter of huge inspiration to her. In any case, she'd guess soon enough. The resemblance *is* remarkable.'

Julia was silent.

'Besides,' he added more quietly, 'I want her. I want her. Don't you understand that? She's my only child.'

Julia made no answer to that, for his last words had opened her like a surgeon's knife. She felt her life building up, snowballing down on her to destroy her, everything she had ever said or done coming inevitably to the climax she ought to have been able to foresee. Every act has consequences, she thought, and that's what life is – a series of consequences, coming home to roost. She had done this to herself, through her own deeds – her sins, her mother would have said – and the responsibility was hers. Who should suffer but herself? It had the symmetry of music, as when, after long wanderings in the minor, the motto comes again to its home key and its resolution.

They pulled up in front of the house and got out, and she stood looking up at the lighted window.

'What is it?' Peter said gently.

'Coming home with you,' she said. 'It feels so natural. Everything hurts so much.'

He took her hand and pressed it, pouring his strength into her.

'It's the most natural thing in the world,' he said.

Twenty-Two

June, 1979

M artin, Julia and Catherine were invited for lunch on Saturday at the Kanes' house in High Wycombe, and they accepted with varying emotions. Cathy was excited; Martin suspected a trap and was determined to thwart it if possible; Julia expected a trap and hardly knew what she was to do about it.

He had played them like fish for the past few weeks, drawing them in gently, and Julia, knowing perfectly well what he was about, had somehow delayed action – though what action was open to her was doubtful. But her self had shelled another, and while one was being gently tamed and led towards the cage, the other watched cynically, knowing every move before it was made.

Catherine was in a state of rapture that the famous Peter Kane was not only an old friend of her mother's but actually her *uncle*.

'He's not your uncle,' Julia said flatly. 'He's your aunt's husband.'

To Catherine that was a distinction without a difference. 'But why didn't you *tell* me?'

'Yout aunt and I had a – a falling out, years ago,' Julia said. What a useful expression that had proved. Aunt Ethel was dead many years now. Julia had gone to *her* funeral.

'What about?' Cathy wanted to know.

'Private. Grown-up things.'

'Well, she must want to be friends again,' Cathy suggested, 'if she's asked us to lunch.'

And Julia could hardly say that the invitation had nothing to do with Sylvia and everything to do with Peter and Cathy. He had her tied, hand and foot.

So the trap was neatly laid, and sweetly sprung, and Sylvia, knowing or unknowing, was the one who sprang it. The luncheon went pleasantly, innocently. Afterwards, replete with good food and softened with good wine they relaxed in large armchairs while Peter and Catherine played a duet. It was an extraordinary experience for Julia to watch them together, so much attuned to each other that they seemed to be able to anticipate each other's movements and play as one, without rehearsal; leaning and looking together as they played, so much alike in appearance that Julia felt Sylvia must surely guess at last.

But Sylvia's expression betrayed nothing but pleasure and a kind of proprietory pride, and finally, when they had finished, she invited them to come down with her and Peter to their cottage in Dorset. They were leaving that evening and were intending to stay a week.

'Oh, could we? Oh how lovely!' Cathy exclaimed at once, clutching her fiddle to her chest and whirling round on her mother with her face glowing. '*Dorset*, Mummy!' It was her home, after all, and she had not forgotten it.

Julia was very reluctant to deny her such a pleasure, but she said, 'Darling, I have to go to work.'

'Oh, you could take a couple of days off, surely?' Peter said reasonably. He saw Cathy's eyes fixed on him and knew who his allies were. 'You must have a holiday entitlement. Or Sylvia could phone up and say you're ill. You look as if you need a rest.'

'Oh Mummy! Oh couldn't we, *please*?'

Julia looked from him to her and back, and Peter made the next move. 'It's a lovely little cottage, near Lulworth—'

'Lulworth! But that's where we lived, before we came to London! Oh Mummy?'

'If you really can't manage it,' he went on sweetly, 'perhaps you'd let us take Catherine, anyway. It is half-term, isn't it? Nicer for her than being stuck in the flat while you're at work.'

You bastard, Julia sent a thought-wave at Peter. How could she refuse the child now? With the ease of a chess master, Peter now manipulated Martin, while leaving Julia to realise her position.

403

'How about you, old man? Care to come down for a few days and take the sea air?' He knew perfectly well that Martin could not take time off even as easily as Julia might, but he also knew perfectly well that he would not stay behind if Julia went.

Julia was well up to this stage, and made her last protest. 'But we haven't anything with us – no night things, or clothes.'

'Oh, that's no problem,' Sylvia said. 'Peter can drive you back and you can pick up whatever you need. We can stay here tonight and go down tomorrow.'

Julia looked at Martin. *It's up to you*, his look said.

What can I do about it? hers said.

It all fell into place, exactly as Julia knew Peter had planned it. Peter was to drive Julia home to collect their things, Martin was to drive himself home for the same purpose, and Cathy was to stay and keep Sylvia company.

Why couldn't Martin drive Julia and save two cars going?

Martin lived nowhere near Julia. It would take too long. Anyway, it was no trouble to Peter.

Julia yielded, almost more amused than exasperated. Martin drove himself off feeling that he had come badly out of the whole affair, and Julia waved goodbye to Sylvia and Catherine in the doorway and climbed into the two-seater. Peter engaged reverse, backed fast down the drive and out on to the road, and as soon as they were out of sight of any windows, he stopped and regarded Julia with a whimsical smile.

'Well?' she said severely.

'Oh no,' he said, tongue in cheek.

'What are you up to?'

'Nothing, nothing.' He threw his hands up in the air with a gesture of wounded innocence and drove on.

'It's beautiful country around here,' she said after a moment, wanting to stay on neutral ground. She let the window down and breathed in the air from the old woods through which they were driving, the damp, sweet-rotten smell of leaves and earth, and the peppery fragrance of grass and nettles. 'Such a cool smell.'

He smiled, looking ahead at the road. 'I bought the place for you,' he said.

'You lie.'

'I did! I imagined you having a horse and riding through the woods on summer mornings, and hunting in the winter. I knew how you'd feel about it. And the place in Dorset, you can't doubt *that* was for you . . .' He broke off, and looked troubled for a moment. Then he seemed to gather himself. '*Why* did you leave me?'

'What do you mean, why?' she said, surprised. 'You know why.'

'Just for having Sylvia – that was no reason.'

'It was reason enough for me.'

'It couldn't have been that. Not you, Julia – you are above such mundane considerations.'

'What an impossible idealist you are,' she said.

'*Me*, an idealist?'

'Oh yes, you are. You can play the cynic all you like but I know you. I know what you search for through your music. And in life – you want life to be symmetrical. You expect there to be a perfect, logical reason for everything.'

He yielded. 'Well, why not?'

'There's hardly ever a sufficient reason for anything, let alone a logical one. Picture to yourself a talented young man, starting a brilliant career, well-connected wife, two nice kids, house, car – why should he throw all that up to run off with a grubby schoolgirl?'

'You were neither. And stop changing the subject,' he said. 'There's no sort of parallel there. Answer my question – why did you leave me?'

'I've told you the reason.'

'Just that?'

'It wasn't "just" to me. What choice was I left with? I'm a very proud person, you know. I couldn't give up my dignity.'

'It's one of the things I love about you,' he acknowledged.

She ducked her head as if avoiding a blow. 'I know you had to marry again, afterwards. You're not the sort of man to live alone. But I wish you hadn't chosen to marry Sylvia. She isn't right for you, nor you for her.'

'There's one thing which you don't know, one way in which she is ideal.'

405

'And what's that?'

'She's insignificant. I can ignore her. I could never ignore you – that's why you were so wearing.'

'I wouldn't call your treatment of my sister "ignoring". What else do you want to explain away – your infidelity?'

'I was never unfaithful to you – never!' He said it so vehemently he startled her. He went on more quietly, 'Never in any way that counted.'

'Very convenient.'

'You're supposed to believe me – I gave up everything for you.'

'Oh, I know what you mean – or what you want to mean. And in that way, I was never unfaithful to you.'

'You were never unfaithful in any way,' he said gloomily. 'Oh well . . .'

'I suppose so,' she said.

If there had only ever been Joyce, he could not have spoken like this. If there had only been Joyce, he would not have been what he was today, an artist, a renowned soloist. Julia had loosened him, extended his comprehension, and at the moment when he had finished with his initial need of her, she had left him. His need had become wider-ranging, the need simply to know she existed, to justify his new airy freedom when it became too heady.

He had taken her as a child, removed her from all other influence, moulded her like clay into his shape – but if he created her, how could she simultaneously have created him? He remembered times when he had tried to quarrel with her, and she had merely observed him, smiling, refusing the bait. Secure in her inner convictions, she had not needed to fight, had not needed to win. An odd sort of pride, that was, that had to prove things only to itself. But she had had the other sort too, the ordinary pride that could not bear to be less to him than before – and so she had walked out.

And now she sat mocking him, looking at him with the easy arrogance of an aristocrat, the pride he could never bend his way. She had courage, she had strength and though he knew he might have her at the snap of his fingers it was no triumph – she came consenting, not conquered, and while she would love him mind and body, give up life or freedom for him, she would never bend her will to him. There remained always one part of her he could not have. That, perhaps, above all was her endless fascination.

As long as he loved her, she would remain all these things to him; and as long as she remained all this, he would love her. And now, of course, there was Catherine. He had the uneasy feeling she knew all the moves of that game before he played them, and that, playing along, she would take the shine out of it for him, and still win in the end.

When they reached Julia's place, she insisted on stopping at a shop a few yards down the road to buy some food.

'If we're going to be some time here, we'll need something to eat,' she said. Peter stared, and then laughed.

'How well you know me,' he said. 'If someone told me you know everything that is to happen for the rest of time, I wouldn't find it at all surprising.'

'Don't flatter yourself,' she said. 'You aren't so hard to read.' She was covering up a fluttering of excitement that she didn't want to admit to – but after all, it was natural enough. She hadn't had a man for a very long time, and she was a normal healthy woman, in the prime of life and desires.

She cooked first, from the conviction that she wouldn't feel like it afterwards, and while she cooked, Peter wandered around the studio, picking up things and putting them down, and humming to himself. She listened with a little half-smile. He still had not learnt that the beginning of an affair is always exciting, though the lesson had been repeated for him often enough, she was sure. He called out something to her which she didn't hear above the sound of sausages frying.

'What?'

He appeared at the doorway, holding one of the many pictures of Cathy. 'Why do you make her look so much like me?' he asked. She was amused. 'No, I mean it,' he said. 'Look, here's one of me, and here's one of her – now aren't they similar?'

'Martin says all my pictures look the same. It's just my style. I never was much of a painter, you know.'

407

'You were.'

'I was not. Come, admit it now.'

'You're one hell of a human being, though,' he said, coming over to kiss her neck.

'All right, go and put the paintings back and take your tea, or supper, or whatever you want to call it.' She held out a plate to him and he stared at it blankly.

'Sausages and eggs?' He looked up at her with a quizzical smile. 'I haven't had anything like that since – well, I suppose since we moved out of the mews flat, and I hate to think how long ago that was.'

'Don't be such a dilettante. Cathy likes it. It's good plain food, and you've been too long on a fancy diet. I wonder you're not sick of it. It would do you good to have to bring up a child on a limited . . .'

She stopped abruptly, cursing herself for her clumsiness. He walked away without a word, and she followed with the food. They sat down and ate in silence. When they had finished she made an effort to get near him again, seeing his averted eyes and downcast expression.

'What is it, Peter? Is it Nathan? Which one of them?' The last was faintly humorous, hoping he would respond, but he looked up at her with a naked misery in his eyes that hurt her.

'All of them,' he said. 'All my children, Julia. I have nothing, nothing.'

'Peter, don't.'

'What's it all worth? After all, I'm worse off now than I was at twenty-one. Then at least I had youth on my side, and everything before me.'

'You're a famous soloist and a great artist. That's worth something.'

'There are plenty of soloists as good as I am, and better.'

'You're a musician,' she said, making a nice distinction.

'For a little while,' he said. 'Now – the end is nearer than the beginning.' He didn't complete the thought, but she understood. It was immortality, wasn't it – what they all sought? Music was an ephemeral art, LPs notwithstanding. When a concert ended, there was nothing left where it had been. And when he was gone, would even his recordings be played, his name remembered? But a child – a child was the part of you that did not die. Joyce had his sons, Nathan was dead, and there would be no more children for him now, it seemed. He was left with the hollowness of a thin, piping tune played on an empty heath.

As she stared at him, thoughts, remembered words, ran through her mind: George saying that his greatest achievement was Cathy; Martin saying that he had loved her for twenty-five years; Rowland saying, 'He's my brother, and I love him, but he's a bastard'; and Peter – Peter carrying Michael up to bed, pick-a-back, Peter sitting by the hospital bed, holding Nathan's hand as he died.

All their lives, she had striven to match Peter, strength for strength and blow for blow, and now she had gone past him, and he had come to her knee like a child, asking for reassurance. She walked round the table and took his hand and led him to the sofa, and he went with her blankly and sat down, still looking at her.

'Julia, everything I've ever done has hurt you,' he began. 'It would have been better for you if you'd never met me.'

'Oh Peter. Oh my dear,' she said. 'I've loved you all my life – only you, only ever you. Don't doubt it now, not after all this time. That would make it all a waste, a waste of all our lives . . .'

She did the only thing she could in the circumstances. She took him to bed, and held him and reassured him, and they made love, more out of loneliness than passion, but remembering as they did how it had been. Their bodies knew each other, were old friends, and in the end it was something like the old love that had kept them awake night after night. He came into her with a sense of unutterable relief, and almost immediately afterwards fell asleep, just as he used to, with a leg across her and his hand at her throat, as if to stop her escaping.

Julia held him, unsleeping. She was tired, so tired, and needed to be near him, enough and little enough not to care about the danger of the trap she was walking into. But she had not yet given in, and after a while she woke him and made him assume his recognisable persona for the journey back to High

Wycombe. They arrived late, to find that Sylvia had put Cathy to bed, and she and Martin were playing cards and talking. It seemed unnatural to have to walk in with Peter like a stranger, and when Martin looked at her with an odd expression she could not translate, she began to wonder what they had been talking about before she came in.

Peter stopped the open car in the narrow lane. Cathy, beside him, was wind-battered and drunk with speed. As the engine noise dropped to an idle mutter she found she was being deafened from all sides by a mixture of birdsong and silence. Her hair, which was tied in two bunches over her ears, was curled and matted with the wind.

'You look like a black spaniel,' Peter said affectionately.

'I can smell the *sea*,' Cathy said. 'We passed by where we used to live with Daddy. I tried to tell you, but you didn't hear.'

Oh, he had heard all right.

'Here come the others,' he said. 'Jump out and open the gate for us – the white gate, that's right.'

Martin's Rover, with the two women as passengers, followed Peter's car through the gate and stopped while he picked up Cathy again, and drove on up the narrow, steeply-mounting drive. It was so overhung with burgeoning trees and bristling hedges that they had no view of the house until the cars pulled up on the gravelled parking place below it.

'Cottage!' Julia snorted as she climbed out of the car and stood beside Peter looking up. The big, square, white house was wedged into the top of a mound, and a flight of steep steps led from the gravel where they stood to the green front door. The sloping ground on either side of the steps had been terraced and planted as a rockery, and all around tall trees and thick hedges flourished, cutting out the view, and acting as a windbreak so that the heat was trapped in.

'Just a little place in the country,' Peter said airily, looking up at the Georgian face of the house as he might at a friend.

'Not the place for cripples, obviously,' Martin said.

'There are two other entrances, without steps,' Peter said, 'but this is the only way to approach by car.'

410

'It's not the place for nervous mothers, either,' Sylvia said. 'No neighbours for about ten miles, and just wait until you see the terrace out at the back!'

Inside the house was cool and spacious with polished wooden floors, old comfortable furniture, and hundreds of books lining the walls of almost every room. While the landward facade of the house was Georgian and cream-washed, the seaward side showed its true age, presented a face like a fisherman's cottage to the weather: grey stone, two feet thick, with small double windows set deep into them against the winter gales.

The long drawing room was the exception to this, for it had French windows which led out on to a sort of balcony with a high stone wall. This terrace was built over the cliff, and when Julia leaned over the wall she saw a sheer drop to the tumbled rocks and hissing sea far below her. To her left, the madly overgrown cliffside was a riot of bracken and gorse, knapweed and thistle, stunted trees and bushes rollicking down to a green spit into the sea; to her right beyond the cliffs was a small, crescent-shaped beach.

'That's our own private beach,' Sylvia said proudly. 'It belongs to the house.' It seemed odd to Julia that Sylvia should be the hostess here.

Catherine was racing madly about, skidding on the polished floors – the first time it had been an accident, but now she was pretending to be a dog, and Julia wondered what had brought that on. There was a pleasant kind of anarchy for a while as everyone looked round the house at his or her own speed, and so it happened that Peter was with Julia when she discovered the other balcony. It was on the upper floor, leading off someone's bedroom, and was only just big enough for two people to stand on, close together. It was on the side of the house, and looked over the luxuriant woodland that hid the house from the road. In the middle of all the greenery, Julia could see a neat rectangular lawn with a circular patch of rose bushes in the middle.

'It looks like a badly-shaven chin,' she said to Peter as he came up behind her and looked out over her shoulder. 'The little tuft in the middle left by a blunt razor.'

'That's the sun lawn. One can get a remarkable tan lying there – it's a sun trap. And, of course, it can only be overlooked from the house, so we sometimes lie out there in the nip. I'll take you there later, if you like. There used to be tennis courts, too, between the lawn and the sea – over there – but the last of them fell in two years ago.'

'Fell in?'

'Into the sea. The house used to be quite far from the edge on both sides, but the land is receding, and every winter a bit more falls into the sea. That's why I got it so cheaply – it's a diminishing property. You can still find traces of the tennis courts amongst all that,' and he gestured towards the scrubland of bracken. 'We call that the jungle.'

'What about the house – is that safe?' She turned her head to look at him. The clear light from the sea reflected in his eyes and face, making him luminously beautiful. He put his arms round her waist and rested his chin on her shoulder so that their cheeks were together.

'Safe for the moment. The rock it's built on doesn't recede as fast, fortunately. We have some chaps down every year to do tests and see if it's still safe. One day it will go, though. One day they'll say "we can't be sure any more". Then we'll move everything out of the house, and it will lie deserted, perhaps for years, the abode of spiders, decaying a little, and getting mossy, until one winter's night, at the height of a storm, it will crack, slip, and crash down on to the rocks and into the sea.'

'And someone will walk past next day, and stop, and stare.'

'And there'll be no house there – as if there never had been.'

'He'll wonder if he's lost his way, because the whole headland will look different.'

'Not for a long time yet,' he said, kissing the tip of her ear.

'And a little piping ghost will wander about the clifftop.'

They turned away and started downstairs.

'Whose ghost is that?' he asked. He still had his arm, absently, round her waist.

'Oh, mine. I'm going to haunt this house when I die.'

412

'I thought it was only people who die violent deaths who haunt places.'

'Not necessarily. You don't think I'd leave you unsupervised, do you? No, you'll never get away from me until you die too – then I might be able to lie down.'

He withdrew his arm and shook her shoulder roughly. 'Don't,' he said. He was as superstitious as an actress.

The days at the house passed sweetly, drowsily. Julia felt as if she were drowning painlessly in honey. They woke early, breakfasted in the sunny morning room, and then scattered, each to his own occupation, to sunbathe on the lawn, to bathe or bask on the little beach, to walk along the windy clifftops, or to sit in the cool of the house with a book and the magnificent view.

Catherine spent most of her time, when she was not practising, with Sylvia, charmed with the novelty of a newly-acquired aunt; and Sylvia, with the energy of a childless woman, played with her, accompanied, instructed and amused her.

She said to Julia, 'It's marvellous to have someone else's child. It means you can have it when you want it, and give it back when you've had enough.'

But behind the flippancy Julia could see enough to recognise the hunger for a child that had eaten Sylvia thin. If only she could have a child, much of what was wrong between her and Peter would be put right. That was part of the reason Peter wanted Cathy, of course, though he may not have realised it. She wondered, just a little, why he did not have children by Sylvia, but was rather uncomfortably glad that he did not. She knew what Peter's plan was – he would gradually get Cathy to love him, which wouldn't be difficult, and then would offer to teach her, knowing that Julia could not refuse that, not able herself to pay for or provide anything like it. As pupil and teacher their relationship would become so deep and intimate that it would seem the most natural and wonderful thing in the world when Peter eventually revealed his kinship to her.

It was a good plan, and she knew that by it he meant to avoid hurting the child. But she knew Peter too well: he was emotional and impulsive. He would not be able to carry the plan through. He would break out with the news before Cathy was ready, and do God knew what damage. For the moment there seemed little danger. Peter was being circumspect, went off on his own, and only seemed to reappear when Sylvia had just left with Cathy. Even Martin, seeing that Peter and Cathy were always apart, was lulled into a sense of security, and spent his days working relaxedly through Peter's enormous library.

On the Tuesday, Martin had to go back to London to play in a concert, but he promised to come back the next day and finish his week. On Tuesday, too, Sylvia was to go and visit friends in Portland, and stay the night with them. How did it come about?

'Honestly, Peter, I sometimes think you're a magician,' Julia said, perplexed, as they stood out on the terrace after breakfast, having waved Sylvia and Martin off in their separate cars.

'Why so?' Peter breathed out the last smoke from his after-breakfast cigarette and watched it rise slowly in a mass until it caught the breeze, swung sideways and down like a chorus line curtseying, and was whisked away.

'The way you manipulate people.'

'Oh, most people don't care what they do, one way or the other. I just give them a bit of a push in the right direction.'

Julia shook her head. 'There's your wife, who has every reason to think ill of you, and Martin who knows perfectly well what you're up to, and they both drive meekly away and leave you with a clear field to work your evil designs.'

'And what about you?'

'What about me?'

'What are you going to do about my evil designs? Or are you caught up in my magic too?'

Julia sighed, but not unhappily. 'I think I must be. After all, I'm not protesting, am I?'

'Do you love me that much?' Peter mocked her.

'Oh, it isn't a question of love, is it? If I had the choice of being blind or losing you, I'd choose to be blind. I could live without the sun, but not without you.'

That struck him as odd coming from a person who had lived without him for about as long as she had lived with him, but he said nothing. He was watching her turning her face to the sun, closing her eyes to slits and smiling with contentment, as if she were savouring the last of it. He shook off his superstition again, angrily.

'However,' Julia said suddenly, opening her eyes and looking straight at him, 'don't think that because I'm not protesting you're going to have it all your own way.'

'I don't,' Peter grinned. 'I learnt a long time ago to beware of the crocodile when it smiled.'

'Quite right. They have eyes in their eyelids.' She looked around her, and sighed again. 'I love this place.'

'I knew you would,' he said. 'When I bought it, I knew you'd come home one day. It's your house, all of it.'

'Tell that to Sylvia,' Julia said, but she smiled all the same. Suddenly oppression seemed to be lifted from them, and all that day they were free, the three of them, to be happy. The weather was perfect, one of those utterly brilliant June days, and Julia packed a picnic lunch and they set off along the cliffs, determined to make the most of it.

They walked westwards until they came to a place where the cliff was sufficiently crumbled and broken for them to climb down on to the stony beach. There they changed into their swimwear, and spent a happy couple of hours paddling around the rock pools, investigating crevices and poking under tattered curtains of weed. Peter showed his daughter how to catch the little crabs that lived there, but they quite failed to catch any of the fish, which flicked away from their fingers and under rocks whenever they came near.

'Aren't they an*noy*ing?' Cathy said, pushing back her black curls with a hand on which the salt had dried into white tidemarks. 'They wait until you've just nearly got them—'

'And then they zoom away,' Peter finished.

'If we had a net it'd be different,' Cathy said, looking hopefully at her mother.

'You're right,' Peter said. He raised his voice to a squeak and said, 'Mamma, we want a fishing net. Please, Mamma.'

Cathy stared at him in astonishment – this was *Peter Kane*, after all – and then snorted with laughter. 'You are silly!'

'Don't call me silly – I'll push you in,' Peter said.

415

'You wouldn't!'

'I would.'

'I dare you, then.'

'I'll fight you for it.' He put his fists up and pranced. Cathy began to giggle. He pretended to get bitten in the toe by a crab, and flailed about, only saving himself from a ducking by sitting down heavily, and then jumping up as if he'd sat on another crab. Cathy was helpless with laughter, and Julia watched, smiling, from a distance. She had never seen him with a daughter before, of course, but she remembered his clowning with the boys years ago.

'Tide's nearly in,' she said after a while, and then squinted up at the position of the sun. 'We'd better go back up or we'll be cut off.'

'Oh, not yet!' Cathy protested.

Peter gave her a gentle cuff and said, 'No arguments. Mother knows best.'

'We should really get out of the sun while its at its height,' Julia said. 'We can eat up there somewhere and then come back down when the tide's turned.'

Their limbs felt heavy as they climbed up, and even Cathy was glad to find a grassy spot to sit down, not too far from the cliff edge, where the breeze cooled them and an outcrop of rock and gorse shaded them. Julia laid out the food, and though they did not feel hungry in the heat, they ate all the same with slow pleasure.

They didn't talk. The sun was at the middle of its parabola, and everything was overlaid with an extra quiet, as if nature were observing Sunday. The wind made a continuous small noise against the ears, but when you turned your head out of it, underneath the other little noises – the tiny rustle of grasses, the intermittent whiz-whiz of a cricket, the warm drone of a bee, and very far away, more felt than heard, like a pulse, the sea – underneath, the silence became audible.

'Listen!' Julia said. The man and the child tilted their heads out of the wind and listened with her. 'You can hear the silence. It's almost deafening.'

They did not say *don't be silly*, or *you can't hear silence*. They felt it too, that particular stillness – she had simply

416

put it into words for them. She sat a little higher than Peter, and for him was framed by the impossibly dark-blue sky. He stared at her, unable to speak or move, for she seemed like something almost holy: perfect, golden and silky, like a wild animal, resting against the sky, chosen to harbour some special grace, and he caught his breath at her. Then a gull mewed, high up overhead where the wind currents were, and she moved her head to look at it, and the stillness was alive again.

As soon as the tide had receded enough to expose an edge of beach, they went down again, and made their way barefooted along the slippery ledge. Not a place for nervous mothers, Sylvia had said – but Julia could not have been afraid today, not if she tried. Catherine balanced along the perilous way a foot behind her father, as fearlessly and securely as if she had wings. Their progress was slow, for the tide had left new treasures, and everything had to be seen and examined. There was a clutch of tiny shells of the most perfect turquoise colour, some real mother-of-pearl, little crabs flushed rosy pink as if they were blushing with the shame of being uncovered in their retreats, a seahorse, long time dead, with proudly arched neck like a charger.

They came round the point and found a higher beach of small pebbles where they could walk on the level and three abreast. Cathy was still carrying the seahorse, and Julia began to tell her an old story she had heard somewhere, long ago, about the white horses of the sea who gallop in at midnight and come right out of the sea, lapping up the shore like waves of luminous mist. Cathy listened to it, liking the romance of it, but feeling she was too old for fairy stories, glancing now and then at Peter for his reaction. Then when it was over she picked up a flat stone and ran down to the edge of the water to skim it.

'Watch me, Mummy!' She flung it badly and it sank.

'You can't skim stones!' Peter shouted derisively.

'I used to could!' Cathy shouted back, agitated, and picking up another stone threw it so wildly that it shot backwards and narrowly missed Julia's face.

'Hey!' she protested.

Peter said, 'Just hold on there, young lady. I'll show you how to do it.'

He took her hands in his and corrected her grip and stance, as he would have corrected her fingering or her holding of the bow. He paused in his work then to look at them, and then at her, and to say seriously, 'You must take care of your hands. They are your most valuable possession.'

She looked up at him, serious too, almost breathless. 'Do you think I can – I can be a violinist – a soloist?'

'I think you have great potential. And I can help you realise it.'

Julia, watching, saw the look that passed between them and thought, she's his now. Was it as easy as that?

'But first,' Peter continued in a very different voice, 'you have to learn to skim a stone properly!'

The three of them made their way slowly along the water's edge, skimming anything that approximated the flat and round. Julia was very good at it, and picking her moment could get the stone to hop neatly from wavetop to wavetop until it disappeared. In fact, she was better at it than Peter, whose stones never did more than two or three hops; but Cathy wouldn't allow her prowess, and turned always to Peter for applause or help. Just for today, at least, he could do nothing that was not perfect.

The cliffs picked up their voices and flung them, high and hollow, out across the water; the exhausting, sliding banks of stones were like glass under their feet. The gulls turned in the air above, keeping up a continual, mournful complaint. Sometimes they landed and sat here and there on the beach, huge as geese and so white they might have been freshly bleached that morning and set out in the sun to dry. They walked away rapidly when the humans approached, looking at them sideways and with loathing from their glittering obsidian eyes.

The sun began to slant more, and an afternoon feeling came over them, a slight pastel tint of melancholy along with the bright chrome tints of happiness. Cathy ran about still, indefatigable, but Peter and Julia went higher up the beach where the going was easier and trudged along hand in hand, watching her pick things up and drop them again, or throw them, high and sparkling, into the sea.

418

'You've done well with her,' Peter said.

'But?'

'I didn't say but.'

'I heard the one you didn't say. You meant, not as well as you could have done.'

'Wrong, for once. I meant, not as well as *we* could have done.'

They walked on, thinking about it. Just then it all seemed possible.

'I'd like her to go to boarding school,' Julia said after a while.

Peter shook his head. 'I don't think that would be the thing. I think she needs to stay in London for the moment, for the sake of her music. She can get a better teacher there than elsewhere.'

'You really think she has talent?' Julia asked. She had always believed so, but it was good to have it confirmed by an expert.

'You're asking a biased source,' Peter said, 'but yes, I do think so. I think she can be very good.'

'How good?'

'Very good,' he repeated, and looked at her solemnly. 'I think she can be a musician, to give you back your own distinction.'

She closed her eyes a moment in pleasure.

'Why is that important to you?' he asked.

'I don't know. I suppose I feel it justifies me, though heaven knows why. If I thought I'd spoilt her—'

'You can believe me. I'm Peter Kane, the famous fiddler.'

'I never think of you as the famous fiddler,' she said, laughing.

'What, then?'

'Oh, just my love.'

He threaded an arm round her waist and they walked on happily, discussing Cathy's future with unemphatic disagreement, wrangling for the sheer pleasure of it.

It was just another part of the perfect day when Catherine found the dog – or when the dog found her. It was a large, bushy, black and white mongrel. Peter and Julia didn't see it

419

arrive, but suddenly it was there, frisking round Cathy and giving short, sharp barks of inducement to play.

'That dog knew we were coming,' Julia said. Peter looked enquiry at her. 'She's been agitating for a dog ever since she was about five years old, but of course we've never been in a position to have one. I must say, she was consistent in her desires.'

'So, we've been lent the dog for the day by . . .' He rolled his eyes skyward.

'Why not? Nothing can go wrong today. I feel like Mary Poppins.'

'Not practically – you are perfect.'

They felt timeless as they walked along, the enduring family group of man, woman, child and dog. After all their years of conflict, they had suddenly come over on to the same side, and all this long day they were in accord, and a silent bargain was struck, that it should never end.

The house loomed grey and solid and welcoming above them, and as they neared it the dog slipped away without warning, bounding up the overgrown path into the jungle as if, coming to the end of its script, it had left the stage to take up its ordinary life again.

Cathy watched it go, her back eloquent, and then she turned and ran back to her mother with a tragic face.

'Oh, Mummy . . . !'

'Yes, I know – you want a dog, exactly like that one.' Julia and Peter were still hand in hand, and she felt the unspoken communication flow between them. 'Well, I don't see why you shouldn't have one.'

There was a second's time lapse before it registered, but then the joy on her face was a once in a lifetime thing, like the perfect performance of the Tchaikovsky violin concerto. She jumped up to fling her arms round her mother's neck.

'Oh, Mummy, you darling beautiful Mummy, thank you!' She swung on Julia's neck for a moment, and then jumped down, landing heavily on Peter's foot and saying all in the same breath, 'Sorry, Daddy!' before she expressed her excitement in a round and round dance, like a dog chasing its tail.

It meant nothing, it was the merest slip of the tongue, but

Peter looked as though he had been hit with a spade, and Julia drew her lip in between her teeth. Then she called Cathy, and they each took a hand, and the three of them climbed together up the rough steps to the house.

The perfect day was ending. Cathy was in bed and asleep, and Peter and Julia had bathed and changed, and then eaten at a table on the terrace. Now they were leaning on the parapet watching the blood-red and gold sun sink into the sea. It was a sight as gorgeous as an emperor's wedding. The sky streamed with luminous feathers as the east deepened from turquoise to blue-black, and the sun disappeared inch by inch, from a blob like molton glass to a bright fingernail, and then only a shining. And then it was really gone, and the luminosity drained out of the sky leaving it solid and suddenly close.

After a long silence it was hard to speak again. Julia heard Peter sigh in the darkness, and then he took out a cigarette and lit it, and the fragrance drifted across to her, mingling with other night smells, dew and earth and night-scented stock.

'Look, there's the lightship,' Peter said quietly. She drew nearer to him as he spoke, and he put his hand on her shoulder and felt it cool, as if she were drinking in the dew. He kissed it, smelling the faint flowery scent of her skin, and then drew her against him, under his shoulder.

'I know what we'll do,' he said.

'What?'

'We'll bring the record player over to the window, and put on some dance music and dance on the terrace.'

'And drink wine . . . ?'

'And get drunk, divinely drunk like we used to.'

'I don't remember ever getting divinely drunk.'

'Perhaps it was two other people then?'

'On two other terraces?'

'Moonlight can be terribly deceptive.'

They found some old 78s and put them on, and danced slowly to the sweet, plangent sound, their cheeks together, the corners of their mouths just touching. They drank old red burgundy, and it tingled in their bodies with the same kind of pleasurable melancholy as the music. Sometimes they

421

sang, and sometimes were silent, and sometimes they forgot to dance, but swayed on the spot, out of time, breathing mouth to mouth, no distance anywhere between their bodies.

Towards dawn they went down to the beach and stripped off and swam, hardly noticing the coldness of the water. He splashed her, and she ducked under the water and came up behind him and pulled him down, and he chased her back to the shallows and pushed her down on the slope between the tide marks where the water was breaking and made love to her while the sky slowly brightened and at last the sun came up, young and cool to light them home.

But now the house was dark, in shadow, and they were reluctant to go in, knowing that once in they must separate to bathe and dress for breakfast, after which the others would be arriving back. The world, having let them breathe for a day, was crowding in again, and as they entered the house she dropped his hand, and he drew into himself and would not meet her eye. The silent battle was resumed: with one bound they were on opposite sides again, and their time together was over.

She waited for him to speak, wondering how he would say goodbye, but he was silent, and when she looked up, his head was turned away, he was staring out at the sea to avoid looking at her. But for all that, he could not help seeing the old gesture of pride with which she drew herself up, and he clenched his hands at his side to stop himself reaching out for her, and after a moment she turned without a word and walked out of the room.

Twenty-Three

That was Wednesday morning. Now it was Friday. Time was running short, and the battle was growing more bitter. Julia was tired, she wanted to relax, to rest, to be loved, and sometimes she could not remember what she was fighting for. Why not let him have Catherine? But the thought of Catherine always roused her to one more effort. Cathy, her beloved, her daughter! Cathy must not suffer; and for Peter to win without Cathy suffering, Sylvia must suffer. She kept fighting.

Peter would scarcely talk to her now, almost hating her because only her will stood between him and what he wanted. It had always been that way – in all his life, only she had ever thwarted him; but now his confidence was growing. He felt, as hand-to-hand wrestlers will feel, the quality of his opponent's endurance: he felt her flagging.

This, combined with an excellent dinner, made him feel genial, and the atmosphere became almost party-like. He and Cathy played another duet – a piece of unaccompanied Bach – and the others gathered round in the drawing room to listen. With one or two stops for him to correct or help, they got through it, and the two intertwining strands of music drifted out of the open French windows and into the darkness, to mingle with the hush and sigh of the sea far below. Julia stood at the windows and looked out, away from the bright room, for she could not bear to see them together like that, intensifying her dilemma.

When it was done, they put away the instruments and Peter lounged in his favourite leather armchair and treated them all to his indolent good humour. Sylvia sat on the leather chesterfield – matured like good wine, now, that sofa –

423

doing a piece of her elegant, useless embroidery, with which she occupied her childless, Peterless hours. Everyone, Julia reflected, needed some way to express their creativity. Martin sat in the opposite chair, with Cathy on the arm, blowing smoke rings for her. The atmosphere relaxed, and Julia turned back inwards, remembering all over again how charming he could be when he tried.

'I love this place,' Julia said suddenly, during a pause in the idle conversation.

Sylvia looked up. 'Do you? I thought you would.'

'Now I'm here, I never want to leave it,' she said, stretching a hand out at the night. 'The sound of the sea—'

'Pretty comfortless in winter,' Martin said practically.

'Oh, no!' Julia merely refuted, shaking her head.

Peter watched her with a small smile of private amusement. 'I'll leave it to you in my will,' he said. Then: 'No I won't. You might be tempted to bump me off to gain possession.'

'Julia wouldn't do that. She's too soft,' Sylvia said.

'I don't know about that,' he said. 'No, I'll leave it to Cathy.'

Cathy looked across at him sharply, and then decided it was a joke and gave an impish grin. 'How do you know I might not bump you off?' she said.

Julia felt – what? – time, or fate, or something, catch its breath and listen. It was a sensation like pricked ears. Suddenly there was tension, danger in the room. Peter was still relaxed and smiling, but Julia could almost hear the machinery of his thoughts.

'Well, I don't, of course,' he said with easy humour. 'I'll just have to make sure I keep my eye on you all the time.' He held his hand out as he spoke, and Cathy went across to him trustingly and stood at his knee, looking down into his face and smiling.

To Julia, it was as if the child had picked up a snake to play with, and she said abruptly, 'It's about time you were in bed, young lady.' It was clumsy. Even to her it sounded clumsy and harsh. Cathy turned her head to look at her mother in surprise at what seemed from the tone of voice to be a rebuke, wondering what she had done wrong; and at the same moment Peter put

424

his arms round her waist and swung her round to sit on his knee. Recognising an ally, Cathy leaned back against him, letting her legs dangle, and put her hands over his, which were clasped at her waist. She looked comfortable there, enthroned like a queen, her dark curly head against Peter's dark smooth one.

She said, 'I'm not tired, Mummy.'

'Oh, it isn't late enough for bed yet,' Peter said casually.

Cathy hastened to consolidate her position. 'I'm going to teach my dog to lie down when I whistle, and go left and right, like a sheep dog.'

'Better learn to whistle first,' Peter said.

'I can already,' Cathy protested. 'Look –' she pursed her mouth to demonstrate, and Peter tightened his arms convulsively, jerking the breath out of her. 'Stop it,' she gasped, giggling. 'That's cheating! Oh, stop it, I *can* whistle!' But between giggling and being squeezed she could not get more than a weak husky blow out in one piece.

Julia could not bear it any longer. 'Catherine, it's time for bed,' she said sharply. 'I won't tell you again. Get up now and go and clean your teeth.'

Cathy's laughter stopped. Her face was next to Peter's, and two pairs of bright blue eyes were turned on Julia, side by side, one pair with a mocking challenge, one pair hardening in rebellion. Another word, and she'll hate me, Julia thought.

'I mean it. Now.' She saw Peter's arms tighten again, encouraging the protest. 'Peter let her go. Cathy . . . !'

'No,' Cathy said, half-frightened at herself. The four blue eyes burned like lamps but the rest of the room seemed to be deep in a mist, and Julia heard her own voice very far away.

'Let her go.'

'I'll have her,' he said.

She felt the hair rising on her neck, as if the room were full of electricity, and something was winding tighter inside her, winding up to bursting point, so that she wanted to scream.

'No,' she said, and her voice was the thinnest sound, twisted out of her.

Cathy was suddenly frightened, seeing how strangely her mother looked, and she tried to wriggle away, off Peter's lap. But Peter tightened his grip so that she squeaked under it,

425

and then she was really frightened. She began to whimper, still struggling, looking first at her mother, and then towards Martin, and from him to Sylvia, for help.

'I'll have her, Julia – I will,' Peter said slowly, with mounting emphasis. 'You can't stop me. There's nothing you can do.'

'No! Peter, no. Peter, don't – don't—'

'She's mine,' he said, his voice rising, pressing down Julia's exultantly. 'You've kept her from me all these years, but your time's up. You've had it, Julia.'

Cathy struggled again, but Peter stood up, still holding her, with no more effort than if she had been a puppy, and she dangled from his strong, violinist's hands, unable to cry out from lack of breath. 'She's mine now – my daughter. She's my daughter. My child – my daughter!'

Julia clung to the doorpost, white and wild, and the room seemed to swing round her and clamour like a bell. She saw Sylvia start up, going to Cathy's aid, trying to loosen Peter's hands. 'You're hurting her. Peter, you're hurting her.'

But he brushed her off as carelessly as if she had been dust. Martin took a step towards him, turned then to Julia, and then back again, swinging between the two in fatal indecision, not knowing where to pit his strength or place his loyalty. While he hesitated Peter touched Cathy down briefly, turned her and hoisted her up in his arms, all in one movement, so that her face was level with his. He began to speak to her in a low voice.

'You didn't know that, did you Cathy? Stop it, stop struggling. I'm not hurting you. I would never hurt you. Listen to me! You're my own, my own Cathy. I'm your father. She didn't tell you that, did she? She lied to you, Cathy. That man you called your father – he wasn't your father at all. He was your mother's husband, but she came to me, she came to me and I made you, I am your father, and no one will ever part us again. You hear that, my Cathy? You and me. No one can take us away from each other – not her, not anyone – not ever again.'

Catherine stared at him, half-hypnotised, while around them silence clamoured. The room was full of pain, but no one moved or spoke now – too late to try to repair a situation gone past breaking point. Cathy twisted her head round to stare at her mother, white and strange in the blackness of the doorway, and it seemed a face she did not know, comfortless. Silently she asked for the truth, and her mother's eyes closed, her head turned away. It seemed to Cathy as though her mother was dying, and the world was whirling away, drawing with it everything she knew, leaving a black hole, a nothingness, out of which came a sense of grief so huge that she gasped for breath, and then began to cry. She jerked her head away from the figure in the doorway, turned it this way and that, seeking for comfort. The man's face was close to hers, and looking into it she saw a mirror of something she knew – her own image perhaps – at any rate, a comprehension. Here was someone who understood what she was.

'Cathy,' he said, and it was like being called home. 'Don't be afraid.'

She pressed against him, and buried her face in his neck, and his arms were gentle now, strongly protecting her. Across her bent head, Peter's eyes met Julia's, and there was no more conflict between them, only a stillness. It passed out from them across the room, and they all stood like actors in the last scene of a play while he walked out, carrying Catherine, and closed the door behind him.

They watched his exit, and stood still long after he had gone, waiting for the curtain to come down. But the stagehands had gone home, and they were left stranded on the brightly-lit stage, embarrassed, not knowing how to end. At last they moved, awkwardly. Martin muttered something about 'fresh air' and 'walk', and hurried out, avoiding all eyes. Julia turned away to lean against the door jamb and stare out across the sea. Sylvia moved towards the other door, wanting to escape more than anything; but then hesitated, looked back at Julia, and came to stand near her.

She thought Julia was crying. Her back was to Sylvia, and her shoulders were hunched, as if she had received some hurt, but after a moment she held her hand out behind her, and when after a pause of uncertainty Sylvia took it, she squeezed it and said quietly, 'I'm sorry. I'm so sorry.'

427

'Oh Julia,' Sylvia said helplessly. Julia turned, and she went on, 'Why didn't you tell me?'

'How could I?'

Sylvia stared a moment longer, and then of the same impulse the two sisters embraced. Sylvia was crying now, but not for herself – for Julia, who had no tears, whose face was as calm as sleep.

'I knew,' Sylvia said. 'I knew somehow, when I first saw her, but I didn't want to believe it. I tried to hide it from myself.'

'You know that I never meant to hurt you,' Julia said.

Sylvia pushed back and stared into her face. '*You* hurt *me*? But it was my fault! I was the one who did wrong. I should never have . . . done that . . . with anyone's husband, least of all yours! But it didn't make any difference, you know. He was always yours, Julia, always. Never mine, never for one moment. He never left you.'

'Oh dear God,' Julia said softly. In anguish she stroked the hair back from her sister's wet face.

'I couldn't give him children. It was like a punishment from God. I couldn't give him anything. All I did was take him from you,' Sylvia said. She gasped through a fresh access of tears. 'It hurts, but I'm *glad* you did it. She's lovely.'

How could she make Sylvia see? Julia could hardly speak past the constriction of her throat, but she stroked Sylvia's hand and said, 'She looks so much like him – she's nothing like me, nothing at all. She could be anyone's child, and his.' She hugged Sylvia once, hard, and then put her away from her, forcing her attention. 'Be a good mother to her, Sylvia, please. For her sake, if not for his. Please?'

Sylvia stared, and she saw the great loneliness in Julia, and it awed her so that she stopped crying. Slowly she began to understand what it had all been about, gradually pieces fell together. Julia kissed her hand, gave her a faint, troubled smile, and left her. Sylvia stood just as Julia had left her, thinking, until Martin came back in to disturb her reverie with a hesitant cough.

Julia was up very early, before the sun, while everything was

428

still milky-grey, waiting for the first spark of gold over the rim of the world to give it colour. She wanted to go out in the air, into the white perfect morning, to swim and feel the silky water on her skin. She put a thin robe over her naked body and walked out of her bedroom. She had not seen Cathy since Peter carried her out of the room the night before, and she longed to slip into the child's bedroom and look at her; but Catherine was a light sleeper, and might wake, and Julia did not know yet how things were with her. She had no idea what Cathy might say or ask, or how she could answer. She hesitated, stood at the door listening for a moment, but then passed on.

She had a curious desire to see someone, and it seemed terribly important, as if she would never make human contact again if she did not now. She walked along to the next white door, turned the handle softly and opened it. The bed was under the window, and they slept like reversed bookends, each hunched on the extreme edge of the bed with their backs inwards. Peter still slept naked – she saw his bare shoulder where he had pushed the covers down in the heat of the night – but Sylvia was dressed politely for sleep in something lacy and expensive-looking. They breathed quietly in sleep, not touching, but not giving the impression of being separate. Julia felt she had been right. Peter had said he could ignore Sylvia, but something, age or custom or something, had crept up on him and bound him to her. Whatever they were, they were a couple now, and most of what was wrong between them would be put right if they had a child. She suppressed the longing to hug them, and backed out, closing the door quietly.

She felt strangely light as she went downstairs, almost without substance. She crossed the drawing room and opened the doors to the terrace, and stepped out into the morning. The sea was calm and silvery and made soft noises to itself like a dog sleeping; the sky was turning from silver to white, brightening, and high up, very high, a gull hung on the air, silent, scarcely moving.

The gull seemed the essence of life, of reality to her just then, marvellously rounded and solid with the pre-dawn effulgence gleaming on the curve of its pearly body. For the first time she had no urge, however slight, to draw or paint it. She was not an artist any more. She was not Julia any more. She was unreal: the fabric of her seemed to be wearing thin; light might begin any moment to pass through her – light or time or something. She was the little, piping ghost she had imagined, casting no shadow, bending no blade of grass as it passed.

She stretched out her arms and turned round, and laid them against the cool stone of the house, needing to touch something solid. She loved the house, and would be glad to stay here, winter or summer, never leave. She didn't want to think about leaving. What did it feel like to be free? She had only been free once, for that brief period between her divorce from Peter and her marriage to George, and she had enjoyed it – but she had been younger then. Now she was older, and there was nothing more to work towards – now it only felt like being masterless.

She looked at her hands, flattened on the stone – they could work to earn her living, as they had done before. I never was much of a painter, she thought, but I could always earn a living. She thought then of George, of his hands, his brown soldier's hand, blunt and sure, touching her as if she were the sword he had fought with all his life. His death made her sad, to think that he could never again see such a morning as this. He had loved being alive – his death had been so out of keeping.

She thought of Cathy – her darling girl. How could she bear to part with her? But she must not be selfish: Peter could give her so much more, all she wanted. He could open the doors to music for her, and she was ready for it: a little girl, yes, but an artist too, and every artist was born old, as old as the art itself. Music was the most important thing in her life, more important than a mere birth mother.

And Sylvia? She hated to think what she had done to Sylvia. Her tears last night! Sylvia loved Peter, and Julia had torn her life open. She could not hurt her again. But how could the three of them co-exist now in the face of all this knowledge? She knew that the only way she could resist Peter was not to see him. If she was in daily contact with him, they would become lovers again, and there would be a return to the concealment, the lies, the guilt. The two most vulnerable, Cathy and Sylvia, would suffer unbearable hurt.

Her life was a complication not just for her but for everyone. Her removal from the scene would make everything smooth. Peter and Sylvia and Cathy. Sylvia would be a good mother to Cathy – a devoted one, having no one else to lavish her affection on.

Ah, but would not Cathy feel devastated and rejected if her mother abandoned her? How would it be possible to make her understand? How would it be possible, in the first place, to leave her? Julia felt the bull's horns, ugly dilemma, tearing her. Two possibilities, both of them impossible. She could not go away. She could not stay.

Loneliness slipped down into the hollow she had become, finding its level, like cold water. She remembered her childhood, the solitariness of the child without friends, without family. She had not minded it then, knowing nothing else, had walked complete and unperturbed within the bubble that shut her off from the rest of the world. But she had been young then. The thought of it now was something to be dreaded – to be alone again, without Cathy, without Peter. How could she endure it?

It was all too much, too much to cope with, too much to think about. Her mind shut off in self-defence. She placed her hands on the top of the parapet, and with a jump hitched herself up to sit on it. Colour was beginning to enter the day, and away to the left of the terrace the jungle was growing greener as the world woke up. A butterfly flickered past her, and she felt a tired surge of pleasure. 'You're out early,' she said. It hovered as if it had heard her and had turned back, flickered about, and then alighted on the wall of the house just above her. It was brilliantly coloured, the first reds of the returning spectrum in its wings – a red admiral? She was not much on butterflies, but she knew one or two.

She wanted a better look, and with infinite caution, not to disturb him, she drew her legs up under her, eased herself into a crouching position on the parapet wall, and slowly, carefully stood up. It flexed its wings, but did not fly off; it remained there, palpitating gently, letting her get a good look at its velvety royal colours.

It was wonderful up here. She turned away from the butterfly to look out at the sea as it wrinkled, scarcely moving, below her, too full for sound or foam. The air too was still, no wind. She felt a peace return, dropping slow balm into her wounds. It was not a peace of joy, but of stillness, and it was what she wanted just now – for nothing else ever to happen again. Everything hurt too much. She wanted just to sleep, to escape from the circularity of her thoughts, from the dread of the future, from the sad beguiling spectres of the past. It would be so easy not to feel anything more, so easy.

The butterfly darted away from the wall and up, and as she turned her head with the movement, she lost her balance. Her bare foot slipped away from her on the slight sheen of dew on the cold stone, and she teetered. In that split second she knew that she could not regain her stability, and her heart contracted with shock and fear. Reality jumped back into her like a bolt of electricity.

She ought to flail her arms and try to throw herself backwards in the hope of falling on to the balcony. But it seemed wrong to make a violent movement that would mar the white stillness of the morning. And suddenly it did not even seem like a choice, but simply a letting go of everything that pained and perplexed her. Fate had overtaken her. Nothing more to decide. The image of herself as a child, locked in aloneness, was in her mind. Julia alone; then and now: always. So much easier to let go, to go quietly, to be one with it.

All this passed in the split second, shock, fear, resignation; and already it was too late anyway. No help. Alone. Be still, now. She did not flail. She stretched her arms wide as she fell, away and out – and at the last almost joyfully, the wind in her hair, to lean like a gull, briefly, on the still air.

It seemed to Sylvia as though the afternoon would never end, like those Sundays when they were children, back in Milton Street, when each hour between lunch and dark had seemed as long as a week. Tearful, restless, bored, she had tried to read a book, and it felt as though nothing would ever happen, nothing would ever happen again, that they would stay forever like this, trapped in pain in each other's company with nothing to think of or talk about but the one subject they wanted desperately to avoid.

They had scarcely missed her before she had been found. It was not until around midday that they discovered Julia was not in the house. A quick search of the grounds and the beach had been followed by the discovery that she had taken no clothes with her, and they had begun to be alarmed. Martin feared a swimming accident – Peter, perhaps, something worse – and given the events and emotions of the night before they had felt it right to telephone the police.

Around two o'clock, before they would have had time to make any serious enquiries, the police telephoned back to say they had found her. The ebbing tide that had taken her out in the morning had brought her back in into the next bay and wedged her amongst the rocks at the flood. At least, they thought it was her.

They had wanted Sylvia, as next of kin – barring Cathy – to go, but she had become hysterical, and Peter had gone instead. One of the things she would never forget was his face when he returned. The body had been easy for him to identify, but not the face. The doctor had said that the injury could not all be attributed to being rolled around by the waves amongst the rocks – he was of the opinion that there had been a fall from a great height, perhaps from the top of a cliff. It had not all been post-mortem damage.There was no water in the lungs. She had not drowned.

She had not drowned. The words were the first that sounded in Sylvia's head when she woke this morning, feeling heavy and dull from the sleeping pills they had given her last night. The heaviness had kept her from crying during the morning, but she had cried again all afternoon, and now she could cry no more and felt empty, scraped out. She wondered how she must look, red-eyed, and remembered Catherine's swollen face as she had stared at her for a moment with flamed eyes before burying her head again in Peter's chest.

Sylvia glanced across at them. Peter had not moved since he first sat down with Catherine on his lap, and Cathy seemed

433

to be sleeping now with her face pressed against him. Sylvia's arms ached for Cathy with a power of longing she had not known herself capable of. But Catherine would not leave Peter. Peter had become for the moment the only foothold in the world that did not cave in under her. Her mother was dead, had died twice over for Cathy, and nothing would ever be the same, but Peter was warm and real, he was something to hold on to – her father, made in her own image.

From the child, she looked at the man – her husband! That was almost, but not quite, a joke. Sylvia had grown up late in life, and on emerging from the dream of her adolescence, she had fallen in love with Peter – too late. She had then to discover that he did not love her, that he had married her out of perversity and spite, and loving him still she had borne with his malice and contempt, even with his neglect, hoping he might change, hoping that one day she might win his mind over from the preoccupation that absorbed it day and night. He had been Julia's – always. She had had less of him than he would have given a dog.

But he was her husband, and now Julia was dead. Dead. So final, that word. Julia had lost, was beaten, had been betrayed over and over, and now, finally, was dead. The victory was to Sylvia – Peter was hers. He would not leave her now, not now she was needed to take care of Cathy. He would be a husband to her now, perhaps even learn to love her. Hollow, all hollow. Her eyes were open at last. She did not want him. But she had promised, that was the irony – Julia had made her promise to be a mother to Cathy, and that included, she saw it now, being a wife to Peter. She must never show him contempt, never leave him. Julia had bound her to him by dying, very conveniently.

Conveniently? How had she died? *She had not drowned.* A fall, not drowned – but how? Had she escaped them? *Was it deliberate?* Julia was not beaten, only dead – and dead she still had power over them all, she would still rule their lives. My sister. Not drowned. Sylvia put her hands over her face and wept again, hopelessly.

Peter saw the movement, and it irritated him. What right had Sylvia to cry? She had never loved Julia – she was

434

simply making the stock response to a situation. She was regulated like a machine – but behind that show of hands she was busy working out the advantages that had accrued to her in the matter. His wife, he believed, was trivial, selfish and pragmatic. She would cry the requisite tears. but she would believe Julia's departure convenient.

He made a movement of irritation, but Catherine stirred slightly in his arms and he was still again. He looked down at the sleeping child. He had won, then – this was his prize. But he had to have Sylvia as well. He had forgotten that in the heat of the battle. He had fought either for Julia and Cathy, or for Cathy alone, but he had forgotten Sylvia. He could not leave her now – Cathy needed her. She needed a mother, and he had seen the affection that had grown up between her and Sylvia in the past few days.

As she grew older, the affection on Cathy's part would become more like the affection she would have bestowed on an animal – a pet dog – but it would suffice. This, then, was his future. Here was the thing that, with his music, would make his life worth going on with. Cathy growing up, becoming a woman, becoming a musician, growing in his likeness. He had noticed in his daughter's eyes a faint light of battle that promised him he would not find life with her dull. She would plague him with her will, her India rubber obstinacy. She was not so unlike her mother after all.

He had been trying not to think of Julia, for he would keep seeing again and again that corpse, which was not her – did not even look like her. Didn't look like anything human, broken in places humans ought not to break. He hauled his mind away by main force. That was not Julia – Julia was what he remembered of her, a film that had come to the end of the last reel. Yes, that was a good way to look at it, for though there would be no more, the film could be rewound and played again, nothing was lost, it was not over. He could not cope with it being over. Desperately he tried to evade the finality which laid a blow to his mind whenever he remembered that it was the end – that never again would he see her, or speak to her, never make her laugh, or reach out and touch her, know her to be near him. He had always thought he held her on a thread, but it turned out

435

to be the other way round. For a quarter of a century he had lived his life in the context of her: present or absent, she had defined him. They had been apart before, but this time there was the knowledge that there was no way he could ever come to her again, no telephone number to ring.

He remembered how she had looked the last time he had seen her, standing over there by the window, and that strange look of peace that had passed between them, as if she was glad it was all over, and that he had won. Why had she fought? He would never understand it. What happened was an irony – having survived the battle, she did not live to enjoy the peace.

But what would she have done in the peace, he asked himself suddenly. Cathy had turned against her. If he and Sylvia had taken Cathy, what would there have been left for Julia to do? She could neither have stayed nor gone. Her death had been the easy solution, saved her the problem of making a decision. Did she kill herself then? Was that what he was trying to tell himself?

The thought sickened him, and he stood up to shake it off, putting Cathy down gently on the sofa. She continued to sleep, curled and abandoned like a city before an earthquake. The room was so still that any movement caught the eye, and both Martin and Sylvia watched him as he walked across the room. He hated them – they distracted him when he wanted to think about Julia. He knew, quite certainly, that one day he would stop dreaming about her, and that, when he woke up and tried to bring her to mind, he would find that she had gone. He would not be able to remember what she had looked like, and every image he called up after that would be unreal and forced, and would not comfort him, but make him sadder. He knew this – it was inevitable – and he wanted to think about her now, before she was gone for ever, while he could still call her back, vivid and warm and real.

He walked round the room, his hands behind his back twisting together restlessly. Here she had sat reading, holding the hair back from her face with one hand; here she had stood on the night they had danced, vivid and starry, laughing at him; here she had clung to the door jamb, fighting for Cathy – no, he didn't want to remember that. He closed his eyes and

436

called her up differently, young and sleek, feeding the baby – sleeping beside him in the mews flat.

But there was little comfort in those early memories – it was here, where she had last been, that he could find her most easily, and he stood at the terrace door and looked out at the sea. He never wanted to leave this place. She had said she would haunt him – oh, please God that she would! He understood Heathcliffe. It was cruel to be the one left behind. It was bitter. It was as he had known it would be – she had won, in the end.

He swung round and looked back into the room, and saw the other two still watching him, and he needed to vent his anger on somebody.

'What are you gawping at? Do you think I'm a side-show?' Martin looked away but Sylvia kept staring, a frown between her brows. 'Why don't you go and do something? You don't have to sit there with your hands in your laps because someone's died, you know. No one will notice if you don't observe the two minutes' silence. Nobody's interested in your reactions. She's dead – can't you get that through your heads? She'll always be dead from now on. It doesn't matter if you carry on with what you were doing now, or six months from now.'

They looked at him with slight distaste as if he were something they were too polite to mention. He clenched his fists.

'God, you make me sick, the pair of you! You never cared for her, either of you, not a bit. You never loved anyone but yourself,' – to Sylvia – 'and as for you . . .' Martin looked up and met his eyes with an indefinable expression, almost like pity. 'You wanted her, but you were never more than half a man. You couldn't have her, so you trotted round after her being her mother. You – ach!'

He made a sound of disgust, and turned away again, hating the sight of them both. Only Julia had ever understood, it was only her he had ever been able to talk to. Oh Julia, why did you leave me like that? It was a dirty trick, not like you. You used to fight me tooth and nail, but you never fought dirty. Despair seized him, and he was afraid of it, and he fought against it, whipping up anger again in defence.

'She won in the end – she turned the tables on the lot of us. She killed herself, and left us here with our hands in our laps to do the dirty work work for her. She's got us all just where she wants, and we can't get back at her. What did she make you promise, Martin, eh? You can't break a deathbed promise you know.' Damn you Julia, he thought. You're out there laughing at us. I can hear you.

He lifted his head and shouted out at the sea, where the waves turned over endlessly and the high gulls hardly moved on the thin airs. 'Julia! You won, didn't you? But you cheated. Oh God, it was a dirty, rotten cheat!'

There was a strange harsh noise, and then silence. His face was aching, it was screwed up in a kind of grimace. In a moment he said, quietly now, 'I didn't love her.' His voice sounded surprised. He rolled his head from side to side wearily, and said it again – explanatory. 'I didn't love her. I *was* her.'

He turned slowly round to face them – slowly, because he didn't seem to have proper control of his limbs. Cathy was sitting where she had been lying, her face in her hands, but the other two were standing up, staring at him. He couldn't see them very well, they were misty. He blinked and tried to think what was that expression on their faces – anxiety, pity perhaps? – but mixed with something else, something like horror, as if they were the witnesses of a road accident.

He put his hands up to touch his face. It was twisted, it was wet, and for one moment he saw reflected in their eyes what he must look like. He looked at his hands, bewildered. Tears, they were tears!

'I'm crying,' he said.